THE FOURTH
ENEMY

HEADLINE

First published in 2022
by HEADLINE PUBLISHING GROUP

First published in paperback in 2023
by HEADLINE PUBLISHING GROUP

1

Cataloguing in Publication Data is available from the British Library

ISBN 978 1 4722 9439 5

Typeset in Adobe Garamond by Palimpsest Book Production Limited,
Falkirk, Stirlingshire

Printed and bound in Great Britain by Clays Ltd, Elcograf S.p.A.

MIX
Paper from
responsible sources
FSC® C104740

Headline's policy is to use papers that are natural, renewable and recyclable
products and made from wood grown in well-managed forests and other
controlled sources. The logging and manufacturing processes are expected
to conform to the environmental regulations of the country of origin.

HEADLINE PUBLISHING GROUP
An Hachette UK Company
Carmelite House
50 Victoria Embankment
London EC4Y 0DZ

www.headline.co.uk
www.hachette.co.uk

To Theresa Curtin

Character List

Daniel Pitt – junior counsel at fford Croft and Gibson
Miriam (née fford Croft) – Daniel's wife, a forensic scientist
Sir Thomas Pitt – Daniel's father, head of Special Branch
Charlotte – Lady Pitt, Daniel's mother
Marcus fford Croft – retired head of fford Croft and Gibson
Dr Evelyn Hall – Miriam's boss, a senior pathologist
Impney – chief clerk at fford Croft and Gibson
Gideon Hunter KC – leading counsel at fford Croft and Gibson
Rose Hunter – Gideon's wife, a suffragist
Toby Kitteridge – head of chambers at fford Croft and Gibson
Malcolm Vayne – newspaper proprietor and wealthy benefactor
Nadine Parnell – Vayne's bookkeeper and personal assistant
Peter Rollins – Vayne's personnel manager
Richard Whitnall – Vayne's international liaison
John Sandemann – Vayne's acquisitions manager
Callum McCallum – Vayne's social director
Boyce Turnbull – courier for Vayne
Geoffrey Wallace – senior minister in the Foreign Office
Lucas Standish – officer with MI6

Inspector Ian Frobisher – police officer
Sergeant Billy Bremner – Frobisher's junior officer
Mr Justice Abbott-Smith – presiding judge
Fergus Dalmeny KC – counsel for the defence
Agnes Ward – prosecution witness
John Alvey – minister in His Majesty's government
Moncrieff – Alvey's senior secretary
Johnson – police bodyguard
Minnie Maude – the fford Crofts' maid
George – maître d' at Gideon Hunter's club

Chapter One

Daniel smiled at his wife. 'Your father might forget people's names, if he doesn't particularly like them, or office meetings entirely, but he's never late for dinner.' He passed by Miriam and did not even try to resist the desire to touch her, kiss her cheek again and feel the softness of her hair before leaving to go upstairs to wash and tidy up a little before dinner.

Marriage was still a new and wonderful adventure for him, a happiness so intense he found it hard to accept. He and Miriam had known each other for some time, but only realised it was far deeper than friendship, or even collaboration of their separate skills, in the past year. He recalled the end of the last case on which they had both worked, and how, as they were standing in the torrential rain in the graveyard, he finally understood that it was love. Now they were together, and this was rich, new and infinitely sweet to him.

As expected, Miriam's father, Marcus fford Croft, arrived exactly on time. He was standing on the doorstep, smiling, when Daniel answered the bell. At this time of the year, it was still full daylight, and Marcus practically glowed in the slanted rays of the evening sun. He was wearing a yellow-gold

1

velvet waistcoat under his light jacket, and his bow tie was a deep bronze. He was smiling with sheer pleasure.

'Come in,' Daniel invited him, standing back so that Marcus could step into the hall.

Marcus hesitated for a moment, looking at the paintings Miriam had brought from his home, where she had lived all her life. It clearly pleased him to see her old childhood belongings here in her new home. It was a sign that she felt this was now where she belonged.

Miriam came out of the kitchen and greeted Marcus. She hugged him quickly, met his eyes for a moment, then turned and led him into the sitting room where she poured him a glass of sherry. They kept it especially for him, knowing how much he enjoyed it. The doctor had said that one glass was acceptable, but since Marcus's first heart attack, not more than one – and definitely not the much stronger brandy he preferred.

Miriam brooked no argument. She loved her father deeply. Her mother had died long ago, leaving the two of them together. But Miriam was strict about him obeying orders where his health was concerned. It was the only issue on which she always prevailed.

Marcus settled in his chair comfortably, glancing at his daughter, and then back again at Daniel.

Daniel could see that he had something to say. It was there, in the way he sat, a certain tension in his shoulders.

It was Miriam who broke through the pleasantries. 'You have news.' It was a statement. 'Tell us, before dinner spoils,' she said with a smile. 'Don't put my cooking to the test. Please.' It was a sincere request.

While she had lived in her father's house, she had never concerned herself with any domestic tasks at all, including preparing meals. All her time and her passion went into her study of pathology. Daniel had learned by trial and error what to say regarding domesticity, and what to leave unsaid. But Marcus had never learned, nor, indeed, had he tried to. But then, Miriam would take a lot of criticism from her father because they adored one another, and she was secure in his acceptance of her eccentricities, as she accepted his.

Daniel was still discovering how easily he could hurt her, sometimes without realising it until it was too late. She was older by fifteen years, and his admiration for her was immense, but admiration was quite different from love. Their marriage was new, exciting, frightening and comfortable, all at the same time. It touched emotions he had not known before.

'I have news for you, yes,' Marcus said, breaking what had been a few moments of silence. He was smiling, as if he anticipated their surprise . . . and pleasure.

Miriam drew in her breath, as if preparing to speak, then apparently changed her mind.

Marcus said, 'I have decided to retire. I think perhaps, finally, it is time.'

Miriam drew in another sharp and audible breath, but Daniel saw that it was relief, not apprehension. She was only too aware of the danger of another, more serious heart attack – perhaps fatal this time. After that first one, she had come home from Holland, interrupting her studies, and she had not gone back until her father was out of immediate danger, regardless of the lectures she was missing, and the exams awaiting her.

Daniel looked at her and saw her shoulders relax.

Whatever might happen to the chambers of fford Croft and Gibson without her father's leadership, Miriam regarded it as secondary to his health. She was smiling now. She glanced only briefly at Daniel, then back again at Marcus.

'Good!' she said firmly. 'They will have to learn to manage without you. And you must let the new head of the chambers – whoever he turns out to be – take the lead.' She smiled, as if to soften the words. 'You must not lean over his shoulder and second-guess his actions. Let him make the important decisions, as if you had complete confidence in him. He will not do everything as you would, but that is not necessarily a bad thing. He must be allowed to have his own ideas, or he will not be much use.'

Daniel knew that she meant every word; she was looking at her father sternly, despite the gentleness in her face. He knew, too, that she was thinking about Marcus, but also about whoever took on the extremely difficult task of following the brilliant, erratic and eccentric man who had led the chambers since its inception. There had never been a Gibson. The name had been added to bolster public confidence, so people would think there was more than one man at the helm.

There were undoubtedly several extremely competent barristers, some of them well established. Daniel could not think who Marcus would choose to succeed him. Toby Kitteridge, Daniel's closest friend in the chambers, was extremely able; he was far cleverer at the law than he realised, and he was very good in court, but he had a long way to go to develop the assurance required to lead. Maybe, one day, Daniel would take his place as head of chambers, but not for ten or fifteen years, at the very least – and possibly not ever. His chief ability was to lead in court, as well as carrying out the detective work usually done by one of the solicitors. It was an area of expertise in which he hoped to become known.

Daniel was watching Miriam, who seemed to be waiting for her father to go on. Instead, Marcus turned to Daniel, a flicker of uncertainty in his eyes. Surely he was not going to ask for Daniel's opinion? That would be absurd. Daniel had been with the chambers no more than a couple of years. Daniel reconsidered. Marcus might not ask his opinion regarding his successor, but he would want his support for whatever decision he was going to make. No one would be particularly surprised by his choice, with several very skilled men in the chambers, but they might be disconcerted. At the same time, his staff would be relieved. Marcus's health was of paramount concern to all of them.

Whoever Marcus appointed, it would be a big change. And it would be a hard job at first, no matter who took over the leadership.

The silence dragged on too long.

'Who are you going to choose?' Miriam asked. 'Have you decided yet? Or are you asking Daniel's opinion?'

'Or yours?' Marcus said, his smile now a little less certain. 'Neither, as it happens. I have thought about it long and hard, and have already decided. Although it is too late for you to disapprove, I value your opinion, and your love even more. But I will not change my mind.' He took a deep breath. 'You may, of course, disagree with my choice. But it is a fait accompli. And – he has accepted.'

Daniel glanced at Miriam's hand resting on the arm of the chair, and saw the knuckles were white. He let out his breath very slowly. 'And who is he?' he asked. 'Do we know him?'

'The new man?' Marcus raised his eyebrows.

'The new head of chambers.' Daniel was wrong-footed. Surely he was not bringing in an outsider to lead them?

'No,' Marcus said quietly. 'But we need a new barrister also. You are good, but we need a King's Counsel, a silk! To make a splash. You will do that one day, but you are not ready for it yet.'

'Then who?' Miriam demanded, her face tense. 'Who have you invited in?'

'Oh, you will know of him,' Marcus replied. He was smiling, his voice a trifle husky, as if his mouth were dry. 'Gideon Hunter KC. He has been second at Mitchell Dawson for years, but he will never be a member of the family – and they are a family chambers, and a trifle stuffy. I found he was looking for something more . . . more adventurous.' He smiled again, seeing the tension in their faces. 'We will suit him excellently.'

'And who will be head of chambers?' Daniel asked. He was confused, even worried. Was that going to be someone new also? It was too much change. He liked everything as it was, and he was comfortable with the familiar team.

'I think Toby is ready for that,' Marcus replied. He lifted his shoulders in a slight shrug. 'Of course, he did not think so when I told him, perhaps he never will. Daniel, I wish for you to help him. He trusts you. Perhaps more than he trusts himself.' His face was intensely earnest now. 'He has the skills. He is very clever – far cleverer than he knows, or accepts – but he hasn't the confidence or the courage that you have. Nothing in his life has yet given it to him.'

Marcus appraised Daniel, before continuing. 'I expect you to take on a leadership role in future. You can, and you will! The position of senior barrister will be yours one day. When you are ready. You are an actor, a crusader! You are not an administrator.' He stared at Daniel levelly. 'Do I have your word?'

Daniel was stunned. Marcus leaving was one thing – he had expected that, and wanted it, for Marcus's sake – but a new barrister, to take all the leading cases? An ambitious man. A silk. A King's Counsel! Daniel had heard of Gideon Hunter. Everyone had. A brilliant, erratic, yet charming man. But coming into fford Croft and Gibson to take the major cases? Of course, Daniel was not yet ready for that, but he would be one day. At least, he aimed to be.

And Toby Kitteridge! Quiet, often painfully shy, Toby must have been horrified at the thought of leading the chambers. But could he do it? Was Marcus right, that he was brilliant, but lacking ambition? Toby Kitteridge was awkward, clumsy, wrists always poking out of his sleeves, hair falling over his forehead. But, yes, clever, seeing further ahead than others could, recognising details they missed; understanding their significance before anyone else did.

Marcus was waiting. So was Miriam. They were both looking at him.

'Yes,' he said. 'Of course. I'll give the new appointments my full support.'

Marcus stared back at him, meeting his eyes quite candidly. 'Good, I want fford Croft and Gibson to retain its distinctive character. Gideon Hunter will either be a great success, in which case you will all thank me for my perspicacity, my daring and my wisdom, or he will be a disaster, in which case people will say that no one could follow me! Or, they could also say that I had lost my wits and made a catastrophic mistake.' He smiled, and there was both humour and tension in his expression. 'But if you help Toby, have confidence in him, and make him believe you do, then he will be rock solid. He will make mistakes, as we all do. But they will not matter. His achievements will outweigh them.'

Daniel forced himself to smile. 'It could be brilliant,' he said aloud, although he did not sound as sure of it as he wished to. 'And the new line-up will certainly attract attention!'

Marcus nodded. Suddenly, his eyes were as sharp, as bright and forceful as they had ever been. 'Precisely,' he said, almost under his breath. 'Everyone will sit up and take notice. It is up to you to make the most of it. Do your best. Take chances! Now is the moment when everyone will be watching you. Be seen! Don't play everything safe, as if I were watching over your shoulder. Throw yourself into it!'

'You are doing this on purpose,' Miriam said quietly, but with certainty. 'Striking out to where it's roughest, to see whether you will sink or swim!'

Marcus nodded his agreement. 'I'm too old to play it safe,' he said to Daniel. 'You are young enough to take chances. If not now, you never will. If you only do what is safe, you will eventually become boring. You must wear scarlet velvet waistcoats so people know who you are!'

'If I wear a scarlet waistcoat, people will think I'm trying to be you,' Daniel said immediately, with a half-smile.

'And aren't you?' Marcus asked, his eyes wide.

'Oh, yes,' Daniel said, now smiling fully. 'But not yet. I want to be myself first!'

Marcus hesitated a moment, then burst out laughing.

Miriam relaxed into her chair, her clenched hands letting go of the arms.

'You will approve of Hunter's wife,' Marcus went on, turning towards Miriam. 'You have much in common. She is an ardent fighter for women's suffrage. Indeed, you will agree with her about a lot of things. And disagree on some, no doubt.'

'I hope so,' Miriam said fervently. 'I shall learn nothing from anyone who already thinks as I do.' She looked at Daniel with a smile. 'Not that I'm in any danger of being bored.'

He felt the warmth burning his face at the memory of their rather heated differences of opinion the evening before, and the intense pleasure of making up afterwards.

8

Miriam turned to Marcus, a slight blush on her cheek as well.

Daniel knew with happiness what she was remembering. He recalled it also, vividly.

Marcus relaxed even more, sinking down further into his chair, and taking another sip from his glass. 'Good,' he said. 'Very good. So, are we having supper?'

Chapter Two

The following day, Miriam worked at the government laboratory and morgue as usual. She had done so since her return from studying in Holland, now accredited as a fully qualified forensic pathologist, an ambition she had held since the age of eleven or twelve. While in Holland, she had missed England, and above all she had missed her father . . . and Daniel. The time had finally come when she'd admitted to herself that she was in love with Daniel, but still dared not consider that he might feel the same about her.

Miriam was painfully aware of the fifteen-year age difference between them. It would have been nothing, if he had been the elder: such matches were quite common and thoroughly approved of. But she was the elder, and it hurt her more than she cared to admit; it created a deep sense of futility and pain, knowing that all that was most precious to her, this source of her real happiness, could so easily slip away.

Not that she looked her age. She was often mistaken for being a decade younger, in her early thirties. She was a striking woman in her own way; some might even have said beautiful. For better or worse, her hair was the same flaming auburn as Marcus's had been in his youth. But, of course, now his was dazzlingly white. The kindest thing she could have said about her own face was that it was 'individual', that it showed her intelligence and it registered every emotion, whether she wished it to or not. Daniel had more sense than to tell her she was beautiful, for she simply would not have believed him, although she had always felt she had lovely eyes.

Before leaving for Holland, she had worked under Dr Evelyn Hall, whose guidance had not only added to her sense of confidence, but had actually enabled her to go to Holland to study further. It was Dr Hall – affectionately referred to as Dr Eve – who had insisted she pursue her studies in the one country in Europe that would grant a Forensics degree to women.

In Holland and in Britain, Dr Eve was highly respected. Miriam knew that it had taken time for her to prove herself, but the scientific community had come to consider her a leader in her field. With her cropped hair, husky voice and rather shapeless body, she struck Miriam as the personification of the eccentric scientist. Dr Eve was forthright, candid to a fault, and brilliant. That the woman not only liked Miriam but also believed passionately in her ability, was of no importance to the British authorities, but to Miriam it was the highest possible accolade.

Since her marriage to Daniel three months ago, Miriam did not often work the long hours she had before. In those days, she had had no particular reason to hurry home to the house she shared with her father. Now, it was different. Daniel often worked long hours too, so their evenings at home – time to talk, or just sit together and watch the waning light in the small garden, hear the whispering of the leaves in the wind – were infinitely precious.

This evening, Miriam wanted to be home early to hear

from Daniel about the new barrister, Gideon Hunter. They had never met him, as far as Daniel could remember, but he knew his reputation. Everyone did. There were not so many lawyers who attained the honour of King's Counsel, the highest of honours bestowed by the Crown on outstanding barristers of fifteen or more years' experience. Like the best of his peers, Gideon Hunter had both prosecuted and defended cases in court, as many barristers chose to do. He was spoken of as clever, unpredictable, highly articulate and, on occasion, even colourful. Which was almost exactly what had been said of Marcus fford Croft when he was in his prime.

Miriam wondered if Gideon Hunter was anything like Marcus. She resisted the thought. No one was like her father! He was the only relative she had known since her mother's death when Miriam was still a child.

Now, of course, there was Daniel. Please God, that would be for ever! She could hardly believe it when she woke in the morning and felt his warmth beside her in the bed. Once she had even woken him, just to make sure it was not a wishful dream. Of course, she did not tell him that. It sounded so insecure, even demanding.

Now she was coming in from the soft summer evening to make a quick supper and hear what he had thought of Gideon Hunter, on what was the man's first day at fford Croft and Gibson. She was eager to learn how Toby Kitteridge was handling his sudden and extraordinary rise to leadership as head of chambers, a position she believed he had never dared to imagine for himself.

She must remember not to give advice to Daniel, but to listen. And not only to his voice, but to his choice of words, his intonation. And, of course, watch the expressions on his face.

She thought of her father's relationship with her husband.

Marcus was not only Daniel's father-in-law, but they were friends. He liked Daniel very much. He had given Daniel a position in the chambers, his first real job after university, at least in part because Daniel was the son of a man Marcus had known and liked for years. Sir Thomas Pitt was now head of Special Branch, the department of the government that dealt with terrorism within the country, rather than from abroad, tackling violence and the threat of insurrection and anarchy, which seemed to be on the rise all over Europe. Miriam felt it all around her, and read about it: civil unrest was growing, along with calls for overdue and desperately needed reform.

But for now, her concerns were closer to home: this new barrister at chambers, Gideon Hunter, and how he reacted to Daniel, the son-in-law of the founder. She was anxious to know how Daniel had fared on this, his first day in Hunter's presence.

She turned in at the gate and went up the path quickly. She had her own key, of course. She was later than she had meant to be. There had been some tidying up to do at the lab. Dr Eve had said she would do it, but that was a pattern Miriam was not willing to set, as it would be all too easy to fall into. Dr Eve was her benefactor and her superior, and she should never take advantage of that. Or only when absolutely necessary. And even then, never take it for granted.

'Hello!' she called from the hallway.

'Hello!' Daniel replied from the kitchen.

Miriam felt as if her heart skipped a beat. She was a pathologist and knew very well that her heart did no such thing. And if it did, it was a happy skip, not a lurch to be feared!

She wore no coat. It was high summer and the sun was warm. There was nothing to take off except a light jacket. She hung it on the coat stand in the hall, then hurried on.

Daniel met her in the kitchen, sunlight streaming through the windows. She walked straight into his arms and hugged him hard. It was no surprise to see him, but it still astonished her that she could walk into his arms and be hugged, deeply, softly. It was such an exciting thing to do. And always would be. Perhaps for a very long time.

'How was your day?' she asked, not yet willing to let go of him. 'What about Hunter? And in particular, how did Toby deal with it?'

Daniel leaned back and looked into her face. 'Hunter did not come in until quite late,' he replied. 'I think he was tidying up at his old chambers.' A shadow crossed his face and he stepped away. 'But Toby is pretty shaken.' He breathed in, and then out again slowly. 'I think he's amazed that Marcus imagines he could possibly do this. He wants it to be true, but he's terrified of failing.' He smiled ruefully. 'It's one of those things that you dream about, and really want, but not yet. I don't know if he will ever feel he is quite ready for it.'

'We can't pick the time,' she said quietly. 'Marcus needs to go now. He says he's feeling fine, but I know him well enough to see through that. He smiles and comes into the office, but it's getting harder for him.' She gave Daniel a steady look. 'Please, help him to believe you can all manage without him, even if you don't really want to.'

She knew she was asking a lot. She was expecting Daniel, who was only twenty-seven, to build the bridge for Toby to cross, and take command before he believed he was ready. Because if Marcus did not believe his appointed successor would be all right, he would have to stay, even if it exhausted his strength and brought his death much sooner.

'I know it will be a heavy burden,' she went on. 'But if Marcus has another attack, it could be fatal this time. You will feel dreadful. And so will Toby. He won't be able to forgive himself.' She saw in his eyes the understanding of everything that she was saying – and even beyond her words, to what was implied. She did not bother to finish the thought. There was no need to spell out the future. 'You'll help him. If anybody in the office gives Toby a hard time, you will rein them in, won't you?' she urged.

'No,' he answered. 'But I'll tell Toby to do it. I'm not going to look as if I'm the real boss. That wouldn't help anyone.'

She knew he was right, but she wanted to protect all of them, and she felt Daniel was the least vulnerable. Was that unfair? Or wishful thinking, because she did not want him ever to be at fault? Confidence, protectiveness, vulnerability, respect, not taking away people's courage or opportunity, their right to try, and sometimes to fail. Loving people was so very complicated.

'And Hunter?' she asked aloud.

He smiled a little ruefully. 'I don't know what I expected, but he wasn't it. He looks . . .' He reached for the right word. 'Aristocratic. And bland. Until you look at him more closely, and stop noticing his pale hair, and his elegant face, but see his eyes. Dark blue, steady, and very bright. I don't know what to make of him. He has a sense of humour, which I didn't expect. And he's cleverer than he sounds—' He stopped, as if he had discovered that he was surprised at his own thoughts. 'I don't know,' he admitted. 'At least it won't be boring.'

'That's what you're worried about? Being bored?' It was not that she believed him – she certainly did not. He was being flippant, so as not to worry her.

'No,' he admitted. 'I thought he would fall into one of the categories I understand. At least mostly. But he doesn't. And I think I might like him.'

'That's a start.' She touched his cheek, then withdrew her hand. 'Supper?'

They had barely finished eating, and Miriam was taking the dishes through to the kitchen, when the doorbell rang. She went to open the door and immediately recognised the man on the doorstep.

Ian Frobisher was tall and fair haired, with a very direct stare. Miriam had met him earlier in the year, when he was pursuing a violent and frightening case. It had ended in darkness, rain, and very nearly in death. But it had also renewed the old relationship between Ian and Daniel, which was a bonus. The two men had been friends – first at school, and then at university, in Cambridge – and, in a fashion, had picked up the threads of their old friendship this February. The passage of time had not clouded their old beliefs, nor had it quietened their laughter and shared memories.

'Ian! How are you?' she said with pleasure. Stepping back, she opened the door wider to invite him in.

'I'm fine,' he said, smiling. 'And I can see that you are, too. Is Daniel in?' He stepped inside and closed the door behind him.

'He is. Would you like a cup of tea, or coffee?' she asked, leading him through to the back of the house. It was a soft, warm evening and they had not lit a fire. 'Daniel!' she called. 'Ian is here to see you.'

Daniel came in from the garden and closed the French doors. 'Come in. Don't tell me you were just passing this way.' He slipped back into the old familiarity with ease, before motioning his friend into the sitting room.

'No,' said Ian, 'I didn't just happen to pass this way.' He smiled.

'Thank heaven you're not on your way to anywhere,' Daniel shot back with a laugh.

'Tea or coffee?' Miriam asked again, enjoying the banter.

'Tea,' Daniel said at the same moment that Ian said, 'Please, coffee.'

'How about something cool, like home-made lemonade?' Miriam suggested.

'Oh, yes,' they said in unison.

She returned in a few minutes with a jug of lemonade and three glasses on a tray, as well as a dish of chocolate biscuits. She remembered that Ian liked them, and Daniel would never refuse chocolate. She set the tray down on the low table and then took a seat on the couch, which was drawn up to the fireplace. At this time of the year, the hearth was concealed by a tapestry screen.

She passed round the lemonade and waited for Ian to explain why he had come. There was a gravity about him that made her certain it was not merely a visit of friendship.

Ian did not equivocate. He sat forward a little in his chair and put his glass down on the table. He looked very serious. 'This is something confidential. It may become public very soon, but—'

'Between us,' Daniel assured him.

'Thank you. You will have heard of Malcolm Vayne.'

'Of course,' Daniel acknowledged. 'Don't like him much – which is completely unfair, because I've never met him. I just don't like the social views of his newspapers, and the way they express them.'

'I don't like a lot of his views,' Miriam commented. 'He's got a finger in just about every public pie, but I'll forgive him that because he supports women's suffrage. And I mean he really supports it, not just with words, but with money.'

Malcolm Vayne was fabulously rich, and was generous towards many causes, most notably the right of women to vote for members of parliament. Not all women – but then not all men could vote, either. A man was required to have certain property, and a standing in the community. Until now, this requirement for property and standing applied only to men. No women could vote . . . at all. Strong feelings about women's rights had come to the forefront of debate lately – and in clear public view – and Malcolm Vayne was one of those men of wealth who had given a considerable amount of money to the cause. Even more importantly, and despite significant public resistance, he had said he would continue to do so.

But Vayne did not limit his support to women and voting. It was well known that he also gave generous amounts to other causes, such as free clinics for the poor, heavily subsidised housing and soup kitchens. As the owner of two of the most widely distributed and popular newspapers in the country, he had the platform to paint a highly favourable picture of himself for the public.

Miriam felt a chill run through her at the thought of what Ian might be preparing to divulge. Whatever it was, she was certain it was important enough to bring him to their home unannounced. She had come to know and respect him, and not merely because he was Daniel's friend. Friends can change, especially during the years from childhood to maturity. But Ian had proved his worth, even though she had met him only a few short months ago. And she knew a lot about him and Daniel, and their long, shared history in childhood and youth.

Ian had been married and had loved his wife dearly, but he had lost her during the birth of their only child, a little girl. Tragedy seemed to have left him mercifully devoid of

18

bitterness, but he was troubled by the deep knowledge of what it meant to be alone. His work schedule was demanding, and he had turned to his family to help him with his daughter. Perhaps it was his way of dealing with his own painful loss, but he had a dedication to his job that he had not shown before. It was more than ambition for himself and his career; it was an anger towards all forms of loss that could have been avoided, and all greed that made others suffer.

When Miriam had first met him, she was drawn to him immediately. But she also feared that his fierce dedication to his work might drive him to hide the emptiness inside him. She liked him not only because he was Daniel's friend, and a loyal one at that, but because he was a passionate and vulnerable man. Now there was clearly something that was deeply troubling him.

'What about Malcolm Vayne?' she pressed. 'Do you suspect him of something?'

'Fraud,' Ian replied. 'Very complicated. And far reaching, with one fraud designed to cover and feed another.'

'I suppose you must be pretty sure, or you wouldn't be bothering to pursue it,' Daniel said slowly.

'How sure are you?' Miriam asked. 'Fifty per cent? Seventy-five?'

'I assume you mean something provable – something you can trace back to him?' added Daniel.

'I don't know,' Ian admitted. 'Morally, I'm certain he's crossed the line.'

'Well, you'd better be at least seventy-five per cent sure, before you take it any further,' Daniel said, with a slight tremor to his voice. 'Be careful, Ian. Malcolm Vayne is not a man to offend. Everything I have heard about him says he doesn't forgive easily.'

Ian took a long breath and let it out slowly. 'Wrong, Daniel. He doesn't forgive at all. I wish it were someone else who'd discovered this new information about him, and not me. But now that I know it, I can't just let it go. And I certainly can't pretend I didn't see it. Or that I saw it, but didn't understand its significance. My man Bremner, in particular, knows what I was told. No,' he said, smiling lopsidedly, 'I have to act.' After a long silence, he added, 'That's the trouble with wanting to lead. When you get the chance, you have to take the bad along with the good.'

Billy Bremner was Ian's second-in-command, a tough, dryly humorous northerner who pretended to despise the soft southerner that Ian was, and yet at the same time deeply admired him. But if asked, he would always deny it. Everyone who knew Ian understood that he did not mind being teased. However, Bremner was far more sensitive than he let on, so Ian was careful whenever he mocked him in return.

'What are you going to do?' Daniel asked.

'If what the witnesses say is true, and the paperwork backs it up,' Ian answered, 'I'll have no choice. It's a clever scheme. Vayne invites people to invest in his company and promises a high return. He also promises his investors that there is little or no risk, because the profits come from an already successful business.'

Daniel and Miriam remained silent.

'That successful business doesn't exist,' Ian said. 'It's no more than a series of fronts.'

'So how do the investors get paid?' Miriam asked.

'The money they're paid actually comes from the next group of investors.'

'But if there are no new investors . . .' said Miriam, her voice trailing off.

'Exactly,' said Daniel. 'There will be no profits. I know about this sort of scheme, and how much of the investors' money goes into the pockets of the man running it.'

Ian nodded. 'Yes, there are inflated promises of returns. The rub is, the returns are excellent. That is, on the face of it. But while a lot of early investors are paid damn good returns, they're not paid from profitable investments, but rather from the pockets of later investors. It's a financial structure that can't be sustained. Eventually, it all comes tumbling down.'

'And what about Vayne?' Daniel asked.

Ian shook his head. 'So far, the scheme hasn't failed, but some of the more experienced investors are concerned, and we're getting more than a few queries about where the potential profits are coming from.'

'Who's asking?' Daniel pressed.

'Insurers, where buildings are concerned. And bankers, where investments are held against loans.'

Miriam leaned forward, closer to Ian. 'So, if investors are paid returns on their investments, but that money is coming from other investors, it seems that eventually the whole thing has to collapse. Many people will be ruined!'

'Even if Vayne can keep it going for years,' Daniel added, 'there is no real wealth created, no investment in something that will grow. It has to implode. Ian, is that what you're expecting?'

'There may be something real behind the scheme,' Ian replied. 'And it may be making money, but nothing even close to what Vayne claims.'

'Men like Vayne know to get out before the collapse actually happens,' Daniel countered. 'He'll take his money with him to whatever country won't extradite him back to England.'

'Exactly,' Ian said grimly. 'And the people who invested? They won't see any of it, ever again. The money doesn't even have to be sequestered in Europe — although it looks as if it is — it could be anywhere. The least we can do is try to stop him.' Ian looked grim when he said this.

The three of them knew that it would be a monstrous task to prosecute a man of Vayne's wealth and standing, not to mention his popularity among those who read his newspapers.

Ian was caught in a tight spot, and Miriam could see that. Even if he could not prove his case against Vayne — and it was very possible that he could not — he had to try. And what if he succeeded? He would ruin Vayne, and those who admired him would hate Ian for crushing their dreams, showing the clay feet of the man they had trusted and believed. And what if he tried and failed? Vayne would emerge from the investigation even more influential, more powerful, and Ian might find his career severely damaged. If he were extremely unfortunate, he too would be ruined.

'You must be very careful,' Miriam said urgently. 'I suppose your superiors are hell-bent on pursuing this, or you wouldn't even be considering it, just based on your and Bremner's feelings.'

'Yes. And they are right. We don't even know who has invested money in this!'

'You haven't put any money into it yourself, have you?' Miriam had no business to ask Ian, but she did anyway. She saw the shadow flit across Daniel's face and knew that if she had not raised this question, he would have.

Ian smiled a little tightly. 'Haven't got anything to spare. And I wouldn't invest right now anyway.' He stopped and looked away.

Miriam glanced at Daniel. Was he thinking the same as

she was? That there was so much uncertainty in the air. There could be a war in Europe, perhaps within a few short years. Wasn't that a nightmare, rather than a reality? But terrible and impossible things did happen. After all, in April, the colossal, invincible *Titanic* had sunk to the bottom of the Atlantic, carrying God knows how many souls with it. There were survivors, but they would never be the same again. What nightmares they must have! Icebergs, vast mountains of ice floating in the sea. Freezing water stretching endlessly in every direction, sinking down to an unfathomable depth, beyond the reach of any light at all.

'Miriam?' Daniel's voice cut across her thoughts.

'Oh! I'm sorry,' she apologised to Ian. 'I was thinking how hard this is for you, and for everyone involved. Vayne seems untouchable. I suppose you have to do something? That is, you can't—' She stopped, as if unable to continue.

'I suppose I would leave it, if I could,' Ian said quietly, not looking at her but focusing instead on the curtains, and the garden beyond.

'Be careful!' Daniel said urgently, echoing Miriam, and then bit his lip. It was clear in his face that he regretted the words the moment they were said. There was a shadow of doubt in his eyes. 'We'll need witnesses in court who know what they're talking about. That is, we need to be certain that these accusations aren't built on envy or rivalry. Or someone's attempt at revenge.'

Ian winced. 'Do you suppose I haven't thought of that?' he asked, with some bitterness. 'Vayne has enemies, of course. Anyone that rich and powerful always has. We're relying on written evidence only, on things that can be proved, not just by words. We're not there yet, but I have a sharp and rather painful feeling that we're not far off.'

'Painful?' Miriam asked, with a sinking sensation inside her.

Was Ian reluctant to charge Vayne because he liked him? Not possible, from what she knew of Ian. Did Ian admire him? That was not likely, either. But he knew what immense power the man wielded. There were so many people whose lives would buckle and fail without his generous gifts. With so many charities and public causes, he was wildly popular. If Ian were seen as the man responsible for Vayne's downfall, he would make uncountable enemies for himself: the rich and powerful supporters, the middle-class donors who followed in Vayne's wake, and the countless poor who benefited from the charities he supported.

'But his public standing does not mean he should be excused, if he committed a serious financial crime like fraud. Or, perhaps, to some it does?' she said aloud.

'No, of course not,' Daniel replied before Ian could answer. 'That's what the courts are for.'

'But by the time his case gets to court, much of the damage will have been done,' she pointed out.

'Not if he is found not guilty,' Daniel argued. 'Then he is cleared, not only of that charge, and his reputation restored. The police will think very hard before they charge him again. He will be free and clear.'

She swallowed back her first words. She had so much more experience of life than her husband. Sometimes he sounded impossibly idealistic. So young. She wanted to protect him, yet knew she must not. It would hurt him to be reminded of the age difference. The relationship between them was tender, and so precious. She had never, ever imagined being so happy, or allowing one person to govern so much of her emotions. As if she could help it! But every so often came the nagging reminder that she was fifteen years older, fifteen years more experienced in the disappointments and sudden reverses of life, and the injustices. Fifteen more years written in her face!

She forced the thought away.

'Miriam?' her husband said. It was definitely a question.

She had been so careful to guard her secret thoughts. Surely he had not read her mind? She must not tell him the truth, but neither must she lie, ever. 'There will always be some people who believe the charges,' she said carefully. 'Enemies. Opportunists. Journalists who grub around after any story that's entertaining. They'll be very careful not to name him, but they will skirt within an inch of it, and most people will know who they mean.'

'Don't worry,' Ian answered, with a twisted smile. 'My superiors won't let me charge Vayne if we don't have a very solid case, with documents, witnesses, everything necessary. For their own sakes, not mine. He has powerful friends. And powerful enemies. And a lot of people who will go whichever way they think wisest for themselves. There will be carrion crows thick on the branches of every tree, waiting for him to fall.' His face mirrored his distaste for such creatures. 'And God help those who guess wrong,' he added, with a wince of pain.

'He won't forgive them,' Daniel said ruefully. 'But neither will you be forgiven by those whose dreams you destroy.'

'Are you suggesting we refrain from prosecuting anyone who's made ill use of other people's dreams?' Ian asked bullishly, but his face reflected sadness rather than blame. 'A lot of things are built on dreams,' he added wistfully. 'Good things, as well as bad.'

Miriam nodded. 'I know. Think of the poetry, the art created by those whose dreams are—' She stopped, uncertain of exactly what she meant.

'Beautiful?' Ian said curiously.

'Not necessarily,' said Daniel. 'Some dreams are unfulfilled. Warnings, if you like. Show me a rich poet! Or a duplicitous and profiteering playwright. I'll show you ten who starve instead.'

'Dreams can be dangerous,' Miriam agreed quietly. 'But not to dream is worse. Good poets show us beauty, and give our own dreams a voice. They understand our pain, and share it. Thieves take our money and give us nothing back but, eventually, disillusion.' She looked directly at Ian. 'But you've got to prove Vayne's guilt, so his victims can no longer doubt the evidence. And that is going to hurt, if they actually believe you. And many of them won't appreciate you for having done it.'

'Would it be better to let them go on being duped and robbed?' Ian asked, perfectly seriously.

'No,' she replied. 'Just don't expect to be thanked for it!'

Ian shook his head slightly. 'I don't. But thank you for listening.'

Chapter Three

The next day was Saturday, and Daniel and Miriam drove in her bright red car out of London, heading south into Kent and towards the sea. They left early, before there were too many cars on the road, and by midday they were sitting where the famous white chalk cliffs of Dover plunged into a dark blue sea below. There was silence, except for the whisper of the wind in the grass, and the faint sigh of the sea on the rocks below.

Daniel leaned back, his head on Miriam's lap, his eyes closed, feeling the sun hot on his face, stinging a little. He had not imagined he could ever be so happy.

He carried that sense of peace through Sunday into Monday, when he was back at work.

He was looking at the morning's post when there was a knock on the door. Almost immediately, Toby Kitteridge opened it and came in, then closed it swiftly behind him.

Toby was a few years older than Daniel, but he always looked as if he were still growing. His jacket sleeves were at least an inch too short, but his tie was knotted more neatly than usual, and his collar was absolutely straight. For Toby, this was a noticeable effort. Marcus had always accepted him as he was, because he valued nonconformity. It remained to be seen how Gideon Hunter would react. And more importantly, how Toby felt about being the new head of chambers in fford Croft and Gibson. Daniel believed his friend could grow quickly into the role, but he knew that Toby himself was far less sure.

'Good morning,' Daniel said, with a smile. 'You brushed your hair. What's the occasion?'

'I always brush my hair!' Toby said. His answering smile was uncertain, but knowing he was being teased, he relaxed a little. 'Have you heard the news?'

'No.' Daniel felt a sudden sinking sensation in his chest. 'What is it?'

'Malcolm Vayne has been arrested! For massive fraud. Hundreds of thousands of pounds, maybe even millions.'

So, it had happened after all. And so soon! Only three days ago, Ian Frobisher had lacked the proof he needed. And now, on this Monday morning, he had made the arrest and charged Vayne.

'What do the papers say?' Daniel asked, with some apprehension.

'All sorts of things, which pretty much amount to nothing,' Toby replied. 'Seems that no one expected it. And no one believes the police have any firm evidence because, as far as they can see, there isn't any. Someone must have invented the allegations. It is entirely fantastical for the man to be charged. And beyond the realms of possibility for those charges to stick.'

'Still,' said Daniel. 'Won't any suspicion of improper conduct severely harm his reputation?'

Toby thought about this, but only for a brief moment. 'He has an entire country of supporters, many of them practically worship him. He's not just a successful businessman, Daniel. He's a major benefactor! How could all these people whose lives he's bettered think ill of him?'

Daniel nodded, as he began to understand. 'And if he's found innocent, it only strengthens the public's feeling that he was being hounded for showing others up by his good deeds.'

'Exactly.'

'And he will be able to get massive damages for his name being tainted.' The true picture was dawning on Daniel. 'Do you think that could be what this is really about? That he's exploiting his arrest and trial by jury, to gain maximum publicity? And he's certain he'll be found innocent? That sounds . . . crazy!'

'Guilty or innocent, he'll profit from it.' Toby added, 'I've been looking him up. His investments are enormous. Businesses, import and export, a vast amount of real estate. Blocks of flats and the best gentlemen's clubs. And at the other end of the scale, factories that employ thousands of people. In the long run, even if the police manage to dig up evidence against him, they're unlikely to be believed. The jury will laugh them out of court.'

Daniel closed his eyes. When he opened them, he stared at Toby. 'The Stock Exchange could go into a tailspin. And the police will be blamed for that as well.'

Toby moved his weight from one foot to the other. 'All of that will be reported in Vayne's own newspapers, of course. His arrest happened after the morning editions were out, so the headlines I've seen so far are projected for the evening papers. I'm sure they're intended to make people rush out and buy up every copy, the minute they hit the streets!' He shook his head with a bewildered expression. 'Do you know anything about this, Daniel? I understand the police officer was Inspector Ian Frobisher. That is your friend, isn't it?'

'Yes . . .' Daniel wanted to say more, but words were flooding his mind and he didn't know where to begin. What had Ian found out this weekend that had tipped the balance so completely? What was it that he could not ignore, however much he wished to? 'Ian came to see me this weekend and told me about the investigation into Vayne. But he said he didn't have enough to make a charge stick, and it was all confidential so far.'

'Well, apparently he thinks he has proof now,' said Toby. 'There will be wild speculation in the papers. Imaginations gone berserk. Did he tell you any of the details?' He pulled over the chair Daniel kept for visitors and sat down on it, as if he intended to stay.

Actually, Daniel was pleased to prolong the discussion. The news of Vayne's arrest was something he did not want to hear, and particularly not so soon. He had agreed with Ian that any arrest should wait until all the evidence was solid, and the witnesses lined up. But this was not really his problem. Let someone else worry about defending Malcolm Vayne! His immediate concern was to be there for Toby, supporting him at the start of his first full week at the helm of fford Croft and Gibson. Vayne had nothing to do with them.

He smiled at Toby. His friend needed reassurance, a reminder that he was more than suited for this new and important role in the chambers. Better to keep the conversation light. 'Let's be honest, most of the major newspapers are owned by Vayne! Do they actually know anything, or will they be printing innuendo and saying how wrong the police are?'

'I'm not sure. Ask Hunter.'

'Hunter? Why?' Daniel said. 'What would he know?' Then

a chilling thought struck him, like ice on the edge of the wind. 'God help us, don't tell me Hunter is going to offer to defend him . . . is he? You'll have to speak to him, make sure he isn't! In fact, you'd better make sure he isn't. Just . . . just commiserate with whoever is!' He realised, in a rush of alarm, how little they knew about Hunter, apart from reports of his skills in the courtroom. Where was his steady core? His morality? His judgement!

Toby's eyebrows shot up. 'I hope not. But I think Hunter has met him on several occasions, related to his philanthropic work. Hunter's wife is involved with several of the same organisations as Vayne.' Then he added, 'Vayne is a complete bounder!' That was his new word for someone who had no saving graces at all. 'He says vile things about other people in his own papers. Which, of course, doubles his sales. Nothing succeeds like scurrilous gossip; any demagogue knows that.' His face creased with anxiety. 'He can write any damn thing he likes, and loads of people will believe him. Does Ian really know what he's doing?'

'He didn't mention any of this on Friday,' Daniel replied, wondering what had happened since then to cause Ian to make such an about-turn.

Had he been given no choice? Was Ian being used by someone else – someone who was hiding behind the police? Some political enemy of Malcolm Vayne, and clearly someone with little sense of self-preservation. Or was there something else about Vayne that the police had just discovered?

Toby was staring at him steadily.

'A cat's paw?' Daniel mused. Perhaps Vayne was using Ian to achieve some unknown end. If so, would it fall on Ian to take the blame, if it all went wrong? It was a justifiable question, and one that made Daniel very wary indeed.

'Is it a case of political envy?' Toby went on. 'Perhaps one of Vayne's own men is trying to topple him – someone who actually hates him? I wish we knew more about Hunter. I don't want to have anything to do with this, even temporarily.'

'Is someone – Vayne or one of his cronies – using Ian to hide behind?' Daniel continued his earlier train of thought. 'It's possible, don't you think? But there's nothing to be done about it, even if that's true, considering the power that Vayne wields. Ian knows the pitfalls. He wouldn't have got himself into this if he could've seen any other way out.' He sighed. 'Damn!' he said quietly, and yet fiercely. 'I can't think of a single thing we can do to mitigate the dangers for Ian, even less to stop the case proceeding to trial!'

Toby nodded, but remained silent for a moment, as if hoping this conversation would go away. He finally spoke. 'So, what do you think of him – our new chap, Gideon Hunter?'

Daniel smiled, sure that Toby was changing the subject to move away from all discussions of Vayne.

'Tell me, Daniel! Do you know anything about him, other than what we read in the paper? I assume he's a bit different from Marcus, and—' Toby left the thought trailing in the air, unfinished.

'No idea yet,' Daniel replied. 'You must have formed some impression of the man.'

'Yes,' Toby agreed, as if reading Daniel's mind. 'He strikes me as formal. That is, based on our one introduction. Outwardly conforming. But inwardly?' He shook his head. 'I don't know. From what Marcus says, he's anything but. I think Marcus is expecting someone colourful, even dangerous.' He stopped. 'Perhaps that's the wrong word. He might mean exciting. Marcus was very much a nonconformist in his youth.'

Daniel stared at Toby. He knew this man quite well. He had seen him in times when he was so tense that he stammered and was physically awkward. Toby never seemed to know what to do with his hands. But once he got started on a subject, he was brilliant. Perhaps his greatest virtue was that he never took things for granted, and he underestimated his own skills. And he cared intensely. Daniel suspected that this adjustment was going to be hard for him.

'He's new here,' Daniel said. With more confidence than he felt, he added, 'We are here already, and we know what Marcus expects of us. We don't win every case, but we win quite a few. And we don't do anything idiotic.'

Toby shrugged his shoulders, almost apologetically. 'I don't like change. I suppose that's a bit stick-in-the-mud of me, isn't it?'

'Yes,' Daniel agreed, with a broad smile. 'And we knew it was coming, this retirement announcement. Better that Marcus goes while he still has quite some time left to enjoy life. We don't want him to die before his time because he wouldn't take it easy. He'll complain like hell about taking a back seat. But honestly, I'm sure he's relieved.'

If Toby knew that, he was more tactful than to say so. 'Gideon Hunter is supposed to be brilliant,' he said. 'Even if he takes a few chances.' He stopped. Always cautious, Toby often doubted the wisdom of voicing his opinion, and especially so soon. He took a deep breath. 'Anyway,' he went on, 'I don't expect it will make all that much difference, at least to begin with. Thank goodness we've got a lot of steady clients who will stay with us, as long as we don't do anything radically different. They will be loyal to Marcus, if nothing else. And Hunter will see to it that we satisfy their needs and keep them loyal to the chambers. No doubt he'll bring in new people as

33

well.' He stopped again, as if too uncertain to carry the thought any further.

'I hope he isn't too conservative,' Daniel said, with sudden feeling. 'Marcus had all sorts of qualities, and I suppose weaknesses too, but he knew what they were, and could make up for them. And he was never a bore. Ever!'

'Be careful what you wish for,' Toby said, with a lopsided smile. 'I'd settle for just survival, at least to begin with.' He shrugged his shoulders again, but this time it was less of an apology than an expression of uncertainty, the gesture suggesting that his jacket was too tight when, in fact, it was perfectly cut.

It was not a busy day, merely a matter of doing a little work on familiar cases, and Daniel was able to be home before six in the evening. Miriam, too, had had a quiet day, and she was there to welcome him.

'Did you hear the news?' he asked, still holding her closely after the first greeting. She was slender, but so alive, so strong. It was a feeling that was still exciting. Perhaps it would always be this good, this gentle, even when he became used to it . . . if he ever did!

She pulled away a little so she could meet his eyes. 'About Malcolm Vayne?' She frowned slightly. 'When he was here, Ian didn't sound as if he meant to arrest him this quickly. Do you suppose he was forced into it? Or has something new happened? The news I heard from Father was very vague. It was such a muddled account of the charge against Vayne that I wondered if the journalists even understood it themselves.'

'I bought an evening paper on the way home,' Daniel replied. 'It was the first newsstand I passed, and it's one of Vayne's. The paper is complaining indignantly about false charges of corruption, claiming that Vayne is the victim of political lies, forgery. It's pretty well what you would expect. They're trying to make a martyr of him, suggesting the police are manipulating evidence to make the charges stick.'

'Do you think that's possible? That it could be a mistake?' she asked. 'Perhaps a frame-up orchestrated by an enemy? Vayne is powerful enough to have quite a few. And he helps some causes that many people are against.'

'Like women's suffrage?' Daniel asked, with a wry smile. 'I suppose it's possible, but it seems a clumsy way of going about it. It will be far more effective to keep on saying that a woman's place is in the home, raising children, cooking and sewing, making new things out of old. Don't say it!' He smiled at the look of disgust on her face. 'I know, and I agree. Everybody should have a vote, even men who don't own property, or pay taxes. We'll have a better chance of our system working if we all have a say. Even if we're only choosing between one rich man and another, when it comes down to it!'

'But is somebody trying to destroy Vayne?' Miriam insisted.

He let go of her, reluctantly, and followed her through to the sitting room that faced south-west. At this time of the evening, it was still filled with sunlight. It faded the carpet a little, and showed the patches of wear on the sofa, but he didn't see them any more, and he thought neither did she. It was a home lived in, familiar, not shining new. He liked it this way, as if it had always been here, waiting for them.

'Probably it's politically motivated, or there's a financial incentive. There is a vast amount of money involved,' he answered her question. 'But that doesn't mean he's innocent . . . or guilty. He'll have enemies because of his political views, and because of where he donates his money. If the charges are valid, there will be people – innocent and trusting people

35

– who've lost their homes and income because of him. I'm glad it's not our job to defend him.'

He sat down on the sofa and sank into its familiar comfort.

'So am I,' she agreed. 'I just hope they don't make his support for women's suffrage part of the case against him, or an example of his irresponsibility. It shouldn't be a side issue . . . to anything!'

The following morning, Daniel was at fford Croft and Gibson by nine o'clock, but as Impney informed him, he had arrived later than Gideon Hunter.

He had just sat down at his desk and started to look at the post, which Impney had opened and placed there for him, when there was a knock on his door. Daniel had no time to answer before it opened. It was not Impney again, as he expected, but a man he had met only once before, and very briefly.

Gideon Hunter was slender, but appeared to be strong and graceful, and he was immaculately dressed. His clothes looked personally tailored for him, something Daniel would like to afford for himself one day. This man also had a highly individual face: interesting and intelligent, not handsome. His nose was too long, his mouth a bit large. A kind person would have described it as 'generous'.

'Good morning,' he said to Daniel, coming into the room as if it were also his.

Daniel rose quickly to his feet and took the man's outstretched hand.

Hunter smiled. 'Please, sit down.' He waved his hand at Daniel's chair, and then pulled up the visitor's chair and sat down on it without being invited. 'I suppose you have heard this morning's news?' It was a question, but the assumption of an answer was in his face and his manner.

'Yes, sir, if you mean about Malcolm Vayne,' Daniel replied, sitting also, and wondering why Hunter had come to see him, if only to mention that.

'I do,' Hunter agreed. 'It's going to be one of the most important cases to be tried in a decade at least, possibly far longer. It will be a fierce battle.' He was watching Daniel surprisingly closely.

'Will it?' Daniel asked dubiously. 'Do you think they have much evidence?'

Hunter looked surprised. 'Don't you?'

Daniel hesitated. Should he tell what he knew to this man he had only just met, but who might well be his superior for years to come. He hesitated too long.

'You doubt it?' Hunter asked, and this time it was a challenge accompanied by a bright interest in his eyes.

'Yes, sir,' Daniel replied. 'I went to school with Ian Frobisher, the policeman who's heading the investigation, and we were at university together as well. He visited me at home only recently, and he mentioned the case. He said he didn't have enough evidence to do anything.'

Hunter's eyes widened. 'Really? What else did Frobisher say regarding Vayne?'

Daniel did not hesitate. 'That he didn't respect Vayne very much, although he gives a great deal of money to causes we both believe in. He didn't say anything concrete.' He waited. Why was Hunter mentioning it at all? Was he hoping fford Croft and Gibson would be asked to defend Vayne? He pushed that idea away. No, if they were asked, it would be Hunter who would be leading counsel. It was a huge case, even if it turned out to be easily defended. Perhaps that was exactly what Marcus had wanted.

'Then something must have happened over the weekend,'

Hunter concluded. 'Otherwise, Vayne would not have been arrested yesterday.'

'It's all over the papers,' said Daniel.

'Yes, and Fergus Dalmeny called me about half an hour ago.'

Daniel knew the name immediately. Fergus Dalmeny was another King's Counsel. An imaginative, meticulous man who made no secret of his ambitions.

'Is he going to defend Vayne?' Daniel asked curiously. 'Surely it's too soon for such a thing to be decided? Unless, that is, Malcolm Vayne saw this coming and had already retained counsel, perhaps the best counsel in London. Or anywhere else. Is that possible?'

'Yes,' Hunter agreed, smiling slightly.

'Already?' Daniel said. 'So, Vayne was expecting it! That's interesting.'

'Isn't it!' Hunter agreed.

Daniel felt both relief and disappointment. He did not want to defend Vayne. As much as he appreciated his financial support of many charities, he disliked the man himself. It was completely unreasonable, because he didn't know him personally, but there was something about his public persona that made Daniel uncomfortable. Still, it would have been an exciting challenge! The fford Croft and Gibson name would become known to every lawyer or aspiring student of the law in London, and places far beyond. But, at the same time, failure to defend Vayne successfully would be expensive, both in terms of reputation and public opinion. However, if Ian could not prove his case beyond all doubt, he would not have moved to arrest him.

'Thank you for telling me, sir,' he said to Hunter. 'It will be one to watch.'

Hunter's eyebrows shot up. 'Watch? For heaven's sake, Pitt, I don't want you to watch it! We're going to prosecute!' There was a lengthy pause that weighed heavily, and then he learned forward in the chair. 'Did you hear me? We are going to prosecute,' Hunter repeated carefully, as if Daniel hadn't understood the first time. 'As you observed, this is going to be one of the most prominent cases of the decade.' His voice rang with excitement. 'Possibly even the century. Although we're only twelve years into this century, and God knows what could happen in the next nearly ninety years. Time is a fascinating gauge of our lives. Think about it: a century ago, Napoleon was Emperor of France and the Battle of Waterloo was still to happen!' Hunter remained leaning forward, his eyes bright, his body rigid with excitement.

'But, sir, is there enough evidence to prosecute?' Daniel asked, although it sounded much like a protest.

'For God's sake, man! I didn't send Frobisher to arrest Vayne, the police did!' Hunter said hotly. 'I don't know what made the difference between when Frobisher spoke to you and when the arrest was made, but it must be a major development, or they wouldn't have arrested anyone, let alone Malcolm Vayne.'

Daniel felt his heart sink. What could Ian have possibly discovered? Did it really make that much difference? Perhaps he had been forced by the political powers to move so soon. And if so, why?

'It's a mess,' he said aloud.

Hunter leaned back and sat perfectly still. 'A mess that we are going to tidy up,' he said, suddenly very serious again, all excitement gone. 'I have connections. I used them to get this case. Not that so many people wanted it! Don't forget that Frobisher thinks Vayne is guilty.'

'Yes, but that's a far cry from having to prove it in court,'

Daniel argued. 'As recently as Friday, he didn't think he had enough evidence to proceed.'

'Then we'll have to work hard, won't we?' Hunter replied. 'So . . . I lead, and you will be my junior counsel. Are you ready for the challenge, Pitt?'

Daniel's head was swimming. This was too quick. But Gideon Hunter, their new leading barrister, was seated on the other side of his desk, looking at him expectantly. What could he say? To prevaricate would make him look indecisive and weak. That would be Hunter's lasting memory of him, derived solely from this first meeting.

He took a deep breath. 'I'm ready for the challenge, sir. But I'm a long way from ready to prosecute Vayne. I have very little idea of what evidence there is against him. We need to know what it was that made the police move so quickly. I just hope it wasn't political rather than legal.'

'Of course, it could be that,' Hunter agreed. 'Vayne is a highly political animal. As I said, this is going to be the biggest trial of the decade, and it could lead anywhere.'

'Yes, it could,' Daniel agreed. 'And it could bring a lot of people down, if he really did commit fraud . . . and money is actually missing.'

Hunter chewed on his lower lip. 'I want this case, Pitt,' he said earnestly. 'Win, lose or settle, it will make us the highest-profile chambers in London. At least, for a little while. It's time we played big! Otherwise, we'll just get smaller and smaller, until we end up like a magician's trick, disappearing up his own sleeve.'

Daniel was amazed. It was an insult to Marcus to say that, and undeserved. Or perhaps it wasn't. They had been a little comfortable recently. Too comfortable? Daniel had been appearing in court sporadically. He had won, but any competent lawyer could have prevailed in those cases. It was months or more since he had won a complicated or high-profit case. Both he and Toby had been careful of Marcus's reputation, perhaps too careful. Did Marcus know that? Was that why he had invited Gideon Hunter to join the chambers, so that someone who had earned the title of King's Counsel would force Daniel and Toby to take chances, to stop being protective and assume risks now and again?

When one of the senior partners, Jonah Drake, had been alive, they had handled all sorts of cases, and they never played it safe. But Drake had been murdered because of one of those cases, over a year ago. Daniel wondered if Hunter knew even a fraction of the truth about that.

Hunter was watching him, waiting.

'I'll go and see Ian Frobisher and find out what he has.' Daniel looked straight back at Hunter. 'We must know everything there is, good or bad.'

'You know this Frobisher well enough for that?'

'Since I was about ten,' Daniel answered. 'Lost touch with him for a while, after we left university. I came here, and he went into the police. Met up with him this February.'

'The Rainy-day Slasher,' Hunter nodded slowly. 'He caught the chap.'

'Actually, I did,' Daniel corrected him. 'That is, we did it together. I know him quite well enough for that . . .' He paused, and then asked, 'So, have we committed ourselves to prosecuting Vayne? We have, haven't we?'

'Yes, we have,' Hunter said, without hesitation. 'We're in for the duration of the battle.'

Daniel nodded. 'The police and our chambers are now in this together, so I'm quite sure Ian will tell us everything he can.' Daniel stood up, and Hunter rose also.

'What if there really is enough evidence?' Daniel asked. 'Or what if it is more of a political issue involving those who outrank Ian? If it came down to a personal quarrel, I'm sure Ian and his superiors would not have recommended prosecution. Someone as influential as Vayne will have plenty of enemies,' he went on, almost as if speaking to himself. 'In my experience, men who are rich and powerful can also be vindictive, and they almost always have enemies. We don't want to get caught on the wrong side of this, legally.'

'Then we won't!' Hunter answered. 'Anything you are unsure of, come to me. Otherwise, get on with it.'

'Have you checked with Toby Kitteridge? What does he say about it? It's a hell of a case to dump on him. It's his first week in charge and—'

'No, I haven't,' Hunter cut across him. 'He has to take care of the rest of the work, all the other cases, the bread-and-butter kind that we can't do without. I'm sure Kitteridge will agree that I am leading counsel and that you're my junior. Do I have to explain that to you, or do you understand me?'

Daniel took a deep breath and let it out slowly. 'I understand you, sir. And anyway, it's up to Toby Kitteridge, isn't it?'

'Of course it is. But I prefer you to agree. It will be a rough ride.' Hunter smiled, and went out of the door, closing it softly behind him.

Daniel went straight to the police station. If Ian was not there, in all probability someone could tell him where he was, or at least where he was expected to be. He explained, when asked, that it was regarding his current case.

'Sergeant Bremner is here, sir. Perhaps you could give him your information?' the constable at the desk suggested.

Daniel accepted. At the very least, he could get an idea of

what Ian had learned that changed his view in such a short time.

Bremner was alone in the office he shared with Ian. The desk was tidy on his side, while Ian's side was covered with a mountain of papers. Daniel smiled. Ian was wildly untidy, and yet he always knew where every piece of paper was, and could remember most of them by heart. It reminded him of his father, Thomas Pitt, whose pockets were always bulging with odds and ends.

'Good morning, sir,' Bremner said, with a flicker of curiosity in his blunt, expressive face. His auburn hair was brushed neatly off his brow, for now. It was his habit to push his fingers through it whenever he was deep in thought. His accent was fairly broad Northumbrian, with an individual lilt of the north-east coast in it.

'Good morning, Sergeant,' Daniel replied. Ian was Bremner's immediate superior, and it might be illuminating to get his opinion of the Vayne case before he heard Ian's.

But Bremner interjected quickly, 'I'm afraid Inspector Frobisher won't be back for a little while. Can I help you?' He said it as if it were mere politeness, and he did not expect his question to be followed up.

'Yes, please,' Daniel accepted, sitting down in Ian's chair as if he'd been invited to. 'Ian came to see me on Friday. Told me about Malcolm Vayne. Said he didn't have enough to arrest him. Now I hear that he has done it. And I dare say you don't know yet, but we've got a new head of chambers, as well as a new barrister, a King's Counsel, who will be taking on major cases.' He saw from Bremner's expression that, indeed, he did not know. 'The new man is Gideon Hunter. Mr fford Croft has retired, and Toby Kitteridge is the new head of chambers. What is important is that Mr Hunter is going to head the prosecution against Malcolm Vayne.' He stopped, judging Bremner's reaction.

Bremner looked stunned. In truth, *aghast* would not have been too strong a word.

'Yes,' Daniel went on, with a bleak smile. 'That just about sums up how I feel, too. I would have suggested to Mr fford Croft that we think about the whole matter a good deal harder before committing ourselves, but both Toby and I have just met Mr Hunter for the first time. If it goes as planned, I'm to be junior counsel. If I turn down the opportunity, I'm going to rather rapidly slide down to the bottom of the heap. Mr Hunter is not noted as a man who only takes the easy cases, and I suppose that is what Mr fford Croft wanted. He said as much to me. I understand his not wanting to play it safe, but this is a bit extreme.'

Daniel heard his lengthy explanation, but it mattered to him that Bremner understood.

Bremner caught on immediately. He had worked with Ian Frobisher for two or three years now, and he considered Frobisher and Daniel Pitt to be cut from the same cloth. 'Yes, sir, I see. So, you'll be wanting all the evidence we have – and rather more importantly, an indication of what we may find in the future?'

'Yes,' Daniel agreed simply. 'I'd like to know what changed Ian's mind since Friday. Do you know?'

'Crisis,' Bremner replied. 'We heard that Vayne and his people were aware of our investigation, even if we've kept it quiet. We're sure that evidence was going to be destroyed if we didn't seize it, which we could only do if charges were brought. It was a matter of acting now, before anything vanished.' He lifted his shoulder in a rueful shrug. 'We have a few people who seem prepared to testify, mainly out of desperation, a fear that Vayne will swindle them out of their savings. Or maybe they're willing to testify from hatred. Who knows? But if we didn't move,' he went on, 'we could have lost our chance. And before you ask: no, we didn't want to make the arrest so soon, but there was no choice. Move now, or it's gone.' He gave another shrug, although this one suggested resignation.

Daniel thought through what Bremner had just revealed. 'Did Vayne prompt it – the arrest – do you suppose? To gain public sympathy early on? If so, it looks like he's the one making the decisions, not the police. Rather a bold move, isn't it? But clever. Puts us on the wrong foot.' Daniel meant this as an oddly phrased compliment. It was one step towards respecting Vayne. If not his morality, at least his intelligence. Or that of whoever was advising him.

'I don't know,' Bremner admitted. 'And if he did make this arrest happen, I have no idea what his motives are. Maybe he thinks we don't know as much as we do, and we'll be left looking like fools.'

'Or perhaps he assumed that Ian didn't have the nerve to make an arrest?' Daniel suggested.

'Could be,' Bremner conceded, with an almost remorseful smile, but his words sounded more like praise. 'Mug of tea?'

Daniel knew the tea would be served in an enamel mug, and by this time in the morning, it was probably stewed. It was a far cry from the elegant tray of fresh, fragrant tea that Impney would have brought to Daniel's office. In any case, what was being offered by Bremner would probably be drinkable. 'Thank you,' he accepted.

It was another half an hour before Ian came back, carrying his jacket on his arm, his hair blown chaotically over his forehead by the warm wind. He did not look surprised to see Daniel, now sitting in the visitor's seat near his desk. 'Thought you might be here,' he remarked, turning to hang his jacket on the coat hook. He sat down in his chair. 'Heard that we had arrested Vayne? His papers are screaming about it already.' He pushed his hair back with one hand. 'Got the morning edition out and they're already yelling blue murder that he's been arrested on a corrupt charge because of lying witnesses, police bribes, forged evidence, and anything else you can think of.'

The man looked miserable, but Daniel was beginning to understand how Ian had been given no choice but to act. He began to feel as if he had also lost his own grip on these latest events. Were the police in control, or had Vayne orchestrated this so that his defence would be fully constructed before the prosecution could even assemble the facts?

'Was he warned, do you suppose?' Daniel asked his friend.

'I don't know,' Ian admitted. 'We're charging him with operating a scheme to defraud people of their savings. He's been very clever, the way he's appealed to their needs, or their greed, and has persuaded them to invest something with the promise of extraordinarily large returns, and fairly quickly. The description given to potential investors is phrased so that all of the profits appear to be the result of skilful money management. And people certainly do believe that Vayne has skill, pretty well amounting to genius. How tempting to believe his investment fund could earn the same sort of fortune for his investors as he did for himself. But what nobody bothers to mention is that it's a scheme, and an illegal one at that.'

'People believe what they want to,' Daniel commented.

Ian looked up sharply. 'Some are just greedy, certainly, but a lot of them are desperate. They want to secure their homes,

46

give something to their children, or just stop worrying about their debts – the sort of debts that decent people collect without realising how quickly they add up.' He sighed loudly. 'It's not greed and it's not dishonesty, Daniel. It's just people seeing the chance to stop worrying day and night about money. And Vayne? Well, he's not stupid! Most people who don't lie don't assume that others are lying. Especially if those others are respected, wealthy, well dressed and articulate.'

'Could he be innocent?' Daniel asked, as tactfully as he could.

He did not want to sound critical, but he was now seriously wondering if Hunter had made a profound error, and had manoeuvred Toby into agreeing. Was this, as Vayne was apparently suggesting, a private vendetta being waged against him, to punish him for his success? Was it possible that the police were being manipulated as tools in someone else's war?

Ian shook his head. 'I listened to these people, Daniel. They are a strange mix. Many are frightened, but clinging on to courage. Others are busy denying what they know, and stumbling onwards in spite of fear. It's not going to be easy, it never was, but I can't go back. I'll give you all the information, the evidence that I have, and I hope I can prove the charges. I'll even give you the names and addresses of witnesses. But Daniel,' he added, 'don't get in my way.'

Daniel wasn't sure how to respond. Get in Ian's way? How? 'Do you think you've got him? Really got him?' he finally asked.

'I don't know,' Ian admitted. 'I thought so, but I've had to move a lot sooner than I wanted to. I'm not sure we have all the facts.' He gave a slight shrug. 'I fear there are some nasty surprises ahead.'

* * *

47

When Daniel arrived home from the office that evening, Miriam had been home for a couple of hours and was beginning to be anxious. When she came into the hall at the sound of the front door opening, her face flooded with relief.

'Sorry,' he said immediately, closing the door behind him, and then putting his arms around her. 'I should have telephoned to say I'd be late, but I kept thinking I would only be a few minutes more . . . and then I wasn't.' He held her a little too tightly, and then realised it after a moment or two and let his arms loosen a bit. 'This case is going to be worse than I thought,' he said, stroking her hair, and at the same time pulling the pins out. 'Something happened that made Ian move before he was ready, but I don't know whether it was by chance or design. Vayne is a very big fish indeed, and maybe we should have had all of our evidence lined up before we let anyone know about it.'

She pulled away a little, so she could meet his eyes. 'We?' she asked warily.

He took a deep breath. 'Hunter has taken the case for the prosecution. We've no choice now.' He always assumed she knew what was happening in her father's chambers. It wasn't unusual for Marcus to confide in her.

'Is that wrong?' she asked. 'Someone has to prosecute.'

'I know. But I don't think Hunter knows enough to have decided so quickly.'

'If he waited, wouldn't he have lost the chance?'

'Yes.' He took a deep breath. 'But we know so little about Vayne's likely guilt or innocence.'

'Then it's your job, your responsibility, to question people, get papers, find the evidence, and build the case, brick by brick.'

She was right, but he still felt that the police had been too quick to make a charge, although it seemed as if they had been forced into it. 'It was always going to be the same result,' he answered. 'Even if we'd been clever enough to disguise our enquiries as something else. The guilty flee where no man pursueth!' He gave her a tight smile. 'If he really is guilty, people tend to see an investigation before it happens, because they're expecting it. But whether he's guilty or not, we need more evidence ahead of going to trial. He's already lashing out at the police. His newspapers are full of indignant accusations of greed, persecution, political opportunism, and anything else they can think of. It's the first day, and the battle lines are already being drawn.'

'His newspapers,' she repeated. 'Yes. Vayne has his own public forum, doesn't he? He can give his readers his side of everything, slanted and self-serving.'

'Yes, but there will be several papers against him. I'm not sure how many readers that equates to.'

'Come into the sitting room,' she said. 'I've had the windows open until a little while ago, and the room smells of summer in the air. Are you hungry?'

He shook his head. 'Not really. Maybe a sandwich, and a decent cup of tea. One that hasn't been sitting in the pot for hours.'

He let go of her and followed her into the sitting room. She was right. It was filled with garden scents, flowers, and one of the neighbours must have been mowing grass. It was a fresh, green perfume, almost as heady as a bowl of flowers, but less overwhelmingly sweet.

'I'll bring a tea tray,' she said.

Ten minutes later, they were seated side by side, the doors open just enough to let in the lingering aromas. Outside, the evening wind was stirring in the trees.

They discussed all that had happened, with everything

leading back to the fact, or at least the assumption, that Ian had been manoeuvred into arresting Malcolm Vayne before he had assembled all his evidence.

'Orchestrating his arrest – if that's really what he did – without all the facts, is a smart thing for Vayne to do,' said Miriam. 'It leaves him all sorts of opportunities to accuse the police of smearing his reputation.'

'I hadn't thought Vayne was so clever,' Daniel admitted. 'It's a bad mistake, and one I'd better not make again.'

'Perhaps it's preferable to make it now rather than later?' she said hopefully.

Her observation was of little comfort to him. 'I think Vayne is more prepared than we are.'

She looked at him, with a slight frown. 'Do you think he's guilty, and that he'll get away with it because he's had plenty of time to plan? Or to trip you up? Or are you afraid that you have fallen into a trap of your own making, and he could be innocent?'

He made a little gesture of regret. 'I honestly don't know,' he replied. 'He has so much money, so much influence, with his newspapers and his philanthropy, that he could be as guilty as hell and we'd have to be very clever to prove it.'

She smiled. It was a soft, sweet smile, but her gaze was direct. 'Then don't go to trial until you have everything as prepared as possible,' she said gently. 'As prosecutor, you have some say about when the trial begins, yes? On the one hand, if you begin it as quickly as you can, he'll have less time to work out his defence. And he knows that he's being investigated, but the onus is on you to prove his guilt. Not just in the eyes of the law, but even more importantly, in the eyes of the people. On the other hand, if you wait until you're fully prepared, he'll have that extra time as well.'

Daniel nodded, but said nothing.

'There will be two arenas where this trial will play out,' Miriam continued. 'In the public, and in the courtroom. Perhaps this is both to Vayne's advantage and his disadvantage, I'm not sure.'

He looked at her steadily, realising she meant far more than the words implied. Vayne's trial – whether he was eventually found guilty or innocent of the charges levelled against him – could have far-reaching consequences for Daniel's own career and for the reputation of fford Croft and Gibson. He was overwhelmingly grateful to have her there at the end of every day, always on his side. And Miriam never prevaricated. For Daniel, this was the deepest possible meaning of not being alone.

Chapter Four

Sir Thomas Pitt stared at the newspaper lying open on his desk and resisted the temptation to tear it up. It would serve no purpose, except perhaps to release feelings of frustration . . . and a rising anger.

The headlines were black, in bold letters that seemed an inch tall. He knew they were not; they were just designed that way to catch the readers' attention.

The police had arrested Malcolm Vayne for fraud. There was a photograph of him, taken in happier times, smiling and waving to his supporters. He was a good-looking man, in his late fifties, with what appeared to be thick, light-auburn hair. In the picture, he was wearing an immaculate dark and well-tailored suit.

His was a face that everyone who opened a newspaper would recognise. Malcolm Vayne attended functions, celebrations and society weddings; he gave generously to all manner of charities. His newspapers never failed to display a photograph of him at every opportunity.

And now . . . he had been arrested for fraud!

It was not the arrest that made Pitt so angry; it was the timing of it. This was a subject of increasing interest to Special

Branch, for reasons that had no immediate connection with fraud. It was unlikely that Pitt's case would be seriously impeded by it.

The dismissal of the case against Vayne would only increase the man's confidence, and his popularity. If the police had waited another three or four weeks, giving Vayne extra freedom so that he might believe he was untouchable, or too big to be brought down by petty details, then conviction would have been certain. As it was, with a good lawyer – and Vayne could afford the best – he would emerge a free man, shedding the skin of accusation as a snake sheds its old skin and emerges renewed.

Pitt was head of Special Branch, that part of the system that dealt with threats of anarchy, terrorism and sabotage within the country. It had begun as a defence against the Irish Fenians' bombings, and remained as a powerful force, ready to deal with anything that fell within its remit. It was highly secret, as well as secretive. And with parts of the world becoming increasingly accessible, Special Branch was very respected around the globe. And, by some, even feared. The identity of the head of this department was kept secret; only Pitt's family knew, and selected people in the government.

The crimes that fell under Pitt's jurisdiction were becoming regrettably larger, with the dangerous rise of social violence all over Europe. The threatened violence of anarchy was everywhere. The overthrow of governments was a constant spectre, stalking the edges of Pitt's vision, glimpsed and then gone again.

Pitt thought of Malcolm Vayne. The man had far more power, and thus influence, than most people realised. Everyone knew he was rich. He gave away more in a year than most people earned in a lifetime. But where did it come from, and to whom was it given? Much of it was to well-known charities. His newspapers trumpeted that news regularly.

Now that this arrest had taken place, Pitt needed some time to learn the facts. His private information from the police had said they were far from ready to act. So, what had happened to change that? He had known Ian Frobisher, on and off, for years. He was a close friend of Daniel, and he could still remember Ian as a boy of ten, a little thin, growing too quickly; his long legs giving him a lanky appearance, and floppy hair always over his eyes. There was a certain innocence to the boy that Pitt had always liked. He was pleased when Daniel had chosen him as a friend.

The years went by . . . and then tragedy had struck. It saddened Pitt that, since the death of Ian's wife, their infant daughter was being looked after by Ian's mother. Pitt could not imagine how he himself would have fared, had that happened to him. He had a daughter, Jemima, now married to an American policeman and living in New York. Then a son, Daniel, a constant source of pleasure and anxiety, hope and fear, and tremendous pride.

None of this was related to why Ian had moved, ahead of plan, and arrested Vayne so soon. There must have been an overpowering reason, beyond Ian's control.

At the same time, Pitt had not told Ian, or anyone else, his true motive for wanting Vayne arrested. Special Branch operated on secrecy and discretion. They did not have to explain themselves to anyone except the Prime Minister. There were still many details he needed to clarify about Vayne's activities, none of them having to do with financial fraud. He knew that Vayne moved huge amounts of money around, and that the actual dishonesty was difficult to find, let alone prove. But that was all domestic lawbreaking, within Ian Frobisher's purview.

It was the job of the police to uncover the evidence of fraud; the pyramid scheme that took people's money, with the promise of huge rewards, then gave the first 'investors' the money paid by the second wave, and the second by the third wave, and so on. None of it produced income. That was the scam. However, while deeply dishonest, it was for the regular police to deal with, not Special Branch.

Pitt's interest was focused on the power that came with such an enormous flow of money. And all power could be dangerous in the wrong hands. What did Vayne plan to do with it? And more importantly, who else was involved? Special Branch had uncovered information suggesting that Malcolm Vayne was linked to a small number of very powerful men. The name of the Seebach Group had been mentioned, but his people were finding it difficult to pinpoint who they were.

His job was to identify Vayne's contacts, and find out about the transfer of money. Pitt suspected that massive sums were being deposited in one of Vayne's secret personal accounts. Where these accounts were remained a mystery.

And who was the Seebach Group? Rich and powerful men who invested in Vayne's companies for the profits? Or was it something else? Vayne rubbed elbows with men of great power, from members of parliament to officers of the Treasury. He hobnobbed with ministers of major government departments, specifically Defence, and both the Foreign and Home Offices. How did Pitt know this? Vayne's newspapers never missed the opportunity to splash photos of Vayne with these people on the front pages. Some of his so-called friends were from old families with inherited wealth, although one never knew how much of that still remained in the hands of the family, or how much had been spent, squandered or gambled away. To the public, it didn't matter. Power was power. And if some of these famous people secretly had more debts than assets, the public would rather not know.

Pitt opened a folder of secret documents and leafed through several pages. It was his job to know everything he could ascertain about Vayne and his finances. He already suspected fraudulent dealings – probably with this Seebach Group – but there were other possibilities, and they all needed to be explored.

Unlike Ian Frobisher, Special Branch was not yet ready to charge Vayne with anything. Pitt thought about this; he was worried that Ian might have been railroaded by his superiors into making this untimely arrest. If Ian had not been pressured, then what had he uncovered to justify it? Or even to make it urgently necessary.

From Pitt's point of view, there were far too many unknowns to make a good case against Vayne. He also believed that if they did bring charges, and then failed to prove them, Vayne would have made himself practically invincible. He would be the wrongly accused! The hero of the common man. The modern-day Robin Hood who squeezed donations out of the rich to give to the poor. The collapse of the case against him would only enhance his reputation even more, and he could very well emerge from the fiasco with the public firmly on his side and donating to his causes in even greater numbers.

What if the 'cause' was Vayne himself? Pitt shook off that thought. The last thing he wanted was for Malcolm Vayne to become even more popular than he had been before his arrest. His own newspapers would certainly make him out to be the man of the people! More powerful in the public eye, and even wealthier.

Pitt questioned if it really would have been wiser for the police not to show their hand now. Should they have waited for another chance, after all the facts were assembled? But he knew the answer to that even before he framed the question. No. It would have been seen as manipulating the facts, in a sense playing the system. The papers would have had a field day, and for good reason. Something had occurred which had left Ian no choice but to act.

These days, people were showing more respect for the police. Pitt could well remember in his early days, when he was even younger than Daniel was now, being obliged to go around to the back door of a house, as if he were a debt collector, or a rat catcher. There was an unspoken order to the servants: for heaven's sake, don't let the neighbours see! But he had refused to be treated like that, and had reaped the unfortunate consequences more than once. Over time, however, things had changed mightily.

After many years moving up the ranks in the police force, he was dismissed on a false charge. He had been immediately recruited to Special Branch by Victor Narraway, then the head of operations. On Narraway's retirement, Pitt had been appointed head of Special Branch. Not so very long ago, he had been knighted by the Old Queen, in the last years of her life, for services rendered to the Crown, with the utmost discretion. While he was no longer a policeman, he was a part of the government that people respected.

Pitt reached into his pocket, always stuffed to nearly overflowing, and took out his pocket watch. He smiled wryly. He knew better than to believe the social acceptance he enjoyed was linked to his position. Everyone who knew him understood that his acceptance into all levels of society, and especially the ranks of the aristocracy, was thanks to the charm, distinction and family status of his wife, Charlotte, now Lady Pitt.

Pitt was no fool. He also understood that he was feared by

those few who knew about his position in Special Branch. It brought with it almost unlimited power, and access to secrets many believed should never be disclosed. Not necessarily secrets related to any crime that had been committed, but to matters that were private: matters of debt, indiscretion, a vulnerability of any sort.

Still, simply knowing so much made him dangerous in the eyes of some, which explained why he was quietly discreet about his position, and always looked over his shoulder with a careful and vigilant eye. Not just for his own safety, but that of his family.

In truth, Pitt would rather not have known people's private weaknesses. He felt more pity than anger for most of them. He understood vulnerability; he was only too aware of his own. And for that reason, he loathed Malcolm Vayne, a man who seemed more than capable of extorting things from people – money, power, social standing – who had secrets they wished to hide.

It crossed his mind again that it had been too early to spring the trap. He assumed Ian Frobisher must have been forced to do it, and that was what worried him. It worried him gravely.

Chapter Five

The front page of the newspaper had a picture of Malcolm Vayne smiling as he walked out of police custody. He was on bail. Since he had not been charged with a violent crime, he was not kept in jail. He was waving at the camera. The caption quoted him as saying that he was about to blow wide open the conspiracy against him.

'We need to be on top of the facts,' Gideon Hunter said grimly, staring at Daniel. 'God knows why the police arrested him so soon. Something forced their hand.' He bit his lip. 'Has Frobisher taken leave of his wits?' He looked bleak. 'Either that, or he's been bought. And before you take offence, which I can see in your face, the other alternative that comes to mind is that, for whatever reason, he felt he had no choice. I need to know what the hell is going on. This is bad, Pitt. Either Vayne is extraordinarily lucky or, more probably, he is very clever indeed.'

'Lucky?' Daniel asked doubtfully.

'Of course, lucky,' Hunter replied. 'That is, if he forced the police to act before any of us are ready. If we're not prepared to give the reason for his arrest, which means detailing the charges against him, it makes us look incompetent and spiteful. Find out, Pitt!' His voice grew sharper. 'We've got to know! We're acting in the dark, blindfolded, and God knows what we'll trip over, and then fall flat on our faces in the end. Find out!'

'What changed?' Daniel asked as he entered Ian Frobisher's office at the police station. 'On Friday, you were working on finding proof before you moved. Then, on Monday morning, you arrested Vayne!' He sounded more accusing than he had meant to.

At the same time, Daniel felt what he believed to be a reasonable hope. If the police had proceeded intelligently, carefully, and this had resulted in the arrest of the man himself, rather than one of his lackeys, perhaps Vayne would not get away with it.

'Ian,' he said, and then he stopped. He noticed that Ian's face was tense, paler than usual. 'What's happened?' Daniel asked, gently now. He sat down, a knot tightening in his stomach.

'Nadine Parnell,' Ian said quietly. He looked bleak and unhappy in his ever-messy office. It was clean, but shabby.

Daniel ran through information stored in his mind. Nadine Parnell. 'Do you mean Vayne's personal assistant, or whatever she is?'

Nadine Parnell was well into her seventies, perhaps closer to eighty.

Ian smiled rather grimly. 'She refuses to mention her age, even to acknowledge it, but she's still sharper witted than most people decades younger.' His smile disappeared. 'And she had the courage to say she'd testify against Vayne.' He held up his hand, palm facing Daniel. 'And before you ask: yes, she knows a lot. She's not only Vayne's assistant, she's in effect his chief accountant. And after decades working with him, she not only knows her job, she knows where all the bodies are buried; most of them so well hidden that they'd be impossible for anyone else to find. She was prepared to sit in court and tell us everything she knows.' He looked away for a moment, sadness crossing his face. 'Unfortunately—'

'Don't tell me she's ill!' Daniel declared, cutting Ian off.

'Worse, I'm afraid. She was knocked down by a car.'

Daniel felt as if the earth under his feet had suddenly yawned open.

'She's not badly hurt,' Ian said quickly. 'A few nasty bruises, and a cut on one leg. But she's shaken. She's certain it was not an accident and—'

'Certain . . . or just believes?' Daniel asked, interrupting again.

'Knows,' Ian said firmly, leaning back a little in his chair. His face was tired, but he seemed perfectly in control. 'And witnesses agree. The vehicle wouldn't have hit her, had it kept to its course, but it turned sharply and drove straight at her.'

'Did you get the driver? What did he say?'

'No, we didn't get him. He accelerated and was lost in the traffic within minutes. Everyone close by was too busy either trying to help Mrs Parnell or calling for an ambulance.'

'Ambulance? I thought you said she wasn't badly hurt.'

'She wasn't, compared with what she might have suffered. But she was very shaken, and that cut in her leg was deep. They were afraid that she would go into shock. She was taken to hospital to get the wound cleaned and stitched, and kept under observation for a day or two.' He paused and gave a little smile. 'She might be elderly, but she seems full of energy, and she certainly hasn't lost her memory, or any of her wits. And she's very, very angry!'

'But still, the trauma—'

'She's an old woman, Daniel, but she seems to be fit as a flea and mad as a hornet. I believe she's more shaken up than she'll admit. And before you argue with me, that's her doctor's opinion, not hers.'

'A warning?' Daniel asked. He felt cold, and everything seemed suddenly dark, as if the sun had slid below the horizon and robbed the sky of light. 'Just the thought that someone would deliberately injure an old woman so badly. The shock could easily have killed her.'

'I'd say it was a warning, very clearly,' Ian admitted.

'You're not—' Daniel began tentatively, then stopped what he had been going to say, which was to ask if Ian was planning to dangle her as bait to tempt Vayne to make a move. But he said nothing, finding the thought offensive. And, in truth, frightening.

'I'm not,' said Ian, as if he knew what Daniel was about to say, but had chosen not to. 'Even if I had any doubt, which I don't, I couldn't afford to ignore this. She knows plenty about Vayne that is damning. If not, he wouldn't have taken such a risk. And am I sure? Not absolutely, but she is.'

'More than sure,' said Daniel. 'She's also brave.'

'That she is,' Ian agreed. 'I don't know whether she'll feel the same way if he tries again. Next time, he might kill her.' His face was hard and bleak. 'Not Vayne himself, of course. I'm sure he has people who would do that sort of thing for him.'

'Isn't there someone else who would know what she knows? She can't do all that bookkeeping alone, can she?'

'Of course not,' Ian explained. 'All of the financial work is done in many separate places, by different individuals working in different departments of his companies. One hand doesn't know what the other is doing. Except for Nadine. She oversees it all, and has done for years, before he became so rich. That makes her the only one who can put it all together. She is indispensable to our case against him. If we're talking financial ledgers, money in and out, she knows it all.'

'Isn't that a hell of a risk?' Daniel was grasping at anything that would deny the reality of the threat. Suddenly, it was so much more than a matter of money, regardless of how clever the scheme, or how much Vayne had taken from his victims. This was about deliberately trying to murder someone, an old woman, because she might testify against him. 'I think we can assume that it wasn't Vayne himself who drove into her.'

Ian nodded. 'One of my men has looked into Vayne's whereabouts. He was miles away when she was hit. We'd be crazy to accuse him. Imagine what his counsel would say in court! And what he would do to Nadine, for bringing about such an accusation. Her testimony would be worthless. A foolish old woman imagining things.'

'She didn't say it was Vayne, did she?' Daniel asked.

'No, of course not!' Ian replied, fairly sharply. 'She's not some daft old woman you can dismiss. She told the police she lost her balance because a man bumped into her on the pedestrian crossing and she fell in front of the vehicle. She couldn't say for certain that it was an accident, or that it was intentional.'

'Then—'

'I went to see her. She's our only witness who will reveal anything meaningful against Vayne.'

'And she still will do?' Daniel had already asked this, but he felt the need to ask again. He had to know.

'So far,' Ian agreed. 'As I've said, she's a very brave woman, and a very angry one.' A swift flash of humour crossed his face, and then vanished completely. 'She's waited for the chance to expose Malcolm Vayne for a long time. She's had suspicions about his financial dealings, and Vayne has always managed to assuage them. She never pushed it with him. Instead, she's brought it up as possible bookkeeping errors, but she knows better. And she also knows that most people who work with her would lie to protect him, and themselves. But this time he has gone too far, and she can prove it. She's sharing with us solid evidence about the scam he was running, including the names of people he cheated. As I said, Nadine Parnell is more than a bookkeeper: she collects returns from all the various enterprises and counts them meticulously. I don't think Vayne has any idea how much she understands and remembers.'

'But if she really has evidence against him,' Daniel said, 'and Vayne knows this, then he'll have no choice but to silence her. Hide her away somewhere . . . or have her killed.' He was surprised how calmly he could say that. 'She's not safe anywhere.'

'Then I suggest you get your evidence together as soon as possible,' Ian said, with an edge to his voice. 'Once she has given her testimony in writing, and has signed it, she will be a little safer, please heaven. And she could do this now.'

'Surely Vayne is clever enough to know that if anything happened to her, it would be damning?' Daniel said, as if talking to himself. 'The most he could do would be to discredit her, so that no one believes her.'

'Then go and get her statement now, Daniel! And be sure to get everything you can, in case they try to hurt her again. I think Vayne is far too clever to incriminate himself by going after her a second time, but he's also clever enough to do it in a way that might look like an accident. Something he can't be blamed for . . . and of course, untraceable to him.'

'Isn't it risking too much?' Daniel asked dubiously.

'I hope so, because that might force his hand. But let's assume that it isn't,' Ian replied, his voice as stony as his face. 'If I'm wrong, I want to err in the direction of overestimating Vayne, not underestimating him. As to getting himself blamed, he'll get one of his loyal servants to do it for him. And yes, even be hanged for it. The killer and the witness, all dealt with in one blow.'

Daniel hated appearing to attack Ian, but he felt he was getting this rather seriously out of proportion. 'I'll go to the hospital and see her. I need to know exactly where she is, so when I arrive, I can look as if I know her. And you'd better call the hospital and have them let me in. I'll go now and take down her evidence.' Another thought suddenly rushed into his head. 'Is there a policeman with her, to keep her safe?'

Ian nodded. 'Yes, of course. And don't forget to have her sign it, every page!' He stood up. 'And I hope I'm overdramatising this, Daniel, but I don't think so. Which is why I've got one of my best men guarding her room.'

Before Daniel left, Ian handed him a list of names. 'Investors,' he explained.

Three-quarters of an hour later, Daniel was standing at the door that opened to Nadine Parnell's room. As Ian had said, there was a guard at the door. Johnson was his name, and he was very large, muscular. In Daniel's estimation, no one was going to get by him.

Daniel introduced himself, then went in and stood at the bedside of Nadine Parnell, an elderly woman with soft grey-brown hair. Her face was at least half-masked by several large gauze bandages, all placed at different angles to cover the dark purple bruises. Despite their presence, the deep discolouration was visible wherever the gauze was only a single layer thick. Her brown eyes stared at him with interest.

'Mrs Parnell, I'm Daniel Pitt, junior counsel to Mr Gideon Hunter, who is leading the prosecution against Malcolm Vayne. How are you?' He stared at her steadily, and with a very slight smile, so she would know that he was asking not out of courtesy but genuine interest. At the same time, he wanted an answer.

'It hurts,' she said. 'But I'll settle for that. Most things worth doing can hurt at some time or another. Or anyone could do them. If you've come to see if I'm still well enough to testify, I've got some questions for you. At least one, to begin with.'

'May I sit down?' Daniel glanced at the hard-backed chair drawn up to the bed, clearly for visitors.

She smiled bleakly and nodded, as if these were merely games of courtesy. Daniel sat, reminding himself that she deserved the truth, unabridged and unvarnished.

'In the end,' she said, 'the truth wins. Prevarication is merely the chance to dictate the play. Mr Pitt, did you say? We had two prime ministers called Pitt, you know? The younger was particularly good. Napoleonic Wars. Got rid of the slave trade; made it illegal. Should never have been allowed in the first place.'

'Yes, I know about the prime ministers,' he replied. 'I got teased about it at school. But despite being the younger, I am not nearly as effective or successful as my father. He holds an important position in government.'

'Modest, are you?' She sounded almost disappointed, as if he had somehow broken her expectations. 'That is a trait that might be becoming in front of strangers, and perhaps your father appreciates it, but I don't care for it. As some poet or another said, a man's reach should exceed his grasp, or what is heaven for? Or something like that.'

Daniel smiled. 'Mrs Parnell, I'm not a policeman, I am a lawyer. I don't hold any position of power.'

'A barrister or a solicitor?' she asked immediately.

'A barrister. The sort who makes you reconsider every case, and only takes an open-and-shut case if there's nothing better.' He thought it was a bit bold, but then again . . .

'Starting with Malcolm Vayne?' Her eyebrows rose. 'So, this is why you have come to see me.'

'Continuing with Malcolm Vayne,' he corrected her. 'I've taken some very interesting cases before!'

'Did you win?'

He smiled. 'Not always. And if I said yes, you might think I only took the easy ones.'

She settled a little more comfortably against the pillows and smiled at him, as if she were about to begin an excellent meal. 'Get out your pen and paper, young Mr Pitt.'

'Yes, ma'am,' he said obediently, although he had them out already. He waited for her to speak.

She gave him a list of names; the same names Ian had given him, and then, from memory, she revealed numbers associated with those names. All these numbers were new to Daniel.

As he was writing them down, she asked, 'Did you already know their names?' And then she smiled. 'You did!' It was not an accusation, merely a remark. Her smiled broadened.

'I did,' he admitted. 'But I couldn't know if they were correct until you gave them to me. And I have never seen these numbers.'

'Most of them represent the amounts invested in Vayne's

scheme, money those poor people will never get back. Unless, that is, they were early investors. They got paid, you know. And do you know how?' Before Daniel could respond, she said, 'By the next level of investors. Which means that anyone who's invested recently is out of luck . . . and out of a lifetime of savings, poor people.'

He patted the paper that was now filled with information. 'As I said, I'm a lawyer, and I shall be junior counsel to Gideon Hunter KC, when we take this to court.'

'Sure of yourself, aren't you!' It was an observation, not a criticism.

He smiled. And it struck him that perhaps this was the only expression that could not be challenged.

Nadine Parnell robbed him of any advantage by smiling back, a charming and perfectly natural smile. She must have been very attractive in her youth, and she still held considerable charm, when she wished to.

'Who else are you going to speak to?' she asked.

'No one,' he replied. 'I have spoken to you—' He allowed her to finish the sentence for herself, as to whether she was the most important, the one who was going to provide the bedrock on which he would build the case, fact by fact.

She gave another smile, but this time it reached all the way to her eyes. She nodded, then began to tell him about Peter Rollins, working in the main office in London and acting as a liaison with Vayne's other offices in Bristol, Manchester, Liverpool and Newcastle upon Tyne. Apparently, this Rollins had attended the same public school as Vayne, and was a team player of some skill. Daniel knew from his own experience how some of these friendships became lifelong bonds. There was a trust, a common heritage that could not be mimicked by anything else. He shared much of this with Ian Frobisher.

68

'Sharp as a needle, Peter Rollins is, when it comes to details,' she went on. 'Never forgets one. Knows everything, and where it fits, who thought of it and when. Only problem with him is that he can never stand far enough back to see the whole picture.' She shook her head. 'It's always the same thing for breakfast every day. And for lunch. Saves having to think what to order, so he says. Not a stitch of humour in his entire make-up. Which results in him never telling a lie, because he has no imagination to think of one.' She did not smile as she said it, but there was a bleak amusement in her eyes.

Daniel thought for a moment, trying to visualise in his mind such a man. 'You find this hard,' he said, watching her face.

'I think perhaps you mean difficult,' she countered him. 'It will not hurt him emotionally. Peter Rollins, for example, will not be able to put himself in Malcolm Vayne's shoes and imagine the fall of an empire. He will see the stories crumple, one by one . . . and will never envision the whole picture.' She shifted a little and winced. 'And I doubt he can imagine the suffering of those Vayne has cheated.'

Daniel realised that she hurt more than she was prepared to admit.

'No imagination for the jury,' she went on. 'Or the distress Mr Vayne will feel, just as he would never imagine the empire he was preparing to build.'

'But you can,' Daniel said quickly.

'Oh, yes.' She smiled. 'That's why I'm useful to Vayne, why he had me scared but not killed. I can see the next move, and the move after that, and even the outline of the one after that! I can see which investments are going to profit and which are going to fail, and very often when. He takes my advice, when he makes a legitimate investment of his own money. He has quite a lot, you know.'

'And he takes your advice?'

'Didn't I just say so?'

'Yes. But why are you willing to tell me? I'll use it in court. And he will know that you told me.'

'I hope so,' she said, with satisfaction. 'Right thing to do, but little pleasure in it if he doesn't know it came from me!'

'And there is satisfaction in this?' he asked.

Suddenly a shadow passed over her face and she looked very old. 'Not really. I've had to save money for him before, but this time it's too big, and there are too many other people in it. What did you say your name was?'

A finger of fear tugged at him. She had seemed so sharp, so on top of things. She had forgotten his name? He shook this off and turned back to their conversation. 'Did he tell you what happened to the money, or did you work it out yourself?'

Nadine Parnell gave a little grunt of impatience. 'I can see it for myself, young man. What did you say your name was?' she repeated.

'Daniel.' He omitted his surname this time, it was more familiar. He forced himself to smile.

'What are you smiling at?' she demanded.

That caught him off-guard. The last thing he wanted was to upset her. Or worse, offend her. 'You remind me of my grandmother,' he answered honestly. 'She was quite stuffy, very Victorian. But after my grandfather died, she married an actor far younger than her, and is extremely happy . . . and outspoken.'

'You say this as if you approve!' she told him, keeping all expression out of her eyes, except amusement.

'I do,' he replied. 'She's doing what she wants, not what

70

other people think she ought to do. And my mother, who was from a wealthy family, married a policeman, when that was all he was. But now he's Sir Thomas Pitt.'

'Have you any siblings?' Now she was interested.

'Yes. A sister. She married a New York policeman, and lives in America.'

'And you? Have you the courage and imagination of any of the rest of your family?'

'I married the woman I love.'

'Promising so far, but how far does it go? It could be very unimaginative, or merely convenient.'

'She's a forensic pathologist.'

'Can't do that in England, God help us!' she snapped.

'I know. She qualified in Holland.'

'Dutch?'

'No, English. But persistent.' He smiled at the thought of Miriam.

'Are you persistent? And brave? You'll have to be, to catch Malcolm Vayne.'

It was time to return to his purpose for this visit. 'Mrs Parnell, tell me about the other witnesses.'

'Give me a name and I'll tell you what I know.'

'Richard Whitnall, to begin with.'

'Whitnall is Vayne's international liaison. Trouble is, he's got connections all over the world, Vayne has. Especially in Europe, so Whitnall is always on the go. Speaks several languages. He reminds me of a damn octopus: I don't know how far, or where, the tentacles reach.'

'Whitnall?'

'No, Vayne, you're not paying attention. But Whitnall knows about it. If he wants to think hard, he could put it all together and take Vayne down. Didn't want to, until now.

Too many hostages to fortune. But his wife and his children, three of them I think, are all away, overseas. Either Australia or America. Don't know. Long as they're safe. And I'm sure that's why he sent them away, for their safety. He knows everything about Vayne. Doesn't want to understand it, but with Vayne arrested, he can't help it now. Always thinks the best of people, even when the worst will be far closer to the truth. But I don't think he'll lie to protect anyone. He has any amount of courage, maybe much less of sense.'

'Perhaps I should see him now?' Daniel suggested.

'And take someone with you. Like this Mr Hunter, if you can manage it.'

'Being a silk will impress Richard Whitnall?' Daniel asked curiously.

'I doubt it. Knows a lot of important people. It's about respect, not fear. Lots of political friends, and many respect him – that's useful to Vayne.'

'How useful?' Daniel asked, with a sudden, much sharper interest.

'Political power is based on who you know, and what you know about them. You can't possibly be so young as not to understand that!'

'I want it in your words, Mrs Parnell, not my own.'

She smiled at that. It took the weariness, and perhaps a little physical pain, out of her face. She looked years younger, as if the light had changed.

Daniel listened, and took many notes on what she said about Richard Whitnall. And then notes about John Sandemann, who was apparently the acquisitions manager for Vayne's companies. And for an investment company like Vayne's, one that owned properties all over England, that was a very important position indeed.

'Over the years, Sandemann bought and sold millions of pounds' worth of properties for Vayne,' Nadine said. 'He almost always seems to make a profit. Or should I say, *they* did. It was always Vayne's money, his advice, his direction.'

'And what about Vayne's right-hand man, Callum McCallum?' asked Daniel.

'An unfortunate name, don't you think?' she asked, her eyes twinkling.

Daniel smiled and gave a little shrug.

'McCallum's an interesting man,' she said. 'He seems to have nothing to do with buying or selling, or money in general.'

'Then what does he do?'

'He's been the company's social director. That is, he arranges fabulous parties which high society, even minor royalty, attend. And they are pleased to be seen, especially when the other guests include ministers of government and famous artists. Ballet dancers, opera singers, stage actors! But don't judge McCallum too quickly,' she added, with a sudden, hard note of warning in her voice. 'He is more than he appears to be. These parties of his are sought after by some surprising people. Those with money want to be seen with those who have beauty or power, and vice versa, of course. These parties have raised millions of pounds, over the years, for so many worthwhile charities. McCallum organises them all, then makes sure Vayne is present for all to see.'

'Which charities?' Daniel asked.

She named a few, several of them known to Daniel. 'If you want to know, I'm sure a good deal of what he raised went into Vayne's own pocket. But you will be very clever to prove it!' She gave a bleak smile. 'Much of it will have been written off as a tax credit, of course. And people boast, or overestimate how much they have given, for all sorts of reasons. It is a Gordian Knot. You know what that is?'

'Yes,' he smiled. 'I believe the only way to undo it is with a sword?'

'Quite,' she agreed. 'Have you a sword, young Mr Pitt?'

'I do, and I'm sharpening it,' he replied.

'Well, be careful, and don't you cut yourself! Vayne has friends everywhere. And more important than that, he has influence, people who owe him, and people to whom he owes favours. It's important to know which is which.'

'Do you know?' he asked. 'In what way is it important?'

'In any way. There's no use telling you what he's like today, because tomorrow he could be different.' She said it without emotion, just a statement of fact.

As she gave him her opinions of all the other witnesses, he duly noted them down. He felt the power of her mind. And even more, her personality. But he could not ignore her thin hands on the sheet, and the slenderness of her neck, or even the old-fashioned nightgown. Was she safe? From what? Time? No one could be sure of that. From attack? He had seen the policeman outside in the corridor, and the man had demanded Daniel's identity before he had allowed him in.

'And you are going to question Boyce Turnbull . . . is he on your list? He could tell you a lot, if you ask him the right questions.'

He froze. 'Turnbull? What does he do? Nobody mentioned him.'

'Travel,' she replied. 'A sort of courier. Employed by the job, it seems. But, actually, I'm not sure he works for anybody else, except as Mr Vayne tells him to.'

'Courier?' Daniel asked. 'Carrying what?'

She put her head slightly to one side, but her eyes were very direct. 'Money. Or money orders. Private letters. Things that would fit into a small attaché case, manacled to his wrist. I suppose it could be diamonds, or even gold, but I think it's mostly papers that he wouldn't want to fall into the wrong hands. In some cases, I believe he carries things he could destroy, if forced to.' She shook her head very slightly. 'He knows a lot, does Mr Turnbull, but you'll have to work hard to get it out of him. He knows which side his bread is buttered on.'

Daniel's mind raced. He would tell Hunter as soon as he could. This Turnbull would have to be handled very carefully.

'You didn't know about him, did you?' she observed.

'No,' he admitted. 'But I do now.'

'He's not as daft as he looks, young Mr Pitt. He'll have to think Mr Vayne's going down before he'll give you what you want to know.'

'I'll remember that,' he said. 'But before I go, Mrs Parnell, I need you to sign each of these sheets of paper.'

'Afraid I'll croak before the trial?' she asked, her head tilted slightly and a little smile playing on her lips.

'Never can be too careful,' he said, hoping she shared his humour.

When she laughed, he thanked her, watched her sign the documents, and said goodbye.

After he stepped out of the door, he warned the policeman guarding her room that her evidence was vital, and she was very frail.

'Yes, sir,' said Johnson. 'Believe me, if anyone goes in there and goes for her, he'll have to be big and brave, or she'll have him on toast for afternoon tea!'

Daniel smiled back at him. 'You'd better see that doesn't happen, or you'll be somebody's dinner. Possibly mine! And I'm sure about that.'

'Yes, sir!' Johnson grinned.

Daniel saw how his eyes blinked quickly. Despite his grin, Daniel was certain he understood the seriousness of the situation. The safety of Nadine Parnell was paramount.

Chapter Six

The following Wednesday, Daniel went into the office early. They were just over a week into the case, and there was still a great deal to do. He needed to sort the evidence he had so far, and then plan the questions they would be asking anyone who had not yet been interviewed. And, of course, find out about Boyce Turnbull.

He was surprised to see Hunter's office door open, and Hunter himself sitting at his desk. There were papers spread everywhere. Daniel hesitated, not sure if he should interrupt him, but Hunter looked up.

'Good morning,' he said. 'How did it go yesterday? Better come in and tell me what you made of it. Take a seat?' He indicated the chair near his desk, clearly put there for visitors.

'Good morning,' Daniel replied. He had not expected Hunter to be there so early, but he had no choice but to obey him. While the invitation to sit was phrased as a suggestion, it was clear from Hunter's expression that it was a polite order.

Daniel pulled the chair a little closer to the desk and sat down.

Hunter leaned back in his chair and looked at Daniel expectantly.

'I've met with Nadine Parnell,' Daniel told him. And then he went on to describe her fragility of body, and her strength of mind. It was still a chilling thought, that she could so easily have been killed. 'The whole incident would have been written off as an elderly woman feeling a little faint,' he said. 'And then tragically losing her balance at the wrong moment. Everyone at the crossing was looking where they were going, not at other people.'

Hunter nodded, concern in his face, but he said nothing. 'No one would have known,' Daniel finished. 'Just an old lady having a dizzy spell.' He met Hunter's eyes and was startled by the gravity in them.

Daniel assumed that Hunter was keenly aware of being the new man in the office, working with people who would have to learn to trust him. It wasn't so easy to put your faith in someone before understanding how they worked, what they thought, but Daniel had a sense that Gideon Hunter was a man he might be able to work with very well.

Daniel still questioned if it had been a mistake to take on such a high-profile case, one which would not only draw attention to the chambers but would stir deep emotions in people, even those who did not know Vayne personally. It seemed that everyone had an opinion about him. He had made money for so many people, and now it was alleged that he was also losing it. And far more than most could afford to lose: their life savings, the cost of many of their dreams. No one wanted to believe this was happening, or that someone as respected as Malcolm Vayne could be at fault.

Daniel forced this thought from his mind. The prosecution of this case had been accepted; it was a done deed.

Hunter was watching him. What did he want to know? Was it possible even now to back out of this case and pay the cost of admitting a mistake? Would he lose the respect of everyone in chambers?

How would Toby deal with it? Daniel felt a sudden chill in the air as the thought crossed his mind.

Hunter was waiting.

'There is evidence of fraud there,' Daniel said. 'Nadine Parnell has deduced what's been happening for a long time, but earlier on she didn't think anyone would believe her. She was the only one in the company prepared to speak out. Now, she's—'

'I understand,' Hunter cut across him. 'An eccentric old woman. I've already heard that from two or three people.' A bleak smile crossed his face, but not without humour. 'A woman rejected or passed over, who has been waiting for any opportunity of revenge. Why has she suddenly seen this fraud now? A trifle opportune, don't you think? Perhaps a very personal interpretation of the evidence?'

Daniel knew that Hunter wanted him to mount a defence against any negative comments about Nadine Parnell, as if they were in court. 'Puzzles change,' he said. 'Sometimes the picture doesn't make sense until a final piece is added. And if you speak out before that, you give people the chance to hide the connections that matter, and then—'

'Good,' Hunter interrupted. 'We'll take that approach in court. Is she all right? Not going to weep, or faint?'

Daniel laughed outright. 'Believe me, she'd have young men like you or me for breakfast, along with toast and a pot of tea! She's been pretty nastily hurt, and she's aware how lucky she is to be alive. But she's as sharp a tack, and about as much fun to stand on!' His face became suddenly serious. 'She told me about another witness, an international courier called Boyce Turnbull. If we could persuade him that it's in his own interest, he might tell us a great deal about Vayne's business dealings. Turnbull didn't always know what he carried for Vayne, but he knew that it was valuable, and not to be trusted to the postal service. And no doubt he remembers the delivery addresses.'

Hunter hid his smile. 'Excellent. We'll get hold of him. We'd better take Mrs Parnell's detailed testimony before the trial, signed and witnessed, just in case anything happens to her. And we'll make damn sure it doesn't happen intentionally. You took notes, I assume?'

'Yes, sir, but very brief. However, I had her sign each page.'

'Good. Then have them typed up and signed by you, and make damn sure you know where the originals are. Good thinking, Pitt, having her sign everything.'

Daniel felt a heavy weight inside him. 'You mean, in case she dies before the trial? Do you really think they'd hurt her again?' He pictured Nadine, with her bright eyes and quick mind. The thought of someone harming her, or worse, was obscene and painful.

The way Hunter looked at him, Daniel felt that the years between them were wider and deeper than he had assumed. Would Marcus have believed the threats? Or had he lost touch with the ugly reality of threats, violence, even murder? He had had some heavy, dangerous cases in the past, but most of them were long ago, before Daniel's time.

'I think Vayne is a very rich, very powerful and very greedy man,' said Hunter. 'And I don't know what his ambitions are. Not knowing is dangerous; we need to know. And we also need to know the stakes in this game, which we do not. At least, not yet. Who's next on your list to see?'

'Peter Rollins, the personnel manager,' Daniel replied. 'He's—'

'What do you know about him?' Hunter interrupted. 'Apart from his job.'

Daniel smiled bleakly. He explained, although he was quite sure Hunter probably already knew. 'He went to the right schools. Not Eton, but Rugby School. Then on to Oxford. Old school ties, as you know, can last a lifetime, especially if you want them to. As far as I can see, he's never made any bad mistakes, nor does he have enemies that amount to anything. Married into a well-to-do family. Not aristocracy, but definitely gentry. He fits in well.' He began to embellish his explanation, but Hunter cut him off.

'I may be new to ffordd Croft and Gibson, but not to London society!'

Daniel felt the heat rise up his face. For a moment, he was lost, and began searching for the right words. The last thing he wanted was to offend his new boss!

'So, Peter Rollins is in the right job for a man with connections and good instincts,' said Hunter. 'But he does not necessarily have the means to set out on his own, and certainly not the imagination. But he knows the ropes?'

'Yes, I believe he does.'

'And he's likely to remain loyal to Vayne, in your opinion?'

'Yes, sir. Unless he sees a lifeboat very close by, he might choose to go down with the ship.'

Hunter smiled. It gave his face a different look. One could easily see what he had looked like twenty years ago. When he was Daniel's age. Keen, almost innocent. What dark or painful things had he faced since then?

'Before you throw him a lifeline, let me know,' said Hunter.

'I will, sir, yes.'

Hunter nodded. 'Good. And who's next?'

'Richard Whitnall,' said Daniel. 'He's the international

liaison between all of Vayne's companies, and oversees their connections.'

'Ah!' Hunter sat forward only a few inches, but his interest was obvious.

'Whitnall travels quite a lot,' Daniel explained. 'But the police warned him not to leave the country until the trial is over. I imagine quite a lot of Vayne's business is on the back burner for the time being. Of course, they can always communicate by letter.'

'What do you know about this Whitnall fellow?'

'He has an excellent reputation,' said Daniel. 'He's a little older than the others. A widower, and all three of his children have gone abroad. Two daughters married men whose careers took them to the United States, and his son went to Canada.'

'Is it relevant?' Hunter measured each word carefully. It was not a casual question.

'Might be,' Daniel answered, meeting Hunter's eyes. 'With them out of Vayne's reach, Whitnall might feel more likely to testify against him.'

Hunter breathed in, and out again slowly. He clearly knew what Daniel meant. 'Is he the kingpin, this Whitnall? He's got no people to disgrace, or to protect? No hostages to fortune?'

Suddenly the room seemed a little darker. 'I don't know,' Daniel replied. 'His reputation is excellent. But I'll find out.'

'Be careful.'

Daniel shifted uncomfortably in the chair. 'It's not likely to be dangerous.'

'No.' Hunter's face lightened. 'But even people who are not vulnerable, because they apparently have nothing to lose, can be dangerous. And Vayne won't have got this far in his greedy and self-serving career without knowing that.' He winced.

'Don't be free with your information, Pitt, don't tell anyone else. But do let me know what Whitnall tells you, if anything. And I'll look for this Boyce Turnbull.'

Another thought occurred to Daniel. 'Do you think Whitnall might name a price from Vayne in return for his discretion?'

'It's possible. What I do believe is that this is a bigger game than you realise. There are several fortunes to be made and lost in this little kingdom Vayne has built for himself. I've been working on the international angle, and it goes further and deeper than I thought, and I'm sure than you thought as well. I can't say I would have had the nerve to take on this case if I'd known. But either way, we are too far in to back out now.' He gave a very slight shrug of his shoulders. It was curiously elegant, and vulnerable. 'Backing away, or even showing reticence . . . that's a certain way to fail.'

'Whereas now it is only a possibility?' Daniel asked wryly.

Hunter smiled again. 'Precisely.'

Daniel decided to go out for lunch. He was hungry, and it was getting late. He did not have a great deal of time, and he had hardly seen Toby Kitteridge. Which meant they hadn't discussed Toby's elevation to head of chambers. This position would put Toby in charge of all of their cases, and presumably Hunter was discussing Vayne with him.

He knocked on Toby's door.

'Come in,' Toby responded.

Daniel entered and found Toby at his desk, busy as always, but showing his normal disorder. Today was particularly chaotic, and Toby looked frazzled. The first expression on his face was close to despair. 'What is it?' he asked, as if he expected disaster.

'Had lunch yet?'

'No. At least, I don't think so.'

'Neither have I,' Daniel said, making his voice suddenly gentler. 'You look as if you could use a break, and a pint of beer. Come with me.'

'I haven't time, Daniel. This all has to be—'

'Of course it does,' Daniel agreed, cutting him off. 'But not necessarily by you. Delegate! It's one of the most important arts of leadership. Marcus would say the same, and you know that.'

'I should learn to trust people,' Toby said. 'I do understand—'

Daniel finished for him. 'That if you act as if you don't know how to delegate, sooner or later everyone will stop doing their best, or go where they are trusted.' He saw the look of dismay on Toby's face and felt a pang of guilt. He drew breath to apologise, but how could he undo what he had just said? And then he knew. 'Toby, Marcus thinks a lot more of you than you do of yourself. And he's right, you're wrong! You make mistakes, yes, but so did he. Need I remind you that you and I covered for some of them?'

Toby shrugged, almost apologetically.

'You've made mistakes, and you'll make more. We all do. In fact, I'm wondering right now if we've made the worst one ever, taking on this case.'

Toby stiffened, and there was a moment of real fear in his eyes.

'We are going to dig like crazy to get out of it. But we will, I think.'

'Vayne?' Toby asked.

'It looks as if he might be far worse than we thought.'

'Daniel, are you saying I should have gone over Hunter's

head and declined it? I think this is the sort of big chance that Marcus would want us to go for. It's the sort of thing Hunter is known for.'

'I know,' Daniel agreed. 'But we have no choice now, we're the official prosecutor. Still, somebody tried to murder our chief witness.' Daniel saw the shock on Toby's face and admonished himself for being so abrupt. Toby Kitteridge had enough on his plate; he didn't need more. 'Come and have lunch. You need to eat. And you need to stop thinking about all of this.' He indicated the papers spread out on the desk. 'Get someone to help you. You'll only have half the work. And anyone you ask will be delighted to know that you trust him. And now you have the power to promote him as well, which is another way to show your trust. Didn't you feel a fool until Marcus promoted you?'

Toby gave a bark of laughter.

'All right,' Daniel conceded. 'Maybe you felt that way, until you saw that you could handle it.' He smiled. 'And if you do promote someone, be sure to pay him more.'

'We are a little—'

'You won't win if you don't play,' Daniel said. 'And if that needs interpreting for you, let me put it another way: you need to invest if you want to earn.' He pulled a sour face. 'Although, I admit that the subject of investing is rather a sore one right now, considering Malcolm Vayne's disastrous scheme.'

'Can you salvage something out of our association with Vayne?' Toby asked doubtfully, as if he already knew the answer. His pleasant face was full of doubt and self-mockery, the humour rueful.

'Oh, yes,' Daniel said decisively, but with a twisted smile. 'The name of fford Croft and Gibson will be on everybody's lips, whether in praise or blame.'

Toby ran his fingers through his hair, and then stood up decisively.

Daniel said nothing, but felt both relief and satisfaction when he turned and walked out of Toby's office, and heard his friend following close behind.

His challenge was not only to prepare for the Vayne trial, leaving nothing to chance, but also to make sure he gave Toby the support his friend needed in this new and potentially overwhelming position.

Chapter Seven

'Anything new?' Miriam asked, looking round the large laboratory to see if there was more work to be done while she'd been away.

'Anything?' she asked again, going into the large, scrupulously clean examination room where she worked on corpses, human flesh, limbs, and any other job that needed to be studied.

The room smelled of lye and carbolic. In her imagination, she could always smell the other less sharp, more clinging odours of human body parts and liquids. And yet, the miracles and the vulnerability of the human body always fascinated her. She needed to find the answers to all these mysteries, especially when they might reveal vital information about crimes or tragedies, and bring some kind of resolution to the living.

Evelyn Hall was busy writing up a report. She was sitting at a long table crammed with papers and books, and with barely enough space to put down the mug of tea that was still steaming. She was wearing an ill-fitting white coat over her grey trousers and shirt. Her grey hair was badly in need of a trim or two and was curling around her collar. 'Done?' she asked, looking at Miriam's eminently readable face.

Miriam had just returned from a quick visit to her father. There was really nothing to say. It was taking the time to visit him that mattered. She'd made a habit of it in recent weeks, since he'd announced his retirement.

'Yes, thank you,' Miriam replied, walking over to the kitchen table beside the gas ring, and testing the teapot. It was too hot to touch, except for an instant. Good. That meant the tea was fresh. She poured a cupful, adding a dash of milk, then went over to sit beside Eve. 'He'll have to find something to meddle with soon, or he'll get bored. But at this moment, he's still reading some of the books he said he would, if he ever retired. He's currently attempting Gibbon's *Decline and Fall of the Roman Empire*.'

'That should keep him occupied for a couple of years,' Eve said. 'You ever tried it?'

'Once,' Miriam admitted. 'But I gave up after the first hundred pages or so. I hadn't realised there were so many words in the English language that I didn't know! And Gibbon has a highly creative way of finding how to use all of them. But what matters is that Father is well, and he knows I am happy. That means a lot.' She hesitated to add more.

Eve was looking at her. 'And?'

'And . . . he told me a little about Rose Hunter, the wife of the new leading barrister in chambers. She sounds interesting. Apparently, she's very keen on women's suffrage.'

'But you're worried.' Eve made it a statement, not a question.

'I am,' Miriam admitted. She had tried once, early in their friendship, to be evasive with Eve, but it was a mistake she did not intend to repeat. 'Her husband, Gideon Hunter, seems to be charging into this case against Vayne without having much of an idea about what can be achieved, never mind what our particular chambers can do.'

'By *our particular chambers*, do you mean Daniel?' Eve asked. 'Nobody knows what they can do until they try. Would you prefer that he only engage in battles he is certain he can win?'

'Of course not,' Miriam said fiercely. She knew that this was what Eve expected her to say, had primed her to believe, but she still rose to take the bait. 'We never grow if we don't attempt something bigger, and more challenging, than we've already achieved. We mustn't get into a situation where some people are above suspicion, because we fear we might not convict them!'

'Precisely,' Eve agreed. 'I would hate to find that your newfound happiness had made you too afraid of losing anything, and that you now want to play it safe. That's not who you are. At least, it's not who you were.' She stopped, as if seeing in Miriam's face a quick flash of anger. Or was it the fear that she could one day be right?

Miriam knew that she had so much more to lose now. And Eve was right: she was protective of Daniel. 'It's going to be a hard case to win,' she said quietly. 'Did you know that Vayne is very much for women's suffrage?'

'Yes.' Eve's face puckered. 'I've often wondered why. What difference does it make to him?'

'Couldn't it simply be because he knows it's right?' Miriam suggested.

Eve's expression was fierce. 'I doubt it. I'd say it's far more likely he's taken that position because he knows it's a hot subject, and those who are against it haven't got a decent argument and will end up looking ridiculous. It's quite an interesting political battle to get into; I'm wondering what he expects to get from it. Other than a lot of newspaper coverage – and he certainly loves to see his name in rival papers, still more with a picture. Some people are like that. They feel that if nobody is talking about them, they have ceased to exist.' Her face reflected her contempt.

'He owns newspapers,' Miriam pointed out. 'And since they all seem to cover the same issues – even if viewed differently, according to whoever the intended readers are – he has plenty of people hearing his point of view . . . and agreeing with him.'

'There is no sense in merely shouting,' Eve said, her mouth turned down at the corners. 'You have to have something to shout about. If Vayne wins the battle on suffrage, he'll be made for life! Even if he loses, if only in the short term, there will be many women who won't forget that he went to battle for them.'

'But does that have anything to do with the case of fraud being brought against him?' Miriam asked. It was a serious question. How much of this case was real, and how much was merely a way for Vayne to make himself appear both a victim and a hero? 'Do you think he'd run for parliament?' she added, a sudden chill running through her. It was a reasonable next step for a man who loved power.

Eve stared at her. 'That is a cold and dangerous thought,' she said. 'And a very timely one.' Her voice dropped a little, losing some of its characteristic certainty. 'Perhaps the real purpose in all of this is concealed behind what appears to be a weak case against him, which your husband and his team may find difficult to prove. I hope your new silk is as clever as he thinks he is. You should get to know him. Gideon Hunter, is it? Learn about him through his wife. She might know nothing, but on the other hand she might know him better than he thinks she does. There is a big suffragist meeting tomorrow afternoon. I'm quite sure Rose Hunter will attend. You should attend, too. Look, listen!' It sounded more like a rousing call to arms than a mere suggestion, and Eve's eyes held no softness of indecision.

'But I have work to do!' Miriam protested, although she was not sure why. The thought of Vayne's manipulation of women who wanted to vote – and some so passionately they would even give their lives for it – frightened her. It gave her the sense that she'd been left with no choice.

Eve looked at her sharply. 'I am quite capable of covering for you. And if I'm not, then you will simply have to work harder to make up the time afterwards. We have all kinds of duties, and I don't just mean what our work requires of us. Getting to know Rose Hunter – finding out more about her husband's abilities, and where Malcolm Vayne truly stands on the subject of women's suffrage – will affect all of us, eventually.'

Miriam's eyes widened.

'Not as pathologists!' Eve snapped. 'As women with brains, knowledge and judgement. And we cannot fight, if we don't know who is on which side, where the battle lines are drawn, and what weapons we have to hand, or can hope to gain. Don't tell me you have lost the stomach for it?' Suddenly, there was something akin to misery in her face, as if she had been struck an unexpected blow.

Miriam felt a sharp stab of pain. Had her own happiness made her so utterly selfish? If so, Daniel would surely become not merely bored with her, but disgusted that she had lost all her courage, her belief in what mattered, and the need to fight for it. In truth, there was not much courage needed, or even conviction, if she only entered the battles she felt assured of winning. 'I had better prepare myself,' she said quietly. 'I will read up on the latest disturbances, so at least I'll sound as if I know what I am talking about.'

Eve gave her a sudden smile, one that warmed her face until, in a certain light – and with a certain generosity of thought – it could have been called beautiful.

Chapter Eight

There were a large number of women already gathered in the spacious and very beautiful private home. Its surrounding gardens were clearly tended by someone who loved nature. Miriam wondered what kind of money one must have to own such a place.

She joined the group with a degree of nervousness. She had dressed carefully, to look like a woman who cared, had intelligence and taste, but was not playing, dabbling, or looking for a cause to fill her otherwise empty time. Nor did she want to appear to be one of those earnest, rather frightening women who talk too much and too seriously because they have nothing else to feed their passion.

The women appeared to be from all social classes. At first, she had feared they might be rather humourless women, with nothing else to do. But now she suspected that many of them might have sacrificed an afternoon's pay so they could participate, even if they could ill afford it.

She guessed there were two hundred people here, at least. In addition to appearing to be from all social classes, they looked to be all ages, which was a pleasant surprise. She saw one or two people she recognised, and nodded and smiled at them, but her primary goal was to find Rose Hunter.

Miriam cared a great deal about the women's right to vote. She wanted very much to see women treated as equals to men, and in all sorts of ways. She knew from her own experience how limitations on women's ambitions in certain areas – in science, for example – could destroy hope and confidence. She believed strongly that if women could take their part in choosing who had the privilege of representing them in parliament, they would have to be listened to a great deal more than they were now. Granted, perhaps far fewer women than men understood the subtleties of politics, but a sense of right and wrong was not the preserve of either gender, whether rich or the poor, young or old, even educated or not. People who could neither read nor write could still tell the difference between what was fair and what was manifestly not. In fact, sometimes those who could read were more easily misled by lies than those who could not.

She spoke to several women and had some interesting conversations, which made her realise how much time she spent in the laboratory and at the morgue. The constant proximity to death had narrowed her thinking. She should rectify that, listen more to the living now.

Eventually, she almost bumped into Rose, who was engaged in earnest conversation with a tall woman with wild grey hair.

'I really do think, Mrs Hunter,' the woman began, making a forward movement which caused Rose to take a step back, unable to look where she was going.

'I'm so sorry!' Rose exclaimed as she knocked against Miriam, quite hard. 'I do beg your pardon, I—'

Miriam smiled. 'Miriam fford Croft,' she said without thinking, then suddenly blushed. She drew in her breath sharply, trying to think of a gracious way of explaining herself.

'Oh, fford Croft? I must introduce myself. I am Rose Hunter.' The woman held out her hand, as a man might have done.

Mrs Hunter was not beautiful, she was far more than that: she was interesting, even commanding. Her face was full of character, and her pale golden hair was marvellous, not tidy, not tamed at all, but seemed quite naturally to fall in elegant waves, even when coming loose from its pins.

Miriam took the proffered hand. It felt like a natural gesture, even if it was not the way most women greeted each other. She must correct her mistake. 'How do you do? I'm actually Miriam Pitt. I keep forgetting! I have to be fford Croft professionally.' That was not exactly true. People were learning that the two were one person, but it still needed a clear explanation.

Rose's erstwhile companion now directed her attention elsewhere, having suddenly spotted an acquaintance. With a nod, she disengaged herself and walked away.

'Thank goodness,' Rose murmured. 'You will never persuade her of anything! She does not listen.'

'Were you trying to persuade her?' Miriam asked curiously.

'No. Actually, I agree with her, but she didn't give me the opportunity to tell her that.'

Miriam smiled. 'That must be trying! I've met a few like that here.'

'Very trying,' Rose agreed. 'I haven't seen you before. Is this your first meeting? If I just wasn't looking carefully enough when I barged into you, I apologise.'

'Yes, it is my first meeting,' Miriam replied. She preferred to be honest right from the beginning. She instinctively liked this woman. 'I have been far too busy to come before. I'm new in my position and didn't feel it was appropriate to ask for any time off. Today, my superior, knowing the occasion, insisted that I come, and then report back to her.'

'But your husband is Daniel Pitt, yes?' It was a gracious gesture, as if there might be some doubt about it. 'My husband, Gideon Hunter, has just joined your father's chambers.'

Miriam smiled. 'And we are most fortunate to have him.' She hoped profoundly that this would turn out to be true. At the moment, it was still just a wish, and with some doubt attached to it.

Rose smiled quite candidly. 'Let us hope that proves to be so. But I assume you are interested in steps towards securing equality for women. If women have the right to vote for members of parliament, those elected will have to take far more notice of the issues we care about.'

'Exactly,' Miriam agreed, with a sudden wave of emotion. 'But equal access to education for women, to begin with!'

Rose looked a little uncertain.

'I mean that if women study a subject, and prove skilled at it,' Miriam explained, 'then they may take the same exams as men. And be granted certification, if they have earned it!'

'Such as in . . .?'

'Mathematics, science, medicine,' Miriam began, and then realised how fierce she sounded. 'Chemistry or engineering, astronomy, anything else we might be good at. I . . . I am interested—' She stopped, realising that 'interested' was an absurdly mild word. This was no interest or mild concern, it was passion, and rage at injustice. 'I had to go to Holland to get my qualifications in pathology, which meant having to be away for quite a long while, more than a year. Had it not been for the support of an extraordinary woman, and the encouragement from Daniel, I'm quite sure I never would have finished my studies. Between being gone, and now working in my field, I'm afraid I'm not fully up to date with what's going on in England. It's not that I'm uninterested.'

96

Rose's eyes were wide. 'And that is why you must ask permission of your superior to take time off? And he agreed? Despite knowing where you were going?'

'He is a she,' Miriam said, with no small pride. 'And yes, she did. She's a remarkable woman. She gained her degree in Holland as well. They are rather more enlightened there. What's more, she's a gifted forensics expert, and I feel fortunate to be working beside her, as her equal. I have no idea whether you would like her or not, but I would be surprised and disappointed if you did not find her fascinating.'

'Disappointed? In me, rather than her, I would think.' Rose raised her eyebrows, but there was amusement in her expression, certainly no criticism.

Miriam decided instantly to be candid. 'Yes,' she agreed. 'But I think that will not happen.' She smiled, to rob the words of any sting.

'And you came here today out of interest in women's suffrage?' Rose asked.

'It's a subject in which I believe every woman should have an interest! But I also came hoping to meet you.'

Rose nodded very slightly and then smiled. 'I have made no secret of my beliefs.'

'And Malcolm Vayne has given a great deal of support to the cause,' Miriam added, watching her carefully. 'Do you know him?'

Rose's eyebrows lifted in a quirk of curiosity. 'And you want to know if I like him? And does Gideon know him? Have strong feelings for or against him? Simple answers are possible, but they carry only a misleading glimmer of the truth.'

Miriam winced, without meaning to. Misleading? Did this mean that Hunter had a relationship with Vayne that involved him accepting the case, before even looking at it in detail?

Miriam had thought his haste was possibly due to ineptness. Could he grasp the ramifications of such a high-profile case? But she had later put it down to Hunter's nature. Did he take it on because of ambition, or overconfidence in his own abilities? Or a longing for the limelight, at whatever cost?

Rose was looking at her as if she could read her thoughts in her eyes. 'No,' she said simply. 'It is not what you fear.'

Miriam felt a slight flush in her cheeks. What had she thought? That Hunter was ambitious, above all else? That he would take a higher-profit case, whether he won it or not? And brush it aside if he failed? Blame it on his team?

'You were right in your first thought,' Rose said, with affection in her voice. 'Gideon is rash, brilliant, ambitious, and frequently jumps before he has looked where he will land. But he is agile enough to get out of most trouble, and always clever enough to extricate himself intact, and that goes for his chambers too. He is loyal. The captain goes down with the ship, you know?' Her expression was unreadable. 'Loyalty has to go both ways. But I'm sure you know that. It's not always easy for me, but I've learned that many clever and ambitious men are difficult to live with. Perhaps you have not found that out yet? Or does Daniel Pitt play it safer than that? If so, I'd be surprised. That is not his reputation. He is seen as a man who takes risks, but from conviction, not a desire for glory, or even admiration. Your husband was one of the reasons Gideon was so pleased to take the position. He admires courage more than anything else.'

That was a great deal for Miriam to disentangle. At the same time, she was deeply pleased to hear her husband described in those terms. When she thought about it, Rose Hunter was right. In the cases she and Daniel had worked on together, as well as those he had handled alone while she was in Holland, he had taken some wild chances based on emotion, idealism and the need to pursue a cause. It had nothing to do with being careful! She felt the same way as Daniel about the issues and the people they encountered, and only ever calculated the odds against winning when it was too late to back out. Even in the days when she had been terrified of everything she stood to lose, she wanted to believe that she still would not have chosen to act differently.

It was a strangely pleasing thought, that she and Rose Hunter shared these traits of risk-taking, of stepping forward and taking a stand for what they passionately believed in. It brought them together in ways most women could not reasonably hope for.

The silence had gone on too long.

'No,' Miriam said aloud. 'Neither your husband nor mine has played it safe. And I don't want to play it safe, either. Except when it's late and I'm tired, and I can't see the way out. Then I see only what it will cost if we lose a case. And more than that, what it will cost those people who have trusted us.'

She saw the confusion in Rose's face. 'I'm a forensic pathologist,' she explained quickly. 'Sometimes I get drawn in professionally. But I am always interested, not just for my father's sake, or for Daniel's, but because my emotions are engaged as well as my professional skills.'

'You sound like Gideon,' Rose said, with a rueful smile. 'But rather more candid than he is. I wish he would be honest with me. But he wants to protect me from worry.' She gave a slight shrug. 'As if that were possible. Part of him still thinks of me as fragile! And perhaps I am. But then, if you love someone, you are always vulnerable.'

'Indeed, aren't we all?' Miriam asked. 'If we care enough

to fight for anything that isn't just handed to us!' This woman had just admitted vulnerability, surely the bravest step at the beginning of a friendship.

Before Rose could answer, the general chatter in the room quietened to a hush. Miriam followed everyone's eyes to a dais at the far end, where a large, fair-haired man was smiling and holding his hands up. She had seen photographs of him, mostly attending functions for charity, or entering or leaving a famous restaurant, theatre or hotel. He was easily recognisable as Malcolm Vayne. The way he moved, the wide gestures with his hands, palms upward, were as clear an introduction as if he had spoken. Many might only have seen photographs in black and white, so would have assumed his hair to be grey. Alive, moving in vivid colour, he dominated the room.

He looked around, as if certain he needed no introduction, and waited for none. 'Ladies!' he began, and the last murmur of voices faded away.

Miriam gave him her full attention. He had been released on bail immediately because he was charged with a crime involving no violence. He was behaving as if he knew for a certainty that the two or three hundred people in the room were entirely on his side.

He did not circle the subject. He apologised if anyone was embarrassed, but it was the kind of mistake that happened to any man who dared to be different, to fight for change which to some might seem threatening. People were afraid of change, afraid of the emotional effort it would cost, afraid they would lose something. 'Ladies!' He smiled. He had excellent teeth, even and white. 'Change frightens many people. It can be dangerous, disturbs the known and trusted. But those who do not accept it will ultimately sink into a slow routine of boredom, even of cowardice. It takes courage to accept the new, and you have courage.' He looked around, as if he owned the room. 'Or you would not be here. You would not be fighting for the right to have your say on the future, your future, which we will all live through. Men, women, old or young, rich or poor. Everyone will live through it, so everyone has the right to have their opinion heard.' He stopped for a round of applause.

'Thank you. Thank you. At the moment, men decide everything. For the most part, they are wise.' He smiled again. 'More or less. But they . . . we . . . do not live your lives. We do not know what you want, what you need, what burdens you carry, perhaps even some you don't need to carry. And you are not listened to!' Now there was anger in his voice, and in his gestures. 'You bring us into the world, you care for us and teach us, nurse us when we are sick, give us confidence when we are frightened, encourage us when we are afraid.'

He looked around, hesitating, as if seeing every woman in the room individually. 'And then we make the decision as to what laws you must obey, what privileges you may enjoy . . . or not! How you shall live. And which of us shall govern you. Have we ever asked your opinion? Taken the time to find out what you want or need? Either we assume we know better than you what that is, or we don't care!'

There was a ripple of applause. A few women called out in agreement.

Then Malcolm Vayne addressed controversial subjects such as housing, children's education – with an emphasis on reading, writing and basic arithmetic – before moving on to the need for basic wages for female workers, and increased safety conditions.

'But what else?' he asked, with another sweeping gesture of his arms. 'If you could vote, you could tell us in a way

101

that would force us to listen! We could not dismiss your concerns with polite excuses, or promises that we did not intend to keep.' He raised his voice and added, 'Because we would be put out of office! Not just by far-sighted men, but by you! You would have an equal say! I think that is not only justice, but it would make for a better society for all our children to inherit!'

He did not get any further; he was drowned out by the roar of appreciative shouts and the sound of applause.

He stood still, smiling.

Miriam glanced at Rose and saw approval shining in her face. Ashamed of it as she was, she was quite certain that there was the same flush in her own face, and she had the same urge to cheer.

As Vayne went on detailing other goals, and how they would be achieved with the granting of votes to women, Miriam's attention began to wander. She looked around the room at the admiration shining in everyone's faces. Why was Vayne doing this? Did he think he could force the establishment to allow at least some women to vote? And then what? Capitalise on that victory in order to extend suffrage to more women? Encourage the movement until it became a tidal wave? If he succeeded, he would not be denied office. Not necessarily parliamentary, but perhaps another plum job with real influence.

She was letting her imagination run away with her. The discussion around her was both emotional and tactical, but she had heard all these arguments and obstacles before, and she was only half-listening. Everything he said was a variation on what she had heard others extol. There were always people who wanted to change things, right society's wrongs. As soon as one goal had been achieved, they turned to the next. She wondered sometimes if it was the fight that engaged them, rather than the goal itself. Not that it mattered. The goal of female suffrage, when achieved, would change politics and society for ever.

As well as hearing Vayne's words, Miriam was listening to the emotion in his voice, real or pretended. She watched his gestures, the passion in his face. The longer she observed, the more she was surprised by his skill. Could it be that as well as his hunger for admiration, power and wealth, he also genuinely cared? Or was it part of his skill that he convinced himself, and others, that he did? If it were not suffrage for women, would it be some other cause?

As soon as he ended his oration, Miriam and Rose left, nodding and smiling at people as they passed them, hearing their enthusiasm, and smiling as if agreeing. In many ways, both women did, but Miriam had doubts that she believed Rose did not share.

'They always say the same things at these meetings,' Rose observed, making it sound to Miriam like an attempt at an apology. Perhaps Rose Hunter was more astute than Miriam had first thought? Did she also have doubts about Vayne's commitment?

They went through the hallway, and out of the front door into the shaded avenue. 'I hope I didn't take you away, when you might have wished to meet certain people, or even Vayne himself,' said Rose.

'Not at all,' Miriam said, with a gracious smile. 'I would like to have spoken with him. But how should we have introduced ourselves? "How do you do, Mr Vayne? I'm Miriam Pitt. And this is Rose Hunter. Marcus fford croft is my father, and my husband, Daniel Pitt, is sitting second chair to Gideon Hunter, King's Counsel, who is leading the prosecution against you, hoping to send you to prison." A little awkward, don't you think?'

'Oh, yes!' Rose laughed openly. 'Definitely a little . . . clumsy!' She quickened her steps and they did not speak again until they were at least a hundred yards from the house.

'Thank you,' Miriam said seriously. 'It was very interesting. I am glad to be forewarned. Malcolm Vayne is all art, persuasion, drama. I must learn how to deal with that effectively. Pathology is science, with some astute guesswork, but certainly based on facts, on stating the most likely theory, testing it for proof, and always being prepared to adjust your ideas if the facts disprove them. And, of course, looking for more tests, and choosing to carry out the ones that may prove your theory wrong. It is not about winning or persuasion, it is about the truth.'

Rose looked at her quickly. 'You love it, don't you? Do you like mathematics also?'

Miriam was startled by the perception of the question. 'Yes, yes I do. The ultimate truth, applied. Mathematics is wonderful, useful in a thousand ways, and pure mathematics is sublime, the one thing that must still hold true throughout the universe, but is not even remotely applicable in court. So much of the time we believe what we want to, and use our beliefs to substantiate whatever truth is being tested. And we need to cling to what we already know, because it steadies the whole universe we believe in.' She smiled back at Rose, glanced left and right for the traffic, then set out across the street, with Rose still by her side.

'To say that two plus two equals five is the ultimate nonsense,' Miriam continued, as they reached the far pavement.

Rose looked at her with curiosity. 'I think you're saying that once you cling on to a universe that defies logic, and impose your own reason on it in order to keep your beliefs intact, everything is in danger. There are many enemies – abroad, at home, within ourselves – but the fourth enemy is pure evil itself.'

Miriam thought for a moment. 'Yes,' she said, 'the danger is the same. The difference is that we know about it.' She took a deep breath. 'But I don't think that is how Mr Vayne sees it. He is cleverer than I thought, with his choice of words, with knowing what people want to hear, and understanding how to appeal to their basic instincts without actually naming all of them. I wonder if your husband and Daniel have understood quite how intuitively Vayne reads people. Once the basic emotions of fear or need are engaged, it is very difficult indeed to change people's minds.'

'I know,' Rose agreed. 'But more to the point for us, at the moment, is to understand how the jury might see it. I'm sorry to be prosaic, but we have to deal with reality. You are not going to try and persuade your husband about the logic of the universe, are you?'

Miriam laughed outright. 'I love my husband dearly, and love has little to do with logic. It is neither logical nor illogical. I want to help him all I can. Picking quarrels, or proving which one of us is right, is the road to disaster. Aren't women supposed to be cleverer than that?' She meant it half in jest, but half in all seriousness.

Rose appeared to grasp her meaning immediately, and also burst into laughter. 'And so what happens now? Now that you have seen Vayne?'

Miriam was serious again, almost as if she had turned a corner and encountered a blast of icy wind. 'I imagine he does not forgive,' she answered. 'I think we had better not engage with him on any subject, unless we are positive we can win. We – that is, our husbands – need to pick their battles very carefully.' She had to be watchful about speaking as if she and Rose were the ones about to stand up in court, and not their husbands. Using the word 'we' betrayed how closely she felt herself involved in Daniel's cases, and particularly this one.

Rose shuddered. 'I know.' She said it so quietly that Miriam barely heard the words. 'I think only one side will walk away from this fight. The other will be left in pieces.'

Miriam stopped walking and turned to face Rose. 'Then we must make sure it is not us.'

Chapter Nine

Rose Hunter arrived home, her head in a whirl. Ideas were spinning around with dark shadows at the edges, ideas she had known were there, but she had ignored until Gideon had taken up the prosecution of Vayne. It was not the meeting that remained with her: that had been no more exciting than any other. People cared. And if they did not, they simply stated their support, but did not take an active part. What lingered in her mind was the conversation with Miriam Pitt.

Miriam did not seem to be the kind of person who had strong beliefs, but never acted on them. The very fact that she had chosen an occupation which, above all, dealt with the process of discovering and accepting the truth – uncovering the facts hidden within the facts, always searching for more knowledge – indicated a love of truth for its own sake. And it could not be easy: she dealt with darkness every day. Not the details of law and legacy, the loss inherent in funerals, managing to ensure continuity, subjects typical to the legal profession. Instead, she dealt with the damage to bodies: blood, bones, organs that no longer worked, perhaps had even been torn to pieces. How did she manage that? To face the brokenness of it, the pain there must be, and the fear? Her inner strength must be formidable.

Miriam was living proof that thinking of women as weaker vessels than men was a fallacy. Steeling oneself not to feel horror, pity or fear was not a sign of strength, it was a lack of imagination, even a kind of death already.

Of course, Miriam would not be accepted in a man's world. Even if she proved herself to be at least as good as the men when it came to her professional skills. And in many cases, Rose guessed, Miriam was even better than most men. She had not said so – to be boastful would be a vulgarity that was almost unpardonable in a woman. No, it was there in the very fact that she did not need to broadcast her actions. No doubt, they spoke for themselves.

Another thing she appreciated about Miriam was that she was fun! She had a sharp sense of humour and did not seem to be in the least in awe of society's judgement. The final proof of that, if it were needed, was that she had shown no compulsion to mock, or proclaim her freedom from society's restrictions, or declare them to be artificially constructed. Perhaps that was partly because she was happy? Any virtue seemed easier to espouse when you are happy.

She thought of her own family. Her father had wanted her to marry well, possibly to someone who was heir to a title. And she had received offers. Gideon Hunter was not such a good prospect: he didn't fit in. Her father had imagined her with a secure place in society, facing no stress or difficulties, comfortably fitting into any group to which she wished to belong, never having to concern herself with matters of finance, as her mother had had to. He did not realise how happy her mother had been. Perhaps her mother had thought he knew? Thinking about her parents' marriage, Rose reflected that it was the battles they had faced together, the losses sustained and the victories won, that had made it sweet.

She thought of Miriam, and how she carried herself with confidence. Rose could see that self-assurance in her expression, in the grace and ease with which she walked.

All of this made Rose that much more interested in Daniel Pitt. There must be a great deal more to him than a fortunate name. She knew of Sir Thomas Pitt only indirectly. Gideon had mentioned him a few times, always with great respect. That in itself was worthy of note. Gideon treated most people with due courtesy, but that was not the same thing as admitting respect. It was good manners to treat everyone with courtesy; that was a statement of who you were, and a measure of the man you believed yourself to be. But to regard someone with respect in the way Gideon spoke of Thomas Pitt meant that he saw qualities in the man that he would aspire to for himself: dignity, courage, honour, great mental acuity, all coupled with an ability to mask his anger, avoid even the slightest discourtesy. And always to be in command of one's own temper, because Gideon was not blessed with that attribute himself. If he really despised the person – whether man or woman – it showed.

Gideon had very much wanted to be first counsel in chambers; his seniority would allow him to pick his own cases, even to accept ones that he might not win, but where the battle itself was worth the time and cost. And further, cases that would be a challenge to the law, and to public opinion. Sometimes he frightened her with his ambition, and his need to take on crusading cases, ones that might break new ground, and eventually even change the law. He loved the battle, even if he did not always win. That said, he usually did win. But a case he could win without stretching his wits, demanding little in the way of courage and imagination, was a means of earning a living, but it was of little satisfaction to him.

Rose had learned early in their marriage not to show how intensely she wanted to protect him. It only made it worse for him. He felt more vulnerable than ever when he thought she wanted to fight his battles for him. Leaving him to fight on his own was an art she was still learning.

She smiled a little sheepishly as she went upstairs to the bedroom and changed into a more ordinary, more comfortable and far less striking dress.

As she changed, she thought how Gideon was very seldom boring. But as well as being charming, brave and sometimes very amusing, he could be reckless, even running risks that were selfish and might prove expensive, resulting in the loss of current fees and future clients. His work had earned him both good and bad press coverage. And also, rather more importantly, a good and bad reputation among his peers. And definitely attracted more than a little envy. She could understand that. And also a certain satisfaction that these same peers would seldom admit to, whenever he lost a case. Which fortunately was a rare occurrence.

She was afraid that, this time, he was going to lose. Various causes she supported meant that she knew Malcolm Vayne better than Gideon did. She knew that whatever the outcome of the case, Vayne and his people would take revenge, even if only to make sure no one else ever attempted to prosecute him again.

She pictured Malcolm Vayne in her mind. He dressed very well, and he always remembered people's names, which was flattering to those who regarded him as an important man. He was someone who wanted to be all things to all people. His mind was quick, darting like a bird from one event to another, recalling – or rather, tucking away in his memory for later use – all the errors and slips people would rather he

110

forgot. He rarely needed to mention them; people knew the speed of his mind, and perhaps believed he could recall their mistakes more accurately than he actually did.

This also served to remind her of one of her husband's less attractive qualities. As a boy, Gideon had shown no special gifts. His clumsiness had prevented him from playing sports, especially when a fierce spirit of competition drove the match. And team sports, especially in school, was where boys made friends. He had felt shame about his lack of prowess, so much so that he would not admit it to anyone, nor ask for help. It had left him feeling isolated from his peers. Perhaps popularity had mattered to him more than it should, but she understood that.

When she first knew him, he had been too quick to remind people of embarrassing slips of the tongue, particularly if they were funny. She could recall one incident where his opponent in a case had made an unfortunate joke, which had fallen on particularly chilly ground. Gideon had made a clever pun on it. Everyone had laughed, except the man whose words he had pounced on. The pun was quick enough and amusing enough that it had been widely repeated, and always attributed to Gideon, further compounding the man's humiliation. As her husband grew in his career, he had become more sensitive to others, and more protective of the feelings of his own colleagues.

Malcolm Vayne had recognised Gideon's cleverness and had courted him as a man he might use in the future. The problem was that Gideon disliked him intensely.

Vayne also seemed to recognise Rose as a woman of great charm, a woman who created the illusion of beauty, which is often more powerful than beauty itself. It was contained in the charm of a smile, the effortless grace of movement and understated elegance, a delicate femininity rather than perfection of form. Like her husband, she disliked Vayne, but she never contradicted him. He was a man who was not capable of being persuaded of anything he had not thought of himself. If Rose had rebuked him in any way, he would have taken offence and seen her as the enemy. And he was an enemy neither Rose nor Gideon could afford.

Even when they had first become acquainted, Rose could see far beyond the winning or losing of a particular argument. She was able to judge the man's intent, the final achievement sought. With Malcolm Vayne, she read his emotions, and she saw not just the hunger for victory, admiration and power, but the intense need for it. It was not as a man might desire a piece of chocolate cake, but as he might suffer, even fall apart, without another bottle of brandy. What was it like to be Malcolm Vayne, truly? Did he really want suffrage for women? Or was he only paying lip service to the cause? What did it mean for him? Millions of potential extra voters? To what end? And make no mistake, there would be an end; one that served Vayne's interests. She was just not sure what they were.

She expected Gideon to be home late, so she was not upset when he finally arrived. She sensed that he was pretending to be happy, interested and optimistic. When he sat in his usual chair, he did not ask about dinner. She could see that he wanted to talk, but was uncertain how to begin.

'Would you like a hot meal?' she asked. 'Or a roast beef sandwich that you can eat when you feel like it? There's plum pie, if you wish.'

'Isn't it a bit early for plums?' he asked.

'Yes, they're from last year, preserved.'

The thought of supper clearly pleased him. 'Yes, one sandwich on brown bread, and then plum pie with cream.'

'I'll ask Cook to bring it through when she's ready.' She stood up and went towards the door.

He drew in a breath, as if to say something, but remained silent.

She wasn't sure if he had changed his mind, or had lost the words to frame his thoughts.

She left the room and returned in just over five minutes, carrying a glass of sherry. She put it on the small table beside the arm of his chair. After a few minutes, the cook came in with a tray. It was properly set out, with roast beef sandwiches on a plate, horseradish sauce in a small cup, and a dish of hot plum pie, accompanied by a jug filled with cream. There was a glass dome over the pie, so it would stay warm.

Gideon thanked her, and she took her leave. He started to eat, and Rose could see that he was not only enjoying the food but also using the time to decide how much to tell her. And carefully considering what words to use.

The moment came when he finished the last of the cream, along with the final piece of flaky pie crust.

She did not prompt him. Her father had been a difficult and uncommunicative man, which Gideon was not, although he could be volatile and easily hurt. But she had learned from her mother not to enquire or push too hard; one got further in the end by waiting.

'Young Pitt is a good man,' Gideon said finally. He was looking at her now, waiting for her response.

'I'm pleased to hear that.' She smiled. 'I met his wife today. At the suffrage meeting Vayne was addressing. She's not exactly what I expected.'

He studied her, his eyes sharp and curious. 'Oh? Good or bad?'

Banal answers would not suffice. It would make her look

evasive, something she despised. 'Oh, I think good,' she replied. 'I liked her, really. She's not predictable. That has to be good.'

A shadow crossed his face. 'A suffragette?' he asked. 'Or was she there to see Vayne? She must have known he'd be there. What does she think of him? Or did she not say?'

She let her breath out slowly. She knew him too well to miss the tone he used when he was worried, the minor hesitations so small that, alone, they would mean nothing. He had eaten in silence, and he was now sitting uncomfortably, as if it would sharpen his attention. She noticed that he could not relax. In his mind, he was trying to interpret something. She would not let him see she was aware of it.

'She's exact, precise,' Rose said. 'I suppose you have to be, in her profession. Perhaps she will encourage her husband to be the same. That's what you need in a junior counsel.'

'I need a lot of things—' he began, then stopped. 'Are you referring to a junior counsel in general terms? Or do you mean that precision is what this case needs specifically?'

'Well, is it?' she asked candidly. 'This is no time for word games. Tell me you're not worried about taking this case to court so soon, and I'll believe you.'

He smiled at her. 'I'm not worried.'

She thought for a moment or two, then smiled back. 'I apologise, but I don't believe you.'

'It's early days yet. Only just over two weeks.' He sat back, suddenly looking tired. 'I keep thinking we've got something real, but it's all slippery, capable of too many interpretations. I can't find anything certain to point at, to measure against other things. Vayne has to be guilty of embezzlement. But no one detail sticks out that we can get hold of, and juries need the particulars, not generalities. But so far, everything can be explained away. Each piece of evidence seems to have an innocent explanation, if taken by itself. But not if all the pieces are stacked up together. Nobody has that many close shaves, accidents, double meanings. It's a house of cards that will collapse, if I can just find the one to pull out.' He smiled slightly at the thought, as if in his head he could see it all collapsing.

'Such as what?' she asked. 'That is, what evidence?'

He thought for a moment or two. 'Some of the money that was moved out of the investment fund into something else. Did it go into Vayne's personal account, and then was never repaid? So far, anything that was moved out of the fund seems to have been lost in a complicated paper trail designed to obfuscate.'

'Were you able to track some of it? Is that why you decided to charge him so soon?' she asked candidly. She did not ask if they had actually miscalculated. 'Can't you show that the investment fund had been depleted and money syphoned off?'

'I doubt it, because the trail goes everywhere. They'll simply say the money was deposited somewhere, and then find a way to point to where it ended up.' He shifted in the chair. 'I'm sure Malcolm Vayne doesn't do his own dirty work, he's far too clever, and perhaps even too squeamish for that. But there's a streak of violence there. Perhaps not in the man himself, but in those near him. Witnesses are not refusing to testify, but they are certainly difficult to pin down. You think you've got it, and then it evaporates. Everybody's testimony depends on being backed up by someone else.' His whole body was tense. 'There's something there, but it keeps slipping away before we can nail it.'

'You knew he was clever . . .'

'That's not helpful!' His voice was growing ragged with tiredness, and he looked as if he was already feeling defeated.

'And I didn't charge him, the police did. I would have preferred to wait.'

'So, what's changed?' She was unperturbed. 'Surely it's only that he has forced your hand, intentionally or not.' She leaned forward a little, holding his gaze. 'It will be a test of nerves, my love. Nobody's ever really beaten him, but he's beginning to realise it could happen. You need to get to know, in detail and for certain, what stakes he's playing for. What does he want? What is his goal? I think it's more than money. He has enough of that to afford pretty well anything he chooses.'

'Then it's something else, something that takes more than money to buy,' he answered.

'Power?' It was the only thing she could think of. 'Or admiration? Acceptance as a member of the nobility . . . a title?'

His eyes widened. 'That's something he could buy, at the right price, although you could say it's worth far more than money.'

'You're probably right,' she said, keeping her voice patient.

He had chosen this battle himself, and at the very moment he was also changing offices. At fford Croft and Gibson he knew nobody. While it was true that Marcus fford Croft had specifically chosen Gideon, it must have been seen as a gamble. And quite a big one at that. Gideon could take on a case and win well, or narrowly, or not at all. Affecting the reputation of the same chambers that had taken such a risk in choosing him, and appointing him at so senior a level. She knew that, and so did Gideon. He might not say so, but she knew him far too well to misread his emotions: the fear, the arguments with himself, the realisation of what his loss in that courtroom would cost him.

'Vayne won the first round,' he said quietly. 'He forced my hand, and I don't know how I could have prevented it. Was that luck . . . or skill? Is that why Nadine Parnell was attacked? Not to frighten her, but to force the police to charge him? Whether she was attacked by him or one of his men, it was still a case of cause and effect. The problem is, we can't prove he was involved.'

'Napoleon said he would rather have lucky generals than clever ones,' she said. She was not entirely playing for time, only giving herself a few seconds to think. 'But luck runs both ways, my dear. Vayne will have to move quickly. He has to cover his tracks, in case you stumble upon the one thing you are looking for, and you find out how to use it against him. What does he want, Gideon? You've got to find that out. Otherwise, you're fighting in the dark.'

'Even more worryingly, Rose, this man can get as much money as he wants or needs. And that, in itself, is one definition of power.'

'What about influence?' she suggested. 'That's the real power, not openly bought.'

'Like what?'

'Political office, for one,' she answered. 'That's not hidden power, it's in the open, for everyone to see . . . and admire. I think he wants power, both seen and unseen. Power to change things, and perhaps to promote other people by giving them influence, office, position. People who can benefit him in some way. It's like good wine. The more you have, the more you want.'

She sat with those words and realised that they made sense. In fact, the more she thought about it, the better it fitted in with what she knew of Malcolm Vayne. She had seen it in his eyes, the giddiness of almost unlimited power. In his imagination, anyway.

Gideon looked at her steadily. Was he weighing what she

had said? Or wondering how to dismiss her ideas without hurting her, or angering her? For all his knowledge of the law, his fluency and charm in court, his speed of thought, he sometimes indulged in a form of self-defence, refusing to admit his vulnerability.

Rose knew that he cared intensely what she thought of him. She was careful not to let him know when she was seeing his fragile side.

'That might be it,' he said quite calmly. 'He might imagine his power is far greater than it is.' He frowned. 'Of course, he has achieved his current position by money, not by good deeds, and that can be eroded quickly. You can lose money in a dozen ways. But if it's a matter of blackmail, and if it's well done . . .' He stopped suddenly, as if his own words had frightened him.

'It's time for me to find a new clock for you,' she said, with a smile.

He loved repairing clocks, taking them apart and working out how they functioned, finding what was broken, and then determining how to mend them. It was all at his fingertips, physical pieces that fitted together in a pattern that worked perfectly. Like any intricate puzzle, before you could put it back together, you had to have a plan. If not, elements could be too tight, or too loose. You needed to know beforehand which wheel meshed with which, where each spring should be, what was broken or missing. Somewhat like the law, she thought. The most important work comes before the trial, in the meticulous preparations, research, interviews. Without a detailed plan, nothing could succeed.

She thought of time, and how elusive it could be. Why did some hours fly by in an arc of beauty, while some minutes moved like the slow creep of ice in a glacier?

Gideon reached out and gently brushed a stray lock of hair off her brow. 'Thank you. I don't think I have anything like all the pieces yet.'

She knew he was referring to the Vayne case, and she knew he was right. There were large, ugly pieces he could only guess at. But she trusted him to find them.

Chapter Ten

It had been three weeks since Marcus had announced his resignation, and had named Gideon Hunter as new leading counsel and Toby Kitteridge as head of chambers. It was a task that all but overwhelmed Toby, who was struggling to keep control, but succeeding more than he had expected.

Immediately on top of that had come Hunter's acceptance of the prosecution of Malcolm Vayne, and then Vayne's arrest when the attack on his bookkeeper, Nadine Parnell, had forced Ian Frobisher to act before his prime witness was attacked again, perhaps fatally. In its turn, that had driven the whole affair into the open.

As junior counsel to Gideon Hunter, Daniel was struggling to keep up with the speed and complexity of gathering evidence, and taking down the testimonies of their major witnesses. It was an onerous and complicated task, because so many people knew little bits and pieces, but no one seemed to be aware of the entire picture. That was almost certainly by design, planned by Vayne and his legal counsel, Fergus Dalmeny, to protect Vayne himself.

Daniel was working on the somewhat evasive written testimony of Peter Rollins, the man who acted as Vayne's primary liaison between his many companies, when there was a knock on the door. It was Impney, but not with tea, as Daniel had hoped. He was there to ask if Daniel would see Sir Thomas Pitt.

Daniel knew that Gideon Hunter was not in. Was that a deliberate choice of time for his father to call?

It was close to eleven o'clock in the morning. 'Would you care for tea and ginger biscuits, sir?' Impney asked. This was a matter of formality. Of course, he would!

Pitt came in a few moments later. Daniel immediately noticed a difference in his father's normally relaxed expression. There was a different air about him, perceived by Daniel as a subtle statement that he was here not as a father, but in his position as head of Special Branch.

Unlike Daniel, Pitt was tall, lanky and inelegant, yet there was a kind of grace to him. His balance was natural and he moved with ease. His hair was grey at the temples, but still thick and kept a fraction too long.

Pitt thanked Impney and closed the door behind him. He sat down in the chair on the visitor's side of Daniel's desk and drew it up closer. He did not need to say that this was a serious visit. Everything in his manner said it for him.

'How are you doing with the evidence against Vayne?' he asked. His voice was light, as if the question were casual, but his eyes were steady on Daniel's, holding his gaze without blinking. He was asking as head of Special Branch.

Daniel had risen from his seat, as a mark of respect, and now he sat down again. 'Trying to sort out what's important,' he replied. 'And what is repetitious or just plain rubbish. I never realised how many apparently coherent sentences actually don't mean anything.'

Pitt smiled. 'Sometimes, it's a reflection of people's jumbled

121

thinking, but for others, manipulating language is an art. Is that what you are facing with the witnesses?'

This time, Daniel chose to be direct. 'Yes. Some are harder to pin down than others. I don't know whether they're afraid of implicating themselves or their friends, or Vayne specifically.'

'Which of them has interests overseas? Financial, or otherwise?' Pitt's eyes did not leave Daniel's face. He asked the question without any change in his voice.

Daniel felt a sudden chill. 'Are you . . . are you interested in anything in particular? I thought Special Branch only concerned itself with trouble in Britain.'

'The English Channel is only twenty miles wide, at its narrowest,' Pitt replied, watching Daniel closely. 'And an open boat can make it across quickly and quite easily, if the weather permits. Especially in summer. I dare say a strong man could swim it. We might like to pretend Europe is far away, nothing to do with us, but it's a fiction that is dangerous to rely on. I have my own sources, of course, but I would like to know of anything you turn up. Personal, financial or political, even if it doesn't affect your case.'

'Do you think—' Daniel stopped. It was clear from his father's manner that he was going to tell Daniel nothing.

Daniel was a lawyer, but he had no special relationship to the government, nor to any police service, still less to Special Branch. That left him outside the realm of his father sharing confidences with him. This was going to be another one-sided situation: his father would ask, Daniel would reveal. But not the other way around.

Pitt gave a small, bleak smile. 'Vayne is not your client. You have no duty of loyalty or silence to him. Isn't it part of your legitimate discovery to know of any large amounts of money or standing payments to anyone?'

122

'You didn't mention receipts from anyone,' Daniel pointed out instantly.

'Overpayments would be interesting,' Pitt returned.

'What are you looking for?' The moment he asked, he reminded himself that he would not get an answer.

'I will tell you . . . or not.' There was a slight smile on his father's face, then it vanished. 'But watch Vayne, Daniel. I don't know if he has loyalties to anyone, here in England, or anywhere else. I don't even know how clever he is. But like an animal of prey, he has instincts that are very finely tuned. Instincts that enable him to see fear and greed, or any strong emotion, in other people. And he'll use that against them for his own purposes. He values loyalty towards himself, but he has none towards anyone else. Don't underestimate him.' His expression changed and he appeared suddenly vulnerable, as if he had seen too much that he could not control. 'Just . . . be careful.'

Daniel had been curious, his interest piqued, even a little annoyed at being shut out, as if he could not keep secrets, but now he felt a real brush of fear. 'You aren't going to tell me to leave it alone, are you? Or not to poke too far into things?'

'No.' Pitt almost smiled, just a slight movement of the lips. 'And I would be disappointed if you entertained a request like that, when I could make it an order. Someone has to prosecute him. Don't be surprised if you can't convict, or you can only convict those around him. He'll soon replace them.'

'You're telling me I can't win?' Daniel challenged.

There was a slight downturn of Pitt's lips. 'I wouldn't be so foolish as to suggest that, Daniel. And you can't back out now – nor would you, if you could. I know you: you wouldn't let Marcus down, or your new chap, Gideon Hunter. More than that, you wouldn't let yourself down. Just be careful. Remember that, as far as I can see, Malcolm Vayne has no moral compass, only a sense of what might be a danger to himself. But he understands that only too well. His tendency to overestimate his own intelligence is the only weakness that I can see in him.'

Daniel had a sudden feeling that he had not yet fully understood why his father was here. What was he really saying, couched in his ordinary words? What was Special Branch's interest in Vayne? Certainly, it wasn't the man's grubby scheme to make money.

'He seems to inspire great loyalty in others,' Daniel said, remembering witnesses refusing to give any incriminating evidence. Except perhaps Nadine Parnell, who would no doubt be described by Fergus Dalmeny, Vayne's counsel, as one angry old woman.

Pitt stood up, just as Impney came in the door with the tea tray.

'Sorry to keep you waiting, sir,' he said, putting the tray on Daniel's desk. 'A few telephone calls.' He was looking at Daniel. 'Mr Rollins telephoned to say he would be able to see you at three thirty, in his office. He gave me the address.' He passed a slip of paper to Daniel. The information was written in his usual elegant script.

Pitt drew in his breath to speak, and then seemed to change his mind. He looked expectantly at Daniel.

'I need to talk to him,' Daniel replied, directing his smile at Impney, not Pitt. 'He has a lot of figures which could be interpreted in different ways, and I need to go back over some of them with him, see what he says.' He glanced at the address, which he did not recognise. 'Although, I'd prefer it if he came here.'

'I believe it's best that you go to him,' said Impney. 'He didn't say so specifically, but he sounded nervous. He was quite insistent. Perhaps he's concerned that he'll be seen with you?' He glanced at Pitt, then back at Daniel. 'I assured him that you would meet him at that address.'

Daniel was about to speak, but Pitt interrupted him. 'Very wise of you, Impney. I am glad that you are sensible to the unsuitability of him coming to chambers.' He took a deep breath and let it out with a sigh. 'Not to mention the danger. Thank you for the tea and the ginger biscuits.' He sat down again.

When Pitt had gone, Daniel was aware of a chill. He had a close relationship with his father, a great deal of whose work was now secret. When Daniel had been a child, it had been ordinary detection, frequently murders involving members of high society. At that time, the police were regarded as being on the very lowest social level. Pitt's abilities were considerable, but the landed gentry had little appreciation for that. When they did accept him socially, it was due to his excellent education and his marriage to Charlotte, a young lady of good family.

Daniel smiled at the thought of that, even now. Pitt had earned his knighthood in a particularly delicate act of service to Queen Victoria, in the closing years of her life. And he was so discreet about that affair that even Daniel did not know what his father had done to earn such gratitude from the monarchy.

But what was it about Vayne that alarmed Pitt so much that he had come to visit Daniel? To others, it might appear that it was merely an urgent family matter – a visit that could be explained away as just that, if anyone asked. But Daniel had sensed more than a warning in his father's words. He

125

recognised much more. Pitt could see a darkness ahead that the others involved in this case – Marcus fford Croft, Gideon Hunter, Toby Kitteridge – could not. But he had not named it. That, to Daniel, added to the chill.

Chapter Eleven

Thomas Pitt stood in the foyer of his home. He turned when he heard a slight noise and saw his wife standing at the top of the stairs.

He had first met Charlotte nearly thirty years ago, when he was the young policeman investigating the murder of her eldest sister, Sarah. He had found Charlotte interesting, different. And in the end, he realised that he loved her. She was socially well above him. Her family had wealth and good breeding, the latter even more important than money. Such young ladies did not marry policemen.

Except that Charlotte did. And amazingly, her father had consented to it. Perhaps he knew that, with her family's approval or without it, she was going to marry Thomas Pitt.

They had shared so many wonderful years. There had been failures, of course, even tragedies, but great success, and an intense and deep happiness. He still felt a tingle of pleasure in watching her come down the stairs slowly, so as not to trip on her long satin skirt. It was a plain dark red, but perfectly cut. It did not flatter her so much as make the best of all her natural attributes: her fair skin, dark chestnut hair, her beguiling smile. She looked even better now than she had in her twenties. There was a serenity in her face, a deep happiness.

She was smiling. She knew he was having to attend this particular reception as a matter of business. She also knew he would rather have stayed in, much preferring a quiet evening at home.

They went together to the front door, and then out to the car that was waiting for them.

It was a twenty-minute drive. They did not speak. He glanced sideways at her and remembered countless other times, most of them in horse-drawn carriages. This ride was smooth, but he missed the gait of the horses, and it lost something of the sense of occasion.

They arrived at their destination and were recognised by the attending footman, so they had no need to inform him who they were.

The man bowed. 'Sir,' he said, then he signaled to another footman to open the double doors to the reception room. Standing there, he announced, 'Sir Thomas and Lady Pitt,' and then stood back for them to enter.

Charlotte squeezed her husband's hand gently, and then laid her hand lightly on his arm.

He glanced at her. They had done this so often. He knew that she was preparing to smile, to remember the names of people she knew. And what about those she did not? He had no need to worry; she had the charm to address them in such a way that no one would be able to tell the difference.

Pitt had a list of the possible victims of Malcolm Vayne's fraud. On that list was one name that stood out: Geoffrey Wallace. Pitt had no need to speak to the others on that list, but Wallace was an exception. As a senior minister in the Foreign Office, he was privy to much, including investigations that went beyond the borders of Great Britain. If he had been swindled by Vayne, Pitt needed to know. Wallace had the professional and social weight to hinder the police investigation, which he might attempt to do if he wanted to protect his reputation – and even more importantly, his position – and keep his name out of the public eye.

It was half an hour before Pitt was able to guide Wallace into a corner, where they could speak in confidence, and out of earshot of the other guests.

'Ah, Pitt,' Wallace said, with rather forced warmth. 'Here we are! Better to meet here than in the office, what?' He was a big man, Pitt's own height, but broader, and with dark eyes and a rapidly receding hairline.

Pitt smiled back. He wanted this to be as painless as possible, but he was prepared to pursue it as far as proved necessary. 'Indeed,' he answered, although he was merely going through the motions.

He did not like dressing up and coming to receptions such as this, especially if he had to meet publicly with a man he would prefer to see in private, without the constant threat of interruption and prying eyes. But he understood that Wallace did not wish others – men with offices in the same building, even his own staff – to see that he was meeting with Pitt. The attendees at this reception knew who Pitt was, and were aware of his position as head of the discreet branch of the service that dealt with treason and violence within British shores. Casually, at such events as this, their meeting could be seen as chance.

It was anything but.

The two men did not waste time. They could be interrupted at any moment, either unintentionally or by design; someone might be curious, even frightened about what they were discussing. Wallace had invested in Malcolm Vayne's fund, which meant he was a victim of the scam.

Wallace looked both embarrassed and annoyed. 'Nothing of any importance,' he said to Pitt, with a wave of his hand. 'Just a run of bad luck. Everyone has them from time to time. I knew the risk when I invested. All very up-and-up, don't you know?'

Pitt said nothing. He could see that Wallace was irritated.

'Good God, man, I've lost on the Stock Exchange as well! Did Special Branch step in then, show up at my office and question my friends about it?'

'No,' Pitt replied. 'Have we in this case?'

'Dammit, man, Vayne hasn't lost anything he can't afford. Have you any idea what he's worth? So, I lost a couple of thousand pounds. Maybe that's a lot of money for you, but . . . how can I put this delicately?' He hesitated, as if it were a real question. 'It isn't for me.'

Pitt knew what the man wanted to say, and it hung in the air like the smell of bad food. Wallace wanted to put Pitt in his place by hinting that a man such as himself, and the men they were speaking about, were not in the same bracket of wealth, estate, income as Pitt. Nor would they ever be. He knew that for men like Wallace, a thousand pounds was not the price of two houses, as it was for a working-class family. Still, it was quite a bit to speculate with, win or lose. And if Wallace lost? Well, it was nothing to lose sleep over.

Pitt swallowed the reply that he would like to have given, and kept smiling, albeit rather strained. 'There's no need to be delicate, Mr Wallace. It is not the amount in question that interests me.'

'I should hope not!'

'It is the pattern of wins and losses over a period of time, based upon the financial advice of Malcolm Vayne. I believe you understand,' Pitt insisted.

Wallace's face darkened. 'That whole damn business is a made-up charge. An attempt to destroy a man who does a great deal of good in this country! And don't you forget it!'

Pitt affected innocence, as if prepared to believe whatever Wallace told him. It was not particularly difficult. Wallace was a man who considered those not of his own class to be essentially ignorant of the rules of finance. He could very easily believe Pitt did not understand.

'I don't follow the man's every move, Pitt! But yes, wins and losses are often equal. What are you suggesting?' He looked at him more narrowly. 'Are you saying that Malcolm Vayne is guilty of this ridiculous charge? You'll make a first-class fool of yourself if you go around spouting remarks of that sort, you know. A fellow's temporary debts are not Special Branch's business. Poking your damn noses into everything! It's a wonder I don't discover you in my bedroom!'

'I have no reason to believe I would find anything interesting there,' Pitt replied, and was satisfied to see the blotches of colour in Wallace's cheeks.

The man did not reply. Instead, he turned on his heel and walked out of the room.

Pitt watched him walk away. He understood Wallace's anger. But he also understood that financial misfortunes, whether gambled away on tables or on the Stock Exchange – or in this case, suffered when investing in a fraudulent scheme – could lead to debt. And debt incurred by a government officer was dangerous. For Wallace, it left him open to blackmail or extortion. Would Vayne's people pressure him to deny that he had been bilked? Nevertheless, a debt always had to be paid, either in money or in favours. And Wallace was in a prime position to hand out favours. If he had to borrow money to cover what he'd lost, the interest could mount until it became a debt for life. Would he end up borrowing money from the very man who had cheated him? If so, he could be pressured into using his influence to aid Vayne in some way.

Pitt wondered if Wallace really was a victim in this scheme. If he had been an early investor, he would have received his profits by now. But the man's face, his tone of voice, suggested that he had not been so lucky. No, he had been a loser, and Pitt needed to know the consequences. The first call he would make in the morning would be to the head of the Foreign Office. Wallace had to be watched closely. And judging by Wallace's vulnerable look tonight, and his gruff manner, he was already feeling the pressure to serve Vayne in some way.

Malcolm Vayne was not only running an investment scheme; he was lending money, sometimes at a high interest rate. At other times, more curiously, he charged no visible interest at all. And it was this invisible interest that also worried Pitt. There was such power implicit in Vayne's vast network of financial deals, both known and unknown.

Who else was going to step forward and perhaps save Vayne? Or, on the other hand, perhaps help the court to reach the right conclusion – by whatever means necessary?

Pitt inhaled quickly. If Vayne's counsel could prove that coercion or bribery had been employed to assemble the case against him, and the judgment was reversed, what then? Vayne could act justifiably indignant, claim to be a victim of a vendetta. And this would elevate public sympathy for him, and open the door to more fraud. He could become unstoppable. And no one would dare charge him again.

It frightened Pitt that Daniel was part of the team that was prosecuting Vayne, yet there was absolutely nothing he could do about it. Any meddling would only make it harder for Daniel to do his job.

For the rest of the evening, Pitt pretended to enjoy himself, at least as much as he usually did at such events, which was not a great deal. Like all the heads of Special Branch before him, he knew too much about people. Had these guests understood the extent of his knowledge, they would have felt uncomfortable in his presence. Often, however, the secrets he knew about others were nothing more than petty mistakes – ordinary foolishness, hasty judgements, love affairs – most of which he learned about more by accident than design. And more often still, there were minor misdeeds that he deduced from the very fact that people hid them, or told relatively innocuous lies, and then added more lies to cover the first lies.

Charlotte had been watching him, as if she knew there was something wrong, but she did not ask him about it. That, in itself, was indicative of the seriousness with which she regarded it. Also, being in a public place, he could tell her very little, and she did not want half a story.

'I'm sorry,' Pitt apologised when they were home again, closing the front door after having thanked the driver.

'Is he in danger?' she asked, meeting his eyes.

'Who?'

'Daniel! Who else?'

He had often kept secrets from Charlotte, but he never lied to her. 'I don't think so.'

'Can you do anything about it?' She was controlling her voice, but she could not keep the fear out of her eyes.

'They would be very stupid to stop the investigation now,' he replied, which was true. 'Vayne is protesting, swears he's innocent. That he's the injured party. He would be a fool to use any sort of violence at this point. And—'

'Can't you assign someone to watch him?' she said, cutting across him before he could complete his answer.

He tried to smile, and knew he was failing. 'Watch Daniel, or watch Vayne? Or perhaps Gideon Hunter?'

She took a deep breath, as if to steady herself, before preparing to answer. But instead, she remained silent, as though she could find nothing to say.

'No point in watching Vayne,' he said. 'If there's any violence, he wouldn't do it himself.'

'Could he actually be innocent?' she asked.

'I don't think so,' he said. 'Not fundamentally. But he could be innocent of the precise allegations against him.'

She raised her eyebrows.

'The best witness against Vayne was very nearly murdered. That she was only injured—' He stopped. He had not meant to tell her that, and he shifted the focus away from Nadine Parnell. 'Everybody's watching him. What he needs is for us to fail to prove him guilty. And he has to hope we don't find a more serious charge.'

She gave a stifled laugh, but it was fraught with fear. She buried her head in his shoulder and he tightened his arms around her.

The next morning, Pitt went out early. Not to his office but to the offices of the branch of military intelligence that dealt with overseas threats to Britain. There, he sought out a friend he had often helped in the past.

'I know just the chap you should see,' the man told him. 'I'll call and set it up. Do you need it done right now? I guess they can't afford to charge this fellow Vayne and then fail to convict him. It's like giving him the keys to your house. Wait a moment.'

Half an hour later, Pitt was sitting in the office of a different MI6 officer, a quiet, rather studious man in his late thirties or early forties, with dark hair and the clearest blue eyes Pitt could ever recall seeing. The man, Lucas Standish, was multi-lingual and knew a great deal about foreign affairs. He could call on people in most of the European countries, without raising any eyebrows.

Standish invited Pitt into his office and made him welcome. With a very casual air, Pitt got straight to the point.

'Malcolm Vayne?' said Standish. 'Nasty piece of work. Slippery. One young man in my office has nicknamed him The Eel.' He smiled bleakly. 'Long, slithery creature with enormous teeth. Can wriggle out of almost everything.'

Pitt was at first surprised that Standish knew this much about Vayne's character. How interesting! At the same time, he felt hope rising within him. 'Do you think he'll slither out of this charge?'

'Possibly,' Standish replied. 'He can act the picture of injured innocence very well. And he has a lot of people in his debt, many of whom wouldn't dare give testimony against him. He's a master at that. We haven't any proof, or else we would have used it, but he has a hold over quite a number of people, and some of them would surprise you. As would the grounds for blackmail.'

'Sleeping with the wrong women?' Pitt asked. 'Does anyone really care? That is, enough to pay Vayne to whitewash the charges and maintain his discretion?'

'I doubt it. I'm afraid it's more serious than that, and it's mostly financial. If what he does is legal – and he makes it look as if everything is – then he can receive investments, but also lend money quite openly and above board. And it's all confidential. Most of high society doesn't want it known that they have either invested in a scam or borrowed money from the wrong side of the tracks. If they've borrowed, compound interest builds up quickly. And by the way, he's very clever at covering it up. But the foreigners also—'

Pitt leaned forward. 'What about this pyramid scheme of his? The investment fund. I need more details about the foreigners involved in that, too.'

'Frankly, I don't think it exists, most of it. If he's paying the first investors with the money paid in by the second wave, and the second with the third, and so on – well, it seems to me that this would've become a public scandal much sooner.'

'It has to collapse eventually,' said Pitt. 'Unless he's brilliant enough always to get an astoundingly good return from somewhere.'

'That's where his business acumen comes in,' Standish answered. 'He lends out at one rate of interest, and borrows at another. If his scheme is being investigated, I'm guessing he needs to borrow an enormous amount of money to put into the fund's account, and then send money to his investors. That will make it seem like they're receiving interest on their investments.'

'And why does MI6 care about this?' Pitt asked. This seemed to be growing more complex and uglier by the minute.

Standish smiled, but there was anxiety in his eyes. 'Because we know that he's borrowing from some very shadowy people in Europe. No single country in particular. Austria, Switzerland, Germany, and others in the Middle East. A lot of his borrowings are tied to a group based in Zürich.'

A hideous thought touched Pitt's mind with an icy chill. 'And how is he going to repay all this money?' he asked.

'That's what worries me,' Standish replied. 'If you don't convict him – and I'm not sure you can, because I'm not sure he's cheated anyone in England – we could lose the thread completely. That is, his connection to foreign lenders.'

'But—' Pitt started to ask and was cut off by Standish.

'If he's not convicted, he'll emerge as a man who was falsely charged,' Standish continued. 'Who stood trial and was totally exonerated. What will he do if proven innocent? He'll pass himself off as a victim of the old order. My guess is that he'll run for parliament.'

'There's no empty seat—' Pitt began, then stopped.

Standish smiled bleakly. 'There will be when he wants it. It's not too difficult to arrange. And he'll win. Those people who have overextended their finances will sympathise with him, and make him welcome in their government.'

'Yes,' Pitt said, and then mulled this over for a brief moment. 'I had the same thought myself. Use his prosecution to position himself in the public eye as another innocent man unjustly accused. People will love that. I can paint the rest for myself. The picture is very clear.'

'It would be good if I could tell you otherwise,' Lucas Standish replied. 'But it's our job to look at the truth pretty squarely. I'm sorry. I can't give you any more details.'

'I don't need them,' Pitt answered. 'Thank you for being so honest with me.'

'Is it your son who is handling the case?' Standish asked, with clear sympathy in his face.

'Junior counsel,' Pitt replied.

'Do your best,' Standish said. 'And if I can help, let me know.'

'Yes, I will.' Pitt rose to his feet and shook the man's hand. 'Thank you.'

Chapter Twelve

Daniel had a late lunch, and then met with Richard Whitnall, whom he had not seen before. He recognised the man from the photograph he had been shown.

Richard Whitnall was in charge of Vayne's interests in Europe, dealing with the accounts and investments privately, and managing large sums of money.

Daniel and Whitnall had agreed to a meeting place. They encountered each other as if casually, in Hyde Park, at Speakers' Corner where, as usual, someone was standing on a wooden crate and addressing a small crowd. The people were alternately cheering and heckling. It seemed to Daniel that all was done good-naturedly, with plenty of colourful abuse and shouts of laughter.

Whitnall was waiting at the far left of the open area, as he had promised.

Daniel was aware of the international dealings the man supervised for Vayne; he also knew that the European investments were far wider than they had appeared at first. And even more importantly, they seemed to involve much greater sums of money than were revealed in the official accounting documents. So far, Daniel and his team had managed to identify the main offices of these contacts. The primary office was in Zürich, but there were also smaller offices outside of Switzerland, including addresses in France, Spain, Italy and Germany, with agents acting in Sweden, the Netherlands and Portugal as well.

Daniel approached Whitnall, directing his eyes for the most part towards the speaker, until he was standing only a few yards from the corner.

At first glance, Whitnall appeared to be an average-looking man, not more than about five foot nine in height, slender, and with a very fine head of dark brown hair that was heavily greying at the temples. He was neatly dressed. Daniel thought he could have been a bank clerk or a librarian, except for the very good cut of his clothes and a certain casual confidence in the way he stood, with his attention turned to the speaker.

According to the documents Daniel had read, Whitnall had studied Modern History at Oxford, and had passed with honours. Apparently, he spoke both French and Italian fluently. Daniel guessed that, with his international contacts, he would have a good knowledge of several other languages as well.

Whitnall turned and smiled as Daniel approached him. 'Mr Pitt?' It was phrased as a question, but there was no doubt in his face. 'Shall we walk?' That was not really a question either. He turned, even as he spoke, and began to move towards the long path that led round a curve and out of sight. 'The flowers are quite extravagantly lovely,' he went on. 'I always get a lift from their exuberance.'

'Excellent description,' Daniel agreed, walking beside him along the gravel path and enjoying the sunshine.

The two men walked down a shaded, dappled path beneath the trees and towards a blaze of colour, where the profusion of flowers was so thick one could barely see the earth between them.

'Wonderful,' Whitnall said, glancing at the riot of crimson, scarlet and gold petals. 'All the pleasure of a garden, and none of the work. I can see no space left where more flowers could grow, had they the temerity to try.' His lively choice of words reflected the humour in his eyes.

'An extended English formal garden, as if we lived in one of the great country houses,' observed Daniel. And then he got straight to the point. 'Mr Whitnall, I believe you travel a lot as the representative of Malcolm Vayne and his companies. You must know a great deal about them, and be able to deduce even more.' It was a statement. He was not going to brook any argument.

'I see you're getting right to it.' Whitnall smiled, but he was still looking at the flowers, from the blowsy red roses next to them, to a tall patch of greenery, pale and heavily leafed, providing shade for the more delicate blooms. These were followed by blues and purples, stately delphiniums towering over a groundcover of blues and greens. 'Yes, I do know a great deal about my employer's business interests,' he agreed. 'I've learned much over time, but only recently have I put it all together. It has been rather like assembling the pieces of a jigsaw puzzle, but without a picture on the box to tell you what it is all supposed to mean. A sale in Luxembourg, a loss in Madrid, and perhaps in Rome, and so on. The picture does not emerge easily. And all the less easily if it forms a picture you most certainly wish to see, but do not like.'

'But you do see it?' It was not really a question, just a way to lead Whitnall into giving Daniel more information.

'Yes, but there is so much to be uncovered, brought into

140

plain sight. The accumulation of facts is dizzying. Who owes how much, and to whom? And, above all, in each case, exactly what are the payments for? Advice? Merchandise? Shares in something else?' He glanced at Daniel. 'Precisely what!'

Daniel felt as if the temperature had suddenly dropped. The flowers were brilliant, but there was no longer the same heat in the sunlight. 'If we can trace the money, can you tell us how it was used?'

Whitnall glanced at him, and then away again at the flowers. 'Yes,' he said simply. 'And I have records for some of the transactions – amount and date, et cetera – but not all. I think if you know who paid what, and when, and how much in total, you will begin to see a very different picture from the one Vayne claims.'

Daniel felt his heart beating faster. This was what he needed to hear. Another insight into Vayne's fraudulent scheme.

A few middle-aged men in dark business suits passed them, going in the opposite direction. One of them carried a rolled-up umbrella and used it as a walking stick. They nodded at Whitnall, but did not break the rhythm of their stride.

Whitnall waited for a gap of several yards to open up before he spoke again. 'Flowering cherry,' he observed as they passed a tree in full leaf. 'Should have seen it in the spring. Still, the birches are my favourite, actually.'

'Beautiful,' Daniel agreed, looking up at the leaf-laden branches, motionless against the sky, the leaves shivering slightly now and again in the gentle breeze. 'But I like the beech trees best of all. Clean limbs, like dancers. Do you know those gentlemen who just passed us?'

'Yes.' Whitnall looked straight ahead, not at Daniel. 'This kind of business is all about who you know. And Vayne knows the right people in a dozen countries. And they know him! He loans and borrows money all over Europe. But what, and to whom, that's the key. I think it would surprise you if you knew.'

'But you know?' Daniel said, with a rush of anticipation and even certainty.

'Of course,' Whitnall agreed, 'and I can prove what I know, or I would not have told you.' He smiled with a touch of regret, even pain. 'Do you know the duck pond further along here?'

'Yes, of course. Why?'

'Pleasant creatures, ducks. So much more to them than you think. Ever watch them, newly hatched? They know how to swim straight away. Of course, they float anyway. Oil in their feathers, I suppose. When they get older, you don't see them paddling, but they are. Paddling like mad. They move at a heck of a speed. There's more to a duck than you can see.'

Daniel took his meaning immediately, but he waited to speak.

Whitnall smiled. 'I can give you a list of names. What you need to do is follow the money. Don't look at what each individual payment is, but how much money is paid in total, and to whom. And then ultimately, for what.'

'And what will I find?' Daniel asked quietly. 'Debt? Debt that can't be repaid?'

'Among other things,' Whitnall agreed. 'But mostly you will begin to see the movement of power. The debts that are cancelled because they have been paid by other means. And make no mistake, all debts will be repaid, eventually, at a time of Vayne's choosing.' He gave a short bark of laughter. 'You cannot anticipate the consequences, or appreciate the weight and movement of the tide, the undertow. Yes, undertow is the word for it. At first, you think you are in control. You know where you are going and those you trust: the bank

142

manager, company heads, government ministers. Then you find you cannot touch the bottom with your feet any more. You are in the grip of the current. You are moving more and more rapidly, being carried along with it, as if in a maelstrom. Power, Mr Pitt. Power you do not see, but which you realise is stronger than you are, and it is dictating the movement of everything.'

'The power of money? Debt you can't pay?' Daniel could see the invisible strength of it in his mind's eye, like a light ship caught helplessly in a rip tide.

'Political power,' Whitnall answered. 'The power of money first, then public opinion. That's a current more powerful than anyone's money.'

Daniel had no answer. But these words changed his mind completely. He knew that Whitnall was talking about Vayne. Everything in this case whirled around Vayne. He was the eye of the storm.

The calm sunlight shone exactly as it had moments before, but suddenly it seemed sharp-edged and brittle.

'Is this a guess, a belief, or something you can prove?' Daniel asked, as they passed a huge bed of pansies, velvet-like flowers with heads dancing in the slight breeze.

'There's enough evidence, if you know where to look,' Whitnall answered. His face puckered a little. 'Not easy, because you won't want to see it. Good causes. A lot of people risk being hurt, disillusioned. But everything has a price. The question is, what are you prepared to pay? What is it worth, and who stands to lose?'

'But can you prove Vayne has acted illegally?' Daniel asked again. 'Or is it only a hunch, which could be wrong?'

'Straight to the point again!' Whitnall smiled.

'Yes,' Daniel agreed. 'And what is the answer?'

'Better to begin at the beginning, take it step by step, and get to the end by the careful application of reason. There is no room for mistakes here.' He looked at Daniel for a moment. 'You understand that? Your first mistake will be your last. Vayne is not stupid, and he does not forgive.'

'And what about you?'

Whitnall gave a very slight shrug. 'I'm a widower. My children have gone to make their fortunes abroad. Vayne has no power in the mountains or plains of Canada.' He glanced at Daniel. 'But be careful, Mr Pitt. And I say this for you . . . and your family.'

'I'm not pleading the case in court,' Daniel replied, as if this would exonerate him from danger. 'Gideon Hunter is. He's quite a bit older than me, with an impeccable reputation and much more big-trial experience. He's taken silk, and is a King's Counsel, whereas I've only just started out.'

Whitnall smiled and it filled his face with an unexpectedly youthful charm. 'Then you've got all that ahead of you. But I hope to heaven Vayne is dealt with, and that all this never happens again. It's dark, I promise you.' He gave a shrug and was silent for another hundred yards or so. Then he looked up, watching the ever-moving patterns created by the shadows of the trees towering above them. He smiled, but there was a sadness in it.

Daniel was at home and working late, making as much sense as he could of the evidence, the same evidence he had more thoroughly examined during the day. He sat in the living room, the door still opened on to the lawn. The only sounds were the whispering of the wind in the few trees, and a chattering of birds as the last light faded.

He could see it far more clearly now. Vayne's problem was

that payment was due to his investors, so that they would continue to believe their money was earning the interest he had promised them, when in fact it had earned nothing. Vayne was forced to turn to foreign lenders to provide some of the repayments, and of course they would advance loans at a rate of interest that would ruin his own profit. So, either they were interest-free loans, if such a thing existed? Or the money procured something intangible from him, like future political influence.

Or was it even worse than that? The loans were not to be repaid in money. But when Vayne realised his ambition, he would return the favours? These people would own him, and all he could do for them.

Miriam walked in and sat down. 'Was Whitnall any help?' she asked seriously.

'Yes,' Daniel replied quietly. 'In fact, another day or two of questioning and we will almost certainly have enough information to make sense of all the individual pieces.' He gave a slight shrug, knowing that he was lying to her by omission. Whitnall had painted a darker and far more dangerous picture than Daniel had seen before. 'Whitnall could have overestimated the value of what he knows, but I don't think so. He was quite adamant that all of his information was very real indeed.'

She looked puzzled, and worried. There was a shadow in her eyes, as if she knew she was not being told everything. 'If he really has so much evidence, then why did he not go to the police, or anyone else, with it? This is major fraud. And if it were not a crime, Ian wouldn't have been involved. And don't say his information is crucial, but Whitnall has only just realised it. Or that it has been a cumulative process, over quite a long period of time, and it has taken until now for him to put it together in his mind. Because if that were so, he isn't

145

very bright!' She looked anxious, but her gaze did not waver. 'Or . . . he could be fabricating all of it, to save his own skin.'

It was a perceptive and very pertinent point, one he hoped was not true. 'I don't believe so,' he said, with conviction, knowing that this, too, might not be honest. He wanted to believe everything Whitnall had said. A sharp picture of the man came to his mind: the confidence in the man's face, the humour, the keen awareness of the damage Vayne was doing, and the reach of Vayne's power. 'I don't know,' he admitted.

Miriam smiled. This time, it was genuine, lighting her eyes, her whole face. 'Then you are well on the track towards putting it all together. Hunter will be delighted, because it sounds like you've made a great step forward with Whitnall. You did it!' Suddenly, she leaned forward and kissed him, softly, for a long time, and the colour was high in her cheeks when she pulled away.

He let go of the darkness Whitnall had painted so clearly, and they kissed again.

Chapter Thirteen

It was late in the evening. Thomas Pitt was tired and ready to go to bed, when the resident maid, Minnie Maude, came in a little nervously to say that Mr Daniel had arrived and wished to speak to his father.

Pitt turned round from the French doors where he had been standing, watching the last light fade from the sky. What was wrong that Daniel was calling at this hour? He took a deep breath and cleared his throat. 'Have him come in, Minnie Maude. Is he—'

She knew him well enough to anticipate what he was going to say. 'He isn't upset, sir, just got something to tell you.'

'Show him in, thank you.'

Minnie Maude backed away and almost bumped into Daniel. He looked tired and a little strained. He thanked her. As she left, he closed the door.

'What is it?' Pitt asked. He could not read his son's emotions, nor did he want to. But he could sense that something was distressing him deeply.

Daniel remained silent.

'What is it?' Pitt asked. 'What has happened?'

Daniel walked over to the fireplace and stood there, stiffly.

He looked down for a moment, then up, meeting Pitt's eyes. He spoke quietly. 'I met Richard Whitnall this afternoon. It's worse than we thought, and the scope of the crime is even wider. Vayne is lending and borrowing money all over Europe. Far greater sums than we thought. It's not just the power of money. It's who owes it, and to whom. And why.'

'Why?' Pitt repeated, although he feared he knew already.

'It's pretty surprising, the list of well-connected men who owe Vayne money that we – that I – didn't guess at. Maybe you knew. It's a matter of power, yes. But Vayne is potentially vulnerable, too, given the extent of his borrowing. And that scares the hell out of me. He could bring the government down.'

'We know that,' Pitt said quietly. 'He could also keep the government in power, or any other government he chooses, and dictate their actions. Perhaps lead them openly, in time.' He saw the last bit of colour drain from Daniel's face. 'Thank you for telling me.'

'We've got to win the case against him, haven't we?'

Pitt met his eyes levelly. 'If Whitnall is right, yes.'

The following morning, Daniel went to Toby Kitteridge's office at the first opportunity, when Toby was free from visitors or meetings. He was inundated by papers, decisions, and Daniel knew that he would agonise over at least half of them. Head of chambers was a position Toby had dreamed of, but always as something that would happen far into the future, maybe ten or fifteen years from now. But even then, unless he had changed a great deal, he would still not think he was ready for it.

That was pretty much how Daniel felt about taking silk: being the lead counsel and making all the big decisions in court, prosecuting cases where fortunes were made or lost. And far beyond that, where not only justice was at stake, but life and death. Death meant hanging, and he was not sure if he approved of it. Hanging seemed barbaric, carried out in cold blood, no matter what the crime. And more than once the verdict had later proved to be an error: final, and irredeemable. He did not want to prosecute a capital case. The thought of an error – the result of an insufficient defence, a chance or a doubt not followed – would haunt him for the rest of his life.

But that responsibility was for him far in the future, if it came at all! Now it was a weight for Gideon Hunter to carry. Vayne was accused of fraud, amounting to theft. Massive, but still only the loss of money. Although the loss, too, of all that money could buy, like food, warmth, shelter. For many, these basics were luxuries that others took for granted.

Daniel knocked on the door of Toby's office.

'Come in.' Toby's voice sounded strained, as if he had already been talking too much.

Daniel obeyed, closing the door behind him.

Toby looked up from his desk, which was piled high with papers, but still far tidier than it had sometimes been in the past.

Marcus had spent years in this room, but it was Toby's now. The books on the many shelves were Toby's, and in contrast were neatly arranged in what appeared to be alphabetical order, suggesting that his mind, at least, was tidy. But Toby seemed to know where everything was when he wanted it, which was all that mattered.

Toby sat back in his chair. He appeared tired, his skin pale, with dark shadows under his eyes. As usual, his hair looked as if he had run his fingers through it, rather than used a

149

brush. He had probably begun the day by dressing immaculately, although without any of Marcus's flair. Definitely no velvet waistcoats. And his tie was now crooked, his jacket discarded over the back of his chair, and his shirt sleeves rolled up. They were possibly too short for his long arms anyway. He gave Daniel a half-smile and invited him in.

'Sorry to disturb you,' Daniel apologised, sitting in the guest chair, and then pulling it closer to the desk.

Toby looked at Daniel. 'Trouble?' There was a flat, almost despairing note in his voice.

Daniel instantly changed his mind. This was not the time to lay his troubles before Toby – especially when he knew Toby could not resolve them. 'Not really. Just wanted to keep you up to speed on Vayne, in case Hunter hadn't told you everything. Anyway, I haven't seen him this morning to tell him about my latest progress.'

Toby looked resigned, as if he expected the news to be bad. 'Has he bitten off more than he can chew?'

'Man's reach should exceed his grasp, or what is heaven for?' Daniel quoted, repeating the line that Mrs Parnell had recited to him.

Toby gave a wry smile, but there was a trace of genuine humour in it. 'I can't expect God to deal with such problems as Malcolm Vayne,' he said dryly. 'And he needs dealing with now. How's your grasp on the case?'

It was time for honesty now. It was either that or lies, and he had never lied to Toby. 'I spoke to Whitnall yesterday,' he began. 'He knows where the connections are, ones that we can't see, and we wouldn't necessarily recognise anyway. He's not looking forward to testifying, but he'll do it. That's the first real progress we've made. That is, that I've made. Everyone else I've spoken to waffles around, and doesn't know this or doesn't say that. Except Nadine Parnell. She will spill all the beans, if she survives.'

Toby's fist clenched on the desktop. 'What do you mean *if she survives*? I understand she was bruised and a bit shaken up, but not seriously injured.'

'She wasn't,' Daniel agreed quickly. 'She just looks so fragile. I'm afraid that if the defence is tough with her, they might shake her composure, or trip her up. It might not take a lot, in open court, to make her look a bit eccentric, or seem like an old lady who is losing her grasp.'

'It's your job to make her look wise and brave!' Toby said sharply. 'What does Hunter say? After all, he's the one who will be questioning her. Have you warned him to be slow, and careful? Simple testimony only, just recite exactly what she knows, and how she came by the information.'

Daniel thought that Toby looked surprisingly young for his thirty-odd years, and even a little vulnerable himself. Had Marcus set too heavy a weight on his shoulders, without any warning?

'We need her testimony, Daniel,' Toby continued. 'She is the only one who hasn't wavered yet. Perhaps you'd better question her, if you think Hunter will be rough.' He shook his head. 'Fergus Dalmeny is far too clever to verbally knock a witness around, especially an old lady. But he could politely tie her in knots. And I don't know Gideon Hunter well enough to predict his behaviour.' He brushed his hair back off his brow and it fell forward again immediately, returning to exactly the same position it had before. 'I have read all I can about him, but he's a bit of a closed book. And before you ask, I'm sure Marcus brought him into chambers on a hunch, a feeling that we needed some colour, and passion, unpredictability. In fact, rather like Marcus must have been in his heyday.'

Toby's face took on a whimsical expression. It was a complete change from just a few moments ago. There was affection in it, at the thought of his erstwhile mentor, and humour too.

'Have you read any of his early cases, when he was at his best?' he asked Daniel. 'You should! It's easy to see where Miriam gets her acuity, and her acerbic wit.' He gave a sigh. 'A pity she can't take the stand in this case, but there's really nothing for a forensic pathologist to say about systematic robbery. And I don't wish anyone dead. Except perhaps Vayne himself. That would be helpful.' He gave an apologetic smile. 'Sorry.'

Daniel echoed his sentiment. He was beginning to get some idea of the power Vayne exercised, and the general fear he generated, whether it was disguised as loyalty, a belief in his innocence, or a widespread blindness to the criminality of theft, quite apart from the law. One might not see blood, or bruises, but there was certainly injury. Whitnall's words rang in his mind, the undisguised fear in them. Perhaps he realised the danger to anyone standing against Vayne.

He understood more and more of what they were up against. It wasn't just the loss of a good job, or even popularity in society; the clubs one wished to belong to; the admiration of people in general; and certain men who could further one's career, one's future ambitions. All understandable, but basically selfish ends. No, this was a danger to family, to wives, to children with careers to carve out, perhaps good schools to go to, or influential friends, even marriages to make. That single dark shadow encompassed many pitfalls, accidents, failures and losses.

Looking at the case more closely, Daniel was glad he did not have a choice to make any more. He was committed, inescapably. Wisdom was admirable. Cowardice was not. Not ever.

Daniel rose to his feet, clearly taking Toby by surprise. 'I just came to catch you up,' he said, with a reassuring smile. 'It's movement, at last.'

Toby smiled in return, but he did not say anything, except very quietly, 'Thank you.'

Daniel had lunch with Gideon Hunter, at Hunter's request. He took Daniel to a quiet and extremely nice club. The doorman recognised him with a smile, as did the maître d'.

'It's an excellent place,' Hunter said casually. 'And so close to chambers one can slip in, eat in half an hour, or a couple of hours, if you have a meeting.' He smiled. 'You should become a member. It's also discreet. After you've had lunch today, consider if you would like me to put your name up.'

The maître d' was standing by, awaiting their instructions expectantly.

'Ah, George,' Hunter said, with a smile 'Luncheon for two, if you please. Mr Pitt and I are not expecting anyone, and I would appreciate the time alone to discuss business.'

George's eyebrows rose almost imperceptibly at the name *Pitt*, but he did no more than incline his head a little and smile. 'Delighted, Mr Pitt. I hope we will see you often.'

'Thank you,' Daniel replied. Actually, he rather liked the idea of belonging to clubs like this, comfortably quiet, and with tables large enough for four, but even better for two. The stone fireplace would radiate warmth when the weather changed, the waiters would remember your name, and probably know what you liked to eat. He did not voice this aloud; he must not appear too eager.

They ordered honeyed ham with salad, new potatoes, and warm apple pie and cream for dessert. In winter it would probably be hot roast, or steak and kidney pudding with suet crust.

Before their meals came, Daniel told Hunter what he had learned from Richard Whitnall the previous day.

'At last,' Hunter said, his satisfaction lighting up his face. 'Someone who has actual information and is prepared to give it to us.' He shook his head slightly. 'Everyone else seems to dither around, and ends up saying very little.'

'Except Nadine Parnell,' Daniel reminded him.

'Yes, Mrs Parnell. But nothing matters unless we have witnesses who are prepared to testify, with solid and relevant information.'

Daniel thought about this for a moment. 'Of course. And more importantly, you would not have leapt in to take the prosecution case otherwise, before anyone else could.' The moment the words were out of his mouth, he wondered if he had said too much.

'You think I was wrong?' Hunter asked very quietly, very levelly, as if he were keeping his temper with something of an effort.

Daniel hesitated, uncertain how bad an error he had made, and whether it would be best to retreat. That would look indecisive. But regardless of how it looked, he needed an answer. 'Have we boxed ourselves into a corner?' He was repeating the same question, although now phrased slightly differently.

Hunter smiled ruefully, but his eyes were unreadable. 'He's very definite about women's right to vote,' he said quietly. 'My wife is strongly in favour of his influence on that issue. She believes he has the power to make it happen . . . if he wants.'

'What does that mean?' Daniel needed to know, not only for the case itself, but because it would affect Miriam so intensely.

Hunter's smile was more relaxed, more genuine. 'It means she loathes the man, but she will somehow swallow her dislike of him if it serves the greater purpose.'

'A long spoon?' Daniel observed ruefully.

'What?'

'He who sups with the devil should have a long spoon,' Daniel quoted.

'Oh, yes.' Hunter's face softened, but there was no amusement in it, only an unexplained tenderness.

Daniel wondered if this shift was due to the pleasure Hunter felt at the mention of his wife.

'I suppose that is so,' Hunter continued. 'But if you want to get much done politically, a long spoon is only part of the basic equipment. And, in Vayne's case, we're talking about a very long spoon indeed.'

'And does she?' Daniel could not let it go. 'Your wife. Does she have a long spoon?'

'Yes,' Hunter replied, without hesitation. 'Doesn't your wife also?'

Daniel thought for a moment. There was a certain honesty in Hunter, even if it undercut his own pride, which he was beginning to like. 'Yes,' he answered, with a certain surprise. 'Miriam is prepared to take the harder way round, when she knows the easy one will not do it.' He took a deep breath. 'Whitnall is a good witness. I think he knows that he will risk a lot by testifying, but he'll do it all the same. He has courage, and he's the only one I have spoken to so far who has any idea of what Vayne's deeper motive is – or at least is willing to voice it.'

'It goes beyond just money,' said Hunter.

'Power,' Daniel said quietly. 'It's not the money per se, it's who owes what, and to whom. And in the end, what they expect in return. Blackmail, debts and high interest rates. This is international, not just confined to the domestic market.'

'Is that what Whitnall deals with, international loans?'

'It's not a question of who Vayne lends money to,' Daniel said. 'It's who he borrows it from, and at what rate of interest. I'm quite sure he doesn't pay his lenders back in money. Instead, he gives them power and important information.'

Hunter thought silently for a few moments, then looked up very directly and met Daniel's eyes. 'You believe him?'

'Whitnall? Yes,' Daniel replied levelly.

'So, you think it's not only about money, and the satisfaction Vayne has in flaunting it, but that it's also about power.'

Daniel answered, without hesitation. 'Whitnall didn't say so outright, but I believe he knows much more about this, and he will tell us in due course.'

'Why not now?' Hunter asked.

Daniel thought for a moment. 'Perhaps he has more evidence to collect. Or he wants to make certain that he has definitive proof of everything he says. He could be sued out of existence if he doesn't have the records to back it up.'

'But you think he knows what Vayne is up to?' Hunter spoke slowly, his brow puckered. 'Perhaps he wants immunity for himself. And we can't very well offer it, if we don't know what for. And at what price,' he pointed out.

'I know. There's a hell of a lot we don't know yet,' Daniel said grimly. 'We'll get at some of the facts during the trial, but in my opinion, we need a more detailed knowledge than we have now, or we face a good chance of tripping over our own feet and landing flat on our faces. And—'

'And Malcolm Vayne would be first to kick us when we are down,' Hunter finished for him. 'He has a lot of enemies who would be delighted to see him flattened on the pavement, but he also has a lot of influence with the public.'

'Does public opinion matter, if he's guilty?' Daniel asked.

'You mean if a jury finds him guilty?' Hunter amended bitterly. 'A jury drawn from those who read his newspapers? Or at least two or three who do?'

Daniel felt a sudden chill in the pit of his stomach. 'You mean, they may come to a decision regardless of the facts.'

'Money is a very slippery thing to get hold of,' Hunter said grimly. 'Most people can't even imagine the kind of money he has. Figures, if they're big enough, become meaningless to some people. And he does give a lot of it away. Or, more accurately, he uses it to buy goodwill and influence. And, of course, he benefits from considerable relief on income tax. It is not pure generosity, I assure you.'

'Can we prove it?' Daniel asked.

'That's the nail we have to hit on the head,' Hunter replied, putting his fist down on the table, but softly, so as not to shake the china or the crystal glasses. 'We have to be as clever as he is, which would be quite an achievement. I strongly believe this case will be won or lost on the jury's perception of whether he is a good man, or an evil one. And all of that is tied in to emotion, and whether the individual members of the jury feel affection or sympathy for him, or not. The facts could go either way. Not all rich men are wicked, and a lot of people want to believe Vayne will do all the great things for them that he promises!'

'Does he?'

Impatience flickered across Hunter's face, or perhaps it was fear. 'Really, Pitt! Read his damn newspapers! He promises all sorts of things, and the people believe him. Who else is going to do such things for them? He doesn't need to deliver on his promises; he doesn't even have to believe them himself. All that's necessary is to keep hope alive, for enough people to believe it's possible . . . and then acquit him.'

'And then what?' Daniel felt cold, despite the warmth of the elegant room, with sunlight streaming in through the windows, making the wine in his glass sparkle.

'Power,' Hunter answered. 'I fear it will be in the Houses of Parliament, either directly or indirectly. The power of his newspapers is very great. He tells people what they want to hear, and he is very good indeed at knowing what that is.'

Daniel did not answer. He took the last mouthful of his wine, and it went down his throat like fire.

Daniel spent the afternoon first travelling to Callum McCallum's office, and then sitting in the man's anteroom and waiting. He was prepared to sit there until McCallum could no longer put him off. Finally, he was shown into a large, airy room with a handsome oak desk and leather-upholstered chairs. At least half a dozen of them, as if he held large meetings here.

McCallum was a big man, well over six feet. He had broad shoulders and his distinctively tailored jacket hung well on him, almost hiding the extra weight beginning to show on his hips and stomach. He had regular features, strong bones, but the most striking thing about him was his magnificent hair. It was thick, wavy, dark, but now liberally threaded with silver. It would only be more dramatic, not less, as time passed.

He did not stand when Daniel entered, nor did he offer his hand.

Daniel glanced at the chairs, assessing their positions relative to the desk, and chose the one with the most direct view of McCallum.

McCallum sat behind the desk and leaned back a little,

looking at Daniel. Even before he spoke, the mood was set: this man was granting an audience, but reluctantly.

Daniel stared at him, thought to speak, and then changed his mind. Neither courtesy nor logic were going to make any difference. This man's mind was made up, his loyalty decided.

'Sorry to keep you waiting. How can I help you, Mr Pitt?' he asked, steepling his fingers and looking across them at Daniel. 'I know much of Mr Vayne's personal affairs. I've worked closely with him for some seven or eight years now, and I have never seen anything that was dishonest. Complicated, yes, without doubt.' He smiled very slightly, like a break in the clouds that instantly closed again. 'Hard to understand, unless you are highly schooled in finances. Are you, Mr Pitt? Highly schooled?' The smile on his face indicated that he knew perfectly well that Daniel was not.

For an instant, Daniel was tempted to say, 'Yes, I am,' but knew he would quickly be found out. 'No, Mr McCallum, I specialise in the law,' he said instead. 'What actions break it, what could merely bend it, and what can be got away with by a person who is clever, but basically dishonest.'

McCallum's face darkened. 'You have been in here less than two minutes, and already you are coming very close to slander. Your charge of dishonesty shows both ignorance and bad manners. Or perhaps you would understand better if I said *bad tactics*?'

Daniel raised his eyebrows. 'You asked me what subject I specialise in, Mr McCallum. Isn't that what we are here to discuss? Breaking the law? I came with the intent of hearing from you why that did not happen.'

A dark flush spread up McCallum's cheeks. Whatever wording they used, whatever pretence at civility, clearly this was open warfare.

McCallum stared at Daniel steadily. His eyes did not soften, nor did they change focus at all. 'Really?' he said at last. 'Mr Vayne is the finest man I have ever known. I intend to do all I can to protect his reputation, his safety, and as much of his comfort as I can. Like all powerful and talented men whose skill and imagination far exceed those of others, he has incurred enmities, jealousies, even allegations levelled at him by lesser men who don't understand the world of international finance. They attack because men like Malcolm Vayne show them up for what they are: followers, beneficiaries of investments they don't even understand, much less deserve.'

'Can we stop the speeches?' Daniel asked. 'There's no one listening: I'm not listening to you, and you're not listening to me. But the trial will take place, and we will both be there. If these charges are not based on fact, then let us discuss them now, and you can explain it all to me before it goes any further. If you intend to explain it in court, and I can assure you, you will be asked to—'

'By you?' McCallum interrupted, with a slight smile that reflected both amusement and condescension.

'More likely by Gideon Hunter.' Daniel did not add that he was a King's Counsel. McCallum would know that. 'But I would like to give him an outline of your position, so he does not waste time and make it sound so complicated that the jury doesn't understand it.' He looked carefully at McCallum's face. 'What people don't understand frightens them. Money unaccounted for looks like fraud.' He smiled back, with the same condescension as McCallum had shown. 'If you make it sound too complicated for ordinary people to understand, they will believe it is crooked.'

'All right!' McCallum snapped. 'I'll have it put into words of one syllable for you. And then you or Hunter can ask me on the stand, and I'll guide you through it. Now, unless you have something else to ask that can be answered in terms you already understand, I'll instruct my clerk to write this out for you and deliver it to your chambers.'

'Thank you,' Daniel said, trying to sound as if he had been given something. 'That would provide something to work with.' He smiled. 'A base upon which to construct our own questions.' He rose to his feet before McCallum could, and extended his hand. 'Thank you, sir.'

McCallum was wrong-footed, and it annoyed him. He did not take the extended hand.

'Good afternoon,' Daniel said, and walked to the door. There was nothing more to be gained here.

Anyway, he wanted to leave McCallum thinking that Daniel had got what he came for.

Chapter Fourteen

Miriam had had a long day and was looking forward to a quiet evening, but when Daniel came home very late and looking white-faced, she saw that he was worried and so she pushed her own fatigue aside. She also discarded the idea of an evening of comfortable silence, where they were each happy just to know that the other was there.

They ate supper, but she did not think he really tasted it.

The garden was not big enough to walk around, so they stood on the small patch of grass where they could smell the flowers, feel the cool evening air, and hear the breeze rustling through the leaves of the few surrounding trees. It was warm and peaceful.

Miriam had learned from experience that there was no point in asking Daniel what was worrying him, although clearly something was. It might be that he actually wanted to talk about it. He trusted her and, to her knowledge, he had never made the mistake of assuming that she would not understand.

'Are you worried about Gideon Hunter?' she said quietly. 'That he's bright, even brilliant in some ways, but that he hasn't enough fear to stop the chambers from taking on cases he can't win? That he doesn't consider losing, or what that battle might cost him . . . and all of you?'

He looked at her with sudden and complete attention. 'Is that what you think?'

'I've considered it,' she replied. It was not said with caution. This was not a time when she could afford to be gentle with his feelings.

She was beginning to fear that her father had made a mistake by appointing Hunter, and that Marcus's decision could cause serious damage to the chambers he had founded, served and nurtured most of his adult life. Her thoughts were mostly for him, but of course there was the practical concern too. If the chambers failed, she did not know if Marcus had the means to support himself for the rest of his days. But that was true for Daniel also! No one who was a part of this would walk away unhurt.

But so far, that was only a dark shadow of possibility in her mind. At present, there was a more urgent question of the practicalities to be addressed. No barrister won every case they took, any more than any doctor could cure every patient. She must think hard, and use her intelligence rather than her emotions.

'Have I considered it?' he questioned. He looked earnest. He shook his head slightly. It was not a gesture of denial, rather a clearing of his thoughts. 'Of course I've considered it,' he went on. 'The main issue at stake is Vayne thinking, or knowing, that his arrest was going to happen. That's why he gave Ian little choice but to act before he was ready, so we would lose the case simply by being hustled into acting before we had all the evidence. He knew that would have two results. It would tip Ian's hand, when he was not fully prepared, and force him to show it. And it would also flush out Vayne's

163

enemies. It would make them come out into the open, where Vayne could pick them off. And believe me, he has the skill and the means to do that.'

Miriam shivered. 'You make him sound very clever. I admit, I never saw him that way. Rich, a little garish, impulsive, sometimes generous, quick-tempered, vain. He has to be the centre of attention at all times. He wouldn't take kindly to being upstaged, but—'

'But not all that clever,' he finished for her, with his eyebrows raised, as if it were a question.

'No, I didn't think so,' she admitted. 'But perhaps he is, and that is the cleverest thing of all. To look brilliant to the people who can be more easily fooled; but to the discerning, to look a little less brilliant, and more driven by emotion and pretty lucky instincts.' Another ripple of fear went through her. Had they been lured into battle before they were ready? And would they lose because of that?

She stared at him, trying to read his face. There was strength and humour in it, and courage. At least, that was what she thought she saw. But there was also vulnerability. She ached to protect him. It hurt even to imagine him in real pain, deep and inescapable. And yet she could not love someone who was invulnerable; that would make him somehow less than human. Such a man could never love her as she loved him; he would never understand the true complexities of life, or love.

Daniel was watching her closely.

She shook herself, and looked at him as if she saw only the immediate problem in front of them. 'We need to know him better,' she said aloud. 'I met Rose Hunter, and I like her. She knows far more about him than we do, or Ian Frobisher. I think we need her help.'

'Are we talking about Hunter or Vayne?' he asked.

'Oh!' She realised how lost she must sound. 'Actually, both, but I meant Vayne. Of course, Rose knows Hunter more intimately than we do, but she would never tell us his weaknesses.'

'Wouldn't she?'

'I wouldn't tell anyone about yours!' she said hotly. 'It would be the ultimate disloyalty.' Then she saw him smile, and she felt the blush warm her cheeks. 'I would protect your weaknesses from anybody,' she stated. 'That is, of course, if you had any.'

He laughed, and it was a beautiful, full-hearted sound, and the joy of it lit up his face.

At that moment, she would have protected him from anything at all. Had he any idea how deeply she loved him? Maybe there were only brief moments when he could handle such knowledge. She changed the subject quickly. 'Daniel, I think you need to know exactly how much Ian knows for certain, and what is only guesswork. Did Vayne outwit him, or did he see this coming and he has some sort of a plan? I dare say, you don't want to challenge Ian, but you can't play your part if you don't know what it is.'

He did not fight her. 'I'll see him, the first chance I get.' He gave a little downturned smile and reached out his hand to touch her cheek. 'And no, I don't mean I'll wait until I can't avoid it; I'll go and find him. If he hasn't got any ammunition to use against Vayne, we need to know it now, and not when Hunter is questioning his first witness and discovers that his gun has no bullets.'

Her first instinct was to thank him. But that would imply he had not been going to do it, but had changed his mind to please her. 'I think that's wise,' she said instead.

His face relaxed into a smile. Perhaps he knew exactly what she was thinking. It was at once a frightening thought, and a comforting one.

Before Daniel had any opportunity to see Ian, he and Miriam went to visit Marcus, something they frequently did on a Sunday. After a long, lazy lunch of cold roast beef, fresh vegetables and potatoes – it was the season for the earliest new ones, delicately flavoured and with the skins almost transparent – they all felt satisfied and well fed.

Marcus leaned back and sighed. Eminently comfortable. This was his home, filled with the memorabilia of his life: memories, echoes of achievement, learning, happy relationships.

Miriam was watching him and saw how the wide smile on his face slowly relaxed into something more serious, even sombre. She knew him well enough to see the ease slip away from him, as if he knew the time had come to speak honestly, and was aware that at least some of what he had to say was going to hurt. It was no longer avoidable. She wanted to defend Marcus and Daniel both, but it would be pointless, like putting a plaster on a boil. It hid it from your sight, but did nothing to drain the infection.

'Hunter?' Marcus said bluntly, looking at Daniel, not Miriam.

She knew enough to keep silent.

'What do you think of him, Daniel? Are you ready for trial?'

'No,' Daniel said unhappily. 'But I'm not sure if we ever will be. At this moment, I think the advantage would go to Vayne.'

Marcus looked deflated. Miriam could see the tiredness in his eyes, and in the pallor of his skin. But she must not interrupt. She was the daughter who loved him. All the years of her life he had been there, so often protecting her, teaching her how to look beyond the surface of things and see the reality behind. Now the roles were reversed, and she felt useless.

Daniel leaned forward a fraction, drawing Miriam's attention. 'As for Hunter, I know he is a bit of a chancer,' he began. 'He's willing to take risks and he's brave. He won't quit because the road gets tough. I think he is there till the last dice are thrown.' He bit his lip for a moment, as if undecided whether to say what he was thinking, or not.

'And?' Miriam prompted him. 'Don't stop there.'

'And if we win,' he continued, with a slight relaxing of his shoulders, 'there will be an immense reward professionally. If we lose, I don't know how hard it will be for us. But if Vayne loses, he will land in prison. And even if he wins, some of the smears will stick to him. It's not fair, and it's not a weapon to use, but he'll be frankly terrified by the accusations. Some of them are definitely true. He knows the verdict will be in the minds of the public, as much as in the courtroom, and it will have very little to do with legal right or wrong. He has money, and that makes him friends and enemies.'

Miriam looked at Daniel and saw an older, wiser man than she had expected. Could he see in her face how much she respected him? She looked away quickly. Not from Daniel, but from Marcus. This much at least should be private.

Marcus pressed his lips tightly together. Finally, he said, 'His newspapers will continue to do their best to thrash the police,' he warned.

'I know,' Daniel agreed. 'But if we are clever enough, and I think Hunter is, he will make it look like the thrashing around of a desperate man, rather than the righteous indignation of someone unjustly accused.'

Marcus let his breath out in a sigh. 'I wish you were conducting more of it. The defence, I mean. What do you really know of Gideon Hunter, Daniel? I know you like him. He's a very likeable chap, but how much are you leaning on my judgement, because you are loyal? Or because I am your father's friend – and more than that, I am your wife's father?'

Daniel thought for a moment, then smiled widely. 'So far, to me at least, Hunter is completely unpredictable. I hope he's the same to Vayne.'

'Remember that it's Fergus Dalmeny who is Hunter's opposition, not Malcolm Vayne,' Marcus interposed.

Daniel raised his eyebrows. 'You mean Dalmeny will give the orders, not Vayne?'

Miriam looked away quickly, in case Marcus read the amusement in her eyes.

Marcus smiled also. 'Once you stand up and start to speak, of course it's Dalmeny who will be in charge. Even if Vayne loses his self-control to the point of arguing in front of the jury. And he'll trust Dalmeny. He wouldn't have anyone he didn't have damn good reason to trust! And take that any way you like.'

'And if Vayne fired Dalmeny?' Daniel asked.

'He'd be a bigger fool than I think,' Marcus responded instantly. 'He'd be lucky to find another man anywhere near Dalmeny's quality.'

Miriam felt a sudden lift in her spirits. 'So, Vayne has to keep Dalmeny, however much he might resent his discipline.'

'Yes,' Marcus agreed. 'And Fergus Dalmeny doesn't like to lose either! Don't underestimate him.' He turned to Daniel. 'One thing about Hunter, he takes advice. He might say he isn't going to, or even behave as if he resents it, but if it's good, he will take it, all the same.'

'It doesn't make any difference now,' Miriam said grimly, ignoring the way her father looked at her. 'We have Hunter, and we must make the best of it. And we must look as if we have every confidence in him. Because once we are in court, it's all about confidence, not choice. Our position is dictated. We must argue for it the best way possible. Unless—' She stopped. She knew what she wanted to say, only hesitating over how to phrase it.

'What?' Both Daniel and Marcus spoke at the same time.

Her mind raced. 'How best to present it,' she finished. 'You don't want to sound as if you are uncertain, and at the same time you must not back yourself into a corner that you can't get out of . . . should you have to,' she added.

Daniel looked startled for a moment, then he smiled. 'Easy to say, rather harder to do. I don't know if Hunter will even call me to question any of the witnesses, and almost certainly not the leading ones—'

'And it is Dalmeny's choice whether to allow Vayne himself to testify or not,' Marcus interposed.

'As so often, wise or not, I doubt it will be Dalmeny's choice,' Daniel said. 'Vayne will decide whether he speaks or not, and I'd be surprised if he chooses silence.'

'There are mixed opinions on that,' Marcus answered, while Daniel seemed to be mulling it over. 'Not to speak looks like cowardice to some. As if you can't proclaim your own innocence because you know you are guilty. Whereas, to others, it will look like arrogance if you do take the stand, even though you may appear guilty if you don't.' He shook his head slightly, the light glistening on his bright silver hair. 'And, of course, if you do speak, then the prosecution has the opportunity to cross-question anything you say. Some men would rather not be in that position.'

'I imagine a wise counsel will make the decision for him,' Miriam said, looking at her father. 'But Vayne doesn't have to listen. Would you let him speak, if you were his counsel?'

Marcus thought about this for several moments before answering. 'I'm not sure,' he said, at last. 'Or even if I would have the opportunity to choose. After all, Vayne is the one in the dock, and I loathe the man. I'm not sure I would even have taken his case, but—'

Miriam interrupted him. 'Go out in a blaze of glory! Or crash-dive into the sea!'

Daniel hid a smile, with obvious difficulty.

Marcus grunted. 'If I took the case to defend him, I would fight as hard as I could, so that when he was found guilty, he would have no recourse to claim he had not been fairly represented.'

The conversation continued after Miriam and Daniel got home. It was she who started it again, because the subject of Vayne's prosecution, the fear and the doubt, continued to preoccupy her mind.

Was it something to do with Marcus being so obsessed with the prospect of battle, tactics, the arguments themselves, that made her think he was fighting the whole issue vicariously through Daniel, and perhaps also through Gideon Hunter? Her imagination went much further than that. There was no physical forensic evidence, because there was no bodily crime involved. She knew very little of accounting, beyond what was needed to balance a cheque book. And she knew nothing of banking or sophisticated finance.

How much of this was Marcus being a knight, a type of crusader, looking for a battle to fight? They all disliked Vayne. The man was guilty of greed, and unquestionably of bad taste.

These might be considered offensive, but they were not crimes.

She waited until they were sitting down, relaxing for an hour or so and enjoying the last of the summer evening. The French doors leading to the garden were still at least half-open. There was no sound of wind in the leaves, or traffic from the road. The only movement was a mass of starlings disturbed by something, swirling high in the sky, black dots against the fading light.

Miriam asked herself if she should disturb the peace by asking the question still unaddressed.

'What?' Daniel said, as if she had already spoken.

She smiled. It was a comfortable thing, being known so well. 'Vayne is unpleasant, often catering to people's worst instincts rather than their better ones, but that is not a crime – frightening and revolting as it is. Is he guilty of an actual, prosecutable crime, and one that we can prove?'

He was listening, not interrupting.

'I realise that you've known Ian almost all your life,' she went on. 'And he is a decent, honest man. But even the best of us can be mistaken, especially when we know we are morally right. Vayne is power hungry, but has he committed a crime? In the eyes of the law?' She hesitated, wishing Daniel would say something, but he did not. He just listened. 'If we try and fail, he'll take his revenge. And not necessarily against the people who testified against him. He's cunning enough and amoral enough to take it out on the most vulnerable.' She took a deep breath. 'And sometimes they're not who we think they are.'

She looked at his face, and saw in his eyes that he understood exactly what she meant, and possibly more. There was something there, behind his expression, something darker. Could it be vengeance against Ian for having accused Vayne, for having inconvenienced him, embarrassed him, possibly even frightened him? The last of these would never be forgiven by a man who cared so much about how others saw him, what they thought, what they felt.

Daniel said nothing for some time, and when he spoke it was not what she expected. 'We must support Hunter, not ask him if he knows what he's doing. It's too late to turn around, anyway. I'll ask him if he has all he needs, and if there's anything I can do.'

Miriam reached forward and put a hand over his. Tonight, there was no need for more words.

Chapter Fifteen

Thomas Pitt was sitting in a large armchair at his club, having held a very satisfactory meeting with a government minister. They could have met at the House of Commons in one of the dining rooms there, but both interruption and observation would have been unavoidable, and they wished for neither of those. Now the minister was gone and Pitt was sitting with a glass of brandy he did not wish to drink. His companion had bought it in a friendly gesture, and drunk his own. Pitt looked at it, at the sunlight shining through the dark golden liquid, but he actually did not care for it very much, and he rarely drank alcohol during his working hours.

'Drinking alone, and in the middle of the day, Sir Thomas?' a mocking voice said.

He looked up and saw Malcolm Vayne standing several feet away. He seemed to tower over Pitt, who was seated.

Vayne was immaculately dressed in a suit undoubtedly tailored for him out of what appeared to be a mixture of silk and linen, the sort of luxury very few people could afford, or even have the occasion to wear. His shirt was unquestionably pure silk. It was not ostentatious, just quietly perfect: the cut, the soft sheen of the fabric.

'No,' he answered Vayne's comment. 'I am merely looking at it. It was bought for me. I did not wish to refuse it – that would have been unnecessarily discourteous. I will simply leave it.'

'You so often do the unexpected. I, at least, expect that of you. Brandy too rich for your taste?' Then he raised his eyebrows slightly, indicating an actual question, not merely a comment.

He was telling Pitt that he knew of his very humble beginnings, probably even of his father's conviction and deportation to Australia for poaching a rabbit from the estate next to the one where he had been employed as a gamekeeper.

Pitt wanted to bite back, because the jibe stung, mainly for his mother's sake. She had worked so hard to give her only child all she could. But that was what Vayne wanted, some self-defensive retort. He refused to comply.

'At luncheon, yes, too rich,' he replied. He should be above retaliating, but he wanted to put Vayne away far more intensely than was good for his judgement, or his clarity of mind. 'Why? Do you want it?' This time he met Vayne's eyes, as if it were the natural thing to do, as if they were acquaintances, not enemies.

The corners of Vayne's mouth turned down in distaste. 'I am not in need of second-hand brandy, thank you. I don't know who you mistook me for!' he snapped.

Pitt smiled. 'It's usually considered to be better when it has aged. Who on earth drinks new brandy?'

'Those who need a little pick-me-up during the day,' Vayne said sharply. 'You have a kind of lost look, as if you don't know which way to turn next. I think you are out of your depth. You are not moving, because you don't know which way to turn next.'

174

That was perfectly true. Reading people accurately, smelling their fear or hunger, was an ancient skill, and one of Vayne's abilities. It was also one of the reasons people were afraid of him.

Pitt deliberately smiled, meeting Vayne's eyes. 'I am not moving, because the next move is yours – and the law's, of course.'

'Oh, yes,' Vayne responded after barely two seconds. 'The trial. Your son is junior counsel, so my staff informed me. Promising young man, but very young, very vulnerable.'

'Of course, you don't have a son, do you!' Pitt shot back. 'At least, not a legitimate one who bears your name.' The moment the words were out of his mouth, he regretted them.

It was a low blow. And completely irrelevant to this case. Except that Vayne was subtly threatening Pitt with Daniel's vulnerability. He had meant to frighten the older man, and the fact that Pitt had retaliated showed him that he had succeeded.

Did Vayne suffer from any such vulnerability? Was there somebody he cared for? Somebody whose loss would wound him beyond bearing? Everything Pitt knew about the man suggested there was no one. And no individual item he could not replace with money. And that was truly to be barren. He had created nothing that he loved.

'I'm sorry,' Pitt apologised.

Vayne's eyebrows shot up. 'An apology? From someone in your lofty position? Isn't that against government policy?'

'No,' Pitt replied. 'It is an expression of regret. Pity, if you like, that you have no one you would regret losing.' He looked straight into Vayne's blazing eyes, without blinking.

'You are going to regret that, Pitt,' Vayne said, clenching

his jaw. 'Soon.' And then he nodded, as if the conversation had been pleasant, and strode away.

Pitt knew that he meant it. This was no veiled threat.

He went back to his office with no sense of victory. Vayne had made it perfectly clear that he would strike at Daniel, if he felt it to be in his own interest. That was not really news; it was just something Pitt could do nothing about, and facing the reality of it was almost crippling. To love anyone, anything, was to open yourself to pain. Not to love was to accept a kind of death before you begin.

It was time to look more closely at Vayne's world. His aims, above it all. What did he love, or fear losing? What would hurt him enough to make him change his behaviour?

He had been given access to the files regarding Vayne, and began by going over his assets: the companies he owned, the properties, and even more importantly, the money he had invested in Europe.

By late in the evening, the picture that emerged was not easy to accept. Malcolm Vayne had loaned an enormous amount of money to a wide cross-section of people, some of whom were not going to be able to repay it. That was frightening, because Vayne would no doubt call in the debts in other ways: information, pressure brought to bear on people who could influence others, favours returned in a dozen different ways. It was not so much the recorded loans that troubled Pitt; it was those he suspected, but could not prove.

And what about the money that Vayne owed to others? Some of it was easy to trace: quite ordinary loans, quickly repaid when one of his properties sold, or a cheque was issued in repayment. Some of these loans appeared to have been written off . . . but were they really? Vayne was not a generous man. He collected debts to the last penny. So, presumably he would have expected to repay his own debts in full measure. Why would he have taken out some loans that were never paid back, but written off?

The answer that forced itself into Pitt's mind was that they were indeed repaid, but invisibly.

The man's power was almost invisible. But, like electricity, its ability to destroy was incalculable.

Chapter Sixteen

The trial of Malcolm Vayne began a little more than two weeks later. It had only been a month and a half since his original arrest. The courtroom was buzzing with excitement.

Daniel took the chair beside Gideon Hunter and his mind raced, trying to think of every possibility, and if they were prepared for it. They had gone over all the details, including the questions for each witness, and what answers they were expected to give. Who would stand by what they had said? Who was indecisive, emotional, angry, frightened, or defensive? Perhaps the most important question of all: who was afraid? And if they were afraid, of whom . . . or what? And which fears were justified?

The noise died away like a receding wave as the judge entered the room. He was bewigged and gowned. Mr Justice Abbott-Smith was a very ordinary-looking man; it was difficult to describe anything about him that was unusual, except perhaps his voice, which was crisp and very precise.

Everyone in the room rose to their feet.

Daniel looked at the judge and wondered if the man's name was plain Smith, and he had incorporated his mother's maiden name of Abbott to make himself sound more impressive. If so, this was not a good sign. Anyone who needed to impress others, and sat in a seat of power, was not only pretentious, he could be dangerously unpredictable.

Abbott-Smith was a large man, with a chest that was puffed out like that of a pouter pigeon. Or perhaps his robes were too big for him?

The judge took his seat. Silence was absolute.

Daniel could hear his own heart beating.

He and Gideon Hunter were seated on one side of the courtroom, with Vayne's defence counsel, Fergus Dalmeny, and Dalmeny's junior on the other. They were all gowned in black and, as was customary, they wore white wigs with small pigtails. Both gown and wig were required in the courtroom.

Despite their courtroom finery, they appeared far less imposing than the judge. He wore a billowing robe, and his head was covered by a white wig that fitted snugly on his head and had long flap-like extensions that covered his ears and reached down to his shoulders.

The mounting silence was intense, almost suffocating.

Daniel glanced at the dock, where Malcolm Vayne was standing alone. It was not a violent crime of which he was accused, and he had posted bail, so he was not handcuffed.

Vayne was also a big man, usually a little florid, but today his pallor was evident, as if he had been jailed, kept away from the sun for weeks, even months. Of course, that was nonsense. He had been out on bail, not imprisoned at all. Daniel had been concerned at first, but soon realised that Vayne had far more to lose by fleeing than he had by staying, and then facing and disproving the charges.

There was the matter of his perhaps intending to carry out revenge attacks against those who had dared to accuse him, and this included those who were willing to testify against him. For that reason alone, Daniel had preferred that he be detained in a gaol cell, but the law was on Vayne's side.

Daniel could already spot half a dozen reporters at least, notebooks out, pencils in hand. Some would doubtless be from Vayne's own newspapers.

All spectators and participants resumed their seats. The usual formalities were performed, with all the solemnity due to the majesty of the law.

Gideon Hunter rose to begin presenting his case. He walked forward so that he could address the members of the public as well as the jury. Daniel wondered if he was more nervous than he looked. After all, he had spent a great deal of time on this case, not only investigating Vayne's guilt, but also scrutinising the man's life of honour and service to the public good. Or was it a life of disgrace? The amount of money involved in this alleged fraud was incalculable, and there were reputations at stake.

Daniel could see from the off, looking at both Hunter and Dalmeny, that the men were preparing to duel, and they were accompanied by their seconds. There would be dramatic scenes here, no doubt about it. Beyond the courtroom, Daniel knew that thousands of people were following this case, many of them in some way financially involved, and half the country was backing one side or the other – whether politically motivated, or merely for the spectacle. The phrase 'bread and circuses' came to Daniel's mind. Was all of this taking place simply to soothe the anger of all those gullible people who had been cheated?

If there was one thing Daniel knew with a certainty, it was that this case could make or ruin Malcolm Vayne. There were no wild animals in the arena, but this trial could prove to be just as savage.

Daniel had already spotted his father in the gallery, sitting quietly, just another middle-aged man waiting for the drama to commence. Like everyone else in the courtroom, Thomas Pitt was probably wondering if Vayne would prevail and walk away, or would the giant fall? If he did, who would he take down with him? Daniel's mother, Charlotte, sat beside her husband, not speaking, but watching intently.

Hunter cleared his throat, as if signalling the room to settle down. He had an excellent voice, and he knew it. Not loud, as if he were shouting at the jurors, but certain, confident, every word clear. Even at the back of the room, people were listening, caught up in his oratory.

'Gentlemen,' he addressed the jury.

Naturally, there were no female jurors, although there were plenty of women in the cavernous courtroom.

Daniel wondered if Vayne's counsel would seize on the fact of there being no women on the jury. Would it become the next inequality that he would address? Judged by a jury of your peers? Only if you are a man. That's what Miriam would say.

And what if Vayne were found guilty? He would be in no position to launch a new campaign for women's rights. And if he were found not guilty? He would have no cause for complaint! To Daniel, this seemed like a nice irony.

'This all may look at first to be immensely complicated,' Hunter was saying. 'And yet, when you untangle it, as we shall do, it really is very simple. Ordinary men are persuaded to invest money in a scheme that they are assured is both honest and prosperous. Big Ben Investments.' He shrugged. 'And so it is . . . to begin with. As more and more people invest in Big Ben, the first investors are repaid, plus they're given a nice rate of interest. But here's the problem: they are paid not from profits from the investment fund, but with the money of the second wave of investors! Why is that? Because the money was never invested. The amount entrusted to Malcolm Vayne and Big Ben, along with the breadth of the fraud itself, gets bigger and bigger. And as the fraud continues, the dividends shrink, getting, shall we say, a little less generous. But they are still enough to satisfy the ordinary man, to justify his feeling that he is being prudent, but not greedy. Investors in Malcolm Vayne's scheme never learn that their profits are coming not from the proceeds of legitimate businesses, but from the money of other investors. What is the art in this? There is none, except to know when to get out before the whole thing finally implodes.'

The jurors were staring at him. He had their total attention, and already the understanding that this was morally wrong.

'And, tragically, it does implode,' he continued. 'But that is the essence of a fraud such as this one. We will show you how this has worked so far – specifically, the Big Ben fund – and what ruin and despair it has caused so many people, some of whom will share their stories with you in this courtroom. You will understand how tragedy was inevitable from the beginning, because there was never a legitimate investment. Let me repeat; there never was a legitimate investment! What does that mean? It means there can be no growth! If you were an investor, how would you feel, knowing that you can never get back your money? It is gone.'

A murmur ran through the spectators.

'We cannot magically produce the investors' lost money, but what we can do is gain justice, and see that no others suffer such losses . . . as so many have done already.'

Hunter continued only a few minutes more, and Daniel noted that the jury was listening intently, their faces reflecting pity, and in several cases, anger. But how long could he hold them, if he could not engage their understanding? Facts were vital – amounts and bottom lines – but comprehending the losses and suffering was the key. It was imperative that the jurors be given the important information, but in a way they could understand. Hunter needed to make it feel personal to each juror!

Daniel was certain that Hunter was aware of that himself. He altered his stance just enough to be noticed, and the pitch of his voice changed, became less cultured and more intimate, as he continued to address the jury. When he spoke again, his words were aimed directly at them, one after the other, as if they were the ones who had been defrauded. He needed them to understand precisely what was involved.

'Had you been one of those investors, you would have chosen to put your well-earned money where it would be safe, and where it was earning interest for your future, when perhaps you will be less strong, less vigorous, and you will need your savings. There are many reasons for wanting to draw from those savings. You have a sudden illness. What will happen to your wife? Your children? Even your house? You have a brilliant child. His future could be all sorts of things, if you can afford a good education for him. But there is no problem: you have your savings! What could be a better use for the money you saved over years of hard work? Or what if you have an accident and cannot work for a while? Never mind, that is what your wise savings are for!'

He smiled at each of them, as if only one juror were seated in the massive, carved jury seats. 'You are a prudent man,' he went on. 'You have thought of this, and made provisions. You have savings that are earning interest even as we speak! You may sleep well at night, knowing you have taken care of this.'

183

His expression darkened. 'Only, when you go to remove some of the money because you need it, it is not there. Without you knowing it, your money – your hard-earned money – has been used to make the first interest payments to the previous round of investors. The pot containing your money . . . is empty.'

Hunter made a gesture of despair. 'That is the fact made real. Gentlemen, we are not talking about a possibility, or a theory. This is not an imaginary disaster that may never happen. When we show you the facts, with evidence, papers, testimony from bankers and financiers, and several hard-working people who have lost everything, you will see that this is the consequence, the terrible truth, for these unfortunate people who trusted the promises of Malcolm Vayne.'

He shook his head. 'Or is it not you, but only men who are like you? Perhaps your neighbour? Your friend? The man you work with? Your brother? The old woman whose husband has died and she has invested what little she has because she was promised that it would be protected? Or the newly married couple saving to provide for a family in the future.'

Hunter took a few steps closer to the jurors. 'How do I know it is not you? Because we would not be clumsy enough to ask you to sit on this jury and make a judgement concerning your own case. But even if you are not one of the many who have invested in Mr Vayne's scheme, you are still a victim in all this. Not you directly, but someone in many ways just like you.'

Daniel watched the jurors' faces. They were imagining being suddenly cheated out of what they had planned, what they believed was the security of their money. The anger, pity and fear were increasingly visible.

Those in the gallery were silent. Some of them were just

like the victims Hunter described. They could all imagine it. And some were actual victims.

Daniel was certain Hunter must be seeing this as well. It would inform his final words, the thought with which to leave them.

Hunter gave an almost invisible bow, no more than an acknowledgement, and closed his argument with grace. 'We will show you, step by step, how this was done. How Malcolm Vayne committed fraud against innocent, trusting people . . . people like you.' He glanced at each man and then said, 'Thank you, gentlemen.' He turned and walked back to his seat.

Daniel was impressed by Hunter's opening and paid special attention to not only his phrasing, but the way he approached the jury. Not as if he were one of them, but as if he understood their concerns.

Fergus Dalmeny rose to his feet. He was not a large man, and yet he was a striking presence. He was darkly handsome, and both the wig and gown suited him. He walked with easy grace to the same place where Hunter had just stood. Daniel was sure that he would address the jury politely, but he had ground to make up, and he knew it. They already regarded him warily, and judging by the faces, with disfavour. These were ordinary men, and he was going to try to justify Malcolm Vayne stealing the savings from other men just like them.

Daniel refrained from saying anything to Hunter, only because it might seem a little patronising. The man did not need Daniel's approval.

Dalmeny was as distinguished as Hunter, but the resemblance stopped there. In fact, Daniel noted something utterly different in his manner. He moved with the tense control of an animal, some type of big cat. Definitely an animal of prey.

'Gentlemen,' he began. 'I do not wish to appeal to your pity, or your fear. I do not wish to appeal to the ordinariness in you, but rather to that which is extraordinary, outside, and dare I say, beyond the commonplace. You have been called on to sit in judgement of another man, and that is something few of us are ever given the privilege and the burden of doing. And you are also called upon, indeed required, to judge as well as you humanly can what has been impressed upon your minds to be true, beyond a reasonable doubt.'

He now stood so still as to be mesmerising. No movement whatsoever distracted the attention. 'Did this man, Malcolm Vayne, take people's money, and while promising to do one thing with it, in fact knowingly and with intent to deceive and rob, did something else? If you do not understand – and I must admit I do not understand myself many of the prosecutor's charges – then you must say so, and give my learned friend the opportunity to explain to you . . . if he can. What you must not do, on your sacred oath in this room, and before this judge, and before the eyes of the world, is give a verdict you do not wholly believe to be true. I'm sure you understand me.'

He did not say more. He turned on his heel and then stopped and turned back to the jury. 'You are going to vindicate a man's reputation, his life's work, or you are going to ruin it, leave it in broken pieces here on the floor. I do not envy you. Nevertheless, it is yours to decide.' He lifted his shoulders very subtly in a gesture of abandonment, then walked back to his seat.

Everyone in the room seemed to shift position, let out a sigh. Some even whispered to those next to them.

Daniel was not sure if he wished Miriam were here or not. It would be comforting to imagine her somewhere behind

186

him in the body of the court. And yet it would be a distraction, and he needed all his attention. He might not even be asked to speak at all. He might have nothing to do but notice, listen, remember, and find immediately any reference Hunter did not have at his fingertips, or had temporarily forgotten. It was bad enough that his father and mother were here. In his father's case, he knew that was necessary. He had connections to this case, even if it was not yet certain what they were. Had he not been in the courtroom, that would have mattered to Daniel.

Gideon Hunter called his first witness, John Sandemann.

Sandemann came into the room. Everyone stared at him, shifting in their seats so their eyes could follow him. He was slender, and of average height, his hair the white blond one expected from someone with a Scandinavian heritage.

He looked straight ahead as he made his way between the rows of people who were staring silently at him, and then across the floor to the witness box. His skin was pale, but he seemed perfectly composed. He did not glance at Vayne.

John Sandemann took the oath, promising to tell the truth, the whole truth, and nothing but the truth, and then looked at Hunter expectantly.

Daniel had met him only once. Most of what he knew was based on Gideon Hunter's notes, taken as part of the preparation work. He trusted Hunter to have read this man well, determining how best to approach him. After all, John Sandemann was one of the closest business allies of Malcolm Vayne.

Hunter rose to his feet.

There was a brief rustle in the gallery, where the press sat. Someone dropped a piece of paper and it fluttered down. Nobody spoke.

Daniel glanced up at Vayne, seated in the dock, separate from all the others, as if he were already no longer one of them; he was guilty as charged, in Daniel's eyes, although not yet found to be. Daniel could not tell from this distance what expression was in Vayne's eyes, but he would have imagined it was anger rather than fear. His heavy jowl was hanging slightly over his collar, but there was very little blood in his cheeks. His pale hair must have been carefully brushed, yet it did not look it. It seemed dry, almost like straw. He appeared to be staring with great intensity at Sandemann, as if his eyes could bore into the man and instill fear. And why not? This was a betrayal about to happen. Here, in public, for the spectators to see and hear, and the press to report.

Daniel looked across at Dalmeny and saw how stiffly he was sitting in his chair. Daniel had learned what he could about this defence counsel – his history, his family, his graduation with first-class honours from Oxford. He was in his early forties, and had married into both position and money. He was a member of several elite gentlemen's clubs, had no particular political allegiances, and no financial debts at all. It was exactly what Daniel expected. What was more, there seemed to be nothing rumoured about the man, and no obvious vulnerabilities.

As for Gideon Hunter, he had achieved some spectacular victories in court, but he had also had some failures, which neither his rivals nor Vayne's journalists would allow him to forget. Nevertheless, juries liked him. He had humour and imagination, whereas Fergus Dalmeny had a reputation for frightening juries sometimes, and Daniel could identify with that. The man's presence was imposing, even ominous.

Gideon Hunter now stood in front of the witness box. Sandemann looked at him, his face impassive.

'Good morning, Mr Sandemann. I have several questions intended to educate us – and that includes the jury – on your role in Malcolm Vayne's organisation and, ultimately, the fraud of which he is accused.'

Sandemann nodded, but said nothing, just as Daniel and Hunter had instructed in an earlier meeting with him. It was far better to remain quiet until asked a specific question. This avoided confusion with the jury. Sandemann had been very nervous in their meeting, and Daniel had been worried that he might not be up to the task. Hunter would certainly question him with respect, but there was no saying how Dalmeny would approach him. If he went on full attack, would Sandemann keep his composure? Daniel was not at all sure. At the moment, however, the man seemed calm, composed.

As Sandemann waited for Hunter to begin his questioning, Daniel took a closer look at his demeanour. He was not only composed, but there was not a trace of fear in his face, which Daniel expected to see in someone who was about to betray a powerful man. That lack of visible fear concerned him, but he was in no position to say anything. Hunter was standing a good distance away, prepared to strike. It would be impossible to get his attention. And even if he did, then what?

'Mr Sandemann,' Hunter began. 'How long have you worked for Malcolm Vayne?'

'Twelve years, almost thirteen,' Sandemann replied.

'And in what capacity? That is,' he added quickly, nodding to the jury, 'would you please describe to the jury your position in Mr Vayne's company?'

Sandemann shifted his position a bit before speaking. 'My primary role is representing Mr Vayne and his company in acquisitions.'

'Acquisitions,' repeated Hunter.

'Yes, the buying and selling of properties.'

'In England, sir?'

'Throughout the United Kingdom,' replied Sandemann. 'And most of the European countries.'

'And what about the charities either created by or supported by Mr Vayne?'

'I have little to do with those,' said Sandemann.

'And Mr Vayne's investment enterprises?'

'Yes, of course. I've been part of these for many years.'

'Would you say that, other than Mr Vayne, you are the most knowledgeable about them?'

Sandemann nodded.

'Please answer aloud,' said Hunter. 'For the jury to hear.'

'Yes,' said Sandemann. 'Probably. Different people have different responsibilities.'

Hunter appeared satisfied with this response. From Daniel's perspective, it was the precursor to Hunter laying out one fraudulent scheme after another. He glanced at Dalmeny and saw worry in the man's face. As for Vayne, his expression was not so much blank as icy. He was about to be betrayed by his most trusted associate.

'Mr Sandemann, you have described to me the specifics of those acquisitions and sales. You have also described – and may I say in great detail – the investment fund managed by – or should I say mismanaged by? – Malcolm Vayne, and how investors were defrauded. Some of them lost their lifetime's savings. And lastly, sir, you have given specific information about how Mr Vayne used all of this fraudulent behaviour as a means to enlarge his personal wealth, at the expense of many. Today, I'm going to take you through each of these groups of transactions, educating the jury about the many transgressions of Malcolm Vayne.'

Sandemann nodded, and then quickly added, 'Yes, sir.'

'Thank you.' Hunter smiled.

'May I add something here?' Sandemann asked.

'Of course,' said Hunter.

'You will appreciate that a great deal of what I know is confidential.'

Hunter barely paused before saying, 'I beg to differ, sir.' His manner was gentle, and there was a polite smile on his face, but for all that it was very slight, the softening of the lips, no more. 'This is a court of law. Any information directly related to the charges of fraud must be disclosed. I do understand if you fear that the jury would draw from it something that would reveal private information about investors, and would certainly show the accused in an unfavourable light, let us say. It is perfectly understandable that you do not wish to do that. And as much as I agree that your testimony might reveal certain things about Mr Vayne's business practices that you prefer not to share, this isn't always possible. But we will try to focus on the inaccuracy of financial figures, rather than the individuals who suffered the manipulation of them.'

Sandemann's face flushed. 'As long as you don't deliberately misstate them.'

'Why should I do that?' Hunter asked, his voice sounding innocent.

Daniel sat up straighter. He was not at all pleased with how this was unfolding.

'Because you are prosecuting him,' Sandemann flashed back.

The question that flew from Hunter's mouth caused Daniel to cringe.

'And in prosecuting him, you think I would be underhanded?'

The room was suddenly so quiet that it could have been empty.

Sandemann leaned forward just a bit, but the movement was not lost on Daniel. 'You might well be,' the man said. 'If it will enhance your own career.' He leaned back. 'Your name will be in all the newspapers, on everyone's lips. Or maybe you have interests of your own, in property? Or perhaps – well, you've said that many are envious of Mr Vayne. Perhaps you are one of them!'

There was, yet again, utter silence. Hunter stared at his witness for a long moment, and then smiled, causing a sigh of relief to be released throughout the courtroom. He turned and stared at Vayne in the dock, and then back to Sandemann on the witness stand. 'I assure you, Mr Sandemann, that I have no desire to change places with Mr Vayne. He is guided by ambitions to be rich and powerful, whereas I wish only to bring lawbreakers to justice.'

Dalmeny rose to his feet. 'My Lord,' he began.

The judge held up his hand, as if to stop traffic in the street. 'Mr Hunter, we are a little early in this trial for histrionics. Ask questions of the witness, if you have any, or else turn him over to Mr Dalmeny for the defence.'

'Yes, My Lord,' Hunter said, rather meekly.

Daniel smiled to himself. Clever man! Hunter now had the full attention of the jury. Perhaps that was the purpose of this exercise all along?

Hunter proceeded to draw from Sandemann lists of figures, on each occasion reducing them to a single figure of either profit or loss. At first, Sandemann gave details, but then finally baulked, responding, 'I'm not sure,' or, 'I can't recall.'

Daniel had his notepad in front of him and was writing furiously. Of course Sandemann knew! He had freely discussed these figures, so why claim to be unsure now? Did he suddenly realise something new about them? Or had he been threatened?

Hunter had a slight frown, as if he somehow had missed the point. 'We're talking about financial loss,' he said, as if prompting the witness to recall what he had previously revealed.

'In any investment,' said Sandemann, 'there is always the potential for loss.'

'In this case, quite a big one, wouldn't you say?' Hunter asked.

Hunter walked over to the table where Daniel was seated and picked up a file. He opened it and read from one of the loose pages. 'In fact, according to what you've told me, there were more than a few losses.'

Daniel knew that this was the turning point. Sandemann would now have no choice but to reveal what the jurors needed to hear, if they were going to convict Malcolm Vayne.

'If you look more carefully,' said Sandemann, gesturing towards the opened file, 'you will see that we were slightly ahead of the market, and more than made up for it in the next quarter.' Before Hunter could open his mouth to argue, the witness rushed ahead. 'I see that you are unaware of the skills it takes to be successful in property sales and management. Or in investment funds, for that matter.' He said this with obvious satisfaction.

'In the case of this investment fund,' Hunter responded, 'I'm looking through the documents and have yet to find one year in which a real profit was made.'

'That was early on, before the companies we invested in became profitable.'

Daniel had to restrain himself from jumping to his feet. Sandemann knew damn well that there were never any profits! He glanced over at Vayne. The man looked impassive, but a little smile flitted across his lips. Had fford Croft and Gibson been played for fools? Did Sandemann intend all along to take the stand for the prosecution, and then testify in favour of Vayne? He was pulled out of these thoughts by Sandemann's voice.

'You will note that in the following year we more than doubled profits for our investors. They were very pleased . . . ask them.' He gave a tiny, infinitely satisfied smile.

Daniel glanced at the jury. They looked confused, at sea. Wasn't the prosecution's witness supposed to testify against the accused?

'If these investments were so solid,' Hunter asked, 'how do you account for the near collapse of the fund? How do you explain the hundreds of investors who lost everything?'

Daniel's confusion shifted to anger, and then to pity for Hunter. Wasn't this every counsel's nightmare? To have a solid witness suddenly change his testimony? How in the world could Hunter turn this around and make it anything but the catastrophe it had become? The only answer was to paint Sandemann as a liar, and expose him as someone who became a witness for the prosecution only for the most unethical reasons: to change his testimony in court and save Vayne from conviction.

'Mr Sandemann,' said Hunter, a tinge of disrespect in his voice. 'According to our calculations – which, I might add, are based on the numbers you yourself provided – Mr Vayne not only absconded with investors' money, but he also saved a fortune in taxes. Very clever, Mr Sandemann. Your skills are truly remarkable. And,' he quickly added, Sandemann's mouth already open, ready to argue, 'it seems that you have agreed to testify not because you want to make this right, and not because you have compassion for all these people who trusted you and lost everything, but because you are complicit in this fraud. And now that we understand this, you are also exposed to arrest and prosecution. Well done, sir.'

Sandemann drew in his breath, then let it out again without speaking.

'And I can certainly see how Mr Vayne must appreciate your skills, as well as your loyalty. I can cite several dozen instances where early investors were paid great sums, despite there being no funds in the bank. And how, when this fraud was being exposed, Mr Vayne turned to a phalanx of foreign moneylenders to acquire the cash to make his scheme seem legitimate.'

Sandemann smiled for the first time, and with obvious pleasure. 'I have no knowledge of fraud, sir. I'm good at my job. That is why Mr Vayne trusts me, and not someone else.'

Hunter did not hesitate. 'I wonder if he will be so pleased with you, sir, when we bring you back as the accused. Even more, I wonder if he'll be as loyal, and insist that you've done nothing wrong.' He glanced at the dock, and then at the judge. 'We are finished here.'

Dalmeny rose to his feet. Before he had fully straightened up, he sat down again.

'Mr Dalmeny,' said the judge. 'Have you nothing to say?'

Dalmeny smiled. 'Nothing at all, Your Honour. Mr Sandemann has proved to be a gifted and knowledgeable witness for the defence. He has testified . . . and under oath, if I might remind you . . . and I thank him.' And then he raised his hand, as if asking permission to speak. 'One last issue, My Lord. Mr Hunter asked Mr Sandemann if he found anything, anything at all, amiss with the records of his transactions on Mr Vayne's behalf. And since he has insisted there were none, in spite of all his diligent and extreme efforts, there does not seem to be any reason for me to take up the court's time. Also,' he rushed ahead, 'Mr Sandemann has revealed Mr Vayne's approach to business, and has sworn this

195

has never been used to defraud. He has also sworn that my client is a man of exceptional business skills, a man with widespread influence, whose acumen is felt here and throughout Europe. And most important, that Malcolm Vayne has never turned to illegal practices.'

As if Hunter could stand this no longer, he shot to his feet. 'My Lord,' he declared. 'Based on this unexpected testimony, I have a few more questions for our witness.'

The judge said nothing for a long beat, and then nodded. 'Considering this unexpected turn, Mr Hunter, I will permit it.'

This time it was Dalmeny who spoke, nearly shouting. 'Your Honour! This is highly irregular! Mr Hunter has had his moment in court, and it is absolutely legal for a witness to change his testimony.'

'Legal, yes,' the judge replied. 'But highly unusual. And I imagine it has taken several moments for the prosecution to reconsider how best to approach this witness. This surprisingly hostile witness.'

He turned to Gideon Hunter. 'You may proceed, but keep it short.'

Hunter nodded his thanks and walked closer to Sandemann, as if the man needed reminding that he was in a court of law. 'Mr Sandemann, you are still under oath.'

There was a snicker in the room. He might be under oath, it said, but that was no longer a guarantee that he would tell the truth.

Hunter squared his shoulders. 'This trial is not about sales and acquisitions. It's about an investment fund, where investors gave Mr Vayne hundreds of thousands of pounds of their hard-earned money, if not more, believing that the fund was safe. That their investments would be secured, and they would earn a respectable interest on those investments. And, in fact, none of their money was ever invested, but used in a clearly fraudulent manner, which ultimately benefited Malcolm Vayne. You might say he *lined his pockets* with money those investors would never see again.' He turned slightly to glance at the jury, as if making certain they were listening closely.

Sandemann also glanced at the jurors, and then shifted his gaze to Vayne.

Daniel saw how Vayne's eyes narrowed. Was this a threat? His respect for Sandemann increased greatly. This had to be nearly impossible, testifying against a man he had admired for years.

'Mr Vayne is very clever,' Sandemann said. 'There are many ways he handles funds, whether they flow through his companies or into the philanthropic organisations he supports.'

Daniel leaned forward. Given the chance to redeem himself, Sandemann was going to lie again?

'Yes, yes, of course,' said Gideon Hunter, nodding. 'And?'

'And Malcolm Vayne has never defrauded, absconded, misused or otherwise mishandled these investments.'

'And I am here to say that Mr Vayne's dealings with these funds can be described as fraudulent,' insisted Hunter. 'As you told me before this trial began.'

Sandemann pursed his lips, as if thinking about this.

'Mr Sandemann?' Hunter probed.

'In my experience, sir,' said Sandemann, 'those who accuse him of dishonesty are decidedly inferior to him. He has done nothing wrong.'

There was a collective gasp in the courtroom.

Daniel looked at Hunter, who was clearly stunned by this statement. It was so final. And in its finality, it sounded sincere.

It would take more than a courtroom interrogation to change this man's position. Daniel believed he knew why. Because it was now proven that Sandemann was aware of these dealings, which left him open to arrest. But was that enough of a reason to commit perjury? If he told the truth, and was given immunity for having done so, there would be no charges against him.

And then a far more sinister thought seized Daniel. Vayne could be sitting in a prison cell hundreds of miles from London, or on the other side of the world, and this would not deter him from having Sandemann punished for his disloyalty. Sandemann . . . and perhaps his family. His only hope to guarantee his safety was to change his testimony and lie on the witness stand. And yes, even if it meant that he would be sent to prison.

Sandemann had just betrayed Hunter. In fact, he had betrayed the entire prosecution case.

For the next few minutes, Hunter worked feverishly to take Sandemann, step by step, through the very points they had rehearsed. These included false claims made to investors, hidden assets derived from fundraisers for charitable organisations, any and every illegal activity perpetrated by Malcolm Vayne. And to each and every charge, Sandemann responded, 'No, sir, that was not what happened.'

Daniel knew that their case was beginning to fail. If Sandemann had been the third or fourth witness, following others who swore to Vayne's guilt and gave substantial proof, they could survive this. But to have him first up . . . it was a disaster. They had no choice but to completely rewrite their approach for prosecuting Vayne.

He asked himself, yet again, why Sandemann would do such a thing, but the answer was the same. He would rather be accused of perjury than have to suffer the wrath of Malcolm Vayne.

Daniel looked at Fergus Dalmeny. The man was smug, satisfied. And why not? Sandemann had just made Dalmeny's case for him. Even worse, an evil man was very close to being acquitted. Daniel could only hope that the next witnesses – Richard Whitnall, Peter Rollins, Boyce Turnbull and Nadine Parnell – kept their composure . . . and their word. Then he looked back at Hunter, whose face was ashen in defeat.

Chapter Seventeen

The court adjourned for lunch. Daniel ate with Hunter at the nearest decent public house. Hunter mostly pushed his food around the plate. Daniel himself did not feel in the least bit hungry, but it was easier to eat than to try to think of something useful to say. Encouragement would seem both artificial and patronising, and he had no useful advice to give, no recommendations of how things should now be handled. Hunter was certainly aware of all the pitfalls. The last thing Daniel wanted was to make him more tense than he already was.

They returned to the courtroom and Hunter called for his next witness, Peter Rollins. He was Vayne's personnel manager, but also the man who seemed to know where every donation came from and how it was used. There was more information to be drawn from him, and Daniel thought it was far easier to do it because it concerned people rather than specific facts about places, buildings, amounts of money. Rollins knew who contributed what, how loans were secured, how and what had been repaid, and what was still outstanding.

Rollins swore the oath to tell the truth, the whole truth, and nothing but the truth. In response to Hunter's questions, he made it clear that Vayne had made both good investments and bad, but he always appeared to have come out on top. That was, assuming the figures were correct, and everything he owned was worth what he had found someone to value it at. Rollins thought these valuations were questionable, but any second opinion would have had to come from someone who specialised in determining the value of property.

Rollins proved to be a more interesting man, even if it was largely because his testimony was about people. He had a mild, pleasant face, a quick smile and an easy manner. Daniel could tell at a glance that it was very difficult to make him lose his temper or his composure.

Hunter asked him some opening questions, perhaps unnecessarily.

Dalmeny rose twice to object, and both times Daniel was sure it was because he saw the interest on the jurors' faces. During the second objection, he stopped arguing and said, 'I'm sorry, My Lord. Perhaps I was hasty. I'm sure my learned friend for the prosecution will reach his point, if I allow him a while longer.'

Mr Justice Abbott-Smith looked at him. 'If you interrupt him enough, Mr Dalmeny, he may forget all about it and we can proceed with the case.' He turned to Hunter. 'Do you recall what it was you were going to ask Mr Rollins?'

'Yes, My Lord, I do. But in case the jury has lost the thread, I shall take Your Lordship's advice and repeat it.' He swung around to face the jury.

The judge drew in a sharp breath, but it was Hunter who spoke.

'His Lordship has kindly allowed me to remind you what we were discussing,' he said to Rollins. 'I believe you were describing the staff you have vetted and employed to work for Mr Vayne in his various enterprises.'

'Yes, sir,' Rollins said courteously.

'What particular skill do you have that qualifies you to fulfil such an important role for a man who manages the enormous sums of money that Mr Vayne does? That is, here and, indeed, all over Europe.'

Rollins nodded, still appearing so relaxed that the jury must have seen that he was perfectly at ease. The people at the front of the gallery must have seen it, too, because they looked kindly at him.

Daniel was very aware of it himself. He wondered if his father was watching as closely. For a moment, he wondered why he was here at all, then recalled how important it was for the head of Special Branch to hear the testimony, particularly as it related to Vayne's play for power in Britain and throughout Europe. Only Special Branch would know precisely why, and they never shared their secrets. It could also be that his father was worried about Daniel being a part of this trial.

Daniel wished to turn and smile at him, but knew it was the last thing he should do. Instead, he glanced sideways at the dock and saw Vayne's face, still smug, satisfied. He clearly had no fear that Rollins would betray him, either intentionally or by accident. But what did Rollins know that could be of any use to the prosecution? Was he here to do anything more than take up time, paint a more complete picture of Vayne's business empire? Did Hunter hope he would make some slip, inadvertently? Was it all they had to hope for? Please heaven, they could do better than that. The man was their witness, not Dalmeny's!

'Are you responsible for engaging all the principal staff, Mr Rollins?' Hunter went on.

Daniel looked around the court. No one seemed to be

interested, particularly not the jury. What did Hunter know that Daniel did not? Surely he was doing more than playing for time?

'Yes, sir,' Rollins replied.

'And please tell us, Mr Rollins, what qualities do you look for in such people?' Hunter asked courteously, a look of interest on his face.

Rollins hesitated. 'Well, there are different qualities. Depends on the position they will fill.'

'Architectural qualifications, for example? You buy a great many buildings, some of outstanding beauty.'

Rollins did not answer.

'Roger Bothwell, for example. I see you have employed him for several years now,' Hunter prompted.

'Yes, well, we have many connections among wealthy estate owners like Mr Bothwell,' Rollins answered.

'So, he advises you on the true value of an estate? The amount of upkeep it will require? Structural repairs? General maintenance? That sort of thing?'

Robert Bothwell was a principal landowner and they both knew it. Even Daniel knew it. If this man was employed at all, it was probably to flatter him. He certainly did not need to work for anyone.

'He advises us,' Rollins replied. He was clearly uncomfortable. He had not foreseen the questioning taking this direction.

'And Mr York?' Hunter asked.

'Advises,' Rollins answered simply.

'About what? He is, I believe, a minister in the government, something to do with agriculture? Or do I have that wrong; perhaps there's another Mr York?'

'No, you have the right one. I don't know precisely what he advises Mr Vayne about.'

'But you hired him, didn't you?' Hunter was not going to let it go.

The judge was frowning. This clearly displeased him. They were dragging the names of very important people into this.

Hunter was waiting for the answer, a look of keen interest in his face. Why on earth this mattered, Daniel could not even guess, but clearly it did.

'I introduced him to Mr Vayne,' Rollins said at last.

'Oh, so you knew Mr York, and Mr Vayne did not? I see,' Hunter replied. 'And you thought Mr York's knowledge, and possibly his connections, would be of service to Mr Vayne. Is that right?'

'More or less,' Rollins said grudgingly.

'How do you know Mr York?' Hunter asked.

'We were at university together,' Rollins said. 'At least, at the same time. And I was quite good at cricket. In the first eleven, you know?' Rollins gave a modest, slight shrug.

'Yes, of course,' Hunter agreed. 'At university, sport is the gateway to everything.'

Daniel knew what that cost Hunter, who had mentioned that he had never been in a cricket eleven at all, because he was never good at athletics. Daniel's own ability at sport was not great, but it had been sufficient to get him on most sports teams, second eleven perhaps, but still a player, one who shared the team spirit. At heart, this was what mattered.

Hunter drew in a breath and changed the subject completely. 'You must know an enormous number of people with power, money, influence. Dozens, perhaps.'

'You exaggerate, sir,' Rollins corrected him.

'A score?' Hunter suggested.

'More accurate, yes.'

'So, you just did a small favour for a friend – that would be your various friends – and introduced them to Mr Vayne.'

Rollins was visibly uncomfortable.

'Oh,' Hunter interrupted himself. 'Wait, you were working for Mr Vayne. I had it back to front. You weren't introducing them to him. Instead, you were introducing him to them, these various gentlemen of note. These few. And that is your sole occupation? No, it can't be. We are aware that you purchased a new house, and not far from my own. A large one, where you live with your family, and your household servants, including a butler, and—'

Dalmeny jolted to his feet. 'My Lord, this is inexcusable! Mr Hunter is obviously threatening to make public where Mr Rollins and his family live. The public will—'

'No, My Lord,' Hunter interrupted, his voice quiet but very clear. 'I'm simply pointing out that Mr Rollins provided a considerable amount of valuable information, contacts that proved of major importance to Mr Vayne. He did it very well, and it was his job, for which he was paid. Well paid, but not for a pleasantry here or there. Does Mr Rollins deny that?'

There was only one way the judge could decide, and his face revealed that he knew it. The jurors were staring at him expectantly, as indeed were several newspaper reporters sitting in the gallery, pencils poised.

'You can't have it both ways, Mr Dalmeny,' said the judge. 'Mr Rollins worked for Mr Vayne, or he did not? And if he did not, he should provide some evidence of who else pays him a regular salary.' His face was grim. He was caught in a neat trap. 'Have you something to ask that is actually relevant to this case, Mr Hunter?'

'Yes, My Lord. Mr Vayne has exercised excellent judgement regarding property. If we knew where the great majority of that information came from, we could prove whether or not it was legitimate. Perhaps, after all, it was due to important contacts, rather than anything questionable. Surely, my learned friend could offer proof of that. After all, his client is Mr Vayne.'

'There is no need to belabour the point, Mr Hunter,' the judge said irritably.

'No, My Lord. I will call just three or four of the most outstanding people Mr Rollins has introduced to Mr Vayne, and who will say that they have business with Mr Vayne, and have trusted him with their money.'

The judge frowned. 'You are pushing unnecessarily, Mr Hunter. We take your point.' He turned to Dalmeny. 'Are any of these associations secret, Mr Dalmeny?'

'My Lord, it is—' Dalmeny was stuck for a word.

'If it is difficult, My Lord,' Hunter interrupted, 'we will have other ways of introducing it. I had not thought it was so sensitive a matter, as to who invested with Mr Vayne. I can introduce it in other ways.'

Dalmeny was furious.

Daniel glanced up at Vayne in the dock.

He was pale, and his shoulders were hunched, as if he were preparing to strike someone, if only he could work out who was within his reach. It was a chilling sight.

Chapter Eighteen

The next day in the courtroom began early. Hunter had telephoned and asked if Daniel could be there at least an hour before the trial resumed.

'What is it?' Daniel asked, as soon as he met Hunter in the almost empty hallway.

Hunter was dressed for court and he did not look to be unwell, although he certainly appeared tired and tense. But then, Daniel was aware that he himself looked little better. The trial felt as if it might be slipping out of their hands, and they both knew it. Today, they were slated to put Callum McCallum on the stand, and neither of them expected it to be easy. And yet it was McCallum who could hold the key to what the case was really about.

Daniel had not spoken to his father for several days, nor did he wish to. He did not want those in the courtroom, and particularly members of the jury, to know of his connection with Pitt. They were not aware that he was head of Special Branch, but he was occasionally mentioned in the newspapers as an important person in government. It was painfully at the front of his mind that Dalmeny might somehow be aware of his father's real role, and had worked out ways in which he could use that knowledge, without it appearing to the jury that someone high up in government could possibly be taking an interest in Vayne's business dealings. That would take the lid off a box he could not afford to open.

'What is it?' he asked Hunter. 'Has something happened?'

Hunter smiled bleakly. 'Not yet. But I am hoping it will. God knows, we need to stir up something. Rollins' connections through school and university are at the core of the whole thing. I was watching faces yesterday, and thinking hard about it yesterday evening. You played cricket at school, yes?'

'I did, yes,' said Daniel. He knew that Rollins was Vayne's major fundraiser and organiser, but he had no idea where Gideon Hunter was going with this.

'So, you know how that all works.'

Daniel wasn't sure what he meant. 'Well, I wasn't much good at soccer, and I just missed making the rowing team.' He suddenly understood Hunter's comment. 'But I know what you're getting at, about belonging, being one of the team, that sort of thing.'

'Of course you do!' Hunter said a trifle sharply, and then his voice softened. 'That's how it works, being part of a team, belonging. And I'm quite sure that's how not only Rollins, but most definitely McCallum, do their jobs. It's about contacts. With their backgrounds, they always know somebody who knows a chap who can give them whatever it is they need. Use that, Pitt. You know it better than I ever will. Show that it's the privileged few, and that it doesn't include the men in the jury. Show how they use their connections to do the things the rest of us can't. Make—' He seemed to be searching for the right words.

'Make the jury understand that this excludes them,' Daniel finished for him. 'Them and us.'

'Exactly. And Vayne has got where he is because he is one of them. Someone the men on the jury could never be.'

Daniel's smile widened. There was no need for words, but he could barely contain the excitement, and a bit of anxiety, that Gideon Hunter was trusting him to handle this next round of questions.

He rushed to the nearest telephone and called Miriam. The pleasure in her voice was just what he needed to give him the courage for what lay ahead.

The trial opened exactly on time. The judge clearly looked as if he had been up half the night with indigestion. He seemed irritated when Hunter explained that Daniel was going to conduct the examination of the next witness, Callum McCallum.

As soon as the usual opening formalities were concluded and McCallum had sworn the oath, the preparations were complete and the battle began.

Daniel rose to his feet, took a very deep breath, and let it out slowly.

'Good morning, Mr McCallum. Looking over all the evidence we have, it seems clear to us that Mr Vayne trusted you with a very great deal of information about the workings and the aim of his company. In fact, you could have taken over much of it for him, at least temporarily, should he wish for a holiday, or regrettably, become ill. Am I correct in that?' He knew McCallum would never deny it; he was nothing if not ambitious.

'Yes,' McCallum replied. 'Mr Vayne has never been ill, to my knowledge, but of course he does take a holiday, from time to time.' He would have been foolish to deny it. It was a matter of record. And a man who never took a holiday was alien to the understanding of most people, and McCallum would not wish to make Vayne appear driven to that degree. It might suggest that he did not trust McCallum to take over, even for a week or two.

'A very great mark of his confidence in you,' Daniel remarked.

McCallum nodded. A flicker of uncertainty crossed his face. This was clearly not what he expected.

The judge also appeared puzzled.

Daniel refused to be hurried.

'I have looked at your education and career.' He smiled for an instant at McCallum. 'Very fine, I see you did well at school, both academically and in sports.'

McCallum relaxed a bit and then smiled.

Dalmeny rose to his feet. 'My Lord, the defence concedes that Mr McCallum was both a good scholar and a good sportsman. No one has suggested otherwise, and I see no purpose in the prosecution going over it, detail by detail. He is wasting the court's valuable time—'

'My Lord,' Daniel interrupted. 'Mr McCallum is the prosecution's witness. I believe we are entitled to establish with the jury the excellence of the witness's suitability for this position, and that he most definitely knows what he's talking about, in this connection.'

The judge turned to Dalmeny. 'What is your objection, sir? If anyone, on either side, is wasting our time, I will restrain him.' He turned back to Daniel. 'Mr Pitt, please be as brief as you can.'

'Yes, My Lord,' Daniel said obediently. He turned back to McCallum. 'After school, sir, I believe you went to Oxford University?'

'Yes,' McCallum confirmed.

Daniel smiled. 'I'm a Cambridge man, myself, but I have great respect for the Oxford cricket team, which, being a cricket man, I played against. A little after your time, but cricket itself is always the same, and teaches the best of sportsmanship.' It was not a question, but he wanted to allow time for McCallum to agree.

McCallum smiled, and said, 'Oh, yes.'

'Never forget the men you played with, or against,' Daniel went on, avoiding the judge's eyes.

McCallum agreed, again with a smile, and then said, 'Yes.'

The judge fidgeted noticeably. Everyone must have seen it.

'And you must remember the names of the members of your team who won such good victories in your last year,' Daniel continued.

Dalmeny rose and started to object. 'My Lord, this is absurd.'

Daniel turned to the judge. 'My Lord, I'm about to draw the facts together and relate them precisely to the work that this witness has done for Mr Vayne.' He deliberately did not refer to Vayne as 'the accused' or 'the defendant'.

'Then do so, Mr Pitt. This meandering down memory lane does not seem to be relevant in any way at all.' The judge's voice was sharp and his face showed his mounting irritation.

'Yes, My Lord,' Daniel said meekly. He turned to McCallum. 'I believe your most successful team included Ronald Baisden, now Lord Baisden, John Colchester, now Sir John Colchester and serving in the War Ministry, and also William Charnwood, now serving in the Treasury. Also, Mr Walter Devenish, secretary to the Minister of Defence, Michael Hilton, assistant to the ambassador to Spain, Richard

Lampton, who is Secretary to the Minister of Trade.' Daniel knew he had the full attention of everyone in the gallery, and he hoped the same was true for the jury. 'And many other men who have moved on to extremely successful careers, positions of influence . . .' He left the sentence for the imagination to finish.

'Is that a question?' McCallum asked.

'No,' Daniel replied. 'I am trying to show the court how excellently placed you are to make superb social contacts, political contacts, even contacts with people of influence in the capitals of Europe.'

This time, McCallum answered with a good deal more emotion. 'I never pretended anything other than—'

'Of course not,' said Daniel, cutting him off. 'And that was your extraordinary value to Mr Vayne. You were able to introduce him to men of great power, because you knew them personally, and certainly shared happy memories with them. It was easy for you to arrange parties, connections, even gain their trust. In many cases, your confidence in them was sufficient for them to trust anyone you recommended.' He stopped, as if any answer was unnecessary.

'Yes,' McCallum agreed. He could do nothing else.

Daniel ached to look at his father, but knew he must not waken in anyone the suspicion that his attention was anywhere but on McCallum. 'One can easily see how you have been of immense service to Mr Vayne. I believe that you have arranged all sorts of social events for him as well: fundraising to help various social causes, such as extending the franchise to women, giving to orphanages and hospitals, and to other less fortunate souls. I have looked at the amounts he has donated, and he is very generous. I've also studied the names of those who contributed to his investment funds.'

McCallum took a deep breath, as if to speak, and then seemed to change his mind.

Dalmeny rose quickly to his feet. 'My Lord, my learned friend appears to have forgotten on which side he is supposed to be arguing! I am quite capable of producing all of Mr Vayne's records of his generous donations, should the court consider it necessary.'

'Thank you,' Daniel said, before the judge had a chance to speak. 'That would be excellent. Most helpful. Although, actually, my purpose was to show, beyond question, how wide and deep are Mr McCallum's acquaintances, and thus Mr Vayne's influence not only on society, but also on the ministers of government here in England, on parliament itself. And then . . . his influence overseas.'

Suddenly, he understood what his father was looking for. It was Vayne's ultimate goal. The motivation behind his rise to power and his use, or misuse, of his wealth. It seemed that his highest goal, and the most dangerous of all, was his determination to exert influence at the real seat of power: the ministries of government. And not only in Britain, but in other countries as well.

There was a rustle in the body of the court, a low murmur that ran through the room. Daniel felt his father's presence, and he had earlier caught a glimpse of his mother and Marcus as well. He also knew that Miriam had come. Without a hat, her hair was recognisable even at the back of the room. Perhaps Rose Hunter was there, too.

'Mr Pitt!' the judge said, loudly and angrily. The whole thing seemed to have slipped out of his control. 'Stop standing there preening yourself. I have no idea if the jury knows what you are trying to accomplish, but I certainly do not!'

Daniel turned slowly. 'I apologise, My Lord. My purpose

is to show what an excellent position Mr McCallum is in, whereby he can greatly assist the ambitions – social, financial or political – of a man such as Malcolm Vayne, who did not go to any of the major public schools, such as Eton, Harrow or Rugby, or to either Oxford or Cambridge. Many other institutions certainly have excellent academic reputations, but the great schools, added to the great universities, offer not only a chance to make friendships that last a lifetime, but friendships that contribute to the kind of influence that may well be lifelong, too. One shares a common childhood, a common social background, common values. It is an unbreakable chain of ties.'

He left the rest unsaid. He was not praising the old boys' network or blaming it, simply stating its existence as a fact, and one which had far-reaching influence. The jury might love or hate him for that, but they would believe the picture he painted, and see it as empowering, or a lucky chance of birth. But one thing was certain: this society of fellow classmates, men of influence and power, did not include those jurors.

He looked over at Dalmeny. The man's face was pale with anger. The defence counsel had not seen that coming, nor was there anything he could do about it if he had, but it was an important element in the case against Vayne. It was not a crime to cultivate social connections, whatever the end purpose, but nor was it a likeable characteristic. It suggested a motive of self-interest. Daniel wanted more than anything to rattle those who donated to Vayne, and to make their connections plain. If his father was silently making notes of this information, that was fine.

Daniel was aware that calling out such respected figures had, in a sense, kicked a hornets' nest. Did Vayne now see that he had far less control over this trial than he had imagined? And was this what Gideon Hunter had intended?

Daniel turned to look at Hunter and saw satisfaction in his face.

He sat down. Without any doubt, he had achieved that goal.

Chapter Nineteen

The trial resumed the following morning. It was a beautiful day, with mild sunshine and a balmy wind just strong enough to stir the leaves on city trees planted at the edge of the footpaths. Daniel decided to walk part of the way. He enjoyed passing the shaded squares and private gardens, many of them perfumed with cut grass. In the background were the sounds of horses' hooves and the engines of motor cars.

Daniel and Gideon Hunter arrived at the courtroom steps at almost the same time. Both were a little early, buoyed by the expectation of the coup de grâce to be delivered by Richard Whitnall. They had suffered a disaster with Sandemann, and could ill afford to have this repeated. Whitnall was their hope for redemption.

Peter Rollins and Callum McCallum, unlike Sandemann, had proven helpful in establishing in the jury's mind the importance of old school contacts. Vayne had none, but he counted on Rollins, and several other men in his employ, to introduce him to influential men, both in business and government.

But there was still the disaster handed to them by Sandemann. Had it not been for this rogue witness, it would have been reasonable to hope that some of the other witnesses they had might prove to be unnecessary, particularly Boyce Turnbull, although it was good to have them at hand. None of them would be able to destroy Whitnall's evidence. Daniel knew him to be honest, and he would make no claims today which could not be borne out by the written evidence.

It was with an air of partially justified confidence that Daniel followed Hunter up the steps, through the doors and into the hallway, then along the main passage towards the courtroom. Neither was surprised to find it already packed with an eager crowd expecting more drama, even this early in the proceedings. Daniel felt a lift of excitement as he realised that the pivotal moment of the trial could come today. Perhaps only minutes from now.

He glanced at Hunter and saw the excitement in his face, the slight flush in his cheeks. Their eyes met, but neither of them felt the need to say anything. It had all been planned, every contingency, every argument foreseen, every counter argument prepared. No more mistakes; no more nasty surprises.

All eyes were on them as they took their places. Heads turned. The whispers were like an incoming tide over a shingle beach: sibilant, insistent, an expectant murmuring rising to a distinct word now and then. Daniel heard *Will they get him? Vayne? Would never have believed what that Sandemann fellow did!*

The door to the hallway closed. The usher called for silence and gave the order, 'All rise.'

Mr Justice Abbott-Smith came in, swinging his arms a little wide, as if to show off his robes. It was already warm. Daniel thought he must be hot under that black. Not to mention the full-bottomed wig! Was it worth the discomfort to be dignified, impressive?

The judge took his seat, which meant that the rest of the court was permitted to sit down.

Hunter rose to his feet and called Richard Whitnall to the witness stand.

'Richard Whitnall!' the usher repeated.

The doors at the far end opened, but it was just another member of the crowd arriving late, delayed by the crush of people trying to find a seat inside.

'Richard Whitnall!' the usher said yet again, going through the door and calling out the name into the hallway.

Seconds ticked by.

Daniel looked at Hunter, but he did not ask the obvious question.

The usher went out through the doors and disappeared into the lengthy corridor.

In the courtroom, no one stirred.

Irritation darkened the judge's face.

'I apologise, My Lord,' Hunter said, a trifle awkwardly. He took a breath, as if to add something, then let it out without speaking.

The usher came back in, looked at the judge, and then at Hunter. He shook his head.

'Do you know what has happened to your witness, Mr Hunter?' the judge enquired.

'No, My Lord,' Hunter replied apologetically. 'With your permission, I will send my associate to look for him.'

'By all means,' the judge said, a trifle irritably. 'But perhaps, this morning, you will make use of the court's valuable time by calling your next witness. I appreciate that this is not your tactic in this highly contentious trial, but we cannot sit here idly waiting upon Mr Whitnall, at his convenience. I assume he has sent no message to you, Mr Hunter?'

'No, sir. I apologise for Mr Whitnall's absence.'

'So I assume. Have you your next witness ready?'

Hunter swallowed hard. 'Within a few minutes, My Lord. We had fully expected Mr Whitnall's presence. As of last night, he was perfectly well, and prepared.'

'Yes, I appreciate that, Mr Hunter. We will adjourn for fifteen minutes to allow you time to readjust your plans.' His tone made any further explanation redundant.

Hunter simply thanked him. He turned to Daniel. 'At least Turnbull is available, isn't he? Even at such short notice. For God's sake, find him! What a mess!' He looked rattled, but was trying, not very successfully, to conceal it.

Daniel looked at Dalmeny. The man's face registered no satisfaction at this turn of events. And then Daniel realised that if Whitnall had been taken ill, then Dalmeny would be denied the opportunity to cross-examine him.

'Damn it!' Hunter swore under his breath. 'Without Whitnall's evidence to build on, how will the other witnesses react? What will they say now?'

Daniel looked at Hunter and saw dismay. The man was controlling himself, but doing so with obvious difficulty. 'Who else could we possibly call?' he asked.

'Whoever the hell I can find that has relevant knowledge!' Hunter snapped. Then blinked and shook his head. 'What happened to him, Daniel? He was fine last night! See if you can find Turnbull immediately. He's not as good, but we can't just pack up.'

Daniel nodded and turned to leave.

Outside in the hallway, he searched briefly for any sign of Whitnall, or of Turnbull. He even searched the toilets to see if by chance he had been taken ill with pain, cramps, maybe eaten something that had disagreed with him. Please God, it was not a heart attack.

Daniel tried to recall exactly how Whitnall had looked the last time he had seen him. Had he been unusually pale? Or flushed? Did he appear more anxious than could be explained by the situation he was in? As far as Daniel could recall, he looked tired, concerned, but perfectly composed, a man ready to perform a hard but necessary task.

There was no one in the cloakrooms. He asked several ushers he passed, describing Whitnall, but no one recalled having seen him.

Daniel was going back into the main building when he saw a uniformed policeman coming in through the door. The man stopped, hesitated. He looked profoundly unhappy. Daniel was easily recognisable as a lawyer, in his wig and gown.

'Sir! Mr Pitt, sir!' called out the officer. The man looked wretched.

'Yes, Constable. What's wrong?' Did he know the man? It seemed that the man recognised him. 'What has happened?' he said, hearing the edge to his own voice.

'It's Mr Whitnall, sir.'

'Is he hurt? Is he ill?'

The man's face was white. 'Worse than that, sir. I'm—' He took a deep breath. 'I'm sorry, sir, but Mr Whitnall is dead.'

Daniel felt as if he had been struck, as if he were walking along the pavement and it rose up and hit him hard. And then he imagined himself suddenly lying there bruised, in pain, and not sure how it had happened. 'Dead?' he repeated, as if the word's meaning escaped him.

'Yes, sir.'

'How? He wasn't even ill yesterday evening! Was it his heart?'

'No, sir. It was a knife.'

'A . . . what?'

'It was a knife, sir. He was stabbed with a knife.'

'You mean someone broke in and stabbed him? In the night?'

'No, sir, not exactly.' The constable shifted his weight uncomfortably.

Daniel felt as if he were in a bad dream. 'Start again, Constable. Tell me what happened.'

The constable took a deep, shaky breath. 'Yes, sir. Sorry, sir. A gentleman from fford Croft and Gibson called us this morning and asked us to escort Mr Whitnall to the courtroom. The constable had trouble getting anyone to answer the door, so we went round the back and tried to get in through the kitchen door, but it was locked. So, we—'

'Picked the lock,' Daniel said for him.

'Yes, sir.' He swallowed. 'We found Mr Whitnall dead on the floor in the kitchen.'

'Killed by a knife?'

'Yes, sir.'

'What kind of a knife? Kitchen knife? Carving knife? A penknife?' It was idiotic! He was asking as if it mattered.

'I'm not sure, sir. We sent for Inspector Frobisher, since Mr Whitnall is part of his case.'

'Yes,' Daniel said, 'I understand. Have you got a car?'

'Yes, sir, I do, but—'

Daniel did not let him finish. 'I'll go and tell Mr Hunter, and of course the judge. I don't know what to do, but we certainly can't continue.'

'Sir.' The policeman had a solemn look on his face.

'Yes? What? What else?' Daniel said impatiently. 'I have to tell the court. Mr Whitnall was to have given testimony this morning.'

'Yes, sir. There is a suggestion that Mr Whitnall took his own life, but it isn't certain. It will be a good idea, if you forgive me, not to mention this, until we know.'

Daniel looked at the man's earnest, pale face. He was very young. He had possibly seen death before, but he was deeply shocked, as if he might have known Whitnall, even liked him.

The young man was right: they needed to determine if Whitnall had taken his own life, or if he had been murdered. An accident did not seem a possibility.

'Wait here, please,' Daniel requested, hesitating only long enough to see the man accept the request. Then he turned sharply and went back into the courtroom.

Hunter was where he had left him, and looking even more impatient. He was standing about ten feet away from Dalmeny. Both men turned as Daniel approached. The bench was unoccupied. The judge had briefly excused himself. It was not an advantageous moment. Daniel looked from Hunter to Dalmeny.

Both of them sensed the gravity of this situation and stepped closer.

'What?' Hunter asked. 'What has happened?'

Dalmeny missed the glance between them, the complete change in mood. 'Changed his mind, has he?' He turned from Hunter to Daniel. 'Got cold feet?'

'Yes,' Daniel said with a rasping voice, in spite of controlling it as much as he could. 'Cold all over. Whitnall is dead.'

'Dead!' Hunter snapped. 'What the devil are you talking about?' He put out his hand and gripped Daniel's arm.

Daniel swallowed hard. 'He was stabbed during the night. The police don't know yet whether it was suicide or murder.'

'I'm sorry,' Dalmeny said, with sincerity. 'I imagine this alters pretty well everything about your case.'

'I have to speak to the judge,' Daniel said. 'How we proceed is up to Mr Hunter.' He turned to Hunter. 'Do you want me to tell the judge?'

Hunter nodded. 'I'll stay here and talk to Mr Dalmeny. You have the news, so please tell the judge.' He smiled bleakly. 'We'll have to continue with Turnbull, I suppose. He isn't here yet.'

'Right.' Daniel turned and walked over to the usher and asked to see the judge.

Mr Justice Abbott-Smith was standing in his chambers, staring out of the window at the bleak wall of the building opposite. He swung around.

'Oh, Mr Pitt, at last you have—' He saw Daniel's face. 'What is the matter, man? Have you discovered that you have made some appalling error? What—' He stopped again.

'Whitnall is dead, My Lord.' Daniel's mouth was suddenly dry, his voice shaky, although it sounded almost normal to his own ears. 'We don't know exactly what happened yet, but the police have been called in.'

'Did you say police? What in heaven's name for?' Abbott-Smith demanded.

'He was stabbed, sir. Once, as I understand it. But fatally.'

'Murder? Suicide?' The judge at last looked horrified, all anger drained from his face, leaving him looking old and suddenly vulnerable.

'Either is a possibility,' Daniel said quietly. 'I'm afraid we don't know yet.'

'If it's murder . . . why in God's name would anyone want to murder him?' As he spoke, his voice died away.

223

'We don't know,' Daniel replied. 'I am about to go over there and find out all I can.' He did not ask permission, but stated a fact. 'I've only just heard from the police.'

'Why on earth are you going over there? What can you do?'

'I will first call by my wife's office.'

'Your wife? Can't you stand on your own two feet, man? What on earth can your wife do? That's preposterous, so you should—'

Daniel interrupted him. 'My wife is a government-employed forensic pathologist, My Lord. The police would call her in, or possibly her associate, Dr Hall. I can go to her lab and take her immediately to Mr Whitnall's home. The sooner a pathologist examines the body, the better. Getting there quickly means her being able to tell us her findings before someone else starts moving things, unintentionally, and disrupting the evidence, perhaps out of a concern for decency. But still, evidence can be accidentally destroyed.'

'All right! All right!' His Lordship hesitated, a look of dismay on his face, as if the known world had suddenly changed shape in front of him. 'And what in heaven's name is a young woman doing in a job like that? How old are you? Twenty-four? Twenty-five?'

'My wife is a fully qualified and accredited pathologist, sir. As I said, she works with Dr Evelyn Hall.'

The judge closed his eyes, as if by not looking at the whole truth he could wipe it out. 'That explains a thing or two. I suppose she's for women's suffrage, too? How come you are prosecuting Vayne, not defending him? That's one of his crusades – which, if you have done any research at all, you must know?' He made it a question.

'Yes, sir, but I do not approve of embezzlement, fraud, or

224

any other kind of theft. And, actually, I do not choose my cases.'

'Yes, yes, I know! This is not my first choice either. Get your wife, wherever she is, and go look at Mr Whitnall. I want a pathologist's opinion as soon as she has one, do you understand me? I want it verbally first, and then written when she has time. I need to know what the hell we are dealing with here. Tell Hunter to get on with whatever he can. You're second chair. We can struggle on without you, for the time being.'

'Yes, My Lord. I shall report to you as soon as there is anything to say.'

'To me, Pitt! Do you understand? First to me!'

'Yes, My Lord.'

'All right! Get on with it, and stop being a goldfish!'

Daniel resisted the temptation to point out that fish do not have feet, or even legs. He knew the judge was referring to the expression on his face, and what appeared to be a gasping for air. He felt about as intellectually brilliant as a goldfish.

'Thank you, My Lord.' He turned on his heel and went out, closing the door silently behind him.

A little over an hour later, Daniel climbed out of the police car, with Miriam beside him, and they stood on the pavement outside Richard Whitnall's home. It looked exactly as it had when he had come here only a few days ago, when he had visited Whitnall to go over his evidence one final time. The difference was that a constable was now standing on the pavement, and was on guard.

The man looked sombre as he stepped in front of Daniel and Miriam, blocking their way. 'I'm sorry, ma'am,' he began.

'Dr fford Croft,' Miriam introduced herself. 'Forensic pathologist. I believe Inspector Frobisher is in charge of this case. If he is here already, he will confirm my position.'

The man looked momentarily confused, then his face cleared. 'Yes, ma'am . . . Doctor.' He looked at Daniel, who had already made up his mind how to introduce himself.

'I'm Daniel Pitt, officer. I'm in charge of the case in which Mr Whitnall was due to testify this morning.' It was a slight exaggeration, but close enough. 'If you ask Inspector Frobisher, he will confirm that.'

'Does he know you, sir?'

'Since we were eleven,' Daniel replied, not mentioning that they had gone to school together, then to Cambridge, although not studying the same subjects.

The constable said something over his shoulder to the officer standing at the doorway leading into the house, then they both stood aside for Daniel and Miriam to pass. Even as they did so, people were coming down the street and stopping outside the entrance.

A man shouted, 'Bastard Whitnall deserved to die. Papers say he was going to betray Malcolm Vayne!'

'Have a little respect for death,' a woman snapped at him. 'You don't know what happened.'

'He knifed himself, that's what happened,' the man replied. 'Coward!'

'We don't know that, sir,' the constable said, clearly working to control his temper.

Miriam stopped and turned towards the gathering groups of people. 'If anyone here actually knows anything, perhaps a policeman can question you immediately. It would help our enquiries a great deal. The police ought to know it, too!' She looked straight at the man who had spoken. 'You there, sir?

226

I am the police pathologist. You could save us a great deal of time. Of course, if you were the one who stabbed him, you might not be so keen to say so. Was the victim armed also? Or did you use the knife he was holding to defend himself? Did he fight back? Are you in any way injured? Do you need a doctor, too?'

The man swore, and turned away, stumbling along the pavement.

A few jeers and catcalls went up. Someone laughed.

Daniel opened his mouth to say something, and reached for Miriam's arm, then changed his mind. Miriam did not need, or want, defending.

She followed the policeman inside, and Daniel went after them, choked by powerful and conflicting emotions. He was proud of her. At the same time, he was overwhelmed by a sense of loss when he stepped into the hallway. Hanging on the walls were pictures of places Whitnall had been, where important things in his life had happened. There were portraits of people Daniel assumed were his grandparents, renderings painted before photography was available to most people. Daniel had liked the man, and he certainly had admired his courage.

The constable led them into the kitchen. The first thing Daniel saw was Ian Frobisher, and lying on the floor at his feet was the curled-over body of Richard Whitnall, hands over his abdomen as if he somehow could have stopped the bleeding. Everything was scarlet: his fingers, his clothes, his belly and his legs. There was a great, sprawling, thick scarlet pool across the floor. The protruding knife handle was such a bright red that Daniel did not immediately recognise what it was. The room swayed around him and he felt cold, in spite of the warm air.

Miriam was on the floor! Had she passed out?

Then he gained a grip on himself. Of course she had not fainted! She was kneeling on the floor beside the body, touching it gently, as if Whitnall were still capable of feeling at least the horror or pain of it.

'I think this probably happened late last night,' she said quietly. 'Maybe around midnight. That is my initial assessment, at a glance.' She looked up at Ian. 'From the pan of milk on the stove, I'd say he was about to make himself a drink before going to bed. He is still dressed in his daytime clothes.'

'Was his death quick?' Ian asked, clearing his throat a little, as if he were finding it difficult to speak. His emotional reaction of horror and pity was still crippling him.

Daniel looked around the room. It did not appear to have been disturbed while waiting for the pathologist to arrive, and yet he was quite certain that the police had searched the house thoroughly.

'Yes, it was quick,' Miriam answered immediately. 'It may have seemed like an eternity to him, but not more than a minute. The blood loss was catastrophic.'

Ian stared at the body. 'He must have been taken by surprise. Is there any way to tell if he knew his attacker, or not?'

'Not medically,' Miriam answered. 'But since they were in the kitchen, it seems likely they were well acquainted. Unless, of course, whoever it was broke in silently.'

Ian cleared his throat again. 'Could it be self-inflicted? A suicide?'

She hesitated. 'A wound as terrible as this, I would expect to see hesitation marks, as if he had to work up to it, and there don't appear to be any. I'll only know when we get him to the morgue and wash the blood away. I don't think this could be an accident. As for suicide, I'll know soon. I'm sorry.'

228

'Is there anything you can tell us now?' Ian asked. 'Where do we begin? Is there anything we can rule out?'

'Accident,' she answered, framing the word shakily. 'You can rule out an accident . . . and a fight. It seems to be a single blow, without hesitation. When I can look in more detail, I may discover other marks, bruises, stains, small cuts or scratches.'

'And if there are none?'

'Then it's either a swift, skilled and ruthless murder, or a decisive, unhesitating suicide,' she replied. 'If it's a suicide, perhaps we can find some reason why it happened around midnight last night.'

'Perhaps worrying about his testimony against Vayne today,' Ian said reluctantly. 'That could be reason enough for some people.'

'Then look for what changed his mind,' she answered. 'What happened at midnight? What did he find out that altered everything?'

'Does he have a telephone?' Daniel asked suddenly, trying to remember if they had ever telephoned him at his house, rather than an office. Then he recalled that Whitnall had, in fact, called Daniel, and Whitnall was at home when he had made the call. 'Perhaps in his sitting room?' he suggested.

Ian looked blank for a moment, then he realised what Daniel was asking. 'You mean it could have been something said on the telephone that changed his mind. Nobody necessarily came here.'

'Well, something dramatic happened,' Daniel said reasonably. 'He wasn't worried yesterday. We spoke to him, and I would swear to that. We need to know what it was . . . who it was!'

'First, we need to know whether it was murder or suicide,'

229

Ian said grimly. 'When can you tell us, Doctor?' He looked at Miriam.

'I'll start working on it as soon as I get him to the morgue. If I may, I'd like to use his telephone to call for the mortuary van to pick him up. You will want to do all your own work before that. Measurements, pictures, and so on.' She turned to Daniel. Her face was soft, gentle, utterly changed from mere moments ago. 'You will have to go and report back to Gideon Hunter, and I suppose the judge. And Fergus Dalmeny. Let them know that I'll be there as soon as I've finished the post-mortem. I don't know when.'

Miriam walked out of the front door into the sunshine with Daniel. 'Be careful,' she said softly to him. 'This may be a new element. A dangerous one.'

'We'll have difficulty proving our case without Whitnall,' he said quietly.

'Of course,' she agreed. 'A great deal of difficulty. Presumably, that is the purpose. Vayne is accused of defrauding his investors, and concocting various other schemes, presumably even siphoning money from his clients' accounts. That could be a strong motive for silencing Whitnall.'

Daniel arrived back in the courtroom when there was little over half an hour left of the working day. Turnbull had been located and Hunter had questioned him, and now Dalmeny was cross-questioning. He had thought of slipping in quietly, and when it was convenient, letting Hunter know the situation regarding Whitnall. But he was recognised by many in the gallery, and so inevitably by the judge.

Dalmeny turned to him. Seizing his chance for a dramatic moment, he stopped in mid-sentence, as if to speak to Daniel.

'Well, Mr Pitt, I see you have returned to us,' the judge

said, with a slight edge of sarcasm in his voice. 'Do you intend to interrupt us again with news, or have you merely come to see how we are doing without you? If the latter is the case, Mr Hunter appears to be bearing up in your absence.'

'I have no particular news yet, My Lord,' Daniel replied. 'The forensic pathologist has taken the body to the laboratory and will give us her findings as soon as possible. But as you well know, we must be certain.'

The judge raised his eyebrows, sighed heavily, but made no remark. Given the volume of the sigh and the expression on his face, words were unnecessary. A woman's place was not in the morgue.

A heavy silence hung over the room as everyone waited for the judge to speak.

'I assume she is at least certain as to the cause of death?' said the judge.

'Yes, My Lord. He bled to death. But whether the wound was self-inflicted or dealt by someone else, she could not say yet. She's examining Mr Whitnall as we speak.'

The judge's eyebrows rose. 'And if we were to ask a second opinion, perhaps of someone more experienced, might we get a more precise answer?'

Daniel could feel his anger rising. 'It is the laboratory of Dr Evelyn Hall, and she is probably the most respected forensic pathologist in England, or even in Europe. Dr Hall will work with her, and she is far too experienced to leap to conclusions of any sort—'

'My Lord,' Dalmeny interrupted. 'May we ask at least if it could be an accident? I cannot imagine what a senior official whose area of expertise is European finance could be doing in the middle of the night, in the kitchen, with a naked blade in his hand, and which would cause him to fall in such a way as to kill himself.'

Daniel heard a ripple of nervous laughter, and a raw edge of horror, spread through the body of the court.

'If you are asking,' Daniel said quickly, trying to keep the anger from his voice, 'then it appears to be either suicide or murder. It is too soon, and prejudicial for the jury, to make a hasty judgement in the matter. The laboratory will tell us as soon as they have an answer they can stand by.'

'We are aware of the importance of what happened to Mr Whitnall, Mr Pitt,' the judge snapped. 'I trust the pathologist is aware of the urgency?'

'Yes, My Lord. And also, the fact that the answer may well affect the verdict in this court, as well as the reputation and the family of Mr Whitnall.'

The judge opened his mouth, and then closed it again.

Daniel nodded, as if understanding what the judge intended to say, and then as silently as possible made his way back to his seat beside Hunter.

'Are you all right?' Hunter asked with concern, his voice low.

'Yes, but—'

Turnbull was still on the witness stand, awaiting Dalmeny's next question.

'What?' Hunter was half listening to Dalmeny, who was speaking to his second chair, a very dour-looking young man. 'Are you all right, or not?' he demanded with concern.

'I'm fine,' Daniel replied hastily. 'But there was blood everywhere.' He had to wipe the memory from his mind. 'At least it must have been quick.'

'Murder or suicide?' Hunter pressed. 'In your opinion? Dalmeny is aiming at suicide because of the betrayal of Vayne, and Whitnall's guilt in testifying against him.'

'We can't rule it out, not yet,' Daniel whispered. 'But we also can't rule out revenge for Whitnall's betrayal of Vayne. Or more likely still, plain murder to silence him. He was our best witness, and a decent man.'

'I know,' Hunter replied, and there was deep sadness in his face. 'I know.'

Chapter Twenty

Rose Hunter was anxious about the trial and its outcome, but more anxious still about her husband's new position at fford Croft and Gibson, and the stress the Vayne case was putting him under. They had been married for fifteen years, and she knew him far better than he sometimes imagined. She could not recall ever having seen him so tense.

They had wanted children, and she had miscarried more than once. He had been startlingly gentle with her, and it was during these times that she had learned to love him. Not the charming, clever and often very funny man he presented to the public, but the quieter, vulnerable man he was beneath that professional exterior.

She knew that Gideon seldom doubted his skill, his speed of thought or the grace of his delivery, but neither did he take it for granted, or treat it lightly. He was like a swan: on the surface, that most graceful of birds gliding across the surface of the water without any apparent effort, and yet, beneath, paddling extraordinarily hard.

He cared intensely. Unlike many men who are successful and ambitious, he was nervous, at times unbearably tense, although it did not show, except to her.

Like so many talented and very public men, he suffered flare-ups of insecurity. It was her duty, which she performed out of love, to protect him and not allow others to see him in these crises. She would have considered it a betrayal to let it be known by others who might use his vulnerabilities against him, however subtly.

She watched him this morning across the breakfast table, and she knew that he was concentrating on what his tactics would be, now that they had lost their most important witness. They did not discuss it. There was no useful comment to make, but the horror was there at the back of their minds, and almost as vividly as if they had actually witnessed it, their nostrils clogged with the smell of blood. There was an edge to the silence, but it was not uncomfortable; there was simply nothing to say.

Their eyes met, and he smiled. For her, that was enough.

Rose accompanied her husband in the car as they drove to the courthouse. She could think of no way in which she could be useful, yet she sensed strongly that he wanted her nearby. This case was a disaster, no matter what the facts turned out to be. If, indeed, those facts were even provable.

She would have liked to go to the laboratory where Miriam Pitt was working on the body of Whitnall, but that would serve no purpose, and could possibly be a serious error. If Vayne's people heard of it, his defence counsel could claim that she was attempting to influence their findings. In fact, Dalmeny might suggest that Miriam was biased anyway. Rose did not dislike Dalmeny, but he had not reached a position of such eminence without winning a great many trials that a less agile, less tenacious, and certainly a less skilled man would not have . . . and she couldn't help thinking that a less self-confident man would not have even tried.

They arrived at the court and with difficulty made their way up the steps and through the crowds of people, most of whom were unwilling to lose their place in the queue as they shoved against each other, although the doors were not yet open to the public.

'There will be no trial if you don't let us in!' Hunter said loudly, his voice surprisingly clear above the others.

'There should be no trial!' a man shouted back. 'It's hate, that's what it is. You're persecuting him because he speaks for ordinary people like us!'

'Get out of debt!' someone else added loudly.

To Rose's surprise, Gideon stopped to answer the first man, his voice rising above the sounds of noisy pushing and shoving. 'How many houses do you have, sir?'

'What?' the man responded.

'How many houses do you have? Mr Vayne has five, I believe. One of them is in Cornwall, another is in the south of France, with seven bedrooms.'

There was a moment's silence. 'I think you're probably rather more like me,' Hunter went on. 'I have only one, and it has three bedrooms.'

There were a few guffaws of laughter, and some rumbles of frustration, as well as a curse hurled at Hunter, loud and obscene.

Someone shouted back at the man.

Rose drew in her breath to beg Hunter to ignore the crowd, then realised it would betray her fear for him, and that was the last thing she meant him to know. She moved closer beside him.

'Please let me through, sir,' she said more loudly, and with more desperation. 'You are standing so close, I'm about to trip over you!'

'Sorry, ma'am,' the offender apologised. 'Here!' he called out, his voice loud. 'Let the lady through! We ain't ruffians! Get out of the lady's way!'

The knot of people parted and Rose took Hunter's arm, as if she had indeed been about to fall. He grasped her tightly enough to guide her through the crowd, and she leaned even more closely against him.

She did not speak until they were inside. 'Thank you,' she murmured as they passed the usher and entered the court chamber.

There was no one in the witness box yet, but she saw Dalmeny and his assistant in their seats, and Daniel Pitt, also seated, and with his back to them. She would recognise his thick wavy hair anywhere. She had met his mother a time or two, another woman who believed passionately in the rights of women to vote, or do anything else for which they had the skills – or could have been taught them. Rose had liked her immediately. Daniel had just the same touch of auburn in his hair that his mother did.

She let go of Hunter. 'Good luck,' she murmured, and stopped at the row where she intended to sit. At that moment, Daniel turned and saw her. She gave him a brief smile and then took her place.

She looked around the room for Daniel's wife, Miriam. Rose recalled their visit after the rally, and she had liked her immediately. She was not there. And then Rose reminded herself that she was at the laboratory, working on the body of Richard Whitnall. What on earth could have driven the woman to such a grisly occupation? There must be so much more to her than appeared at first meeting. It would be most interesting to find out. And if Gideon were to remain at fford Croft and Gibson, knowing more about Miriam Pitt could possibly prove to be quite important, as well as very pleasant.

That Gideon might not remain with the chambers was a dark thought she forced from her mind.

She had dressed formally this morning, in dark grey with a white lace-fronted blouse, and she wore no hat. It obstructed other people's view. But more importantly, it hid the luminous beauty of her hair. She wanted it to be visible anywhere, so Gideon would spot her whenever he looked around. He had never said that it mattered to him that she attended trials in which he was involved, but she saw the smile in his eyes, and the frequency with which he glanced her way, even if only for a second.

The gallery filled with a rush as soon as the doors were open. The chattering spectators came in like a breaking wave. Rose felt a sudden suffocation, as if the water had closed over her head. Did Gideon feel like that? He had smiled at her, but it was habit. He knew she would worry if he had not met her gaze, and possibly read some meaning into his reticence. But she had seen the expression in his eyes. She knew he was nervous. She wished she did not understand him so well.

The judge came in with his usual pomp, and the whole gallery rose. When the jury was seated again, he reminded them of their solemn duty.

Fergus Dalmeny resumed questioning Boyce Turnbull, beginning where he had left off the previous day. But as Rose had expected, he could not resist reminding them of the reasons why they had not heard from Whitnall.

As he began describing the facts, Hunter rose to his feet. 'My Lord,' he said, addressing the judge.

Rose felt her body stiffen, as if warding off an oncoming

blow. Surely Gideon was not going to complain? The judge would be annoyed. He had already told the jury this yesterday.

'Yes, Mr Hunter,' the judge said wearily.

'My Lord, my learned friend is rewording what you have already said to the jury. I do not believe it can be improved upon. You explained it simply, concisely, and it was easily understood. Rewording it appears to be correcting you, My Lord.' He stopped, as if realising that he had gone far enough.

The judge's face reflected considerable irritation. He turned to Dalmeny. 'I don't know whether you are correcting my grammar or my memory, Mr Dalmeny. In either case, I believe it is not only unnecessary and offensive, it is confusing. Is there anyone here who did not understand me yesterday afternoon?' He took a short breath. 'Good. Then may we proceed?'

Dalmeny had the sense to know that he had lost that brief round. 'Yes, My Lord.' He looked at the witness, and proceeded with the questions he had not asked the previous day. As he spoke, it appeared that he was confusing the witness. 'Mr Turnbull, would you like me to repeat the question?' he said patiently.

Turnbull was clearly confused, and doing his best in what were obviously difficult circumstances for him. 'I don't think it would help, sir,' he replied. 'I can hear you perfectly well, I just don't understand what you want me to say.'

'I don't want you to say anything in particular, Mr Turnbull. Just answer the question in your own words.'

Turnbull swivelled round and looked at Hunter.

'Are you looking to the prosecution to assist you, Mr Turnbull?' Dalmeny said, with a warning note in his voice.

Turnbull blushed.

Hunter wisely remained silent.

'Well?' Dalmeny said sharply.

'Sir, I have already answered you as well as I can!' Turnbull protested. 'I deliver messages that are confidential, or at least private.'

A titter of amusement rippled round the gallery.

'I am not a mind reader, Mr Turnbull,' Dalmeny snapped. 'Neither, I imagine, are most of the jury. If you understand it yourself, surely you can put it into English, sir? That is, of course, unless you don't understand it yourself?'

Hunter rose to his feet.

'Yes, yes, yes,' the judge said wearily. 'You are being unnecessarily offensive, Mr Dalmeny. You will frighten the man into complete inarticulacy if you are not careful.' He looked at the witness. 'If I understand you correctly, Mr Turnbull, you are saying that these messages are complex and often obscure, perhaps an answer to an earlier question, and make little sense on their own? Are some, for example, personal, and it is part of your duty that you are covenanted not to repeat them?'

'Yes, My Lord,' Turnbull said with ardent relief.

'And is there any way of telling whether that was done with intent to deceive, rather than to preserve privacy?'

'No, My Lord.'

'So, it could have been a totally innocent message?' Dalmeny said instantly. 'Secret only to guard the private purchase of property, a request to someone, or a personal loan?'

'Yes, sir,' said Turnbull. 'Exactly, sir. It is my job to be discreet.'

'Thank you,' Dalmeny said clearly, with a glance at Gideon Hunter.

'Do you wish to redirect?' the judge enquired of Hunter.

'If you please, My Lord.'

'Then get on with it!'

Hunter turned to the witness. 'Mr Turnbull, as well as

written messages between private individuals, do you carry others that are possibly of great importance, top secret even, from one government department to another?'

'Yes, sir, on occasion.' Turnbull now looked uncomfortable.

Dalmeny leaned forward slightly in his seat, but as yet did not interrupt.

'Sometimes messages are too urgent for the postal service, good as it is,' the witness went on to explain. 'And they have to be put directly into the hand of whoever it is. You can't guarantee that with the post, only that the delivery will get to the right house, as it were.'

'Of course,' Hunter agreed. 'Most especially, if it were money, for example.'

'Yes, sir,' Turnbull nodded. His expression changed.

Even from where Rose was sitting, she could see the loosening of the tension in him. None of this seemed relevant to the case, as yet. Was Gideon going to tie all of this to Vayne somehow? Or was he waiting for the autopsy report on Whitnall? She had a horrible feeling that without Whitnall's evidence their case was too weak to obtain a conviction. What had looked in the beginning like a house of cards – which, if the right card was extracted and held up to the light, would begin falling down – now appeared to be a structure as strong as a house of steel, at least from Dalmeny's viewpoint.

What could she say that would help? This first case with fford Croft and Gibson mattered so much to Gideon. And Vayne seemed to have outwitted them. If he was responsible for the attack on Nadine Parnell, it had been intended to guarantee her silence. It had been a risky move, but Vayne was known to be a risk taker! The only hope was that Richard Whitnall had been murdered, and Miriam Pitt would say so, swear to it on the witness stand. Had Vayne thought of that?

Was he responsible? Or did it even matter, if someone else had committed the murder for him?

She wondered if Daniel Pitt had thought of that. Or maybe Gideon had? Dalmeny would do his best to tear Miriam to pieces, if she testified that Whitnall was not a suicide, but a victim of murder.

But then, who had actually wielded the knife? If Miriam said it was murder, how would the perpetrator be brought to justice? It was no use Gideon attempting it, without all the evidence. If the police did not follow it up, either because they had no evidence, or lacked the nerve, who could ask the relevant questions?

That came down to who had the power, and the wish to get to the truth. In fact, there was one man who had showed courage in the first place, and had the nerve to arrest Vayne, and that was Ian Frobisher. Would he do it again? Could he, without ironclad evidence?

She watched Dalmeny stand, preparing to resume his cross-questioning of Turnbull. He walked out into the middle of the floor. He looked elegant. And very, very sure of himself.

'Mr Turnbull, it sounds as if you have a very responsible job, carrying messages, packets of documents, sometimes money, for many very powerful people . . .' He left it hanging, as if it required an answer.

Turnbull smiled. He was somebody who recognised importance, and seemed pleased to be included among those being praised. 'Yes, sir,' he agreed.

'You carry messages only for Mr Malcolm Vayne?'

'No, sir. I carry things for anybody as asks. Several gentlemen.'

'I see. Such as ministers of state? Important people in business, banking, investments, and so on?'

'Yes, sir.' Turnbull stood a little straighter.

'Have you any idea why the prosecution thinks that you are carrying packets for Mr Vayne that are of special interest to this case?'

Turnbull blinked. 'No, sir, no idea at all.'

Dalmeny smiled. 'Nor have I. It seems to me only to indicate that Mr Vayne has many business ties with gentlemen of some importance. Thank you, Mr Turnbull.'

'May I go now, sir?' Turnbull asked.

This time it was Daniel who rose to his feet.

The judge leaned forward. 'Do you wish to add something, Mr Pitt?'

'Yes, My Lord, if I may?' Daniel replied.

Upon receiving the judge's permission, he turned to the witness stand again. 'Mr Turnbull, you told my learned friend, Mr Dalmeny, that you carry messages, packets, et cetera, for important people. Many of them are gentlemen who are, or might soon be, in positions of importance in several governments, in Britain, and also in other European countries. Ministers of state, for example, people whose messages might be of national importance?'

Dalmeny rose to his feet. 'My Lord, the witness has already testified to this. Is there any purpose in Mr Pitt merely repeating it? The man is his own witness. In fact, the reason he was called at all is lost on me. I fear this is wasting the court's time because he has no real evidence against Mr Vayne, and that is becoming increasingly clear.'

The judge turned to Daniel. 'Mr Pitt, have you indeed any purpose in these additional questions?'

'Only to draw the court's attention to the fact that Mr Vayne communicates very frequently, far more than most gentlemen in business, with a number of ministers in our government, in prominent and powerful positions. And, it seems, with leaders from other countries as well. He seems to deal entirely, as far as we know, in property buying and selling, and in the borrowing and lending of money in Britain, and yet a great deal of his business is apparently transacted in other countries. It results in, shall we say, great gains for some. And, occasionally, for others, great losses.' He left the suggestion in the air for others to interpret as they wished. 'But I'm confused. Why the need to deal with so many men who hold seats in government?'

Dalmeny opened his mouth, took a deep breath, and then spoke quietly. 'Mr Vayne is extremely good at financial investments.' He left the rest of it unsaid.

'In other words,' Daniel replied, finishing Dalmeny's last thought, 'he lends and borrows a great deal of money, and presumably is familiar with the large gains, but also the losses, of some very influential people.'

Again Dalmeny, who was still standing, drew breath, and then thought better of whatever it was he'd been about to say.

Rose watched the two men butt heads and lock horns, not sure which one had prevailed. If there was one thing about which she was sure, it was that her husband did not look relieved.

Finally, the day came to an end, and everyone stood and stretched, and gradually found their way into the halls and then outside. Rose waited for Gideon just beyond the courtroom doors. No doubt he would want to speak with Daniel, possibly discuss their plans for tomorrow. He might even want to spend the evening revising their tactics, in which case she would take a taxi home, and wait there. She would not go to bed without him, nor would she let him know how worried she was.

He had been so keen to join fford Croft and Gibson, and

he never could have taken this case had he remained at his old chambers. He would not have been permitted to! They would have considered it too dangerous, especially with a victory so uncertain.

Gideon emerged from the courtroom ten minutes later, said goodbye to Daniel in the hallway, and then immediately looked around for Rose. She stepped forward. When he saw her, his face lit up with relief. She smiled at him, and then at Daniel, then took Gideon's arm as they left without speaking, and walked out into the late-afternoon sun, still high in the sky.

It cost all the patience she had, but Rose waited for Gideon to speak first. They reached their car. It was hot inside, almost airless. She allowed him to concentrate on driving. She thought of how he was running through the day's events in his mind, weighing and balancing the positives and the negatives.

He did not speak until they were home and in their own sitting room. The French doors were open and the soft garden-scented air drifted inside.

'We've lost the jury, haven't we . . .' It was not a question; there was no lift of enquiry in his voice.

She had never lied to him. 'I think so,' she replied. 'Not because they don't believe you, but because they don't understand the details. Not many of them caught Daniel's meaning about a government minister being so close to Vayne, and potentially compromised. Or that perhaps he knew far more clients with foreign interests than is healthy.'

He smiled ruefully. 'We have to give the details, and hope the jury will make sense of them, or Dalmeny will blow the whole case apart.'

'Gideon, did you notice the middle-aged man seated just in front of me? He was watching Daniel most of the time.'

'Quite good-looking, in a very individual sort of way? Yes, why?'

'I'm quite sure that is Sir Thomas Pitt, who happens to be Daniel's father.'

'Yes, we've met,' said Hunter. 'He might well have been watching Daniel out of paternal pride, but I think this Vayne case might be of special interest.'

'I would guess it's the Vayne case,' she answered. 'Given the number of government ministers who are lending money to Vayne, or who might be in debt to him, perhaps Sir Thomas might get involved, don't you think? After all, he's quite high up in government, from what I know.'

He stared at her; his understanding was sharp in his eyes. 'Deeper roots to this than we thought,' he said slowly. 'No one can clear Vayne of the taint of suspicion, because I believe the bastard is guilty. But we might end up with a hung jury.'

'So then there'll be another trial? Is that likely?' she asked.

He shrugged. 'I can't see anyone retrying the case. Vayne is already saying he's the victim of envy, and there's strong political bias against him. I think the police would be very glad to leave it alone.' His face looked suddenly pale, and more tense.

'Do you think he's going to run for political office?' she said, finishing his thought. 'Oh, Gideon, he's not, is he? Are we playing right into his hands?'

'God knows!' he said quietly. 'That's something I don't dare think about. But if that's so, he could be building the best political platform imaginable.'

'But what would he run as?' she asked. 'Which party, or will he run as an independent?'

'No,' he said immediately. 'He'd never get office that way. Tory, probably. Or Liberal? Whoever he thinks is most likely to win the next election.' He was staring at her with a steady, wide gaze, as if seeing something for the first time. His face revealed that he was more than tired, or even defeated: he was frightened.

Rose was disturbed to see her husband like this, but she understood. 'Do you think that could really happen – Vayne becoming part of the government?'

'It's possible,' he said quietly. 'We've got to be right about this, Rose. We have to take it to the very end, and prove he's guilty. Or innocent. I hate the man, but we have to prove this, one way or the other!'

Rose thought about this for a long moment, and then said, 'Do you think Whitnall was murdered?' She found the words difficult to say.

'I don't know. Perhaps Miriam Pitt will tell us that.'

She looked straight back at him, meeting his eyes, and there was nothing to say that was wise or hopeful. It was not a time for comfortable evasions. There was too much at stake. Both for her husband's career and, God forbid, the future of the country.

Chapter Twenty-One

Daniel took charge of the questioning again the next day. After yesterday, the air was tense, almost choking with emotion.

He began with Nadine Parnell. He was quite anxious that the old lady would come across as fragile, uncertain, perhaps be seriously put off by the courtroom atmosphere, the rather antiquated white wigs and gowns, and the whole formality of the proceedings. And he was also concerned that the crowded galleries would distress her.

When Mrs Parnell was sworn in and standing in the witness box, he approached her, stopping before he came too close. He knew she was well into her seventies, a smartly dressed woman who held herself with dignity. Today, she was in a dark plum-coloured jacket and skirt, and a shell-pink silk blouse. Her hair was perfectly coiffed, mostly still dark, but with silver streaks at the front.

'Good morning, Mrs Parnell,' he said, with a slight smile.

'Good morning, Mr Pitt,' she replied. 'I am quite ready. You may begin.' She was setting the tone immediately, and he was happy to follow.

'Then I will,' he agreed. He asked her to describe her employment in Vayne's group of companies, and how long she had been there. He also asked her to tell him about the positions she had held over the years.

He was impressed by her answers. She struck him as serious, and lacking a sense of self-importance. She stated the facts without emotion. She outlined quite simply the positions that she had held with Vayne, beginning with bookkeeper and then advancing over many years to his head of accounting. 'I am aware of all the funds that come in and go out,' she said. 'That includes, of course, to whom we send money, and from whom we receive it.' She was smiling very slightly, but there was little emotion in her tone of voice, or her face.

'Thank you,' Daniel said. He knew where he was going next, but he reminded himself to move carefully. He was aware of Dalmeny's eyes on him all the time, watching for the change of expression, lack of confidence, hesitation, the slightest shift of thought.

It was as if Dalmeny scented victory. If so, he might be right! Daniel and Hunter were struggling to find anything in the endless financial figures that might stir the jury's emotions. They had to prove to each member of the jury that there existed a clear line between what was legitimate and what was not. Vayne had crossed that line, and the men in the jury box had to be convinced. They had always known the case would be an uphill battle, but it was proving to be even harder than they had expected.

How could he reveal the damning information he knew this old woman possessed, and do so without exposing her to Dalmeny's power to destroy her testimony? As Vayne's counsel, it was Dalmeny's job to make her look less than professional, to undermine her competence. But what if he did his job too well, and she found herself humiliated, her dignity destroyed in public because she was attempting to bring Vayne down?

Their case against Vayne was constructed from a mosaic of so many tiny pieces that added up to a pattern recognised only by those who understood the complex mathematics of it all.

It had been Gideon Hunter's decision to let Daniel ask the questions. Gideon looked very tired, and Daniel was concerned that he might be ill. When he asked him, Gideon assured Daniel that he was fine. It would have been clumsy and intrusive to ask any further. This was the beginning of a new partnership which Daniel hoped would last a long time, and too many questions might be seen by Hunter as prying. He accepted that, like himself, Gideon was tired, perhaps not sleeping well while the difficulties of this prosecution continued to mount.

Why on earth had Marcus resigned now, and picked Gideon Hunter to take his place? And what reckless lunacy had made Hunter seize the chance to prosecute Malcolm Vayne?

Nadine Parnell was waiting for Daniel to begin.

'Mrs Parnell, your work sounds complicated.'

She smiled very slightly. 'Only when you are unfamiliar with it,' she said.

'And what can you tell us about Malcolm Vayne's financial dealings?'

'Once you understand what he is doing – which, I grant you, may take some time – then it becomes perfectly clear. I'm afraid it took me rather longer than it should have, but when I finally understood, then it was quite simple.' And she proceeded to quote in detail a single example of what she was referring to. It was surprisingly easy to follow. Goods were purchased, but their prices were consistently elevated. 'Good for tax purposes,' she added.

Daniel took a breath. 'You have told us about discrepancies.

I believe you referred to them as *bookkeeping complications*. Could you please explain these, without being too technical? That is, where the errors were, and what they mean? This way, we can understand what, if anything, went wrong. Indeed, whether there is anything beyond a layman's failure to understand a rather complicated subject. At least, complicated to those of us who do not find mathematics easy.'

'Of course,' she nodded. 'There is a very large amount of money indeed going through Mr Vayne's businesses. It is necessary to keep track of income and outgoings, including whatever sums are incurred for payment, whether repayment of loans, or interest on money borrowed or lent. My job is to distinguish what is income, and thus what taxes are due, from what is donated or collected for one charity or another. These donations are not subject to income tax, and must be kept separate from the company books.'

'Thank you,' said Daniel.

'Also,' she added, without being asked, 'all of it is quite straightforward, I assure you. In the case of the company books, even the smallest mistake may well become a larger error, multiplied, if not corrected.'

Daniel cut her off with a shake of his head. 'I see! Or I think I do. Are you saying that even the simplest error might expand into an ever-growing rat's nest of errors and corrections?'

He waited for her response. When she paused, he wondered when it would be the most opportune moment to question her about money loaned to Vayne. Had it really come from foreign sources? And would she know? He shared Gideon Hunter's belief that these massive loans were at the heart of this investigation. Were they also the reason for Whitnall's death?

'Indeed,' she said, nodding. 'It takes only a few errors to suddenly find the books are off by hundreds, thousands, or even hundreds of thousands of pounds. When this happens, the entire process must start anew, but with an intense focus on every number.'

Dalmeny stood up. 'My Lord,' he said, addressing the judge. 'We can hardly condemn Mr Vayne for a bookkeeping error!'

The judge turned to Mrs Parnell. 'Please clarify this for the court.'

'Mr Dalmeny is correct,' said Nadine Parnell. 'Mr Vayne never touches the company books. At worst, his associates have failed to keep on top of the more junior staff. At the same time—' she added, but was cut off by Dalmeny.

'I do apologise for saying this, but are we to take seriously the testimony of this witness? I ask the court to appoint a team of accountants to go over these financial ledgers and make sense of it all. I'm sure we'll discover that my client is very competent in the area of accounting. Without such knowledge, he could never have built such successful businesses.'

Daniel looked at Nadine Parnell, whose face exhibited something he found difficult to describe. If he didn't know better, he'd guess it was humour! Nevertheless, he felt the reins slipping out of his hands.

'You mistake me, sir,' said Mrs Parnell. 'I do not think that Mr Vayne is incompetent.'

Dalmeny smiled, as if savouring this victory.

'Nor do I imagine he does the paperwork himself,' she added.

Daniel saw this as his chance to step in and win a point or two. 'Is it that complicated?' he asked innocently, hoping she would follow his intentions.

'When dealing with such lengthy numbers,' she said, 'errors

happen. Especially if the person in charge of accounts isn't paying attention.'

'Paying attention?' Daniel said.

Mrs Parnell squared her shoulders. It was a long time standing in the witness box for an elderly woman. 'Yes, sir,' she said. 'Human error, you know. Multiplying numbers that should be added, or coming up with a figure that doesn't make sense, but is entered nevertheless.'

'And in the case of Mr Vayne's business accounting?'

'It would be greatly to his advantage if some errors were made,' she said. Before Dalmeny could protest, she rushed ahead. 'How easy to claim that these were simple errors, and then try to wriggle out of prosecution by blaming these errors on an incompetent member of staff. Whether the funds inspected are part of Mr Vayne's companies, or money implicated in these charges of fraud, they must be reviewed, and reviewed again.'

This time, Dalmeny jumped to his feet. 'Just what are you suggesting, madam?' His face turned flaming red as he spoke. 'No one has mentioned your knowledge of any financial situations outside of Mr Vayne's company.'

Nadine Parnell gave the defence counsel a long look. 'My apologies, Mr Dalmeny. I was under the impression that financial dealings outside of Mr Vayne's company are exactly why we're here.'

Daniel looked at the jurors, and he saw that one man's face mirrored what seemed to be disgust. Another juror was looking away, as if trying not to smile.

A certain idea came into Daniel's mind. It had to do with something his father had said about Vayne and foreign money. How much did Mrs Parnell actually know about this? Clearly, her last statement was intended to guide him into that area. Could he do this, step by step, so the jury would understand?

Daniel smiled and addressed Dalmeny directly. 'If Mr Vayne's dealings are as honest as you say, then the witness's comments will not only be in the interest of justice, they will also prove highly beneficial to Mr Vayne. Then there will be no doubt left in our minds, and no shadow hovering over his name. Is that not also what you wish?'

Dalmeny hesitated, clearly not sure how to answer.

'Proceed, Mr Pitt,' the judge said unwillingly, his tone of voice suggesting he had no choice.

'Thank you, My Lord,' Daniel accepted graciously, then turned again to Nadine Parnell. 'Mrs Parnell, if you would explain to us, so everyone can understand? You would be greatly aiding the course of justice.'

She was looking at him sagely, amusement in her face, and then gone again. She reminded him of Miriam. Perhaps, in years ahead, his wife would look like this dignified, clever old lady.

'Certainly, Mr Pitt.' She proceeded to explain very clearly and logically how figures are entered, the various bookkeeping methods used to deal with a variety of expenses, and how figures could be changed to alter or hide actual financial dealings. 'It may seem like a small error, and too easy to brush aside, but added together, the results can be very serious indeed.'

'And what must you do, if an error is uncovered?' Daniel asked.

'If I sense, or know for certain, that a final answer is incorrect, I begin the process all over again. But this time, I work backwards.'

'In the case of Mr Vayne's accounts, Mrs Parnell, what drew your attention to any discrepancies?'

She glanced quickly at Vayne, whose expression was dark. 'The fact that every error suggested a loss to Mr Vayne, and every correction was in his favour. The attempt to hide information was not only unprofessional, but it was not at all subtle.'

'How do you mean?' Daniel asked, catching a glimpse of Dalmeny about to rise in protest.

'These kinds of errors – intended to hide or cheat – are easy enough to find, if you are looking for them. No matter how complicated it is, if there is a pattern, it eventually emerges. Any good bookkeeper can detect it.'

'Do you mean any good bookkeeper who is honestly looking?' said Daniel. 'I assume there are those who do as they are instructed and deliberately choose not to bring such errors to anyone's attention.'

'Just so,' she agreed. 'Accounting, bookkeeping, can be fascinating, Mr Pitt. A kind of science, if approached properly.' She gave him a gentle smile. 'If you have been correctly and logically taught, and you understand it, it will make the most excellent sense. Unlike less precise fields, there is little room for opinion. Answers are either correct, or they are incorrect. If incorrect, it is often because figures have been poorly written . . . or someone wishes to commit fraud.'

'And what do you say to mistakes made when one is over-tired, or when the lighting is poor, or one's mind might be confused by new, extraneous matters?'

'Those are excuses, Mr Pitt, but not good excuses.'

'Would you say it was more a matter of honesty?' he pressed, quite gently.

'Of course,' she agreed. 'We can give a tired clerk the benefit of the doubt, if there is any, but there really is no excuse for so many errors.'

'How do you know this?' he asked. 'Or is it a judgement call?'

'Quite simple, Mr Pitt. As I said, an honest person may

write figures poorly because they are overtired, and may mistake one number for another, but the final solutions will not make sense. If you work with numbers as often as I have, you'll know that patterns of deception are quite easy to spot.'

'Is that what we're talking about, Mrs Parnell?' he asked. 'Patterns of deception?'

'In the case of Mr Vayne's business dealings, there are many small errors, but they all lead in the same direction.'

'Meaning?' asked Daniel.

'Meaning . . . cumulatively, they amount to a far greater sum than is reasonable to expect.'

'Can you explain that in particular, rather than in general terms?' Daniel asked.

She responded carefully, every example backed up with others. She never lost her place, nor did she contradict herself.

Despite her attempts at brevity and clarity, Daniel saw the jurors shifting in their chairs, glancing about the room. Boredom was setting in. The moment she paused, he said, 'Thank you, Mrs Parnell,' and turned to face the judge. 'I believe my witness might appreciate a break, My Lord.'

Mr Justice Abbott-Smith announced a lunch recess with a sharp rap of his gavel.

Daniel and Hunter stepped outside, with Rose joining them. They agreed that one of the local public houses was best. It served a quick and quite delicious meal.

'Do you prefer that I leave you, and take myself elsewhere?' Rose asked.

Daniel looked at her, concerned that she might feel pushed aside, but her expression was pleasant.

'As you wish, my dear,' said Hunter. 'You are always welcome.'

Daniel nodded his agreement. They needed to talk seriously,

go over their strategy. Nadine Parnell might not have access to the funds that flowed in and out of Vayne's fraudulent investment project, but she knew about them, and her testimony could be damning.

'Thank you,' Rose said to her husband, and then turned to Daniel. As if having read his mind, she said, 'I'll eat, but I won't talk. I know you have much to discuss.'

They settled into a little table at the back of the pub, out of earshot of the other diners.

Daniel was looking at Hunter earnestly. What had he missed? Was Hunter holding back something he was going to use dramatically in court? Was he thinking about suddenly producing another new witness who would reveal a new fact? Such as what?

'I hope you have something you haven't yet mentioned to me,' Daniel said, as soon as they were served and the waiter had walked away. 'We've got masses of facts and figures, and Mrs Parnell is making them almost understandable, but the jury has had enough. I can see it in their faces. These numbers, or how they're manipulated, mean little to them. Vayne's accounting practices could be as honest and open as possible, or as crooked as hell, and they wouldn't know the difference. Good heavens, if our accounting expert can't go through them . . .'

Hunter looked blank and then shrugged. 'My tax people know if I'm sixpence out,' he replied bleakly. 'But I can see how they could look at a pile of papers like that and give up.' He made a half-hearted attempt at a smile. 'But I think if anyone knows, it is Mrs Parnell. And so far, the jury believes her. I do think they're trying to understand.'

'Then we have got to make it more accessible.' Daniel leaned forward a little, a sense of urgency gripping him. 'Ensure that it makes sense. They've got to feel something! Anger, intense curiosity, a sense of being laughed at!'

'You think she can get all that out of endless balance sheets?' Hunter asked. 'Aren't you being—'

'We've got to!' Daniel insisted, cutting him off. 'There's no drama inherent in this, and I think that's what Dalmeny is counting on. The jury will be bored to death before he even needs to present Vayne's case.' The thoughts came pouring into his mind, as if spoken aloud. 'That's what I would do, if I were defending Vayne, wouldn't you? Let the prosecution put the jury to sleep, then wake them up with passion, envy, greed, hatred, the fear of big changes, good changes, if this prosecution fails.' He became clearer in his mind as he spoke. 'That's what we are to Vayne. He's the victim of a blind, self-serving power that is trying to break him, for the good of the common man. Hunter, we've got to take that from him, show what a hypocrite he is. That means taking control of the drama. Nadine Parnell is quite agreeable to giving the answers, if we just ask her the right questions. This isn't about a few changes to the bottom line; it's about defrauding innocent people out of millions of pounds!'

Hunter frowned. 'And you think the whole thing could come to pieces in our hands?'

'It's already in pieces,' Daniel pointed out. 'I think she's actually very smart, and she has a sense of humour, and shares the pain of the people Vayne has defrauded.' Memories flashed into his mind of Nadine Parnell's face when she was answering his questions earlier: the intelligence, the weight of the anger. She had handed them the one weapon that might work. She should not have to tell them how to use it!

'All we need to do is give her the chance,' he went on eagerly, his food at least temporarily forgotten. 'But we must do it now. She's not only a sympathetic witness, at least while we've got her, but she may be the only chance we have. All the others are reluctant to testify. She isn't. And don't forget, she was run over and could have been killed.'

'I understand,' Hunter said quickly. 'So, let's do it!'

Daniel felt another stab of guilt. He looked first at Rose, who had remained silent throughout the meal and this discussion. Then he turned back to Hunter. 'Forgive my asking, but you look pale.' Was he being too personal? All sorts of ailments were confidential, too delicate and sometimes too painful for a relative stranger to ask about.

'I'm not ill,' Hunter said quickly. 'Just tired. This case is keeping me up at night. And I tend to drive myself,' he added. 'With no sense of when to stop.'

Another glance at Rose told Daniel that she agreed. He certainly understood, even sympathised. The pressure they were under was enormous. A court battle is always focused on the total defeat of the opponent, or as close to defeat as possible. One should never show weakness, or even fatigue. 'What can I do to help?'

'You're doing it all,' said Hunter. 'Continue questioning Mrs Parnell this afternoon.'

'Any thoughts about our strategy?' asked Daniel.

'When you question her, move around a bit, use your charm. The jurors will have to follow your movements. This will force them to be more alert. And help her work with us. She clearly has no love for Vayne, and more importantly, she wants to bring him down. But above all, engage the jury, make them care.'

'With pleasure,' Daniel replied. It was the usual, courteous answer, but there was excitement behind it.

Theirs was a win-or-lose challenge, and Nadine Parnell's

testimony had to be the turning point in this trial. This was where they would win, or slide rapidly down into an all-out acquittal. A total victory for Vayne. Which would also be an inescapable loss for Gideon Hunter, Daniel Pitt, and the reputation of fford Croft and Gibson.

Chapter Twenty-Two

Back in court again, Daniel rose to his feet to continue the questioning of Nadine Parnell. He could feel a minor stir of interest among the spectators in the room.

At this point, and after her long and rather tedious explanations of basic bookkeeping, anything would have interested the jury, at least for a few minutes. But he had to keep them engaged longer, paying attention and hanging on every word. And he needed to do this throughout her testimony. All afternoon, if possible, stimulating not only their intellect but their emotions. And above all, their anger. Malcolm Vayne had cheated many unsuspecting investors through his fraudulent scheme. The only suitable response was outrage.

'Good afternoon, Mrs Parnell,' he said, with as much charm as he could manage without sounding unctuous. 'If you remember, I first came to see you around the time of your fearful accident in the street, which very nearly cost you your life—'

He was interrupted by a sharp stir of interest in the gallery.

'I hope you are fully recovered?' Daniel continued. 'You look fine, but it must have been very frightening. I do not wish to distress you, but I am afraid I have to ask you about that incident, in case the jury finds it relevant, as indeed I do.'

Dalmeny rose quickly to his feet. 'My Lord,' he said, as if weary from hearing too much unnecessary testimony. 'I realise that Mr Pitt is relatively new to this court, and young, but general enquiries as to the witness's health and well-being are irrelevant. This witness is clearly quite well enough to have talked all morning, as far as I can see, so let us not—'

Mr Justice Abbott-Smith looked weary as well, and sounded short-tempered. 'Mr Pitt, charm is all very well, in its place, which is not here! Please get to your point, if you have one.'

'This goes to the heart of my point, My Lord,' Daniel replied steadily. He briefly glanced at the jury and saw that he had their full attention.

Conflict, even minor, was a spark of life. There was something to fight about! Dalmeny had obligingly already made that clear. The very fact that he objected to Daniel's question had made the jury at the very least interested.

'Then get to it, Mr Pitt,' the judge snapped.

'Yes, My Lord. I will try not to –' and here he glanced across at Dalmeny – 'waste the court's time.' He looked back at Nadine Parnell, and saw in an instant that she had understood perfectly well where he was going with his questions.

'If I understood you correctly, Mrs Parnell, you were standing on the kerb, and there was heavy traffic. You felt a sudden sharp pressure behind you, which caused you to lose your balance and fall forward into the road. You were very fortunate not to have been more seriously injured.'

'Yes. Bad bruises from a collision with a passing motor car,' she replied. 'The driver didn't stop. I was taken to hospital . . .' She paused for a moment. 'It is kind of you to ask.'

'Do you still have pain?'

'Very nice manners, Mr Pitt, but is it relevant?' the judge asked sharply.

'Yes, My Lord,' Daniel said politely, then turned again to Nadine Parnell. 'How did you come to overbalance into moving traffic, Mrs Parnell?'

'I didn't,' she said, holding her chin a little higher. 'I was pushed from behind, sharply, in the middle of my back.'

A gasp rose from the gallery. Daniel had no need to look – he knew he had their undivided attention and sympathy.

'I have a bruise where something hard was shoved into my back. I cannot see the bruise, of course, but the doctor told me it was shaped like the ornamental head of a walking stick.'

'Someone shoved you with a walking stick, presumably accidentally? Or, perhaps, with intent? What did the police say? You did speak to the police after the incident, I presume?'

'They came to see me in the hospital,' she agreed.

'Do you recall who visited you?'

'Yes, a very nice young man. Frobisher, I believe was his name. Yes, that was it: Frobisher.'

'Have you any idea who pushed you?' he asked. He did not look at Dalmeny, but he gave a momentary glance towards the dock, where Vayne was leaning forward, listening intently.

'I have my own ideas,' she said. 'But I have no proof, or I would have told Mr Frobisher, and I'm sure he would have done something about it, Mr Pitt.'

Dalmeny sat up a little straighter, ready to rise.

'But you have not?' Daniel pressed.

'Exactly,' she agreed, but she was looking at him very steadily.

'It is not because anyone has threatened you, and you are afraid?' he asked, with overt sympathy.

Now the jury also was staring at her; their attention was

absolutely rapt. Several of them looked shocked, angry. Others showed concern for her, possibly imagining their own mothers, wives, or aunts.

'Mr Pitt!' the judge said sharply. 'Are you going anywhere with this? I warn you to be careful not to raise an accusation that you cannot substantiate. I would not have you using this courtroom to start rumours and make charges you cannot begin to prove. Do you understand me, sir?'

'Yes, My Lord. I am trying to establish Mrs Parnell's reliability, and the fact that she is not speaking out of fear, and not trying to lay the blame on anyone for her frightening accident.'

The judge sat back. That was not the answer he had expected, and it made him look a trifle foolish.

One of the jurors smiled. Another coughed discreetly into his handkerchief. If anyone thought he also was smiling, they were probably right.

'You are not afraid, then?' he asked Mrs Parnell, aware of the tension in his own voice.

She raised her chin a fraction higher. 'I thank you for your concern, Mr Pitt, but I assure you, I am fine.'

Dalmeny shook his head, as if out of frustration, but he said nothing.

Daniel continued. 'When questioned earlier, Mrs Parnell, you were able to explain the bookkeeping methods very exactly. I'm not sure if my learned colleague understood it all.' He glanced at Hunter, and then back again at Mrs Parnell. And then he smiled rather sheepishly. 'To be honest, I'm afraid that it is I who struggle with numbers. I can add and subtract adequately, and even multiply or divide, but beyond that I am lost. I'm not sure if the gentlemen of the jury are like me.' He turned and smiled apologetically, as if he might have unintentionally insulted them. He was relieved to find amusement, relief and agreement in their faces. 'But I would like it very much if you would explain some of that to us.'

She smiled back at him. 'Of course. It can be complicated for many.'

'Nonsense,' the judge said, glaring at Dalmeny, as if he were offended by the defence counsel's failure to raise an objection himself. 'We do not need another lesson in arithmetic, madam.'

'I have not presumed to give you one, My Lord,' she replied, with something of an edge to her voice. 'Although a lesson in good manners would not come amiss.'

There was a moment of silence, like the gap between a flash of lightning and the roar of thunder, seconds afterwards.

'One more remark such as that, madam, and I shall hold you in contempt!' the judge said, making some attempt to control his temper.

'Very suitable,' she agreed. She refrained from saying that the irritation was mutual, but the thought was in her face, and Daniel could see that the jurors finished the exchange for themselves. He needed to stay on top of this, lest it get out of control.

Nadine Parnell nodded, and then shared a smile of comprehension with the jury.

Daniel watched the men's faces. Clearly, they respected Nadine Parnell and they were sympathetic to her. He was about to enter into the realm of fraud, intentional fraud, and he suspected that Dalmeny would be spending a good deal of time jumping to his feet in protest. However, what purpose was there in having this expert witness, if the floodgates of this fraud were not opened and the truth allowed to spill out?

'Mrs Parnell,' Daniel began, forcing his body to remain

relaxed. Nothing would give away his anxiety faster than clenched fists and a tight jaw. Dalmeny would be watching for those signs. 'This trial, as you know, is not about accounting errors. Nor is it about figures placed in the wrong column. Instead, it is about a massive fraud perpetrated against innocent victims . . . men and women who have lost everything, due to the malice and deceit of Malcolm Vayne.'

Dalmeny leapt to his feet. 'My Lord!' he declared. 'This has not been proven!'

Daniel turned to Dalmeny. 'I believe we're here to do just that,' he shot back.

The judge leaned forward and pointed his finger at Daniel. 'Be very careful, Mr Pitt. An accusation alone does not indicate guilt.'

'Yes, My Lord,' Daniel said, trying hard to appear contrite, but feeling a rush of excitement.

'Mrs Parnell,' he went on. 'Charges have been brought against Mr Vayne for creating a financial scheme . . . a fraud. Only you can explain to the jury how this was done.'

Nadine Parnell paused for a moment before speaking. 'Mr Pitt, I'm sorry to correct you, but there are actually several people in the Vayne organisation who understand how this was done.'

'I stand corrected,' said Daniel. 'Let me rephrase this. Charges have been brought against Malcolm Vayne for creating a financial scheme . . . a fraud that several in his firm know about, but you alone are courageous enough to explain to the jury.'

He could see out of the corner of his eye that Dalmeny was rising to protest again, but then sat down and said nothing.

'In a fraud of this type,' said Daniel, 'how is the chicanery exposed?'

Nadine Parnell thought about this for quite some time.

'Madam?' said the judge.

She glanced his way and then nodded. 'A moment, sir. A quick and incomplete response will not do.'

Daniel feared a rebuke from the judge, and was surprised when he said nothing. In fact, was that a smile playing on his lips? Understandable, considering how knowledgeable and self-possessed this witness was proving to be.

'The steps required to carry off this kind of fraud are several,' she said.

'Could you please take us through them, one by one?' Daniel asked.

'Certainly, but it will take some time.'

'As much as you need,' he replied. 'And, if necessary, we can continue tomorrow.'

There was no need to glance in Dalmeny's direction to know that he was reacting.

'It begins with the announcement of an investment fund,' she said.

'Must it have a name?' Daniel asked.

'Always, or else how would investors recognise it? In the case of Mr Vayne's fund, it was called Big Ben Investments.'

'And can you explain how it was set up?'

'Yes, of course, the process was straightforward.'

'Meaning?'

'Meaning . . . most investment funds follow this structure.'

'And Big Ben . . . can you tell us specifically?'

'You'll be happy to know it's less complicated than book-keeping!' She flashed a charming smile. 'However, there are two key elements to this particular fund. On one side, there were funds loaned out to businesses and individuals who needed more money than the standard banks would provide.'

'And in exchange for this loan, borrowers were charged an interest rate?'

'Always,' she replied.

'Can you give us some examples of why an individual would need to borrow from Big Ben, and not his personal bank?'

Nadine Parnell looked at the judge. 'Excuse me, My Lord, if what I say sounds . . . indelicate.'

The judge nodded.

A murmur ran through the gallery, what Daniel read as a how-we're-getting-to-the-good-part anticipation.

'Gambling debts, for one,' she explained. 'Money for a love nest, or some illicit relationship. There are many reasons why someone would need a large influx of cash, and would want to receive it secretly. For many, the Big Ben fund was the answer to those needs.'

Daniel nodded, but said nothing. To interrupt her now would be madness. The entire courtroom was hanging on her every word!

'So . . . the process,' she said. 'First, an investment fund is established. Its structure is based on fairly rigid legal requirements.'

'And this was done with Big Ben?'

'I'm sure it was, or else the fund could not have been activated.'

'Thank you. And then . . .?'

'Letters go out to potential borrowers . . . and potential investors.'

'You've clarified who the borrowers are. Now, could you please explain the role of the investor?'

'The investor puts money into the fund. This is how a fund builds its assets, and has sufficient money to lend out.'

'And the process?' Daniel asked.

Nadine Parnell nodded. 'Let's say you have fifty thousand pounds that you want to invest.'

The renewed murmur around Daniel reminded him that few people had anywhere near that sum lying around. For most of the people in this room, that was a fortune they would never see.

'Big Ben Investments is one fund to consider,' she explained. 'You invest your fifty thousand, with the promise that your money will be invested in up-and-coming or established companies, and will earn a respectable interest rate. Or,' she added, 'it could be money loaned to an individual borrower. In both cases, the interest payments are an important element. That is, interest paid by the borrower, and interest earned by the investor.'

'Could you please give us an example?'

'Yes, of course. You've invested fifty thousand pounds, with the promise of, let's say, an annual return of ten per cent on your investment. That means that at the end of the first year, your fifty thousand pounds is now fifty-five thousand.'

'That sounds like an excellent investment!' said Daniel, directing his eagerness toward the jurors.

'It definitely is,' said Nadine.

'So, I invest with the expectation of earning interest. But how do I know that borrowers will pay back what they borrowed?'

'When someone requests a loan, there are fund officers who check their financial history, their solvency, and so on. It doesn't do, if money is loaned to someone who can't repay it.'

Daniel took a deep breath. This is where it was going to become delicate. 'Mrs Parnell, can you please explain how a fund, with all appearances of being legitimate and solvent,

can find itself unable to pay its investors their earned interest
. . . much less repay any of their original principal?'

'Objection!' declared Dalmeny, rising quickly. 'It has not
been established that Big Ben was guilty of this!'

Daniel looked squarely at Dalmeny. 'Did I mention Big
Ben? No, sir, I did not. You did.'

The judge raised his gavel, as if expecting to have to quieten
the room, but there was only silence. 'Continue, Mr Pitt.'

'Mrs Parnell?'

'Let's call it the XYZ Fund. You invest your fifty thousand,
expecting to earn interest. And you receive an interest check
at the end of the first year. Let's say it's five thousand pounds.
You are delighted! And you have a choice: take that windfall
and use it for whatever you like, or tell the people at Big Ben
that you want to reinvest it. So now you have fifty-five thousand pounds in the fund.'

'Where can this go wrong?' Daniel asked.

'It can go terribly wrong if XYZ is taking your money but
not investing it.'

'But then, aren't they having to find a way to continue
paying you interest, or even repay the entire amount invested,
should you request it? And if they can't pay you, you'll know
that something underhand is afoot.'

'Yes, Mr Pitt. The result is that there's not enough money
in the fund to pay the investors. And that is where the fraud
comes in,' she said.

'I don't understand, forgive me.' Daniel looked puzzled,
hoping to not only capture but hold tight the attention of
every man on the jury.

'Follow me closely,' she said, sounding like a schoolmarm
teaching a classroom of dolts. 'XYZ welcomes a new investor
– let's say it's you – and you put ten thousand pounds into

the fund. Because your money has been pocketed by the XYZ people, and never invested, they have to find a way to pay you. How? They use the money donated by the second investor.'

'And the money invested in the up-and-coming enterprise?'

'That enterprise never existed,' she said. 'Which makes XYZ a front for fraud.'

'But can't the money paid back by the man with the gambling debts make a difference in the fund?'

'If he pays at all, it will likely be far too little to cover what XYZ owes its investors. But remember,' she added, 'the fraud is never discovered until investors demand payouts. By then, the fund is empty, worthless.'

Daniel closed his eyes for a moment, as if this would muster the courage needed for the next declaration. 'Mrs Parnell, you've done an excellent job describing how these funds work, both for the borrowers and the investors. Now . . . I'd like to turn your attention to the Big Ben fund, established by Malcolm Vayne.'

All eyes turned first to Vayne, and then to his defence counsel. As if by mutual agreement, neither man reacted, but remained outwardly calm, even relaxed.

'Mrs Parnell, based on your many years of experience, and the trust that Malcolm Vayne placed in you for more than thirty years, what can you tell us about Big Ben Investments?'

She lowered her head for a moment. When she lifted it, she looked directly at Daniel.

He returned the look.

Her eyes were blazing. Whether it was anger, indignation, or her opportunity to right a terrible wrong perpetrated by a man she had served loyally for much of her adult life, he wasn't sure.

'Mrs Parnell?' he prompted.

'In my professional opinion,' she said, her voice ringing through the courtroom like a clarion call, 'the Big Ben investment fund was a clear and utter fraud.'

What happened next could only be described as pandemonium. There were shouts coming from the gallery, the sound of indignation and even despair. Journalists raced towards the exit, desperate to file their story, and all of them knowing that Vayne's newspapers would never print the truth.

It was getting late, but there was still half an hour left for the court to remain in session. Daniel wondered if he should stop on this dramatic note and continue in the morning, or forge ahead.

He thanked Nadine Parnell and sat down.

Dalmeny walked out into the open area of the court. He was an elegant man, and clearly he knew it. He also knew better than to be openly hostile to Nadine Parnell, particularly when the jurors so obviously liked her.

'Good afternoon, Mrs Parnell,' he said courteously.

'Good afternoon, Mr Dalmeny,' she replied, equally civilly.

'It is very brave of you to come out in public view of the court.' He turned around and indicated the few press reporters who were still in the room. 'And before the world's press, to make these charges.'

Her smile did not falter. 'I have spoken the truth, Mr Dalmeny. I appreciate that not everyone will believe me. I've tried before, and been disbelieved quite strenuously.'

Dalmeny hesitated barely a second, and yet it was visible. He had lost his impetus, his stride. 'I did not ask you that, Mrs Parnell. Please do not answer questions that I have not asked.'

'I beg your pardon, sir. I thought it was implicit. Had I

272

been in your place, I would have wondered why anyone would wait so long, if they had already seen an injustice, or even an accidental error. Those who overlook such fraud . . . well, it makes me doubt their intelligence, to put it at its kindest.'

A flicker of real anger crossed Dalmeny's face.

Nadine Parnell was smiling and was so polite, and yet she was doing exactly what Dalmeny had asked her not to.

Daniel looked at the jurors, and saw that several of them were quite clearly amused. They liked her, and were on her side in this confrontation. In a sense, Dalmeny had already lost, this time. Did he know that?

Dalmeny changed tack. 'I'm very sorry to bring back your unpleasant experience on the street, which must have been both painful and very frightening to you. Indeed, it is not an exaggeration to say it could have been fatal! Do you believe it was at Mr Vayne's instigation that someone pushed you off the pavement and almost under the wheels of an oncoming motor car?'

There was a sharp intake of breath throughout the room. Then silence.

Nadine Parnell looked at Dalmeny with surprise. 'Good heavens!' she said with amazement. 'I did not know Mr Vayne had such acquaintances. What a hideous thought.' She left it hanging in the air, undenied, as if he had made the suggestion.

Dalmeny was caught out, wrong-footed, as if he had expected her to expand on the thought and, by magnifying it, render it ridiculous. 'I asked if you had imagined him guilty of such a thing,' he said tartly.

She pursed her lips a little and gave it a moment's thought. 'Well, if he were innocent of these charges against him, it would have been a very foolish thing to do. And he's not a fool. Not a fool at all. And if he were guilty, then that would

273

only draw attention to it. So no, I had not thought it was other than exactly what it seemed, an accidental push and a driver's inattention at a most unfortunate time. That is, at first. But the police convinced me otherwise. And now I see that it has clearly occurred to *you* that Mr Vayne might have been behind this . . . so perhaps it is well advised that the police look into the matter in more detail, and leave no uncertainty as to what happened.' She gave a tight little smile. 'Suspicion being as damaging as it is, you cannot afford to leave it hanging in the air.'

Dalmeny plainly had no reply that satisfied him. He had played with fire and now he was suffering severe burns. He retreated.

'Anything further, Mr Dalmeny?' the judge enquired.

'No, My Lord,' Dalmeny replied. 'My learned friend is welcome to make use of any time left.'

'Mr Pitt?' asked the judge.

'Just one quick question,' Daniel replied, standing and approaching Nadine Parnell.

'Mrs Parnell, you mentioned that others might have been aware of the fraudulent scheme orchestrated by Mr Vayne and Big Ben Investments. I know this is difficult, and perhaps very uncomfortable, but could you please give me the name of one . . . or all . . . of those who knew what was happening?'

'You've already questioned the man who knows at least as much as Mr Vayne,' she said. 'Boyce Turnbull.'

This time, Dalmeny shot out of his seat with such force that he nearly fell over. 'Objection! Mr Turnbull has testified, and Mr Pitt had no further questions for him.'

The judge looked decidedly annoyed. 'Mr Pitt?'

'We must have Mr Turnbull back on the stand, Your Honour, if we are to get to the truth here.'

The judge turned, looked at Malcolm Vayne, and then nodded. 'Get him on the stand, Mr Pitt.'

Daniel rushed out of the courtroom and looked for Boyce Turnbull. At the moment, no one was more important to their case. He sent one of the ushers to find him, but the man returned to say that Turnbull was nowhere to be found. This was no problem, at least not yet. Turnbull had not expected to be recalled, so it was natural that he would not be in the courtroom. On the other hand, Daniel was concerned that perhaps they had lost another witness. Perhaps Turnbull was now reluctant. If called, would he show up? A cold feeling settled in the pit of his stomach.

Hunter joined him in the anteroom. Their eyes met and Daniel knew that Hunter had the same thought, the same fear.

Nadine Parnell had just swept them up in a wave of possible victory, but could they build on it? If they could prove that Vayne's entire investment fund was a fraud, and that his motives reached far beyond financial gain, their case against him would be won.

Chapter Twenty-Three

Miriam had not been in court for much of the trial of Malcolm Vayne. She had her own work to do. It was still new enough to be exciting, and she was secure now, no longer a mere assistant whose work had to be supervised. But it was a considerably heavier responsibility, and she could not afford to have her attention divided.

She had asked Daniel how each day had gone, knowing it was of immense importance to him. But she cared about it also, and the present situation was coming towards a climax, which would affect not only Daniel, but also Gideon Hunter and his wife, Rose. And, of course, Marcus, who had retired from the chambers he had founded, but it still carried his name. And, to a great extent, his reputation. He cared about it deeply, and always would, as long as he lived.

Miriam was surprised to realise how much that mattered to her.

She was busy working with Dr Eve on the details of Richard Whitnall's death. Clearly, the immediate cause was that he had bled to death. The question was whether the wound was self-inflicted, or had been made by someone else.

Eve and Miriam were concerned only with the medical

276

facts. What had been in Whitnall's mind at the time of his death was extremely important – and certainly, morally, at the core of a far wider issue encompassing Malcolm Vayne. Miriam understood that Whitnall's death might be related to Vayne's trial. They would have to swear to their findings in court, and they could not afford to be wrong in even the smallest detail.

The court battle would be intense. If they could prove that Whitnall was murdered, then other lives would almost certainly depend on it.

The case was unusually painful for Miriam. She had not known Whitnall personally, but Daniel had, and he had liked the man and his dry humour, admired both his courage and his honesty. When you have seen and known someone when they are alive – feeling, believing, caring – their death feels far more real than that of a stranger.

She stood by the table on which Whitnall lay, with Eve standing on the other side. There were no marks of any kind of struggle. The skin was dry and cold, the body lifeless, as if there was no blood inside it. Miriam knew that an enormous pool of it had spread around his body at the time of death, more blood than an ordinary person might have believed possible.

Now they were examining the terrible knife wound, carefully tracing the path of the blade, the sliced edges of tissue washed clean. Any blood that remained had been removed, leaving the corpse to look oddly like rubber. More like a broken toy than a once-living creature.

Eve was holding a large blunted knife, trying to work out exactly which way it had entered Whitnall's body, and whether it had been a single cut. She needed to determine if there had been any hesitation, perhaps a loss of nerve at the last moment, which might indicate suicide. If there had been an assailant, how would he have been affected by that first gush of blood, or witnessing the shock of pain in the victim's face? And what had been going through Whitnall's mind in the seconds before oblivion?

Miriam looked away from the wound and up at Eve.

Eve must have been aware of the movement, perhaps a change in the reflection of light. She turned to look at Miriam.

'What?' Miriam asked.

'Look.' Eve touched the boundaries of the wound delicately, indicating its edges. 'A single stroke would not make these separate marks. The blade went this way,' she said, holding the knife at a particular angle, and then changing its direction. 'And then it cut again, this way, and far deeper.' She looked up at Miriam. 'Here. Do it yourself, gently . . . gently! Let the blade follow the line of least resistance. Then draw it out, and lean it slightly to the left. Does it go in further?'

Miriam did as she was ordered. And there was no doubt that it was an order. Eve was watching her. First, Miriam's face, to see that she understood; and then her hand, to watch for the movement, to be sure Miriam felt how the resistance was different, and how the blade had taken another path. And all of this without changing the shape of the wound.

Miriam followed the instructions carefully, then looked up and saw satisfaction in the older woman's face. 'Is this proof?' she asked.

'Either of those wounds would have been fatal,' Eve replied. 'The second was to make it look like a self-inflicted injury. This was not suicide: no one would do that to himself twice. No, the first was deeper, and it was fatal. The second was to leave the knife in the body, at a more natural angle for a man stabbing himself. But it's an awkward angle for a right-handed man. Which he was. You can tell,' she said, moving closer to the body. 'The body gives us the evidence: a slightly larger right hand, and the more developed muscles in the right forearm.' She met Miriam's eyes. 'This man did not do this to himself. It's delicate proof, but it is proof.'

'Is it something we can show?' Miriam asked. 'I mean, so a jury could understand? That they would have to accept, even if the science is something they don't understand, or don't want to believe?'

Eve smiled, her expression one of humour, although with a bitter edge. 'The belief in Vayne runs very deep with some people. He seems to represent a hope of change for the better. He's clever enough not to say precisely what he is promising, or how he will achieve it. He paints a rough picture in words familiar to everyone. If people believe what he says, they will cling to those words as long as they can. And they will resent like hell anyone who breaks that dream.'

Miriam drew breath to argue, but what could she say? Those who followed Vayne were certain that he was right. His hold on people was emotional, not logical. The result was that anyone exposing his flaws would earn only hatred. His people knew that, and used it to advance his interests. Whoever disturbed Vayne's popular image in court would have to be very clever, very aware of the emotions he was playing with, and how damaging such testimony could be.

'We need to tell Ian Frobisher,' Miriam said aloud. 'The police have to know, and I have to tell Daniel. And, of course, Gideon Hunter.' She was uncertain how to finish the thought. Finally, she said, 'The defence is saying that Whitnall killed himself because he was ashamed of what he had testified to, and couldn't go through with it.' She heard the anger in her voice, and felt it tighten her throat. 'It's easy enough to ascribe any sort of motive, rational or not, to someone who takes their own life. To some people who have never tasted danger, anyone who commits suicide is mostly mad, or a coward. The fact that they don't know, or understand, doesn't stop them from passing judgement.'

'You don't need to persuade me!' Eve replied. 'Despair is impossible to imagine, if you've never felt it. And if you have, it is not something you want to revisit. But others will imagine guilt, remorse, shame easily enough, if it fits in with their idea of Vayne. Then they'll cast around for someone to blame. Whitnall's death, his accusation of Vayne in the first place – well, there are plenty of possibilities there.' Her face took on a hard, bleak expression. 'We must prepare evidence that is moving enough, and incontrovertible. We must force the jury to believe it was murder. And we must do so without the possibility of escaping the truth. We must leave that jury no way out!'

When she spoke, Eve's voice had the kind of edge someone projects when arguing. 'And yes, Miriam, we'll notify Frobisher at once! Tell him to come here. He has to see this for himself. Daniel could very well call him to the stand, or one of us, or both, and we must be ready with irrefutable evidence. Get on with it!' she added. 'Don't just stand there!'

Miriam obeyed. She understood that Eve's emotion was not directed at her, but at the cruelty of the act, the supreme arrogance of whoever had considered Whitnall's life an impediment to his ambition, and then killed him for it. She knew that Eve Hall was many things – brilliant, stubborn, eccentric, sometimes intentionally very funny, instructive and sharp – but, above all, she was passionate about the miracle and the

280

sanctity of life. But it was Miriam who had the opportunity and privilege of working with such an impressive woman, and was following the trail that Eve had blazed.

She went to the telephone and called the police station. It was Bremner who answered. He was Ian Frobisher's assistant, and she knew him from the case in February. She recognised his lilting accent from the far north-eastern coast. She told him very briefly what she and Eve had concluded, and then asked to speak to Frobisher.

When Ian Frobisher came on the line, she repeated the findings, speaking briefly and powerfully. 'It makes all the difference,' she said urgently. 'He was definitely murdered!'

'It seems so,' Ian agreed.

She detected a slight lift in his voice, but not the whole-hearted relief, almost joy, that she was feeling. It was a great relief to her that Whitnall had been murdered. It exonerated him from charges of cowardice. She was confused by Ian Frobisher's lack of enthusiasm.

'Do you understand?' she asked. 'This means he didn't kill himself, that somebody else did. It can only have been to silence him, so he could not go to court and give damning evidence against Vayne.'

'Yes,' he agreed. 'But we still don't know what the evidence was, nor can we prove it. It doesn't have to have been on Vayne's orders. He could deny it, and no doubt he will.'

'And so, they will believe Vayne,' Miriam said, finishing his thought for him, perhaps more sharply than she meant.

'Miriam, all is not lost yet. Start thinking about how you can convince the jury. I'll be there as soon as I can.'

'Thank you,' she answered. There was no need to tell him how hard she would be working on it until then.

*　*　*

Ian arrived at the laboratory within the hour. It was barely midday, but already he looked tired and a little rumpled.

Miriam saw him and made an immediate decision. 'Good afternoon, Ian.' She smiled. 'Tea? I'm sure you haven't had any recently.' Without waiting for his reply, she turned to walk across the room and make the tea from the gently humming kettle on the gas ring. 'And something edible?' she asked, barely turning round to see his reply.

He sat down on one of the tall stools and nodded his assent.

Eve came in from one of the side rooms, carrying a plate of sandwiches. She set it down near Ian's elbow. Then she swivelled round to face Miriam. 'I'm going to write up my notes.' She walked out without looking back.

Ian relaxed, shaking his head ruefully. 'I think we have our orders.'

Miriam flashed him a smile. She noticed how silently he sat, as if waiting. Possibly, he was glad of these few moments to rest.

She made the tea and set it on the tray.

Miriam liked Ian. She liked his patience and dry humour, his depth of emotion, and she found it easy to see how he and Daniel had been friends since they were boys, and then through junior school, high school, and eventually university.

She placed the tray on the bench, handed him a plate for his sandwich, and poured his cup of tea. He had been to their home often enough that she knew how he liked it.

They both ate a whole sandwich before he spoke.

'Can you prove this about Whitnall's death to someone who has no medical skill?' He did not need to explain what he meant. It was easy to slip back into the kind of communication they had shared before, in the late winter, during the dramatic end of the last case they had worked on together.

'Yes,' she said. 'But I'll make diagrams and photographs so the jury can see how it couldn't have been just one thrust. They need to understand that if you plunge a knife up to its hilt, and you're doing it into your own stomach, you don't take it out and stick it in again. We'll show that, but without shocking them too much.'

'Isn't the very idea of it shocking?' he asked. 'If they imagine it at all, it will be enough to make some of them quite sick.'

'There will be no blood in the photos,' she explained. 'And it's usually the blood that makes it so dreadful. But,' she added, 'I will describe it.' She thought about this for a moment, watching his face. 'I think I'll do it slowly, so they feel the pain, some of the horror, and they will agree that no one would plunge that knife into himself twice, especially after the agony of the first cut. That cut severed the artery. I can demonstrate that, without appalling them too much.'

'If he didn't kill himself, which of his men would Vayne trust to do it?' Ian directed the question at Miriam, but it was aimed more at himself. 'Whoever carried out his order – if that's what happened – that person would then have tremendous power over Vayne. Would he take that risk?'

'I don't know,' she admitted. 'I think he would have to be desperate to trust anyone. Would any of his acolytes commit murder for him?' She saw Ian wince. 'I think you're saying they would. The people I trust most wouldn't murder anyone for me, especially not as brutally and bloodily as the attack on Whitnall.' She thought about this for a moment. 'I take that back. No one would murder for me, in any circumstances.'

'You, or Dr Eve?' Ian asked reluctantly. When Miriam seemed confused, he quickly added, 'That is, which one of you will testify?'

She hesitated, several seconds ticked by, and then she sighed. 'I don't know. I want to do it, but our report might be given more respect if it comes from Eve.'

'It would,' he said, as if he would rather not have to admit it. 'If Daniel is asking you the questions, even if you testify under your maiden name, Dalmeny will certainly make an issue of it. He only needs to make one juror believe that you have more loyalty than skill.'

'They shouldn't be compared,' she began, then stopped, shaking her head. 'Sorry. Not the point.'

'The trouble is,' he replied slowly, as if thinking of each word as he spoke. 'Most of the people loyal to Vayne have their time accounted for, so we need to investigate this more thoroughly. We stopped when it looked like suicide. We just need to carry out some decent police work, check and counter check. You know, get fresh witnesses, write down their statements, and then compare them with each other.'

'Who would you trust?' she asked, returning to Ian's earlier question, her mind reaching for answers. 'Who would lie for him? Who owes him a debt, financial or otherwise?'

'Or who has suddenly been relieved of a debt?' he added. 'Don't worry, we've got some very good financial detectives.'

A dark thought came to her. 'If you paid a man to kill someone, wouldn't you sooner or later – and preferably sooner – get rid of him, too?' She stopped. 'Sorry, that's a hideous thought.'

'Hideous, perhaps,' he said. 'But not so unlikely. If Vayne paid someone to commit murder for him, it makes sense to kill him, too, and in a way that looks entirely unrelated. How else to ensure his silence?'

'It might frighten him,' she replied. 'But not make him feel guilty.'

'I take your point. But there is one thing you seem to have overlooked.'

'What is that?' she said quickly.

'Vayne has been charged with a non-violent crime, impersonal even, in some ways,' he replied. 'He was arrested, but released on bail almost immediately. Murder has never been part of the charge.'

She froze, a hard knot clenched tightly in the pit of her stomach. 'Do you mean he could have done it himself?'

He met her eyes with a cool, soft gaze. 'Wouldn't you, rather than put your neck in a noose held by someone else?'

She breathed out slowly. 'Yes. Yes, I would.'

Ian Frobisher left Miriam after their conversation, and Miriam went back to work with Eve. All their attention was now focused on checking and rechecking their conclusions regarding Whitnall's death, and making sure it was definitely murder.

'I wish we could also prove who did it,' Miriam said, late in the afternoon, when they could not think of anything further to explore.

'Not our job,' Eve replied. 'Point is, if Whitnall was murdered, then his evidence is valid again.' She looked up at Miriam. 'What could he have said? What did he know that no one else did, or would admit to?'

Miriam's mind raced, but it fastened on nothing specific.

'Too damn bad he was killed before he gave his testimony in court. Even if his words are read out from a piece of paper, it doesn't have the same emotional impact,' Eve went on. 'But it still proves that what he knew was important. No one does this to a witness unless he is terrified of what that witness will say if he's allowed to live. As for Hunter, if he can't make the jury believe that, then he's in the wrong business.'

She made it an absolute statement, her voice ringing with certainty. But her eyes were concerned. *Brittle* was the word that came to Miriam's mind.

'The police will have to prove it was Vayne,' Miriam said, but so quietly that she could have been speaking to herself. 'Or maybe it was someone paid by him, or otherwise rewarded.'

'Doesn't matter,' Eve said flatly. 'We've done our part to prove that the fatal wound wasn't self-inflicted. That's all we needed to prove. Someone did it – Vayne, or somebody paid by him, or loyal to him, rewarded by him, with some political or financial interests – but we'll leave that to Frobisher. We can offer proof in court of a terrible wrong having been committed. That's the best we can do.'

It was late afternoon when they began to pack up for the day. They had achieved all that they could and were ready to testify, even if asked as soon as tomorrow morning. No matter which of them was called to the stand, they were ready.

'I'll lock up,' Miriam offered. 'I just have to finish these notes. No need for you to wait. I'll only be another fifteen minutes.'

Daniel would still be in court, so she had time to perform those end-of-day tasks.

'I'll wait,' Eve replied, sitting down in one of the hard-backed chairs.

Miriam wondered whether to argue or not, and decided not to. Whatever she said, Eve would do as she wished. She smiled and thanked her, just as the door to the passage was flung open so hard it slammed back against the wall. A large, handsome man came in. He was well over six feet tall, with a mane of dark, white-streaked hair. He looked straight at Miriam, ignoring Eve.

286

'What do you want!' Eve called out, grabbing his arm.

Miriam realised who he must be from Daniel's description of him, his size and the white blaze at the front of his hair. Callum McCallum, Malcolm Vayne's right-hand man. He seemed enormous in this laboratory, and furiously angry, as if he would break anything he wanted.

Eve gripped his arm with an even greater force. He swung round and lashed out at her with his other arm, his full weight behind it, sending her flying across the floor and landing hard against the double sink and cupboards. She slid to the floor and lay there without moving.

Miriam exploded with anger, running to Eve. 'Have you killed her?' She knelt by Eve, checking for a pulse, and was relieved when she felt the rhythmic beat.

He ignored her and grabbed her wrist.

Pain shot up her arm and she tried to free herself, but he held her in a vice-like grip. She knew that if she tried any harder, she might pull her arm out of its socket.

'Let go!' she said harshly, trying to twist around to face Eve.

The woman was motionless on the floor. Miriam could see shallow breaths, and now there was blood in her hair, with a narrow trickle visible on the floor.

'What have you done?' She was cold at the thought that Eve needed her attention. She could die! The impact of her head against the sink had been so great that Miriam feared there might be brain damage. 'Let me help her,' she pleaded. 'Please, I beg you.'

'You're coming with me.'

'But she's hurt!' Miriam said desperately. 'She's—'

'If she's that bad, there's nothing you can do, and if she's not, then she'll come around without your help. You have a telephone here. She can call for someone.'

He pulled sharply at her arm, throwing her off balance. She stumbled, trying to regain her footing, but he was dragging her towards the door.

'Let me—' she started again.

He turned to face her. 'I don't care whether you have both your shoulders dislocated or not, it's up to you.'

She stared at his face, his eyes, and knew that he would kill her if he had to. Then he would have to kill Eve, too. She did as she was told and stopped resisting, almost as if she were willing to accompany him.

They went into the street, and McCallum closed the laboratory door with a slam. He walked her less than a dozen yards to where a large, dusty black car was parked. He opened the passenger door and pushed her inside.

'Make a fuss and I'll tie your hands,' he said. 'We've a long way to go. You could be very uncomfortable indeed, if you force me to hit you. I will return you, in time, to your husband, whole and more or less functional. But if you fight me, I'll fight you, and I will win. I think you know that already. I have to do this.'

McCallum swung round and climbed into the driver's seat, then started the engine. He pulled out into the street and drove rapidly through the traffic.

Miriam sat motionless, still trying to absorb what was happening. It was less than twenty minutes since she and Eve had been safe in the laboratory, closing everything down for the day, at the same time feeling helpless in a case where they seemed to be blindly groping for answers.

Had McCallum killed Richard Whitnall? Why? There could only be one answer: to prevent Whitnall from giving testimony against Vayne. Which meant his information was damning.

It would have ended in Vayne's conviction, possibly even imprisonment.

Should she try to find out more? They were driving quickly through the streets leading them out of the city. Where was he going? If he intended to kill her, he could have done so in the laboratory. Did he mean to hold her as some kind of ransom, so the charges against Vayne would be withdrawn? Was she of value to him as herself, or as a pathologist? Or . . . as Daniel's wife?

It was the first time she had thought about Daniel. If he had been taken, she would be frantic. How would they tell him? She felt guilty at the thought of his pain, confusion, and eventually his grief, and she was filled with pain herself. It was almost unbearable.

McCallum seemed intent on the road, driving with great care, keeping to the speed limit, so that no one would remember the car. Or, above all, stop him for speeding.

Miriam was not sure what anyone could do. She saw no prospect of escape. It was as if she could feel the violence inside him, but there was also desperation. She realised that he must be heavily involved in Vayne's fraud. Could any money be worth this? Looking sideways at his face, the tight lines, and the muscles knotted in his neck and jaw, she wondered if there was any point at all in speaking to him.

They were still travelling swiftly, but McCallum showed great skill. Miriam saw that he was more than a good driver; he was in full control of the car. She was a pretty good driver herself, and she knew the attention it required. A lapse of even seconds could cause an accident. It could be violent, dangerous, very possibly fatal. But McCallum would not let this happen.

He was heading north, but to where? A place far outside the city? Perhaps the countryside, where he could hold her prisoner and no one would know, never mind care. Then he could contact . . . who? Vayne? Probably, to let him know that he had her, that he was dealing with the situation. And then someone could notify Daniel that his wife was a hostage.

She wondered if McCallum, or someone working behind the scenes for Vayne, would demand that they drop the case. No, that would be too obvious, and it would leave Vayne still on trial, without an acquittal. They would have to follow through with the trial and force a jury verdict of not guilty. Vayne would be the hero of the hour. In fact, he would be even more powerful than before. Especially if Vayne could magically free her, and then he would be more than a hero. He would be a saviour.

And eventually, the political candidate who garners the majority of votes.

Had McCallum thought this through? Did he understand that, if he was doing Vayne's bidding, he would take the blame? Kidnapping, assault on Eve. Perhaps this massive fraud, and the murder of Whitnall. Was that the idea behind it all? Miriam wasn't sure. But to cast all the blame on McCallum would take some very clever planning, and it was risky. Was Vayne as subtle as that? Nothing in his past indicated he was. Perhaps he had always intended for McCallum to take the blame, if he were charged. Did Dalmeny know that? But then, why had Vayne allowed the trial to proceed this far, if McCallum was to be set up as the stool pigeon?

She remembered Daniel's comments. His father had spoken to him about Vayne. If Thomas Pitt was interested in the case, then bigger, more powerful and far more dangerous issues were involved. Foreign influences? Treason? Daniel suspected that Vayne had lent large amounts of money to several people in the government, but it would take intensive research to prove it. If these men were in positions of power and entrusted with knowledge, and if they were beholden to Vayne for those loans, relying on him to keep their secrets, then this would change everything. She tried to push that thought away, but could not shake one reality: if there was no danger from outside parties, why was Thomas Pitt, the head of Special Branch, involved?

She felt the speed of the car, the pounding of fear in her chest. Was McCallum a part of this fraud? Or was he merely a tool? And did it make any difference to anything she could do?

She was cold, in spite of the warmth of the day. Cold, and yet suffocating inside this car.

She wondered how much of this was McCallum's own idea. Could he be the brains behind Vayne's rise to power, his accumulation of wealth, and whatever lay ahead. Were these two men friends? Allies? Partners? Was one of them using the other? Or were they equally manipulative, in their own way, and working towards the same end?

She looked at McCallum again. They were far outside London now, gathering even more speed on the open road, heading north. She saw that some of the tension was easing out of him, as if he had escaped the worst part. His shoulders were less hunched, and his hands lighter on the wheel.

Should she talk to him? Did it matter what she said? Was anything going to make a difference? Might speaking to him make the situation worse? The more she knew or correctly assumed, the more dangerous it would be for him to let her go. If she knew too much, if he felt she understood his weaknesses – or worse, Vayne's weaknesses – that might make it impossible for him to free her.

They were on a main road, still heading north, when he finally broke the silence, as if he felt compelled to speak.

'You're wrong, you know? All of you.' His voice was quite calm, as if they were merely two people taking a car ride together.

He seemed to require an answer. 'Are we?' she asked.

'Yes. You only see the moment, not the future. Vayne is a great man. He will do marvellous things for the country.' His voice sounded curiously empty, as if it were an echo of the real man.

Was this the real man speaking? The next thought struck her like a physical blow; first the awareness that you have been hit, then the rush of pain. He had said *will do*, speaking of future plans.

'Will do?' she said aloud.

'Yes. You can't stop him. No one can.' It was not pride in victory she heard in his voice, it was despair.

'Whitnall tried to stop him,' she said. There was no point in pretending now. 'Is that why you took me, and maybe killed Eve?'

His knuckles turned white when he gripped the wheel. His arms were shaking. The intensity in him frightened her. What was he terrified of? Vayne? The police? The law? That he had killed Eve?

For Miriam, this was her worst fear. It gripped her stomach until she found it difficult to breathe. She was so distraught, she felt choked by her grief.

Was that why McCallum was so afraid? He feared he had killed Eve, and would hang for it? If so, then he would have to kill her as well. She was a witness.

'Why?' she said suddenly. 'Why did you hit Eve so hard?'

When he answered, Miriam felt only shock.

'Vayne has my children.' His voice was so strangled he could barely get the words out.

'He . . .'

'If I don't keep you from taking the stand, my children will die. And as long as I have you, Pitt will do as he's told.'

For the first time in Miriam's life, she felt the dark mantle of death close in around her.

Chapter Twenty-Four

Rose Hunter was deep in thought as she walked towards the morgue, where she was hoping to see Miriam Pitt. It was too late to worry if anyone saw her, or what they thought. After this visit, she would find a taxi to take her home.

She had thought of something she had forgotten to ask, and it could be important. She could have phoned Miriam, but she welcomed the chance to get outside, in the fresh air. It was only a detail about the death of Whitnall. It mattered whether he was left-handed, or right-handed. Were they sure? Could they argue the point successfully, if Dalmeny were to say he was ambidextrous, which he might have been! It was a slender thread, but potentially a strong one. It was such a small detail, and required no special trip, but she felt compelled to go to the morgue and ask Miriam. Perhaps if there was a way to be sure, it could preempt any defence Dalmeny might come up with.

She stopped and looked around her. She was perhaps fifty yards from the morgue. As she stood on the footpath, the door to the morgue opened and a large man came out, dragging a woman with him. She was struggling, but she clearly had no chance against his superior height and weight. And, very clearly, his strength. At first, Rose did not recognise the woman whose face was turned away as she struggled. But when she stepped closer and saw that bright hair, she knew at once that it was Miriam Pitt.

The man forced Miriam into a black car parked at the kerb, then slammed the door and got into the driver's seat. Within seconds, the engine burst into life and the car pulled away, built up speed and disappeared around the corner.

Rose stood frozen to the spot for a few seconds, then ran into the morgue. There must be a telephone there! And where was Evelyn Hall? Had she reported this to the police already? Were they on their way?

Rose reached the door, hoping it was unlocked. She grasped the handle and broke out in a sweat of relief when she felt the latch disengage. Was it normally left open? Surely not. Anyone could walk in off the street!

She pushed the door wide and rushed inside. Walking quickly down the passageway, she read the large sign on the door: MORGUE. She pushed open the door and stepped inside. It was totally silent. There was no one there.

It was when she turned around that she saw the crumpled figure of Evelyn Hall on the floor beside one of the benches. There was a slowly widening pool of blood around her head, now matting her grey hair.

For a moment, Rose thought she was going to faint. Then she took a deep breath, and another, and crouched down beside the woman. She put out her hand, shaking very slightly, and touched Eve's cheek. It was warm. A little unsteadily, dreading what she might feel, she put her fingers to Eve's neck. There was a pulse, but Eve did not stir.

Rose got to her feet, a little dizzy for a moment. She steadied herself and looked around for the telephone. There must be one. Then she saw it. Who should she call first? The ambulance? The police? Ian Frobisher's name came at once to her mind. She picked up the phone and asked the operator to put her through to his station.

It was only seconds before someone answered.

'Ian Frobisher, please,' said Rose. 'It's urgent!'

Before she could catch her breath, he was on the line. 'This is Rose Hunter. I'm at the morgue where Mrs Pitt works. Mrs Pitt has been kidnapped! I saw it happen, but I was too far away to do anything!'

'Where are you now?' he demanded.

'At the morgue! And we need an ambulance! Dr Hall is unconscious on the floor, and she's bleeding heavily . . . from her head! But she's still breathing,' she added, hearing the desperation in her own voice. 'Can you come now? And send an ambulance immediately!'

There was only a moment's silence. 'Yes, an ambulance at once.'

She heard him call out to someone, mentioning the morgue, an attack, and the need for an ambulance.

He returned to the call. 'Are you all right, Mrs Hunter?' he asked.

'Yes, but—'

'Is there anyone else there with you . . . other than Dr Hall?'

'No.'

'Now listen carefully,' he said. 'Does the laboratory have a lock on the door?'

'Wait . . .' She put the telephone down and walked over to the door. It had a lock. Without thinking, she closed it firmly and turned the key, then went back to the telephone. 'Yes, it does, and I've locked it.'

'Good. Wait there. Don't call anyone else.'

'But my husband . . . and Daniel Pitt . . . he needs to know!'

'Someone will get word to them. Now listen, Mrs Hunter, I'll be at the lab quickly, as will the ambulance. And Mrs Hunter . . .'

'Yes?'

'Do not open the door unless you know who's on the other side. Do you hear me?'

'Yes. Yes, of course, I won't.'

'Good. And don't try to move Dr Eve. Leave the ambulance men to do that.'

'I understand,' she said.

'I'll see you very soon.'

She replaced the receiver and sat down. Now she was feeling cold and a little wobbly. The next minutes felt like hours.

She returned to Eve. There was still no movement. She lowered herself on to the floor and placed her hand on Eve's arm. She might not be aware of it, but it made Rose feel better.

She tried to think usefully, make some sense out of this, but her thoughts were filled with fear. What would happen to Miriam? If she had been here, arrived even minutes earlier, the man almost certainly would not have taken her, or struck down Dr Eve. And then it occurred to her that, had she been there, she could be bleeding on the floor as well.

What she should have done, or could have done, was irrelevant.

She would do anything now to help Dr Eve and Miriam, but what? These moments before the ambulance arrived might be the difference between life and death, but she knew that Ian Frobisher was right when he told her to do nothing.

She put her hand on Eve's shoulder. She was still breathing, but she hadn't stirred at all. Was she bleeding inside her skull, where no one could see it? She might not be doing Eve any good at all by sitting with her, but her presence was certainly doing no harm.

There was a loud, reverberating pounding on the lab's door. Before she could stand up, there were several more sharp raps. She ran to the door and was about to turn the key, when she thought to ask, 'Who is it?'

'Ian Frobisher, Mrs Hunter. And the ambulance is here, too!'

With a wave of relief, she turned the key and pulled the door open. Suddenly, she wanted to cry. Her eyes filled with tears of relief, and she wiped them away angrily. The ambulance men went past her, carrying a stretcher.

They went straight to Eve, dropping to their knees and trying to examine her wound without moving her.

One of them checked her pulse. 'Strong,' he said.

'Mrs Hunter?' Frobisher said gently. 'Can you tell me what happened? Exactly what you saw?'

'Is she going to be all right?' Rose asked one of the attendants, ignoring the questions.

'No way of knowing yet, ma'am. Gotta get her to hospital fast.'

Ian touched her arm. 'Mrs Hunter, what happened? And Miriam Pitt? Did you recognise the man who took her? Was she fighting him, or did she appear to go willingly? See what you can remember, please.'

'I'm sorry. I only saw her for a moment, but she walked awkwardly. He was gripping her by the wrist and dragging her across the road. He wasn't guiding her so much as yanking her. I only saw them for as long as it took him to reach the car and push her inside.'

'Have you ever seen him before? Any idea who he was?'

'I've never seen him before. At least, I don't think I have.'

'Can you describe him?'

She thought about this for a long moment. 'Quite tall, I'd say quite a bit taller than Gideon, so over six feet.'

'Anything else?' Ian asked.

'Next to Miriam he seemed very, very large. Broad shoulders. Oh, and I think he was a bit overweight.'

Ian nodded, and then something changed in his face. 'Mrs Hunter, was there anything distinguishable about him?' It was a long shot, but perhaps . . .

'Yes!' she said. 'Now that you mention it, yes! He had the thickest hair, wavy and dark. And there were streaks of silver at the front. My God,' she added, 'how in the world did I forget that?' After a moment she paused. 'You know him, don't you?'

'You've described Callum McCallum, Vayne's right-hand man.' He pulled on his lower lip, as if deciding how to proceed. 'Did you telephone anyone else?'

'You said not to!'

He smiled, but it was an acknowledgement of her obedience, no more. 'Very good. So, we can assume that anyone who knows about this is part of it.'

Rose watched his face, hoping to see optimism, but there was none. And how could there be? She could not expect him to make any promises about getting Miriam back safely, or catching whoever it was who had taken her . . . and possibly killed Eve as well. At the same time, she found it comforting that he was being honest with her. And also terrifying. She feared for Miriam's life. And Eve's, too.

'What about Daniel?' she said. 'He needs to know!'

'I'm going to his offices now,' Ian assured her, his voice gentle.

'I'm going with you!'

'Mrs Hunter, I'm not sure . . .'

'I'm going!' she repeated.

They watched as Eve was placed on the stretcher and carried out. It wasn't until the door closed that Rose realised her own skirt was covered with blood.

There was one thing that Ian Frobisher had not said. Rose understood it was too soon, but it might have helped. He did not say that everything would be all right, or even that any of it would be. She had hoped to hear this.

Squaring her shoulders, refusing to succumb to her light-headedness, she followed Ian Frobisher out of the lab, shutting the door, and the terrible images, behind her.

Chapter Twenty-Five

Daniel was sitting, watching and listening to Gideon Hunter question one of their witnesses. In the overall picture, he seemed to be what they knew him to be: a minor player. After a few choice questions, however, it became clear that he was Vayne's scheduling secretary. He knew everyone who came to his office. Hunter was polite in his questioning, and very clever in making the man understand his importance to this trial.

Daniel could see where the questions were leading, but he was sure that this witness was becoming aware of the pitfalls. He was loyal to Vayne. Beyond loyal, almost hero-worshipping. Getting him to reveal anything detrimental to Vayne's case was presenting a real challenge.

All thoughts of the trial were shattered when the doors to the outer room flew open and banged loudly against the wall. Everyone turned around, shocked by the sudden noise . . . and then the image before them.

Daniel heard the judge begin to protest the interruption, but then even he fell silent.

With one look, Daniel understood why.

Rose Hunter had come into the room, her clothing streaked

with blood. Even her face had a smear on it, and her hair was dishevelled and tumbling out of its pins.

Daniel looked at Gideon Hunter. The man appeared stunned, frozen in place. It was Daniel who shot to his feet and pushed his way out of the front row to rush towards her.

'My God, what's happened?' he demanded, oblivious of the court usher, or anyone else moving forward, either to help, or to prevent her from further disturbing the proceedings. He caught hold of her. 'Rose, are you hurt? Where? How badly?'

Rose caught her breath with difficulty, her chest heaving as she sought to speak. Her husband was suddenly there, holding her. Ian Frobisher was entering the courtroom behind her.

'My God, Rose, what . . . the . . . blood!' Hunter clasped her even more tightly.

'Oh, Gideon,' she answered, her voice cracking. 'It's not my blood, it's Dr Eve's!'

This time, it was Daniel who was stunned. 'Eve? And what . . . what about Miriam?'

Ian Frobisher placed a hand on Daniel's shoulder. Before he could explain, words spilled from Rose's mouth.

'He came to the laboratory,' she said, her voice coming in gasps. 'He knocked Eve senseless, but she's alive. At least, she was when—' She swallowed hard. 'At least, she was when they came and took her to hospital. But Daniel—' She turned to face him, her eyes filled with fear. 'Miriam's gone. He took her.'

Ian grabbed Daniel by both shoulders, as if to steady him.

'I saw it,' she went on, 'but I was too far away to do anything. I'm so sorry.'

'What . . . what did you say?' Daniel could not seem to get the words out.

302

'I ran into the laboratory and called the police. And then an ambulance came.'

Daniel felt choked by panic. He guided Rose to the closest seat. The woman who was sitting there quickly moved aside.

One of the ushers appeared with a glass of water, possibly taken from the judge's desk, and handed it to Rose.

She took it and drank a few sips, nodding her thanks to the man.

Gideon Hunter knelt beside his wife, his eyes wide with fear.

Daniel heard the judge's gavel banging sharply against the wooden bench. Was he calling for order? Not possible! He saw Dalmeny stand, and wondered what he was up to.

'Is there a doctor in the courtroom?' Dalmeny asked loudly, his words rising above the din of voices expressing concern, confusion, even fear.

Daniel felt a rush of gratitude, and then urged Rose to take another sip of water.

At first, Rose gestured, as if brushing it away, but then drank it slowly and carefully, several times nearly choking. She looked at Daniel's face; alarm filled her eyes.

'Who did this?' Daniel asked her, his voice begging.

'Mrs Hunter gave me a description. I believe it was McCallum,' Ian said to Daniel.

Daniel heard the words, but he was fighting the most violent panic he had ever experienced, so severe that he feared losing consciousness. He nearly turned to face Vayne, but could not.

'What?' Hunter asked urgently. 'McCallum? Are you sure?'

'What did he say?' Daniel asked Rose, and then looked at Ian. 'Why would he take her? And where?'

Rose took another deep breath. 'All I saw was him dragging Miriam, and then pushing her into a car.' She pressed her hand against her forehead. 'He must have thrown Eve down very hard. When I found her, she was unconscious and she was bleeding. I felt for a pulse; she was alive. The first thing I did was call Ian Frobisher. They – the ambulance men – took her away.' She struggled to gain control of her breath. 'They couldn't tell me anything, but their faces were very serious, as if she might not recover.'

'Did he leave any kind of a note?' Hunter asked. 'Asking for anything? Demanding something?'

'There was nothing,' Ian replied. He turned to Daniel. 'Even without a note, his message is clear. Either we find Vayne not guilty, or we'll not see Miriam again. He didn't need to spell it out.'

People seated nearby gasped, shifted in their seats. One woman began to weep, but not a word was spoken.

Daniel turned first to Gideon Hunter, and then Ian. 'I'm going after him, as soon as we have any idea which way he's gone.'

Ian nodded. 'Let's go to his office first. This was planned.'

Daniel knew that Ian was thinking as he spoke. His own mind was beginning to clear, and logic was replacing some of the intense fear. Ideas were taking shape. Malcolm Vayne, the judge, the entire legal system could go to hell. He had to find Miriam . . . nothing else mattered.

Daniel saw the fear in Rose's face. He wanted to help, but Hunter would take care of her; he needed to focus on Miriam.

'You think McCallum is doing this on Vayne's instructions?' Hunter asked Ian.

'Does that even matter?' Daniel shot back. 'Whether he is or isn't won't change the danger my wife is in!'

'I'll handle it at this end, Daniel,' said Hunter. 'You go and find her.'

Daniel grabbed Ian by the arm, his heart pounding with terror. 'Come on!' he urged. He was both surprised and dismayed when Ian refused to budge. 'Ian!'

'Slow down a bit,' said Ian, his voice calm.

From Daniel's perspective, it was too calm. 'Miriam's life . . .!'

'I know!' insisted Ian. 'But rushing around like madmen won't get us anywhere. We need to stop, think logically.'

Daniel began to argue, but saw that Ian was right. 'Tell me.'

Ian looked first at Daniel, and then at Hunter and Rose. Before he could speak, Dalmeny joined them.

'Do we all understand the ultimatum?' Ian asked, including Dalmeny in his question. 'Miriam was taken against her will.' He turned to Rose. 'Was she fighting him?'

Rose shook her head. 'I think she was doing as she was told . . . as far as I could see.'

'Clearly,' said Hunter, 'McCallum is saying it's Miriam's life against Vayne's freedom.'

'Conjecture,' said Dalmeny, and then held up his hands. 'Not to minimise the urgency of this,' he quickly added. 'But McCallum could be acting alone. Let's not so easily paint my client as the villain. So far, even the pathologists—'

'Would testify that Whitnall was murdered,' Hunter cut across him. 'If Dr Eve and Miriam were not about to give that testimony, then neither of them would have been attacked.'

When Ian confirmed that, indeed, Whitnall's death was murder, not suicide, Dalmeny closed his eyes.

'We need to hope McCallum contacts us,' said Ian. 'With one expert in hospital and the other taken God knows where, he's holding all the cards. And we have everything to lose, if we don't do as he says.'

Daniel realised he was gripping Rose's arm, and released it.

'You will have to testify against McCallum, when we catch him. In case you're anxious about this – feeling confused or afraid – it's best you make a sworn statement now, before your mind tries to blot out the traumatic events you've witnessed. Do you understand? Are you well enough to go to the police station with Ian and do that?'

Rose looked slightly taken aback. She was straggle-haired, and her face was blotched with traces of blood. 'Of course I understand!' she said, with only a slight catch in her voice. 'I'm not a child!'

'No, you're not,' Hunter agreed, smiling as he said it.

Daniel was sure that smile was to soften any irritation on Rose's part that she was being ordered about, although that was precisely what was happening.

'Make your statement,' said her husband. 'And then you're going to see your doctor.' Before she could respond, he said, 'And don't argue with me! I need to know you're safe and unharmed before I can turn my mind to helping find Miriam.'

That last remark seemed to be a turning point for Rose, who nodded without a murmur.

Daniel spoke briefly with Hunter and Dalmeny. The trial would continue, with Hunter handling everything for the prosecution.

Without conceding any points of law, and not allowing that Vayne knew anything about McCallum's behaviour, Dalmeny offered to give all the assistance he could, while implying that Vayne would do the same.

Ian nearly spoke, but held his tongue.

Daniel knew what his friend was about to say, and the control it took not to say it. The room was still full, although most of the spectators and members of the jury were unaware of the severity of the situation. He glanced over to where

Vayne was seated. The man's face was impassive. If he was part of this unfolding drama, nothing in his face gave that away.

Ian spoke quietly to Daniel, whispering reassuring words that one friend would give another. Despite his calm voice, everyone in that tight little circle was gripped by the emotional power of Rose's account.

Because Ian was not in uniform, he was receiving odd looks. Why was this man at the centre of such intense conversations? One of the ushers actually approached Daniel and asked if Ian should be escorted out. When Daniel quietly explained Ian's role, the man became wide-eyed and rushed off.

Ian left them for several minutes and then returned. 'I have men watching all the roads leading out of London. If anyone sees McCallum, they'll report back to me. They've been told not to approach him. We don't want to frighten him, or—' He stopped.

Daniel knew what had been omitted. Ian didn't want anyone to frighten McCallum, and perhaps force him into an act of violence against Miriam.

The judge banged his gavel once more. 'I have been extremely patient, since a woman is already injured. But would someone please approach the bench and explain!' He was looking directly at Gideon Hunter, but it was Ian who left the group and walked up to the judge.

'Excuse me, My Lord,' he said, and then introduced himself. 'The head pathologist, Dr Evelyn Hall, has been attacked and is unconscious in hospital. The assistant pathologist, Dr Miriam Pitt, has been kidnapped, it seems by Mr Callum McCallum, Malcolm Vayne's assistant. We're about to track them down, but it will take time. Dr Pitt – the wife of Daniel Pitt – is a hostage, and her life is at risk.'

Dalmeny approached the judge and started to speak, but he was instantly silenced.

'These proceedings are set aside for the time being,' said the judge. 'Return to the courtroom Monday morning, nine o'clock, and we'll see where we are.' And without waiting for the defence counsel's reply, he rose to his feet.

Daniel looked at Vayne. He couldn't decide if the look on his face was fear or triumph. Or perhaps something between the two.

Ian quietly thanked the judge. Now that Daniel was formally released from his prosecutorial role, they could leave the courtroom and begin their search for Miriam.

Before they could leave, the judge called Daniel back. 'You are released from your duty to the court, Mr Pitt, since you can hardly be dispassionate when your wife's safety is at stake.'

Before Daniel could thank him, he was silenced by a stern look.

'And,' continued the judge, 'if Mr Hunter requires any assistance, he need only call for it from his chambers. I will allow him time to do what must be done. As for the defence,' he added, gesturing towards Dalmeny, who took several steps closer, 'you will have ample time to accommodate yourself to the changed circumstances.'

'Thank you, My Lord,' said Dalmeny.

'And perhaps you will need time to, shall we say, rearrange your case, in accordance with these new events.' The judge turned back to Hunter. 'I imagine you will need to know how Dr Hall is progressing, and whether she will be well enough to give her testimony in person within the foreseeable future.'

Dalmeny rose to the challenge. 'My Lord, of course we all wish Dr Hall a complete recovery, but it could be a long one, and perhaps even incomplete. We cannot delay indefinitely. Justice delayed, you understand, is justice denied.'

'I am quite familiar with the Magna Carta, young man!' the judge snapped. 'As I have been since you were in short trousers. We will assume that Dr Hall will be fully recovered in a few days, and that Dr Pitt will be returned unharmed. And if there is any evidence that these events are tied into this trial, you can be sure there will be new charges, including, God forbid, one of murder!'

'Dr Hall is still alive!' protested Dalmeny.

Without thinking, Daniel said, 'But Richard Whitnall is not!' He immediately realised his gaffe and pressed his hand over his mouth.

'I will excuse that as the utterance of a man fearful for his wife,' said the judge. 'Otherwise,' he added, leaning very close to Daniel, 'we could be looking at a mistrial.' He stood tall, rapped the gavel again, and announced, 'Court is adjourned.'

Chapter Twenty-Six

Daniel moved in a daze of fear. Everything was both distant and at the same time suffocatingly close. The pain of loss wrapped itself around him like a nightmare of never-ending loneliness. And yet, through it all, as if lit up on a stage, he was aware of Ian Frobisher taking charge of what to do next.

They were preparing to begin their search, but in which direction?

'They could be anywhere,' Daniel said. 'Anywhere.'

Fergus Dalmeny was still in the courtroom. He walked over and had a quiet talk with Ian. Daniel tried to listen, but the two men were huddled together and speaking in hushed tones.

As Dalmeny walked away, Ian returned to Daniel's side. 'The north-east coast,' he said, a sliver of hope in his voice.

'How does he know?' Daniel asked, gesturing towards Dalmeny.

'He's met McCallum many times these past months,' said Ian. 'Including in McCallum's office. According to Dalmeny, his walls are covered with photographs of beaches and rugged coastlines. He said that his favourite place is the Northumbrian coast. It seems his family keep a small cottage there, within walking distance of the old Dunstanburgh Castle.'

'I know that place!' said Daniel, his eyes suddenly brighter. He glanced at Rose, expecting to see her share his optimism, but she looked so pale, perhaps emotionally bruised rather than physically.

Daniel was touched by this, and by her concern for Miriam. She wasn't worried about herself, but for the safety of his wife. That knowledge only strengthened his resolve to get out of the courtroom and on the road. He needed to push aside the sense of emptiness, of living life without Miriam, and channel his energy, his intellect, into finding her.

He suddenly realised that Ian was saying something to him. 'Sorry, what?'

'My car's outside. I have maps, money. Gideon Hunter is calling Bremner now. He'll contact all the police stations up the coast and they'll report back to him. I'll call him at regular intervals.'

'Oh God,' Daniel said. 'Marcus. I need to tell him.'

'Bremner will go to his home,' said Ian. 'We have no time to waste, he'll understand.'

It was a long evening, perhaps the longest of Daniel's life. Ian drove steadily till well after dark, with Daniel for the most part sitting silently beside him. At this time of year, it was after ten when night finally closed in. It did not come swiftly, rather a gentle settling of the shadows. In fact, so softly did it come that Daniel realised with surprise that the sky was glimmering, but not with the last of the sun, rather with a great arc of stars.

Miriam would love this endless sweep of light forever circling the earth. Could she see it? Could she see anything?

'Why Miriam?' he said, almost to himself.

'She would be a star witness against Vayne,' Ian replied.

'Does McCallum really believe Vayne is innocent? And not just of Whitnall's murder, but this whole fraud allegation. How could he believe that taking Miriam would somehow end in Vayne being found not guilty? Really, Ian, what does he hope to achieve, other than a few hours of madness. Or the noose?'

Ian did not answer. His attention was focused on what little traffic was on the highway. Not many cars, but they were moving at high speed.

Daniel stared out of the side window. Did Vayne even know that McCallum had taken Miriam? No matter what McCallum said, or how much he believed he was acting out of loyalty to his employer, he alone would be found guilty. Would he realise that, and understand the price he might have to pay for such a fearful decision? And why? Was he acting out of blind loyalty to Vayne? Or was there more to it?

They pulled into a small village and parked near the green. They had filled the petrol tank an hour ago and used the facilities, so this was solely for a brief rest. 'I could drive a bit further,' Ian told Daniel. 'But I'm losing my concentration.'

Daniel offered to drive, but admitted that his fear and anxiety might put them in danger.

They finally decided to check into the village inn. After a few hours' sleep, they would resume the search, refreshed and alert, early in the morning. Ian persuaded Daniel that they would make much faster progress in the daylight than driving on dark country roads at night.

Before they went to their room, Ian showed his badge to the innkeeper, who allowed him to call Bremner to see if there was any news.

Daniel paced the little parlour adjacent to the desk, unable to sit still. The moment Ian joined him, he asked, 'Well?'

He looked at Ian, who was clearly exhausted. His skin was pasty and his eyes were bloodshot. Despite concern for his friend, all he could think of was Miriam. Was she still alive? Were they on the right road, moving ever closer to finding her? Were they sure McCallum had come this way? And if so, how long ago? The last thing he wanted was to spend a night in this inn, wasting precious time that could be better spent searching for Miriam.

As if reading Daniel's mind, Ian replied, 'They're about two and a half hours ahead of us. McCallum must have a good car if he can cover that much distance. And yes,' he added, 'Bremner says we're on the right road. McCallum was spotted and is heading for the Northumbrian coast.'

They followed the hallway to their room. Inside, they found two beds separated by a low dresser. The dresser would remain empty, since neither Daniel nor Ian had taken the time to pack a bag.

They sat on their beds, but did not speak. Both men were clearly drained of energy. It had not only been a long day, but one fraught with the horror of Miriam's abduction, the attack on Evelyn Hall, and then the long, intense concentration required to drive hundreds of miles on a darkening road.

It was some support for Daniel, knowing that Ian understood better than almost anyone else his fears of losing his wife. In truth, Daniel had been feeling somewhat ashamed that Ian was involved in this hunt for Miriam. His wife had died from illness, not an act of violence, but the profound sense of emptiness had to be the same. Ian was no stranger to grief and loneliness, two emotional states that Daniel feared. What could he say that would help now? Acknowledge Ian's pain. No, that would be presumptuous, despite their long friendship.

'Thank you,' he said very quietly.

313

Ian looked at him, but said nothing.

'For being here . . . and doing . . . this.'

Ian nodded and offered Daniel a little smile.

'Do you want me to take a turn at the wheel tomorrow?' Daniel asked, relieved that his friend had understood the emotion behind his words.

This time, Ian smiled broadly. 'And trust you with a police car? If I have to, I will, but let's wait and see.'

Daniel returned the smile and added a little shrug.

'And thank you for asking,' said Ian. 'Now shut up and go to sleep!'

They slept uncomfortably for four or five hours, just long enough to clear their heads for the journey, and stop their limbs from cramping, and then started on the road again. The sun was just beginning to rise. It was too early for breakfast, and Ian had paid for the room when they checked in. They would have liked to sleep longer, but their minds were whirling, trying to grasp what had happened, and to make sense of it. And anyway, Daniel knew he could never sleep, not until Miriam was found . . . safe and well. Perhaps that was also true for Ian. He wondered what memories of grief were being reawakened in his friend.

They drove swiftly through the empty countryside, deep in ripening wheat, passing meadows with cows already making their way through the grass and towards the gates. They knew it was milking time.

It was a beautiful day. The dew was heavy on the grass that grew alongside the road, and the light was brilliant, sparkling on every rain-washed blade.

In small copses the trees were heavy with leaves, like green clouds resting in fields, rising above hedgerows, some bursting

314

with wild flowers. But the panic of yesterday evening was settling now into a hard kernel of fear. All the more need for reason. Action without thought was worse than no action at all. In truth, it was particularly dangerous.

As Ian drove, Daniel's mind pounded with questions. Why had McCallum taken Miriam to Northumberland? It was hundreds of miles from London.

Why? Reason it through. Think, for heaven's sake! What sense did any of it make? Was McCallum doing anything more than playing for time?

McCallum had definitely attacked Eve and taken Miriam, and it had been a vicious attack. Because Eve was a strong woman and a brave one; if she had been given any chance, she would have fought back. And with all the things in the laboratory that could have been used as weapons, she could well have found one.

But he had attacked Eve first, and disabled her, perhaps silenced her for ever. That had to be because the pathologist could prove that Whitnall was murdered. Daniel was certain that Miriam's first thought would have been to save Eve, stop the bleeding, do what she could to help. But she had been kidnapped.

Daniel could not avoid the thought that the real issue behind Vayne's trial was far bigger than financial fraud. What was it that his father, as head of Special Branch, was looking for?

Why did McCallum want Miriam? He had not made any demands in exchange for her release, at least not yet. Was he hoping to stop the trial? Or intending to compromise the prosecution case? Force them to call this witness, or ignore that one?

Daniel wondered if he was giving himself too much

importance. He was not even in charge. Hunter was. And he could continue perfectly well without Daniel.

A more obvious thought ran through his mind. When he stopped being so self-critical, he thought that perhaps the goal was to make Marcus withdraw the chambers from the whole prosecution. No, that would not work, unless the purpose was to ruin fford Croft and Gibson. And there was no real motive for that; it was too far-fetched. No, it had to be somehow linked to getting Daniel out of London. In a way, achieving that would make him a hostage, too.

Would Dalmeny be willing to exert pressure on Thomas Pitt to make him leave Vayne alone? That would allow Vayne free rein to do whatever he was planning, even if it was damaging to England. Once the head of Special Branch was involved, the potential harm was wide enough and deep enough to precipitate an international crisis.

Should Daniel call his father? Tell him where he was and why?

The case would be in the hands of the Northumberland police, who would make no connection with a trial going on in London, which was the other end of the world to them. Nor would a local murder committed in London raise any interest in the North. And certainly not in time to be of any use to Miriam.

Ian was following the main road. They came to a turn-off to the east, heading towards the sea. Ian stopped at the local police station, told Daniel to wait in the car, and called Bremner again.

He returned within minutes. 'Eastward, to the sea,' he said. 'McCallum is almost certainly heading for Dunstanburgh Castle. Most tourists go to Bamburgh, because it's still intact. Dunstanburgh is a wreck, on the very edge of the sea. Its dungeons are under the water at high tide.' His mouth twisted bitterly. 'Is he up here only to lead us far away from London? Or should I say *you*, and not us? I don't think I make any difference to this case, but you do. And even more importantly, Miriam does.' His voice choked for an instant. 'And Eve Hall may be dead. Or, if she recovers, no use to anyone. God! I want to see that bastard hang!'

That was the first time Daniel had ever heard Ian express such emotion. Like Daniel himself, Ian had followed the dictates of the law, sometimes with anger, quite often with pity. And, thank heaven, with satisfaction. He had never wanted to see the ultimate punishment. It seemed like an admission of defeat for society; it was an act of vengeance, a belittling of everybody.

'Or maybe the point is to implicate McCallum in the whole thing?' Ian mused. 'Is that the idea behind it? Let McCallum take the blame for everything? No,' he said, answering his own question. 'That's stupid. If Vayne were convicted, then McCallum would lose his job, and everything else he has worked so hard to achieve. Or is there something we've yet to discover, another whole thread to this tangled mess that we can't see?'

Daniel struggled to understand the purpose, the endgame. Could it be a chain of debt that his father had suspected but could not yet prove? Was his father right, and it was power Vayne and his associates were seeking, and not money for its own sake? That seemed far more likely.

Daniel thought of the names of the people involved in Vayne's property deals, the losses and debts, and the power already held by some of them. Would that explain his father's interest in them? Daniel already understood that this was far bigger than merely money. No amount of wealth could buy

Vayne high office, but the lack of it – a debt he owed to powerful people who wanted to see him rise in government, knowing they had a hold over him – that could be their investment in almost anything! Then there was no limit to what such influence might buy, piece by piece.

Was Fergus Dalmeny part of it? Or was he merely doing his job and defending Vayne the best way he could? Perhaps he was faced with trying to win an impossible case. In any courtroom battle, win or lose, it was his duty to defend his client. That was true, no matter what crime Vayne was charged with. But it was also true that Dalmeny could not lie to the court without putting his entire career in jeopardy. Was his part in the proceedings in any way affected, or even touched, by the truth? Theoretically, did Vayne's guilt or innocence even exist, until the jury returned their verdict?

Daniel wondered why Dalmeny had taken the case. If Vayne were found guilty, he would swear that he had not been defended adequately. Dalmeny's reputation would be unlikely to recover from such a setback.

If Vayne appealed, or demanded a retrial, then what? Did the government want the expense of further legal proceedings? And all the bad publicity! There would be a loss of confidence in the government, not to mention possible panic on the Stock Exchange.

Or did Dalmeny believe that Vayne was not guilty in law, even if some of his business practices were questionable? Daniel was beginning to think that Vayne was guilty, at least morally, of shady practices, skating close to the edge of dishonesty, but he was beginning to doubt that the fraud charges could be proved. Perhaps the greatest punishment Vayne would receive would be a fine. No doubt, a man like Vayne could find plenty of people willing to pay it for him.

A chilling thought occurred to Daniel. Was it possible that Dalmeny had hostages to fortune – loved ones that Vayne could punish easily, if Dalmeny failed to produce the desired verdict in court? Did he know, as surely as Daniel did, that Vayne was morally responsible for Whitnall's death, and possibly Eve Hall's as well?

When he was finally too tired to drive, Ian reluctantly turned the wheel over to Daniel. As the car raced forward, Daniel's hands ached from clenching the steering wheel. So many questions rushed through his mind. How long had McCallum been planning his moves? Were those plans hastily adjusted in light of Whitnall's murder? Or, in spite of appearances, with the opportunistic attack on Dr Eve and Miriam's abduction, was it all turning out as intended? Either way, it was clever, carefully planned, whether in haste or at leisure, with every cog falling into place.

'Did Vayne study all of us?' he asked, his eyes never leaving the road. 'It looks as if he was deciding which of us – Miriam, Gideon, you, me – posed the greatest threat. Did he wait until he knew us well enough to predict how we would all react? Or did he think on his feet?'

Ian stirred, and only then did Daniel realise that he had been half asleep.

'It looks as if we've all been played, right from the beginning, like chess pieces being moved according to someone's game plan,' Ian replied. 'But one thing is clear: taking Miriam hostage is intended to prevent our carrying on the trial against Vayne.'

Daniel nodded, without speaking. He focused on maintaining top speed. He did not know what he was going to do. But if the police thought Miriam was being held in

Dunstanburgh Castle, he must go there. The thought that she could be there, and he had not done everything possible to find her, was unbearable.

As he drove, more questions flooded his mind. What if McCallum knew too many of Vayne's secrets, and this was Vayne's way of blaming McCallum for everything, and using Daniel to get rid of him? Or Vayne's way of getting rid of Daniel? Or even both? But Daniel did not believe himself clever enough to pose so much of a threat to Vayne. To imagine that Vayne lived in fear of him suggested a deluded sense of his own self-importance.

But what about Thomas Pitt? Was Vayne getting to his father through hurting Daniel? That would be a believable answer. With all of his contacts, it was very possible that Vayne knew that Pitt was the head of Special Branch. It suggested that Vayne's ambitions, both foreign and domestic, were as grand as Thomas Pitt feared. Vayne had power, evidenced by the headlines in every newspaper in the country. If he were found not guilty, with the help of Dalmeny – and using Miriam's safety as leverage to effectively destroy the prosecution – Vayne could emerge as the hero. It was a story that would keep all his readers enthralled.

For Daniel, all of this was plausible. And he had walked straight into the trap laid out for him, blindly. But what alternative was there now?

Daniel realised he was so caught up in his thoughts that the car was losing speed as his foot relaxed on the accelerator. He told himself to pay attention. Also, it was time to stop for more petrol. Then they could get something to eat and be on their way again.

He drew into a place where he could park, and they both ate a sandwich without even noticing what it was, and downed a cup of tea. The little inn had a telephone, but it took some persuasion for the owner to allow Ian to use it.

Before he made the call to Bremner, Ian asked the innkeeper if a large black car had come through in the last few hours. He described McCallum, and was relieved when he was told that yes, the innkeeper remembered a man travelling alone. He was quite tall, and he seemed distressed. He bought two bottles of beer and two large sandwiches. And no, he had seen no one else. Ian described McCallum in more detail, focusing on the prominent silver streak in his hair.

No doubt, it had been McCallum.

Heartened by this information, Daniel picked up the pace to full speed, taking the narrow road leading to the coast.

They arrived at the ruins of Dunstanburgh Castle as the sun was sinking towards the horizon, splashing the incoming tide with brilliant scarlet ripples and shining patches of gold. The dark, ruined towers rose above the waves. There was a brisk wind coming in from the sea, spilling white spume, with some waves curling and crashing over the wreckage of the stone towers, sending foam up into what had once been the chambers and the great hall of the castle.

Daniel not only felt the chill of the sea breeze on his skin; he was cold to the bone.

Was McCallum somewhere around here? Was this what he had intended all along, for them to follow him so he could be on familiar ground, putting them at a disadvantage? If so, where was he? And where was Miriam? Despite the certainty that McCallum was nearby, Daniel feared it was all a trick, an empty distraction. But if not, what could McCallum possibly hope to gain from this now?

He parked and walked quickly towards the ruins of the castle, Ian keeping pace beside him. If McCallum and Miriam were here, they would not be at the water's edge. That was too exposed and, even on a balmy summer evening, too cold.

Daniel felt a wave of nausea that almost choked him. What if McCallum had killed Miriam already? He had distracted Daniel from Vayne's trial, forced him to walk out of the courtroom, abandoning Hunter. Was that all he really wanted?

'I'll go round,' Ian told him. 'Cut him off, if he's down at the water's edge.'

'Right,' Daniel agreed. He turned away. The wind was only cool, but it felt like ice on his skin.

There was a noise behind him. He whirled round. There was nobody there. He looked back again. There was movement, but no more than the motion of the sea, not sudden, but steady, rhythmic, the roar and crash of water rushing in, then being sucking back out again, a little further each time.

Then he saw McCallum. The man was standing near one of the towers that still remained. Before Daniel could respond, McCallum was walking towards him. There was no sign of Miriam.

They were alone. Ian was down below, on the sand.

Daniel stood his ground, waiting, trying to gather his thoughts. He was determined to appear calmer than he felt. McCallum had begun this; he must have some purpose in mind.

McCallum reached him and stopped, eight or nine feet away. He was a bigger man than Daniel had remembered. His face was impossible to read because the brilliant light of the setting sun on the water was behind him, the spume reaching higher with each wave.

'Where is my wife?' Daniel said loudly, above the roar of the water. 'What do you want?'

'Don't be stupid!' Callum McCallum shouted back, taking

322

a couple of steps closer. 'I want you to back off the case against Malcolm Vayne. He's a great man. He'll do wonderful things for the people of England, when he takes control.'

'Takes control?' There was more mockery in Daniel's voice than he meant there to be.

The idea was monstrous. Or was it? Money, fame, the belief that the rich, the unfairly privileged were against him, and that he was fighting for the ordinary man: these were powerful issues in any election. There were stirrings of change all over Europe, but especially in Spain and France. Daniel did not need to ask McCallum if he believed Vayne was part of it – it was plain in his face.

'Whatever your demands, first free my wife,' Daniel said, as firmly as he could. He felt his heart beating too fast. The light was growing pinker as the sun approached the horizon, and the wind was even colder. 'Where is she?'

'I'm sure that—' McCallum said, but Daniel cut him off.

'Now!' Daniel shouted. 'I must have her first, before we talk. How do I know she's still alive?'

'You don't.' McCallum's voice was strained.

He took another step towards Daniel. There were perhaps five feet of earth-covered rock between them, and behind McCallum were the weather- and time-ravaged towers of the castle, remnants framed by a reddening sky and the rising sea. Even the white spume of the breaking waves was tinged with pink.

'But she will be dead if you don't do as I say!' McCallum went on, taking another step towards Daniel.

His arms were hanging loosely by his sides, fists clenched. If he got closer to Daniel and grabbed him, he could break his back. Or, with a clumsy twist, his neck. He was moving closer.

Daniel refused to retreat. A step backwards would be seen as a moral retreat as well as a sign of physical weakness.

McCallum took yet another step forward. A wave crashed against the farthest tower of stone and shot a fan of white foam high into the air. It fell and was quickly dragged out by the undertow, only to be overtaken by another, bigger wave breaking against the ancient masonry.

McCallum lifted his shoulders and swung a powerful blow at Daniel.

The younger man saw it in time, ducked, and let the force of McCallum's own weight take the full impact of Daniel's fist on his chin.

McCallum was startled. He took two short, awkward steps, and then fell to his knees.

Daniel stood there, facing McCallum. Could he kick him, and hammer a foot against his jaw? If he was not accurate enough, he could leave himself open to attack. And in this long summer twilight, with the sun already touching the horizon and sending scarlet tentacles across the water, Daniel knew that the air would soon be colder and darkness would cover everything. He also understood that if McCallum landed even one blow on Daniel, with his weight behind it, it could be enough to finish him. It would throw him into the sea, into the surging water, and he would drown. And when questioned? McCallum could simply say that he had never seen Daniel! No one could prove him wrong.

McCallum was on his feet again, shoulders hunched as he mustered all of his strength, but he was balanced more carefully this time. He had the weight and the reach to beat Daniel, and they both knew it.

There was no point in shouting for help. Ian would never hear him above the roar of the waves. But Daniel was fighting not only for his own life, but for Miriam's. He pulled back and lashed out as hard as he could, putting his full strength into driving the toe of his shoe into McCallum's knee. He struck bone.

McCallum gave out a cry of pain and fell backwards, hitting his head on the rocks.

Daniel felt another wave of nausea. Had he killed McCallum? Then McCallum moved.

Daniel put his knee on the man's chest, but knew that he was not heavy enough to hold him down for more than a few moments. McCallum's desperation seemed to equal his own. What was the source of his loyalty to Vayne? A loyalty so great that he found the strength and passion to kill Daniel, someone he did not even know?

Daniel saw a large piece of driftwood, waterlogged, a dead weight. He leaned over as far as he could and grasped it, then raised it above McCallum's head.

McCallum saw the rage in Daniel's face, and their eyes met. 'Vayne will kill my children,' McCallum said between clenched teeth. His eyes were wild with despair.

Another wave crashed hard against the broken towers and roared over the half-ruined wall, swirling to within five feet of them.

Daniel had not considered this threat against McCallum's family. Was he telling the truth? Even so, his fears remained with his wife. 'Where is Miriam?' he shouted above the sucking, belching roar of the water that was rolling back out again. 'Tell me, and I'll let you go!'

McCallum's body tensed, as if about to throw Daniel off him. Daniel lifted the driftwood. 'Where is she?'

'I'll take you.'

'You'll tell me!'

McCallum suddenly looked like a man defeated. All anger left his face. 'She's further up the coast, you can see the cave from here. Get the hell off my chest! If you kill me, you'll never find her. She's in a tidal cave, you fool!'

'You were going to let her drown!'

'No, I wasn't! I was just supposed to get you out of London, then take your jacket, your identity, keep you hidden until everyone believed you were dead. That's all I had to do.'

Daniel saw no alternative. McCallum might be lying, but he might possibly be telling the truth. Maybe Vayne really was holding the man's children! And if what he said was true, Miriam was in one of the many caves that filled with water as the tide rose.

Gradually, he allowed McCallum to stand up.

The man turned and headed north, towards the caves, leading the way while Daniel stayed close behind him, holding the length of wood, just close enough to be able to strike McCallum hard if he turned on him.

They moved slowly, picking their way over the slippery rocks and smooth sea-worn stones. Daniel glanced behind him several times, but there was no sign of Ian.

They paused as they reached the edge of the swelling tide that was getting closer and deeper with every second.

He wondered if it was true, that every seventh wave was bigger and wilder than the others. The one racing towards them seemed to be. It was huge. The crest curled over them like an avalanche, crashing against them. Daniel was swept off his feet. The water was burying him, thrashing him and then crushing him, rolling him over and over. He was bruised, numbed, gasping for breath. He kicked, fighting the maelstrom. It felt as if the water was ravenous, eager to swallow him in the vast belly of the ocean.

Where was McCallum?

There was water everywhere. He didn't know which way to fight. He rose to the surface and gasped for air, then instantly was caught from behind by another monster wave, but it was the undertow that knocked the breath out of him. He felt its power, mixed with the taste of salt. Everything in his body hurt. Then, when he felt himself losing consciousness, he was lifted up, as if by a saving hand, and thrown clear.

He turned in time to see McCallum being dragged away from the rocks in the belly of a giant wave, sucking him out towards the open sea.

Daniel reached frantically to grab for him, but McCallum was already yards away, visible only when the trough of water swelled and heaved. And then he was pulled outwards, lifted higher, so high he was raised over the rim of the castle wall, the surge immensely powerful.

And then he disappeared.

Daniel found himself clinging to a ledge. He looked around, but McCallum was trapped somewhere inside the open jaws of a lurid, scarlet-infused wave, reflections of the sun sinking behind the horizon.

Daniel clung to the stones as the water drained away, pulling at him, tugging him from the flat edge towards the deep, undersea dungeons. The lowest of them would probably have been underwater even centuries ago, when the castle rose towering over the sea, guarding the Northumbrian coast. How many bones lay there now?

The tide was still rising. Where was Ian? What had happened to him? They must find Miriam and get out of here! He was able to regain his footing, but only just in time, the tide rising rapidly around him.

He ran as fast as he could, jumping over stones, tripping

and slipping over the tussocky grass, shouting Miriam and Ian's names, only to have the words snatched from his lips as if he were screaming into a void.

Where the hell was Ian? Had the sea taken him, too? The thought was unbearable. Everything was out of control. Destroying lives as surely as if the ocean had covered them all. The darkness was complete inside him.

'Miriam! Ian!' He shouted as loudly as his lungs would let him.

Nothing but the oppressive darkness of the sky and the thundering of the waves.

He was on a beaten path now, and it was leading to the heart of the ruins. He tried to run, but his legs felt heavy.

Suddenly, a car was beside him, screeching to a halt. The driver's door swung open.

'Get in!' Ian shouted. 'The caves are over there.'

In the fading light, Daniel could barely make out Ian's face. He stumbled, grasping at the door handle as relief washed over him. The metal felt solid in his grip. He scrambled into the car. Before he could slam the door closed, he felt the force of the wind whipping around the exposed coastline.

'Hang on!' Ian shouted above the noise. 'You all right?'

'Yes, but McCallum is gone.' Daniel looked at the darkening sky. 'Got to find Miriam, before the tide—' He could not finish that thought.

Ian put his foot down hard on the accelerator, while releasing the clutch so quickly that he almost choked the engine. He took a deep breath, tried it again, this time smoothly. The car rolled back on to the little road.

They drove dangerously fast towards the caves. They were visible as dark openings in the cliffs, carved out with hollows and tunnels. Ian drove as close to the water as was safely possible.

When they arrived at the caves, he killed the engine and they rushed towards what was left of the ancient structures.

Ian waved his arm in one direction and lunged into the nearest cave entrance, while Daniel went to the next. It took him three attempts before he could wade into the rising tide, desperate to find Miriam before it was too late. But there was no sign of her.

Desperately calling out her name, he clambered over rocky outcrops and past several caves, the daylight nearly gone. He had his back to the sea, to the last of the daylight fading over the hill.

And then she was there, her face white with fear, her arms and legs bound to the roots of an old tree, the rising water well above her waist. In minutes, it would be over her head.

'Miriam!' he shouted. 'Oh God, Miriam!'

She hesitated, frozen, and then realised that it was Daniel's outline against the last streaks of light on the water. 'Daniel!'

She drew a shivering breath as he worked to release her from the ropes. And then she was clinging to him, as if she were drowning and he her last hope.

He clung to her exactly the same way, as if he would never let her go.

Chapter Twenty-Seven

Daniel had thought he would sleep without even moving, but he woke every hour or two, dreaming of the sea, darkness, and haunting thoughts about the loss of Miriam. But she was there, in his arms, in their little room at the inn. He could feel the warmth of her against his body. And she was breathing; he could feel it because he checked often.

Unlike Daniel, she was soundly asleep, without even stirring.

Finally, he was in such a deep sleep himself that he didn't hear the knock on the door, until it became hard, insistent. He got up and went to answer it, demanding to know who it was before he unlocked it. He recognised Ian's voice and pulled the door open.

Ian stepped in. 'Are you all right?' he asked. He glanced towards the bed, and Miriam, who had not stirred.

'Yes, thank you. Just tired. And you?'

'I'm fine,' Ian replied, but the weariness in his voice and the pallor of his skin betrayed his words as a polite lie.

'Did you sleep?' Daniel asked with concern.

Ian had done all of the driving, not stopping until they had found this inn.

Daniel knew that the near loss of Miriam had reminded

Ian of his own, irretrievable loss, and his responsibility for the little girl growing up without her mother. But Daniel could think of nothing at all to say that was sufficient to express the depth of his emotion and convey that he was mindful of Ian's loss, at least. 'Thank you,' was all he finally managed. It was insufficient, but better than silence.

'You'd better get up and eat something,' Ian said. 'McCallum's body hasn't been washed ashore yet. It may never be. Or it could wash up somewhere else. But I called last night to tell Bremner that we've got Miriam, that she is safe, and that McCallum is dead.' His face looked even more vulnerable and weary. 'McCallum wasn't lying about Vayne having his family. We got them out safely, but it was a messy business. Nothing to prove they were Vayne's men keeping them locked away, and they are not likely to say anything. Someone will have to tell his wife and three children that he's dead. We'll be sure to say that he died in order to save them, and I suppose that's true.'

'What about Marcus?' Daniel asked.

'He was called minutes after Bremner learned that Miriam was safe.'

Daniel nodded. He could not imagine what agony Marcus must have been going through after he learned of his daughter's abduction.

'I hope to hell we get Vayne,' Daniel said, with some force. 'He blackmailed McCallum and was ultimately responsible for him being drowned. I suppose that's better than having him hanged. I never thought I'd say it, because I don't think that hanging is the answer to anything, but I'd like to see Vayne on the end of a rope!' He wondered if he'd repent of his words later. But for now, he meant them.

'Is Miriam well enough to travel?' Ian asked, looking beyond Daniel to where Miriam lay, still asleep.

'Yes. At least, I think so,' Daniel said tentatively.

'Good. I'll finish up here. I've spoken with the local chief inspector, and they'll put you on the train in Newcastle. There's one straight through to London. You'll be home long before dark.'

'Train?' Daniel shook his head, but it was a relief. No more driving on the open road, trying to stay awake. Home tonight! 'What about you?'

'I'll tidy up here, sort things out, and explain fully to the locals what we were doing here at all. I've told them Miriam is a pathologist, and that she was kidnapped to prevent her from testifying in court, and that she must get back to London. They can take my word for it, or check with Bremner if they want to. Also, I'll telephone Miriam's father and reassure him that she's unharmed. I've called your father and filled him in. So, all you need to do is get up, get dressed, and let the police here drive you to Newcastle and your train home.'

Daniel thought quickly. It all sounded so easy. 'I don't know that I've got the fare for the two of us, all the way to London. I didn't even think of that when we left, and—'

'Of course you didn't,' Ian cut him off. 'The police will understand that. I should be able to get home by tomorrow morning.'

'But the fare . . .'

'I'll settle that here, and don't look like that! It's on the police, this time. Now, get Miriam up and have some breakfast. I left you as long as I could, but you need to move it, if you're going to make the train.'

'Thank you,' Daniel said, but it seemed so inadequate. He hesitated, there were no words big enough to carry the weight of all he felt.

Ian shrugged and patted him on the shoulder. It was a

332

gentle gesture, and Daniel knew that it conveyed all he meant. He turned and went out of the door, calling again, 'Get a move on!' Then he added, 'Oh, and Bremner called the hospital. Eve Hall is still alive, but they can't say yet if she will make a full recovery. Now, get on with it.'

Daniel and Miriam were able to catch the train to London, albeit with only minutes to spare. Neither of them was moving quickly; the events of the past forty-eight hours had drained them of energy, leaving very little in reserve.

They settled into their compartment, happy to be together, and in a warm, enclosed and safe place. There was one other passenger, an elderly woman who had tucked herself into a window seat and was focused on the goings-on outside.

Miriam moved as close to Daniel as possible. 'We need to talk,' she said, her voice a whisper.

'You're here, you're alive. What more is there to discuss?'

She took his hand. 'A lot, Daniel. McCallum told me things in the car, and then even more when he had me in that cave.'

'He did? Why would he do that?'

She gave him a crooked smile. 'If I were to guess, I'd say he assumed I'd die and take his secrets with me.'

Daniel could only respond with, 'Oh.'

Over the next hour, she revealed all that she knew. How Vayne had ordered Whitnall's death, and how he had paid off the debtors of the man who had attacked Nadine Parnell. She also knew that Vayne found himself in terrible straits with his Big Ben investment fund.

As Daniel had deduced, Vayne had lied about the investments, yet continued to take money from unsuspecting investors. The only way he could cover the fraud was to deposit large sums into the Big Ben account. He went to the

Seebach Group for that, and they were happy to comply. The more they gave him, the more indebted he was to them. But there was another motive for them. If they kept Vayne out of trouble, and put money into his campaigns, they were certain he would rise quickly in the government. With war being talked about daily, they saw Vayne as someone who would direct lucrative contracts their way. And it didn't matter to Vayne who these men were – hostile Germans, neutral Swiss, or anybody else – as long as they kept him in power and out of prison.

There was another factor that Daniel already knew. In addition to borrowing money, Vayne had also lent money. The recipients were key men in the British government, banking, or industry, who dared not borrow through the standard institutions. Why? Because their debts were related to gambling, mistresses, even extortion. These men were forced to pay enormous sums to support their public image as honest, God-fearing husbands and civic leaders.

So many influential men were beholden to Malcolm Vayne, and Malcolm Vayne was beholden to so many influential men. It was like the shape of a pretzel, twisting and turning, with the ends never actually coming together.

Daniel took notes as Miriam related this information. There was too much to trust to memory, and not a single part that could be omitted.

When she was finished with her lengthy description, Daniel slipped his arm around her shoulder. 'You've just made our case. When the jury hears this, Vayne can't possibly be acquitted.'

'Please heaven, that's true,' she whispered.

Daniel and Miriam arrived in London mid-evening. It had been a long train ride, practically the whole length of England.

As much as they longed to nest in for the night, there were two visits that were necessary.

Miriam insisted on driving, and she was more confident than Daniel had expected.

She gave him a flashing smile. 'Have no fear, I'm in charge of something again,' she said. 'Back to normal.'

He understood and smiled back. There was everything to say, and nothing. It was there in a touch of the hand, a meeting of the eyes.

They pulled up to the kerb in front of Marcus fford Croft's house. Before they could open the car door, he was walking towards them. They exchanged hugs, words of thanks, and Marcus insisted that they come inside.

'We can't,' explained Daniel. Before Marcus could protest, he placed his hand on the old man's shoulder. 'Tomorrow, I promise.'

Marcus didn't look pleased, but it was clear that he understood. They were on the brink of sending a vile man to prison, and this had to be their priority . . . for now.

Miriam gave her father a long and comforting hug, then followed Daniel to the car.

As they drove away, Daniel saw that Marcus was still outside, watching them. A father who loved his daughter.

After a short drive, they arrived at Gideon Hunter's house. It was late to call by, especially uninvited, but that was irrelevant. What mattered was that they had to appear in court on Monday morning, and they had to give him a full account of what had happened, what they had learned, and what Ian had accomplished. It was possible Hunter would need to call Bremner, who was prepared to testify if necessary.

Hunter himself opened the door. He looked pale. The lines of strain around his mouth were deeper, but although he was obviously tired, he invited them in without hesitation.

Rose came into the hall as she heard their voices. She tried to hide her relief at seeing them, or at least disguise it, but she could not. She was genuinely thankful and delighted to see Miriam alive and well. The women embraced, and there was relief and joy in their reunion.

Daniel watched them and saw tears in their eyes. He fought hard to restrain his own tears.

It took several minutes before all of them were fully composed.

'We are losing the case,' Rose said quietly, leading them into her gracious living room. She gave a brief smile towards her husband. It seemed to reflect apology, grief and possibly a little guilt.

'It's slipping away from us, Daniel,' Hunter admitted. 'We can paint all sorts of pictures of greed, deviousness, extravagance, but every time Dalmeny manages to water it down, explain it and suggest that all witnesses against Vayne are motivated by their own political ambitions, or envy, or even just ordinary misunderstanding. We don't have proof of anything.'

'I think we can change that,' said Daniel, feeling heartened when he saw both Rose and Gideon suddenly alert, hopeful.

Over the next hour, Miriam revealed all that she knew about Vayne ordering Whitnall's death and the attack on Nadine Parnell. She explained how it had begun long before that, when Vayne had found himself in terrible financial straits with his Big Ben fund. She outlined his dealings with the Seebach Group, and how they were more than happy to lend him money. They knew that if they kept him out of trouble, and in favour with the public, his place in government was practically guaranteed. As for Vayne, he didn't care who these men were – friends of Britain or, with the possibility of war being talked about daily, potential enemies of the state – as long as they kept him out of prison . . . and in power.

Hunter understood this, and had discussed Vayne's suspected foreign connections when preparing the case against him with Daniel, but this was the proof he needed. 'I didn't have the full picture until now,' he said quietly. 'But it explains everything.' He shook his head and his face was tight with strain.

'Who have you still to call to the stand?' Daniel asked earnestly. 'We must think. Things have changed, since McCallum can no longer testify. The man is dead. At least, that is the only reasonable conclusion, since I saw him swept out to sea. Whether his body will ever come ashore is uncertain.' He sank back in one of the deep armchairs. 'And if a body does wash up, it will have been ruined by the sea, and there may not be any identification on him.'

Daniel looked at Hunter for a long moment. 'It's your decision,' he said. 'And I'm sure Dalmeny will enjoy bringing us up on ethics charges.' After a moment he added, 'But seriously, you'll have to call me to the stand. I'm the only one who saw McCallum swept away, and my word is the only evidence that he is dead.'

Hunter shook his head. 'I wish I didn't have to, Daniel. McCallum knew everything, and now only Miriam has that information. I'm afraid that without McCallum here to argue his case, most of Vayne's wrongdoing – if it can be proved to exist – can all be blamed on him.' He looked bleak.

It flashed through Daniel's mind that Hunter had been carrying this entire case alone for two days, not knowing what had happened to Miriam, or to Daniel either. The trial had been adjourned temporarily but it was only a brief delay before the battle was rejoined, and Hunter needed to have his ammunition ready.

'But McCallum's absence can be interpreted in several ways,'

Hunter went on. 'And Dalmeny has the wind behind him now. I don't know if he is relying on McCallum coming back . . . but maybe not? Either way, he's an excellent person to put all the blame on, poor devil. There's got to be a way around this, but—'

'We're losing, aren't we?' Daniel said, echoing Rose's concerns. He looked directly at Hunter, who had grief written across his tired, almost bruised-looking face.

'Yes,' Hunter admitted simply. 'Dalmeny seems to have an answer for everything. I've got a witness I'm not looking forward to questioning, and I hope I won't have to.'

'Who?' Daniel asked. How could they lose a case when they had gathered so much evidence against the man charged? He looked at Hunter. 'Who?' he repeated.

'Mrs Agnes Ward,' Hunter replied. 'She and her husband put all their savings into Vayne's investment company. Harry Ward had a degenerative disease and knew he would not be able to work much longer. They lost everything. He died, and now she has absolutely nothing.' His voice cracked as he said it. 'I know it's an emotional play, but we've been talking about facts, figures, money, all of them numbers on a page. I want the jury to see what that kind of theft actually means, in poverty, shame, hunger and heartbreak. In destroying people's lives.' He glanced at Daniel, as if daring him to criticise.

'And don't forget me,' said Miriam. 'I'm the one McCallum confessed to. I realise that I'm in a strange position, being the wife of junior counsel for the prosecution, as well as a pathologist working on this case, but perhaps former co-workers, professors and the like can testify to my honesty and integrity. If the jury accepts me, they'll be told every aspect of Vayne's deceptions.'

Daniel blinked and swallowed hard. He still feared for

338

Miriam's safety. And as for this Mrs Ward, they had to have better arguments than emotional testimony. Dalmeny could argue as passionately as the best of them.

'We haven't received the medical evidence regarding Eve yet,' Daniel reminded them. 'With Miriam back, she can describe how McCallum attacked her. My testimony that McCallum admitted to me that it was Vayne's command to hurt her won't be any good. I'm the prosecution, and I'm too close to all of this.'

'But I was there!' insisted Miriam. 'And I saw it all first-hand. And McCallum made it clear that he was doing this for Vayne.'

'The judge might rule it as being biased testimony,' said Hunter. 'That is, McCallum could have kidnapped you for a dozen reasons that don't involve Vayne.' Despite these new possibilities, his voice remained flat, as if anticipating defeat.

'Evelyn Hall is still unable to testify,' said Daniel. 'She's conscious, and it seems she's out of danger, but it will be some time before she can take the witness stand.' He looked agitated, and yet determined. 'But Miriam is here now, and she will testify. She saw the attack on Eve, and she herself was kidnapped by McCallum.' He turned his eyes to Rose. 'And you saw him drag her out of the morgue and push her into his car. Miriam can also testify to his taking her all the way north to Dunstanburgh, where he tied her up in a cave, which is under water at high tide. Ian Frobisher and I rescued her. He has stayed in Northumberland to handle the final details, but he will be back soon.'

Hunter stared at him, a flash of hope completely altering his expression.

'Added to that,' Daniel went on, 'somebody was holding McCallum's wife and children hostage. McCallum was told to take Miriam, or his family would be killed. He told both of us that, and I believed him. And Sergeant Bremner was told the same, by Mrs McCallum, when he led the rescue. We can prove it. If we play this right, we've got Vayne.'

That flash of hope became a positive light in Hunter's eyes.

Miriam turned to look at Daniel. 'Do you think McCallum meant to come back and testify? Or did he know that Vayne was going to blame everything on him?'

Daniel reached out his hand and touched her gently. 'I'm the only one who knows what happened to him, and I can't prove it. I drove north to get you. Dalmeny knows that, and he knows that I was following McCallum, but what I say in court is another matter altogether.'

She shook her head very slightly. 'You're going to tell them about the fight? But then,' she added, 'you can't prove that he attacked you.'

'No,' he agreed. 'Not unless I'm specifically asked. And then . . . I don't think Dalmeny will ask me, but I won't lie.' He gave a little grimace. 'The truth is on our side.'

There was a rueful smile on Miriam's lips, as if she understood. She would never lie about forensics. Honesty was part of their character, something they shared.

He turned to Hunter. 'You must let Miriam testify. And Dr Eve, if she is well enough.' He turned to Rose. 'Have you seen her? How is she?' He should have asked earlier. He had been so badly frightened by the danger to Miriam, he had not even thought of Eve, and now he was ashamed.

Rose smiled a wry, sweet smile of understanding. 'She's making a good recovery, but it will take time. She's still in considerable pain – when he hit her, she struck her head against a very hard surface. But she's mad as a hornet. If she's able to take the stand, and if you pit her against Dalmeny, he may not survive.'

340

'As long as he survives long enough to see Vayne go down, I'm happy with that,' Daniel retorted.

'What do you think we should do?' Hunter asked Daniel. 'Should I put you on the stand so you can tell the jury where you've been, and why?'

Daniel smiled. 'It's far wiser, and less dangerous, to tell what we know, and do so as soon as we can. In any case, we can only afford to reveal what the jury will believe. Don't swamp them with too many details.' He was speaking what seemed to him to be the truth, but he looked quickly at Hunter to see if he agreed. Hunter was now the leading counsel of fford Croft and Gibson, and it would be both clumsy and rash for Daniel to forget it.

'I don't know whether we can win,' Hunter said, seeming to choose his words with care. 'But I do know we must try. Can we find Vayne guilty in law? I want to think we can. But I'm almost positive that we can paint him as being morally guilty. Whoever actually murdered Whitnall, it was ordered by Vayne, and it was a brutal crime, one which the law cannot overlook.'

'This might sound strange,' said Miriam, also choosing her words carefully. 'But I have a strong belief that it was Vayne himself who killed Whitnall.'

'Based on what?' Hunter asked, incredulity in his voice.

'McCallum was insistent that he didn't do it,' she said. 'He didn't come right out and say it was Vayne, but the suggestion was certainly there. Of course, if Vayne is accused, it will take no effort to put it off on to McCallum. And it's very convenient that the man isn't here to defend himself.'

'Which we will point out,' Hunter said gravely. 'A lesson to the jury, and more importantly, a lesson to his other employees and admirers. For him, loyalty is a one-way street.'

'I believe that,' Daniel said, with conviction.

'It's our job to make the jury believe it,' Gideon insisted. 'If we can think of a way. If we don't take risks now, it may be too late.'

Rose put out her hand and placed it on her husband's arm. Daniel looked at Miriam and saw her smile. He stood up. 'I think we need a night's sleep, in our own bed.'

'Will you be all right?' Hunter asked anxiously.

'Of course!' Miriam answered before Daniel could. 'And Gideon, stop worrying. This will be the final showdown! Not only am I not going to miss it, I'm going to be part of it – and with first-hand information.' She glanced at Daniel, then at Hunter. 'We'll get him!' she declared.

Daniel had thought he would sleep longer and more deeply that night, possibly without even turning over. He surprised himself by lying awake far longer than he had imagined, running through his mind every angle on which the case might turn, and how they could ultimately snare Vayne in his own web of deceit. And then, there were images of Miriam in the cave, and how close he had come to losing her.

He fell asleep thinking he had the answer to this case, and then woke again, his head filled with new ways it could all go wrong. Each thought beat a jarring rhythm in his mind. He slept, solved the enigma, or thought he had, and then woke again. It was a cycle that continued until morning.

He was finally sound asleep when he heard the alarm clock ringing on the bedside table.

'Sorry,' Miriam said gently, bending over him. 'I have to get up now. Marcus is going to get Eve. She talked the doctor into releasing her, and now she insists on being in court. But we have to be there soon, which means a quick breakfast. Oh, and then allow time to navigate through traffic. We mustn't be late.'

'I know,' he said, making half an effort to turn over on to his back.

It felt like the middle of the night, even though the bright sunlight was coming through a crack in the curtains, and it was clearly daylight outside. His head was pounding, and he felt bruised all over. Even to move at all reminded him of the beating McCallum had given him.

'Cup of tea,' Miriam said. It was not a suggestion. There was a note of anxiety in her voice. 'Hot bath, shave, breakfast, then out the door. You'll feel better.'

He stared at her. She had fared far worse than he had, yet her voice was clear, sure. She had been McCallum's prisoner for two days, whether he had meant to kill her or not. Her face was still showing signs of the strain, highlighted by deep shadows under her eyes and bruises that no make-up could conceal. Her bright hair, usually carefully coiffed, was in a hopeless tangle.

He put his hand up and gently pushed the hair away from her face. 'We are going to expose mistakes today. All of them, but particularly Vayne's.' He smiled. 'If you can't get the tangles out of this, wear a hat!'

She laughed. 'I'll brush it, don't worry, but first I'll have a cup of tea, and a couple of aspirin.'

'How are you?' he asked.

'Cold and stiff, like you.' She smiled a little lopsidedly.

'Then I'll dress,' he answered. 'I promise I'll look alive and intelligent by the time we get to the courtroom. That ought to put Dalmeny off his stride,' he said, with a smile.

They arrived at the Old Bailey. At the entrance to the courtroom, they parted, with Miriam waiting in the anteroom.

Since Daniel intended to call Miriam as a witness, it was better that she not hear the evidence before she gave her own.

Hunter was waiting. 'I should have thought to send someone for you,' he said. 'Is Miriam better? Last night, she looked exhausted.'

'She's fine,' Daniel replied. 'She's pretty tough.' He said this, and he meant it, but his words could not erase thoughts of what might have been.

Hunter nodded and smiled, then looked around.

'She's out in the hall,' Daniel said. 'We don't want to contaminate her evidence.'

'About being kidnapped and nearly drowned? God help us, if that doesn't shock a few people, I can't think what would! Of course, Vayne will deny it all.'

'Hard to prove,' Daniel answered. 'But it's a damn good piece of courtroom drama.'

Hunter's sombre face broke into a great smile. 'We'll give it the best we have!'

'We certainly will!' Daniel responded, and gave a silent prayer that they would live up to that promise.

Chapter Twenty-Eight

Thomas Pitt was up very early on the Monday morning after Ian Frobisher had telephoned to say that Daniel and Miriam were both safe, and would return home by train that evening. Ian also told him that McCallum had been swept out to sea in the area around Dunstanburgh Castle, and was assumed dead, and that his family, held hostage by Vayne's men, were now being rescued, with Ian's second-in-command Bremner in the lead. Pitt would be informed when the rescue was complete, and then he would be free to do whatever he wished with regard to his professional concerns.

Pitt thanked him profoundly. He was unprepared for the wave of relief that broke through the intense, painful self-control he had been exercising. He had to do his job. Personal emotions did not excuse mistakes, absences, or any other lapse of concentration. If he could not meet that standard, then he should not have accepted the task. That would be letting down Narraway, his mentor and friend until his death a few years ago. And he would be letting down his own family, too.

Charlotte believed in him. She loved him, despite knowing his weaknesses as well as his strengths. The worst day of his life had been when she was kidnapped and held captive, with the threat of a violent death. He remembered only too well the fear he had felt; he was certain Daniel had felt the same when Miriam was in danger.

But Miriam was safe now, and Daniel, too. When he had thanked Frobisher, tears of gratitude all but choked him. He had told Charlotte, of course, instantly. They had held each other close, tightly, but at last had given in to exhaustion and slept.

Now it was morning, six o'clock, but broad daylight. It was the start of a new week. Events were moving swiftly. He needed to focus on doing his job, and there was no time to lose. Today, he had to face the most powerful ministers that had been compromised by Vayne, and it had to be done before Vayne's case could reach a verdict. It would not do if the jury acquitted him! He was guilty of fraud, leaving in dire straits so many people who had trusted him and believed in his promises. Vayne was clever, and he might still manage to put the blame on someone else. Now that McCallum was dead and could not defend himself, or for that matter betray Vayne, he was the ideal candidate to take the fall.

Pitt knew that Fergus Dalmeny was also clever, and could point the finger at McCallum. Had McCallum known the extent of Vayne's fraud, or what it was intended to accomplish? Possibly not, but as Vayne's right-hand man, he was certainly in a position to be privy to all of it. That is, as much as Vayne was prepared to reveal.

Pitt wondered what would have happened if McCallum were to take the witness stand now. It was a natural temptation to deflect blame away from the people one most trusted. Overlooking a few facts was simple enough to do. He might have thought himself mistaken, if those facts apparently added up to fraud. Pitt was quite sure that loyalty would have played

346

a part, and that McCallum might have found many excuses for Vayne's behaviour.

But now McCallum was dead, and his family had been held hostage until they were finally freed by the police. If he had been able to take the stand now, this case might have ended with Vayne's conviction.

This might still happen, but Pitt had his doubts.

Pitt had heard a rumour, not yet mentioned in court, that Vayne had offered to pay back some of the money lost by his investors. If he did this, he would undoubtedly emerge a hero, acquitted by the jury, which would make his chances of being elected to public office all the more achievable.

Was it conceivable that this had been Vayne's reserve plan all along, if he were to find himself caught up in the web of this fraud? Pitt thought yes. Yes, it could very well have been. He was clever enough, and malevolent enough, to conceive such a plan. Deny guilt, then point the finger at McCallum, the scapegoat who could not defend himself.

Pitt reminded himself again that he must act quickly this morning, before Vayne had a chance to testify. In fact, before the court had even assembled.

He was at the Minister's office at nine o'clock. He went alone, because he did not need assistance for what he was about to do. It was unpleasant, but it was absolutely necessary.

'The Minister will see you at ten fifteen, Sir Thomas,' his senior secretary said apologetically. 'He has an appointment in five minutes.'

'I must see him now,' Pitt replied quietly. This confrontation was growing embarrassing, even tragic. But it was also unavoidable.

'I'm sorry, sir, I can't do that. The Minister——'

'This is not a suggestion, Moncrieff,' Pitt said quietly. 'I'm sure you would wish this done as discreetly as possible. Go downstairs, and tell whichever staff member needs to know that the Minister is attending to an emergency.'

'Sir?'

Pitt stared at the man levelly. As far as he knew, this man was not involved in any of the darker aspects of this issue. 'Don't jeopardise your career, Moncrieff, just go.'

Moncrieff's face lost all its colour; he looked mystified. Pitt believed he knew nothing of the connection with Vayne. His own information indicated as much. He waited while the seconds ticked by.

'Yes, sir,' Moncrieff said at last. 'Do you wish me to—'

'No, thank you,' said Pitt, cutting him off. 'I will announce myself. Perhaps it would be advisable if you cancel the rest of today's business. Discreetly, of course. Give no reasons.'

Moncrieff had to force the words out between dry lips. 'Yes . . . sir.'

As Moncrieff went out of the main door into the passageway, Pitt entered the inner office without knocking.

It was a very handsome room, as was fitting for a senior minister of His Majesty's government. It was large, airy, with windows catching the early sun. The walls were lined with bookshelves, paintings possibly borrowed from one of the many art galleries holding centuries of masterpieces often loaned out to be displayed at one time or another. The furniture was classic mahogany, and the mantelpiece and fire surround were of Carrara marble.

The Minister himself, John Alvey, was standing in the middle of the room with a large book in his hand, as if he were returning to his magnificent desk to read it at leisure. He turned and saw Pitt.

'Good morning, Sir Thomas. If Moncrieff is not at his desk, I prefer you to wait until he is. He can't have gone far.'

'He has gone downstairs to cancel your next appointment,' Pitt replied. 'And all others for the rest of the day. On my instructions.'

He hated the necessity for doing this, and he had some pity for the man in front of him. Alvey's opportunities had been great and he had squandered them. But it was difficult to sustain that pity: this was a man who had seen the chance to make money at other people's expense, and he had yielded to temptation. But Pitt also despised him, because he was willing to betray those who had trusted him.

Colour rose to Alvey's cheeks. It did not seem so much embarrassment or shame as it was rage. 'How dare you come in here and behave as if you own the place. You are nothing more than a jumped-up policeman, promoted far beyond your abilities. You should be out there—' He swung his arm towards the window. 'Arresting thieves, pickpockets, or whatever it is you used to do.'

'Thieves are not always out in the streets, Mr Alvey. Quite often, they are inside very comfortable houses, or offices. In fact, very often those who steal the most are . . .' He glanced briefly around the office, then back again at Alvey. 'In the best mansions, or other places of importance.'

'I'll have you not only thrown out of this building, but out of office altogether. Have you taken leave of your senses?' Alvey demanded.

'I will spell it out for you,' Pitt replied.

It was only for an instant that he wondered if he really had all the proof he needed to do this. No, the evidence was unarguable. But who might come to Alvey's rescue? Vayne had woven a very tight net of debt and more debt, loans within loans. Pitt had chosen to start with Alvey because he was one of the most dangerous. If he fell, others would follow . . . like dominoes.

Alvey said nothing. He started to speak, but changed his mind.

It was very complicated, but Pitt was certain of the details, and how each piece of the puzzle connected with the rest. 'You bought a very fine house, now known as Alvey Court, in Buckinghamshire.'

'What of it?' Alvey demanded. 'I could afford it!'

'Yes, you could,' Pitt agreed. 'But you could not afford the repairs it required. You did not look at it clearly enough before you committed yourself. You borrowed the money to mend the roof, the plumbing, some of the basic structure, including rebuilding the entire double staircase.'

Alvey was quite clearly shaken. He drew in a breath, then let it out without speaking.

'You borrowed the money from Vayne to pay for it,' Pitt continued. 'What he wanted back from you was not the money he lent you, but introductions, information – gradually, a little at a time. At first, it looked harmless, social connections only, the minor wealthy Spanish nobility. They were charming. They wanted favours. But it meant that your massive debt to Vayne was obligingly written off.'

'There's nothing wrong in introducing people!' Alvey protested. 'Part of my job is—'

Pitt cut across him. 'To get information and pass it to a blackmailer like Vayne?' he said, this time less politely.

'I didn't—' Alvey started.

'Didn't know?' Pitt asked sarcastically. 'See that far ahead? Then you shouldn't be in a job like this.'

'You can't prove—' Alvey began again.

'Yes, I can prove it,' Pitt cut across him again. 'It's a tangled web, but I have undone enough of the knots to know where the threads lead.'

Alvey straightened up and glared back at Pitt. 'If you charge me, I'll bring down all the others I know about, and there are a lot of them. It will ruin the whole government. Do you imagine anyone will thank you for that? You are a little man, with no imagination. A workman. Born in poverty and with a poor man's lack of understanding of how life works for anyone above your own class. You are a gamekeeper's son! Your father was deported to Australia for theft. Hah! You didn't know I knew that, did you?' He gave a bitter smile. 'That's what happens when a peasant gets promoted above his class, and above his education! Now get out, before I have you thrown out!'

'By Moncrieff?' Pitt sneered. 'I doubt it. He's far more likely to be loyal to his office than to you personally. By the way, did you know that McCallum is dead? It will be in all the papers in an hour or two.'

The blood drained from Alvey's face. 'You're lying!'

'That would be stupid,' Pitt replied. 'It will be in the newspapers, late edition today, probably. Drowned off the coast of Northumberland. That's where he grew up. But I expect you knew that.'

'Why on earth should I know that?' Alvey was grasping at anything he could reach, like a man falling off a cliff and clutching at grass.

'Because you've known him for many years,' Pitt answered. 'Vayne has run half his business through him. And since he's now dead—'

'What in hell are you talking about?' Alvey shouted.

Pitt smiled, but it was more a showing of teeth than any

351

gesture of warmth. 'McCallum attempted to murder the pathologist Dr Evelyn Hall, and then kidnapped and tried to kill the other pathologist, my daughter-in-law, Dr Miriam fford Croft. He was caught, and struggled for his freedom. In the process, he was drowned. I don't know the details. But I do know that Vayne ordered that McCallum's wife and children be held captive until he eliminated everyone who could testify about the cause of Richard Whitnall's death. Whitnall . . . remember him?'

Alvey said nothing.

'He was prepared to testify against Vayne. I'm happy to say that McCallum's wife and three children are safe. Do you want to pretend you didn't know about any of this?'

'Of course I didn't damn well know!' Alvey shouted. 'Any of it! Good God, man, what do you think I am?'

'A greedy and ambitious man who doesn't care what he is party to, as long as it pays, and he doesn't have to look too closely at any of it. Now, tell me I'm wrong.'

'I . . . I didn't know!' Alvey said desperately.

'Then you are a fool,' Pitt replied. 'If you expect anyone at all to believe that, then you must turn King's evidence and testify against Malcolm Vayne. This will allow us to clean up as much of your mess as possible. Your career will be over, but you might avoid prison. Your choice. What will it be?'

'You—' Alvey could not find a word adequate to his rage, and his defeat.

'Policeman,' Pitt said for him. 'Jumped-up policeman.' This time his smile was quite genuine.

Chapter Twenty-Nine

The trial resumed on Monday morning with a new witness, Agnes Ward. Gideon Hunter had prepared her and felt confident she would bring clarity to the plight of Vayne's victims.

Agnes Ward entered the courtroom. She looked elderly, grey-haired, and she walked slowly, as if any movement was painful.

Daniel felt tension grip him as he waited for the dramatic evidence that Miriam would give, but Hunter had insisted on calling Agnes Ward to the stand first. And now that he saw the grief and the dignity of this woman, he too wanted her to have her chance to show the jury exactly what this crime had cost ordinary people, perhaps like themselves, or their parents.

Hunter was gentle with her, as if he knew her personally. 'Mrs Ward, I'm so sorry to have to call you to testify, and to ask you to tell these people who you do not know the pain and grief which, I am sure, you would rather keep private. But injustice is an offence against society, and that includes all of us. If you do not tell us what you experienced, we cannot know what you have suffered.'

Dalmeny half rose to his feet, and then thought better of it.

'I understand,' Mrs Ward said quietly.

The judge took a deep breath. Daniel was sure he meant to tell the old lady to speak up. But the court wanted to hear her, and the instruction was not necessary.

'Please,' Hunter invited.

'My husband and I had saved some money over the years,' she began. 'We knew we would need more. For the small pleasures, after he retired. And we have two daughters and five grandchildren. We wanted to be sure we would not have to rely on them for any unforeseen expenses.'

She spoke with such dignity and pain that Hunter did not interrupt to ask her anything. He might have felt she was omitting a few points, but Daniel assumed he knew she would tell them about the Big Ben fund, without being asked. And nothing breaks a witness's dramatic testimony more quickly than being interrupted.

Fergus Dalmeny made no attempt to challenge her, as if he, too, were looking at the faces of the jury and knew better.

Hunter smiled at her. 'Please, continue.'

'We read of Mr Vayne's investments,' she said quietly. 'We asked about them. I can't remember the name of the young man now. He promised us it was perfectly safe, and assured us that we could take any amount of money out of the fund for emergencies, and put it back when we were able to.' She took a long, deep breath. 'We were saving to put more money in, but then Alfred, my husband, became ill and needed medicine. He recovered, but he wasn't the same. I went back to the same young man we had dealt with – I believe he said he was a broker – and asked him if we could take our money out, to buy things that would make it easier for Alfred to . . .' She stopped, fighting to control herself.

'Did you get your money, Mrs Ward?' Hunter asked.

She shook her head just a fraction. 'No. He said it was all gone. That something had happened, and it was lost.' She wept silently, without distorting her face, the tears simply sliding down her cheeks.

Daniel felt the pain inside him, almost robbing him of breath. Was this really necessary? Surely Hunter could have— No, that was absurd. This woman's pain was representative of all those victims Malcolm Vayne had cheated, and it needed to be seen.

'Was any reparation offered to you?' Hunter asked.

Mrs Ward merely shook her head, and he did not press her. Indeed, he could only ask the final question to which he already knew the answer. 'And your husband, Mrs Ward?'

'He died,' she said simply.

'I'm so sorry.'

Daniel thought that Hunter was either a brilliant actor, or his expression of sympathy was, indeed, heartfelt.

'Thank you for your courage, Mrs Ward. You have the court's sympathy. I'm afraid you have to remain here in the witness box, in case Mr Dalmeny has any questions for you.'

Dalmeny rose to his feet. 'Not for this witness, My Lord. But Mr Vayne has asked me to make it known to Mrs Ward, and to anyone else affected by this loss, that he will be setting up a fund to recompense all who have suffered, and to the fullest extent possible. He has other properties he can liquidate to see that this is done, out of goodwill, to repair some of the damage his employees have inflicted.' He bowed. 'Thank you, My Lord.' He glanced at Hunter.

'The gesture is gracious,' Hunter replied. 'However, we will thank you only after this proposed fund has been established.

Personally, I'll withhold judgement until I know what *to the fullest extent possible* means. Thank you, Mrs Ward. That is all.'

Daniel felt her testimony had gone very well. Who could not feel her pain? Her sense of betrayal? With these thoughts running through his head, he was surprised, and more than a little concerned, when Rose Hunter stood up and walked towards the witness box.

Without asking anyone's permission, she put her arm around Mrs Ward and guided her very gently towards the exit. No one spoke, and all eyes were on the two women.

Daniel smiled to himself. It might have been Rose's nature to show such kindness, but that did not minimise the respect he saw on the faces around him, and the jurors in particular.

The judge called the court to order. He looked grim, as if he knew that, emotionally at least, he had temporarily lost control of the room.

Daniel was almost certain he was right.

'My Lord,' Gideon Hunter said, rising to his feet. 'I have a new witness, previously prevented from testifying to this court. She is here now, and awaiting Your Lordship's permission to testify.'

The judge looked momentarily confused. And then, in Daniel's mind, he made his first judicial mistake. 'Who is this person, Mr Hunter, and why was she prevented from testifying earlier? Do not tell me you have just discovered some revealing new fact. If you waste the court's time, sir, I will see to it that you regret it!'

Hunter managed to look suitably offended. 'No, My Lord, she will explain why she was not able to speak before.'

'Proceed.'

'Thank you, My Lord.' Hunter gave Daniel a sharp kick.

Daniel rose to his feet. He swallowed hard. 'I call Dr fford Croft, My Lord.'

The judge did not protest.

Daniel glanced at Dalmeny, but his face was unreadable. He had no time to look at Vayne, seated in the dock.

Miriam entered through the main door to the court and walked up the aisle between the packed rows of the gallery. There was a rustle of excitement. They had not expected a woman, especially one wearing a trim hat, a highly fashionable dark-blue dress, and with a face encircled by a veritable riot of auburn curls.

She took the stand, stated her name and swore to tell the truth.

For the first time that morning, Daniel noticed the stern figure of his father, seated in the main body of the courtroom, rather than in the public gallery. Was his presence in such a prominent position a gesture of support for his son? Or was it intended to send a message from Special Branch to Malcolm Vayne sitting in the dock? Daniel had no time to mull it over, before turning his attention to his latest, and possibly final, witness.

'Dr fford Croft, of what particular branch of study are you a doctor?' Daniel began.

'Forensic pathology,' she replied.

'Where did you obtain your doctorate?'

'At the University of Amsterdam, in Holland.'

'And where do you work?'

'At the forensic laboratory attached to the morgue.' She gave the address. 'As assistant to Dr Evelyn Hall.'

Daniel turned to the judge. 'Your Honour, Dr Hall was attacked and appears to be recovering, but she was badly injured. Dr fford Croft was a witness to the attack, as well as to Whitnall's autopsy.' It felt odd referring to her by her maiden name, but this was the name under which she had qualified and obtained her employment. Perhaps he had better be open, or the jury might feel he was playing tricks.

'Really,' murmured the judge, a comment rather than a question.

Daniel nodded. 'My Lord, in the interests of openness, I must remind the court that Dr fford Croft owes her misadventures in part to the fact that she is also my wife. I do not wish to mislead.'

The judge's eyebrows rose, but if there was a sarcastic reply on his tongue, he did not express it. He bit his lip in exaggerated self-control.

Daniel saw it, then he turned to Miriam. 'His Lordship has asked why I have called you to testify, rather than Dr Hall. Would you please tell the court all that you observed, so that the court, and especially the jury, will fully understand this far from ordinary situation?' He knew that Miriam understood very well the need to keep her testimony relevant, to hold only to the facts.

'Dr Hall and I were working in the laboratory, which is quite a large area,' she began. 'I was focused on the chemical analysis of a sample when I heard a man's angry voice. I turned and saw this man strike Dr Hall and knock her off her feet. Her head struck one of the sink benches and she fell to the ground. She lay motionless on the floor, bleeding heavily, and unconscious. When I turned to the man, he struck me with much less force, but enough to render me stunned.'

'Do you know who this man was?' Daniel asked.

'Yes. He was Callum McCallum.' She had not yet finished divulging his name when there was a sudden swell of noise in the courtroom, drowning her out.

The judge was more than a little amazed. 'Silence! Quiet. Let the witness continue.' He banged the gavel. 'Silence!'

The noise died down.

Daniel was clenching his hands so hard they hurt. He forced himself to relax. 'What did Mr McCallum do next?' he asked.

'He forced me to go with him.'

'Forced you? Physically?'

'Yes,' she said soberly. 'He gripped my wrist and began to drag me out of the lab. I wanted to go to Eve – Dr Hall – and tried to reach her, but he restrained me. He led me outside and then forced me into his car, where he bound my wrists together. We drove out of the city, northwards, and followed the main road from there.'

'You were with Mr McCallum the entire time?' Daniel asked.

'Yes.'

'Did he say anything to you? Ask questions? Tell you why he had attacked Dr Hall, or why he had taken you by force?'

'I can't remember exactly. It was frightening. I was afraid that he was a bit hysterical. I can't remember it exactly. I—' She turned to the judge. 'My Lord, I can tell the court the main substance of what Mr McCallum said to me. But if Mr Pitt asks me, it could be seen as leading a witness, and this is not permitted. I can relate it all, without being led by counsel. That is, if you will permit me.'

Daniel was startled. He had been prepared to prompt her, and work his way through the facts by asking, without leading, difficult though it might be.

The judge turned to Hunter. 'As lead prosecutor, sir, is this acceptable to you?'

'Yes, My Lord,' Hunter replied. 'Mrs Pitt is an experienced witness.'

The judge then turned to Fergus Dalmeny, who nodded almost imperceptibly.

'Very well,' the judge agreed, looking at Miriam. 'Proceed, but if you give unnecessary detail, or personal opinion, I will stop you.'

Dalmeny looked suddenly irritated, and Daniel suspected that he was regretting his acceptance, and was prepared to give as much trouble as he was legally able.

'Go on,' the judge instructed.

'May I begin with the autopsy, My Lord?' Miriam asked.

'If it is relevant,' the judge agreed.

'It is, I assure you,' she replied. 'We had been asked to do an autopsy on Mr Whitnall, who was meant to give testimony in this courtroom. Our responsibility, if possible, was to determine how death had occurred.'

Dalmeny was on his feet. 'My Lord, this is second-hand evidence from a witness.'

'It is not second-hand,' Daniel interrupted him, before the judge could speak. 'Dr fford Croft was not only present at the request for the autopsy, she assisted Dr Hall at the autopsy itself.'

'She cannot say how his death occurred,' Dalmeny argued, a note of desperation in his voice. 'It is speculation!'

'That is precisely what she can tell us,' Daniel contradicted him. 'And if the court will allow, she will tell you not only the cause of death, but how the evidence proves it . . . and perhaps more.' He turned to Miriam. 'Dr fford Croft, please tell us what you yourself observed during the autopsy, and any conclusions you reached.'

Dalmeny rose again. 'My Lord, according to Mrs . . . Dr fford Croft, she says Mr McCallum took her by force. We have only so far gone a few miles on this journey. Did she continue with him of her own accord? Or not? And where is he now? Did she leave his company willingly? It all sounds very, very odd. I wish for an explanation. Your Lordship might like to hear it; I certainly would.'

Dalmeny was very carefully preparing the ground to suggest that he knew nothing, Daniel thought. But you know what's coming, don't you? Or perhaps you don't!

Daniel turned to face Miriam. 'Dr fford Croft, perhaps you can tell us, as briefly as possible, what happened to you. And . . . where is Mr McCallum now?'

Dalmeny clearly considered interrupting again, and decided against it.

'Doctor?' Daniel prompted.

There was absolute silence in the court, as if they knew how much depended on what Miriam was about to say. Her face reflected the gravity of this. 'I considered trying to escape, but he had me tied up, hands behind my back for most of the time, and then he tied my feet together as well. We stopped at lonely places, off the main road, to eat and perform . . . necessary functions. He locked me in the car, and took the keys with him when he went to buy supplies, or made me lie on the back seat under a rug when he needed to refill the car with petrol.'

'So, you were prevented from escaping?' Daniel wanted to be certain everyone understood that she had had no alternative: she was his prisoner every step of the way.

'Yes.' She knew better than to give more than he asked. Power lay in brevity; short answers lost none of their emotional impact.

'Where did you finally stop?' he continued.

'I wasn't sure then, but I now know, from what I learned later, that it was on the coast of Northumberland, near Dunstanburgh Castle.'

'At the castle?' He wanted some description for the jury, so they could imagine the bleak, deserted ruins that sat on the very edge of the land, brooding over its lost dungeons under the sea. It would be hard for someone who had never been there to picture the scene. But it would be clumsy not to make an effort to awaken the emotions of the jurors, which was what Daniel wanted to do!

'Not exactly,' she answered. Her hesitation was precisely right. It sounded as if she were not sure what he was asking, making it clear that this exchange had not been rehearsed.

'Perhaps if you tell us the important points you can remember?' Daniel asked. 'I'm sure the jury will understand that you were in pain, exhausted, desperately worried as to whether Dr Hall was even still alive. And, above all, why McCallum would take you, against your will, as his prisoner. Did he ask you questions? About the case, or anything else?'

She took a deep breath and then described the ruins, the caves, and how the high tide filled them with seawater. The room was silent; several of the jurors leaned forward, as if not wanting to miss a single word.

After this, she returned to Daniel's questions about McCallum's conversations with her. 'At first, he talked about what a great man Mr Vayne is, and some of the changes he would make when he had the power he soon would acquire. I can't remember all of it. It didn't seem that he was making a lot of sense. Especially about Mr Vayne attaining high office in the government, even aiming as high as Prime Minister.'

Dalmeny rose to his feet. 'My Lord, this is pure hearsay. I cannot—'

'Yes, yes,' the judge said impatiently, then looked to Daniel. 'Mr Pitt, you must not give the witness an open invitation to ramble. Ask a specific question. She is a scientist, I suppose.'

Daniel drew breath to protest at the unfairness of the accusation, especially after the judge had given Miriam permission to tell her story. But then Daniel changed his mind. Arguing with the judge would not improve the situation. But he should remember the judge's ruling, in case Dalmeny tried the same thing. 'I apologise, My Lord,' he said briefly.

He turned again to Miriam. 'Did you stop, once you reached Dunstanburgh?'

'Yes. But as I've said, at first he didn't tell me why we were there, nor did he ask me questions at that time.'

'Did he explain why you were taken against your will, and why he had attacked Dr Hall?'

Dalmeny was standing again.

Miriam turned the judge. 'My Lord, Mr McCallum is not here, nor do I believe he will be. I think this incident is a vital part of the case, and the members of the jury have a right to hear it.' Her voice was dry, as if she had difficulty forcing it out. 'It may be relevant to Mr Vayne's defence.'

Daniel's voice caught in his throat. What was she going to say? Should he guide her? Or would that take the initiative away from her? Was she asking him to interrupt?

The judge stared at Daniel balefully. 'Mr Pitt, are you sure you are adequately prepared to continue? You seem to have lost your concentration.'

'I'm sorry, My Lord. It is distressing to know what Mr McCallum did to Dr fford Croft. But the court deserves to hear the truth, whether it serves Mr Vayne's cause or not.' Had he made a fatal error? He could sense Gideon Hunter stiffening in his seat nearby.

Dalmeny was smiling.

Daniel should not have looked across at Vayne in the dock, but he did. He was smiling, too.

Clearly, both men expected Miriam's further testimony to in some way exonerate Vayne.

He turned back to Miriam. 'Dr fford Croft, did Mr McCallum at any time say why he had attacked Dr Hall so violently as to have rendered her unconscious, possibly fatally, and then abduct you forcibly?'

He willed her to describe it for the jury, but he must not suggest it to her, at least not for the jury to hear.

'I was taken to a cave on the sea, on the cost of Northumberland, very close to the ruins of Dunstanburgh Castle. They—' Her voice wobbled a little. 'They are half-submerged by the tide, when it is high. It is very dangerous. He intended to leave me in one of those caves.'

'In a cave?' Daniel asked, as if hearing this for the first time. 'Was it a tidal cave? The kind that is underwater when the tide is high?'

'Yes.'

'Thank you. Now, I must ask again. Do you know, for a fact – and please, you must not guess, this is terribly serious and a man's life may well depend on what you say. Do you know specifically, based on Mr McCallum's comments made directly to you, why you and Dr Hall were attacked?'

'Yes, I do know.' Miriam's voice was rasping with emotion. 'It took some time, but he finally told me that he had attacked both of us so we could not testify in this trial.'

There was a gasp of indrawn breath around the gallery.

Dalmeny began to stand, his face red and his mouth opened to protest, but Miriam rushed ahead, as if oblivious to the tumult she had just created.

'He also told me that Malcolm Vayne was holding his wife and children hostage, until Mr McCallum showed him proof that Dr Eve and I would not be able to testify.'

'What did you take that to mean?' Daniel asked, a bolt of ice running up his back.

The judge leaned forward, as if he had at last heard something that demanded his attention.

Dalmeny shifted uncomfortably in his seat.

'That we were to be either totally incapacitated . . . or dead,' Miriam answered.

Daniel saw Vayne staring at Miriam. The man could only imagine what was coming next.

'Do you have any idea why Mr . . . why your testimony was unwanted?' He knew better than to use Vayne's name. 'That is, what could you say that would make a difference in this trial? You are a pathologist, not a qualified accountant.' He looked at her enquiringly. At last, he thought he knew. This would be a different victory, perhaps a better one.

Miriam's face was pale. She must be remembering her abduction, and what she had feared would be her death, and then even Daniel's as well.

'Doctor?' Daniel began again.

'We were working on the corpse of Richard Whitnall. We thought, at first, he had taken his own life,' she replied. 'But on further examination – which I could describe for the court, if you so wish – we could see that such a blow could only have been delivered by someone else. It was how the blade had been plunged into his abdomen, then withdrawn partially, and then driven in again. The first blow would have severed the artery, which meant that he could not have made the second thrust himself, even though it looked like one blow, at first.'

'Meaning: it could not have been suicide?' Daniel asked.

'Yes, that is what I mean. Mr Whitnall was murdered.'

There was an eruption in the courtroom. Jurors froze,

horror on their faces, bewilderment, grief – and then understanding.

Any trace of smugness vanished from Dalmeny's face. He looked as if he had been physically struck. He turned to the judge, then looked up at the dock where Vayne sat.

The judge seized his gavel. 'Silence!' he ordered, but it was not said with anger. It was a plea rather than a command. 'Mr Pitt.'

Miriam stood motionless. Daniel knew from the expression in her eyes that she realised even more than they did the significance of what she had just said.

That was it! Daniel could see it so clearly now. Vayne would not be found guilty of fraud. Yes, he had deceived people, played on their greed and their gullibility, but the paper trail was so complicated that few men seated on this jury would be able to fully comprehend the crime. They might see Vayne's actions as more of a moral sin than a provable criminal offence.

Murder, however, was very definitely a crime, for which the punishment was death.

Of course, they still had to prove it!

The judge looked at Miriam with a new expression entirely. 'Are you prepared to swear to that, Dr—?'

'Pitt,' she said, with a faint smile. 'Yes, I am perfectly willing to swear to it. And also, that Richard Whitnall was killed by a large man, taller than Whitnall himself by several inches. We can determine that by the angle of the blade's entry. Also, we know that the murderer was left-handed, again from the angle of the blow. Dr Hall will swear to the same thing, when she can. It is in the evidence and appears clearly in the autopsy report.'

'The killer was approximately the height of Mr McCallum, in fact?' the judge put in.

'Yes, My Lord,' Miriam replied, glancing at Vayne and then back at the judge. 'But the killer was left-handed. Mr McCallum was right-handed. He did not kill Richard Whitnall.'

'What?' Dalmeny was on his feet.

The judge looked at Dalmeny again, as if confused. 'I suggest we dismiss Dr fford Croft from the stand and call Mr McCallum to testify. Although, to be frank, I'm not sure for which side!'

'That's not possible,' said Miriam.

'And why is that?' asked the judge, his voice slightly condescending.

Miriam squared her shoulders and turned, so she could face the judge directly. 'Because, My Lord, Mr McCallum is dead.'

Dalmeny was now on his feet. 'What on earth are you saying? Do you even know what you are talking about? Are you hysterical?' The moment those words escaped his lips, his face revealed that they were a mistake, but it was too late.

'No,' Miriam said firmly. 'I most certainly am not. Mr Pitt could tell you better than I, or Inspector Frobisher, when he returns. As Mr McCallum was attacking Mr Pitt, he was caught in a wave and swept out to sea. He may still be alive, but tossed around in that sea, and with the ruins of those dungeons sucking him back, and then taking him out to sea again, I think it is unlikely.'

The judge took matters into his own hands. 'Are you saying that Mr McCallum first killed Mr Whitnall – or might have done – and then he tried to kill you, and then Mr Pitt, who followed you to Dunstanburgh Castle to rescue you?'

'No, My Lord,' she replied, looking straight at him again.

'I am saying that the evidence of Mr Whitnall's autopsy says that he was murdered by a man of roughly Mr McCallum's height, but left-handed. Mr McCallum knew that, and he was trying to prevent either Dr Hall or me from testifying to it, out of loyalty to Mr Vayne. Or, at least, that is what he told me, before he revealed that Mr Vayne was threatening to harm his family if he betrayed him by speaking the truth.'

There was a rising noise from the body of the court, people gasping, sighing, shifting position, straining their necks to look at Vayne in the dock. His face had gone paper-white.

'Are you saying, young woman, that Mr McCallum admitted to you that Mr Vayne was guilty of this crime?' the judge demanded.

'He admitted to me that he had kidnapped me, and assaulted Dr Hall, to prevent my husband from allowing anyone else to testify that Mr Whitnall's death was not suicide, but murder,' she corrected him.

'Why?' he demanded. 'Why might Mr Vayne be blamed?'

'I assume, from other things he said, that Mr Vayne feared that Mr Whitnall could ruin his reputation, by proving him guilty of the allegations of fraud brought against him. It would destroy his career.'

Dalmeny was on his feet, his face suffused with red splotches at the cheeks. 'My Lord, this is preposterous! Totally without foundation, this witness is defaming my client's name with no knowledge or understanding of the facts. She is a pathologist, not a financier! She knows nothing about the particulars of this case!'

'Possibly,' the judge agreed. 'But I asked the question of her, Mr Dalmeny. When she has finished answering Mr Pitt's questions, you are free to cross-examine her, if you wish. The jury will decide who to believe. However, I do acknowledge that the prosecution has yet to prove Mr Vayne guilty of anything but dubious accounting, and even those charges may rest upon the heads of his professional advisers and book-keepers, rather than his own.'

The judge spoke directly to Daniel. 'If you put it to the jury now, you may very well end up with a verdict of *not guilty*. Perhaps it would be wise to withdraw the charge?' He turned to Gideon Hunter.

Hunter rose to his feet, a trifle awkwardly. 'Yes, My Lord. I think that would be the wisest thing to do. The right thing.'

'Spoken like a gentleman,' the judge said grimly. 'This prosecution should never have been brought.'

The look on Vayne's face made Daniel feel sick. Vindicated. Exonerated. It was all a travesty, and Daniel wanted to have none of it.

For the first time, Daniel saw Ian Frobisher sitting just behind Thomas Pitt. He must have entered the courtroom during Miriam's testimony. Ian looked drained, as if he had abandoned his car, come to London on the night train, and then walked straight from the station to the courtroom.

Daniel watched Ian rise slowly to his feet. What more could happen?

Their entire case of fraud had collapsed. Vayne would not only walk free, but he could resume his shady dealings, loaning money to important people who would thank him with import-ant government appointments. He could continue receiving enormous sums from power brokers, such as the Seebach Group, who would be sure he had everything he needed to win office and move to the top, where he could deliver bene-fits to them far beyond the public's imagining.

Ian took a few steps closer to the judge. 'Inspector Ian Frobisher, My Lord.'

The judge said nothing. So much of this trial was unpredictable, one more surprise was hardly unexpected.

'I have come to arrest Mr Malcolm Vayne on the charge that he did murder Richard Whitnall, and that he ordered the detention – that is, the imprisonment – of Callum McCallum's wife and children, threatening their lives if McCallum testified to the truth. In this charge, there will be no bail, because it is a capital charge. The McCallum family are now free, and being cared for. But the murder of Richard Whitnall is a charge for which, if found guilty, Malcolm Vayne will be hanged.'

The silence in the courtroom was profound. And then it was broken when Vayne lunged forward, out of the box, his face scarlet. He lashed out with his fists, first in one direction and then the other, hitting at people, striking men and women alike as they stood in his way. He was shouting, but his words were indistinguishable.

Ian hurled himself into Vayne's path. Sergeant Bremner appeared from the crowd to assist. Court ushers called out uselessly for calm. There was shouting, hysteria, journalists pushing their way out of the room to reach telephones and call in the story, others racing outside in search of a taxi to take them to Fleet Street; photographers were angling for shots.

Daniel forced his way to the witness box. Miriam was stepping down and trying to make her way back to him.

When he was able to clasp hold of her, he held her tightly. 'Are you all right?' he demanded. 'Are you!'

'Oh yes,' she said breathlessly. 'We won, don't you think?'

'Yes, I do think,' he said, almost choking on the words. Then he kissed her, not caring that most of the spectators in the room were looking at them.

No one paid attention to the sight of a scarlet-faced, desperately flailing Malcolm Vayne being dragged away in handcuffs. Miriam was the one everybody wanted to see, wanted to cheer.

As for Miriam, all she wanted was Daniel. And he was right there, holding her as if he would never let her go.

FOR FURTHER COURTROOM DRAMAS, FEATURING THOMAS PITT'S BARRISTER SON, DANIEL READ **THE DANIEL PITT SERIES**

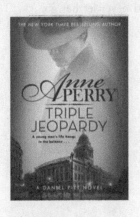

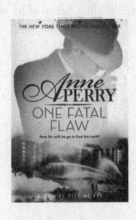

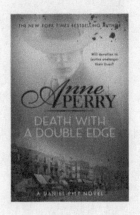

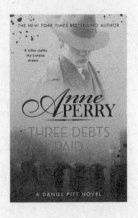

GO TO

FOR MORE FROM ANNE PERRY, TRY
THE THOMAS PITT SERIES

———————

BETHLEHEM ROAD
HIGHGATE RISE
BELGRAVE SQUARE
FARRIERS' LANE
THE HYDE PARK HEADSMAN
TRAITORS GATE
PENTECOST ALLEY
ASHWORTH HALL
BRUNSWICK GARDENS
BEDFORD SQUARE
HALF MOON STREET
THE WHITECHAPEL CONSPIRACY
SOUTHAMPTON ROW
SEVEN DIALS
LONG SPOON LANE
BUCKINGHAM PALACE GARDENS
BETRAYAL AT LISSON GROVE
DORCHESTER TERRACE
MIDNIGHT AT MARBLE ARCH
DEATH ON BLACKHEATH
THE ANGEL COURT AFFAIR
TREACHERY AT LANCASTER GATE
MURDER ON THE SERPENTINE

———————

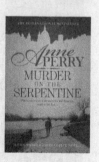

GO TO WWW.ANNEPERRY.CO.UK
TO FIND OUT MORE

DON'T MISS ANNE PERRY'S ESPIONAGE
THRILLERS SET BETWEEN THE WORLD WARS,
THE ELENA STANDISH SERIES

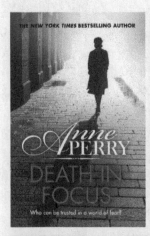

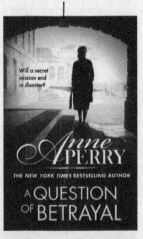

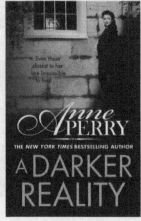

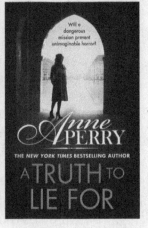

DISCOVER THE
WILLIAM MONK SERIES

THE FACE OF A STRANGER

A DANGEROUS MOURNING

DEFEND AND BETRAY

A SUDDEN, FEARFUL DEATH

THE SINS OF THE WOLF

CAIN HIS BROTHER

WEIGHED IN THE BALANCE

THE SILENT CRY

THE WHITED SEPULCHRES

THE TWISTED ROOT

SLAVES AND OBSESSION

A FUNERAL IN BLUE

DEATH OF A STRANGER

THE SHIFTING TIDE

DARK ASSASSIN

EXECUTION DOCK

ACCEPTABLE LOSS

A SUNLESS SEA

BLIND JUSTICE

BLOOD ON THE WATER

CORRIDORS OF THE NIGHT

REVENGE IN A COLD RIVER

AN ECHO OF MURDER

DARK TIDE RISING

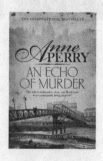

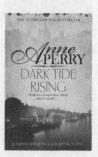

GO TO WWW.ANNEPERRY.CO.UK
TO FIND OUT MORE

  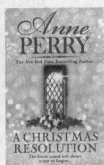